MW01104400

GodSword

GodSword

Emerson Cole

This first world edition published in Great Britain 2006 by
SEVERN HOUSE PUBLISHERS LTD of
9–15 High Street, Sutton, Surrey SM1 1DF.
This first world edition published in the USA 2006 by
SEVERN HOUSE PUBLISHERS INC of
595 Madison Avenue, New York, N.Y. 10022.

British Library Cataloguing in Publication Data

Cole, Emerson
    Godsword
    1.   Brock, Connor (Fictitious character) - Fiction
    2.   Suspense fiction
    I.   Title
    823.9'2 [F]

    ISBN-10: 0-7278-6350-9

Typeset by Palimpsest Book Production Ltd.,
Polmont, Stirlingshire, Scotland.
Printed and bound in Great Britain by
MPG Books Ltd., Bodmin, Cornwall.

Prologue

Unaware that his tranquil world was about to end violently, the elderly monk paused for a moment to catch his breath, exhausted by the steady four-hour climb up the mountainside. He observed with pleasure his young apprentice race ahead, full of youthful vigour and eager to reach the wide ledge first.

The view from the vantage point, a natural promontory jutting out like a giant tongue from an enormous craggy face, stretched beyond the capital Lhasa up towards the majestic foothills of the snow-covered Himalayas and down to the distant monastery below. Ti Rinpoche approached the ledge, slowly shaking his head at Lu Yen, who turned his excited face towards him.

Once, he thought wryly, I was like that: young and nimble like a mountain goat, and as fast as a mountain hare. The ageing Ti Rinpoche smiled. So, maybe he'd become more of an old goat – he glanced at his gnarled forearms and spindly legs – but his muscles felt as supple as ever.

Throughout the previous night, the distant horizon, viewed from the stone-buttressed high wooden terrace of the monastery, had looked like it was on fire. Lu Yen believed, like so many of the visiting nuns and monks who had travelled to the monastery for the week-long prayer festival of Monlam, that this signalled an auspicious new beginning. The boy wanted to boast that he had been the first to witness the sign at close hand.

The wiry old monk joined his flushed apprentice at the ledge, its rough edge smoothed from the centuries of being rubbed by human hands. Together they gazed across the vast undulating expanse that surrounded them, both silent in reverence at the beauty they beheld. The holy man always looked forward to this moment. It had become a ritual ceremony for him, performed

1

for many years following festivals, and, after experiencing the crowds of the past few days, he found that the need to restore the reserves of his spiritual energy was great.

They gazed downwards, both searching out the monastery that nestled far below. The courtyard, usually quiet, with only the resident monks passing back and forth on their business, was crowded with the visiting monks, nuns and travellers setting out on their return journeys after the celebrations of Monlam. Then, slowly, their eyes were drawn to something extraordinary.

'Master,' breathed Lu Yen, pointing at the strange sight unfolding beneath them, 'what is that?'

Approaching the monastery was a long snaking body, khaki-coloured but flecked with red, undulating along the dusty road. It was a procession of men marching relentlessly towards the stone walls. The man and the boy watched in shocked silence as the long line reached its destination and, like some kind of giant centipede, curled out to surround the courtyard and the monks and nuns within. Suddenly, the creature appeared to break apart as hundreds of legs tore away from it in all directions. Red flags, gusted by the speed of the action, revealed a horde of grimy figures that began systematically to attack the harmless, frightened prey who were helplessly caught in a trap. Then, rising to them like a crying aria in a tragic opera, they heard a terrible chorus of tortured screams as the scene below descended into chaos.

Ti Rinpoche turned immediately to his apprentice. 'Stay here, Lu Yen. I am returning at once.'

'Please, master, no! I do not understand – what is happening? Who are these people? Why are they attacking our monastery?' Lu Yen's cheeks had paled and sheer terror showed in his eyes. He put out a shaking hand towards his master.

'There's no time to explain. I must leave.'

'Master, stay here!' pleaded Lu Yen desperately. The chilling echo of the screams below floated up to them. 'Let us stay hidden here – we are safe in this place.'

Ti Rinpoche touched the young boy's hand, trying to calm him. He was little more than a child, he did not understand what must be done. A terrible outrage was taking place and the only place for Ti Rinpoche was among his people, doing what he could for them, protecting them in the only way he knew.

He said firmly, 'You must not follow me, Lu Yen! You are to stay out of sight.'

The scared youth, his fearful wide eyes pleading for reassurance, clasped his dark crimson robe closer to his chest. 'Please, master – tell me what is happening!'

'There is no time – but I will return to you. Now wait here, be calm and pray.'

Leaving the frightened boy, he set out as quickly as he could back down the mountainside.

Despite the remoteness of his ancient monastery, Ti Rinpoche had been well aware of the increasingly oppressive occupation of Tibet by the People's Liberation Army of China. During his ten years as patriarch, he had prayed earnestly for the release of his country, particularly since the visit of His Holiness last summer.

One evening, after sunset prayers, an old friend who had become one of the young Dalai Lama's advisors had shared his alarming suspicions of a looming calamity for Tibetans. Ti Rinpoche listened in shock, a sick sensation in his stomach as he heard the whispered revelations.

'Brother, believe me, the rumours of horrendous atrocities being exercised to intimidate the population are true. There is evidence that crucifixion, disembowelling and castration are taking place. Many of our patriotic brothers have been burned to death, buried alive and dragged behind galloping horses. Those of our more spirited individuals that dared to cry "Long live the Dalai Lama" have had their tongues ripped out with meat hooks while awaiting execution. The terrible thing is that the more we resist, the worse the atrocities against us.'

Ti Rinpoche shuddered at the words, unable to imagine such cruelty. 'It cannot be true,' he said. 'Such things cannot come to pass.'

'They can, and they do,' said his old friend sadly. 'Believe me, a frightful storm is coming upon us.'

Ti Rinpoche had tried to shut the thoughts from his mind, unwilling to imagine such horrors. These were nightmarish stories, and like all bad dreams would fade with the passing of the night. They were things that happened far away to strangers. They were not real.

Yet now the unreal had become reality.

* * *

3

No one appeared to notice the small, wiry old monk as he entered the courtyard. He walked unregarded through the dreadful scene, almost unable to believe what he was seeing. Though breathless with exertion from his rapid descent from the mountain, Ti Rinpoche felt his strength return to him as he began to take in the horror of what was before him. Stretching his arms out, he approached a group of three intruders who had paused from the massacre to watch and laugh as one of their comrades chased a terrified monk about the courtyard, lashing out at the squealing brother with a glinting blade.

'I am Ti Rinpoche, patriarch of this monastery,' he declaimed, his voice authoritative and calm, 'and I demand that you cease this desperate violence immediately. Have you no souls? No pity for your fellow man? Are you monsters? Where is your commander? I must see him at once.'

There was a momentary pause as the aggressors measured the presence of the small man in front of them. Then, with a sneer, one lifted his rifle and, before Ti Rinpoche was aware of what was happening, a savage blow from the butt knocked him senseless.

When a dull consciousness returned to him, Ti Rinpoche was unable to move. He had no feeling in his arms or legs since they had been tied tightly to the wooden steps leading to the grand hall above the courtyard; he felt only the growing pain from a shattered cheekbone.

Through sore eyes, Ti Rinpoche could see that the hall above him had been torn apart. Its ancient artefacts and sacred relics, nurtured over the past seven centuries, had been plundered and thrown into a careless heap. Wincing with pain, as the wooden boards and ropes chafed the naked raw skin of his limbs, Ti Rinpoche dragged his eyes away from the heartbreaking sight, to the cigar-smoking man who stood beside him.

'So sorry to wake you from your sleep,' he sneered. With a nod of his head to one of the nearby soldiers, he said, 'Unbind him.'

Rough hands tore at the old man's limbs, pulling them away from the boards, while a blunted knife hacked away at the ropes binding them. The old man endured the pain, numbed by shock that his fellow human beings were capable of such vicious actions, and in this place of peace and sanctuary.

'There. Now, allow us to make introductions.' The man pulled at his cigar, exhaling a plume of blue smoke through pursed lips. 'I am Colonel Hui Quan of the People's Liberation Army and this gentleman –' he gestured to a young man at his side – 'is Comrade Te Su Lok, representative of the munificent sovereign power that has liberated your country, the People's Republic of China.'

Ti Rinpoche had seen, with a sinking heart, the red emblem on the drab and ill-fitting uniforms of the attackers. He had already guessed that these were the monsters that he had so recently been warned of on that peaceful evening in this very courtyard. He said nothing, not wanting to inflame Colonel Quan. Instead, he nodded patiently.

Anger and contempt flickered in Colonel Quan's coal-black eyes. The cigar, jammed between yellow teeth, protruded from a cruel mouth and glowed menacingly below hollowed, scarred cheeks.

'Five nights ago,' said Quan, lifting his head imperiously as if he was addressing anyone else who might be listening, 'that young puppet the Dalai Lama, permitted by us to remain here on the understanding that he would persuade this province to come under the protection of the People's Republic of China, was found not to have complied with the agreement and has stolen away from Lhasa.

'Our sources believe he crossed the Karpo Pass into India seeking asylum at Tezpur. So – your *venerable* Dalai Lama is now in exile.' Colonel Quan leaned menacingly towards Ti Rinpoche. 'Regretfully much of that cesspool Lhasa is in flames. The unavoidable result of yet another vicious uprising supporting some misguided slander against the People's Republic of China.'

'Praise Buddha he is safe from this,' muttered Ti Rinpoche.

The colonel's eyes narrowed. 'Praise only the glory of the motherland, at last free to govern without the poisoning interference of astrology and religion,' he spat. 'You stupid old man. It will be my pleasure to put out your eyes and cut out your tongue, and then we'll see how much praising of your Buddha you'll feel like doing.'

'We don't have time for this nonsense,' said the colonel's companion impatiently. Dressed also in drab grey, Comrade Lok nevertheless had the air of a civilian rather than a soldier: his

5

clothes were fitted well and the open overcoat that draped around his wide shoulders was of a good thick quality. He was young and lean with smooth yellow skin and predatory sharp black eyes that were constantly drawn to the pile of plunder and treasure mounting up nearby. As the ransacking soldiers continued to add to the hoard, there was the sound of breaking.

'Careful!' Comrade Lok yelled, moving swiftly towards the treasure. Roughly pushing the nearest soldier aside, he stooped over and began to sift through the glittering articles that lay before him. 'You dung-eating imbecile! Have more care, you dolts. The smallest of these things is worth twenty of your miserable lives.'

'What does it matter?' Quan snapped. 'Everything is to be destroyed anyway.' He had been nettled by this young pup's arrogance and calling the men fools was an insult to his command.

Comrade Lok turned slowly back to Quan with a look of contempt. 'It is *I* who will decide what is to be destroyed,' he replied coldly. 'And let me remind you, *Colonel* Quan, that it was your *needs*, as you so delicately like to put it, that made us arrive too late to prevent these rampaging ruffians of yours from destroying what may be of irreplaceable value to the People's Republic.

'Soldiers!' added the young man, pointing slowly around the courtyard. 'More like whoring fools! Now, Colonel, I want you to get on with your work. Instead of standing about talking to this old fool, find the sacred items I know are hidden here. Find them, and then get them loaded so that we can leave.' Comrade Lok paused, almost enjoying the look of anger on the colonel's face. 'Let me remind you that if there are any further delays, General Hai Chuntao will hear of your methods, and your insistence on stopping on the way here to fulfil your base animal needs at the expense of our orders.'

The younger man's last sentence had the intended effect. Quan's rising temper had once more begun to take control and he had been on the very point of launching himself at this young civilian upstart when the mention of the general stopped him. Perhaps it was better if his actions on the road to the monastery remained hidden from official gaze. Any action in the cause of the People's Republic was sanctioned but the colonel's insistence on entertaining that group of nuns they'd encountered on the road ten miles back could very well be frowned upon, even though he'd sent the troops on ahead on their mission of rape and butchery.

Seething with impotent rage, the colonel turned his anger towards the holy man moaning softly at his feet. Placing a boot on one of the old man's fingers, he ground his foot downwards, feeling the bone shatter beneath his tread. 'Where do you keep your *sacred* treasures, you scrawny excuse for a dog? Where are the tools of your poisonous witchcraft? Come on, tell me!'

The old man shuddered and a gasp of pain escaped his lips; then he appeared to master himself and gazed up wordlessly. Something in the depth of his stare incensed Quan and he stamped wildly on the holy man's hand, feeling it break into pieces under the pressure. 'Tell me and the pain stops,' he hissed. 'If not, it gets worse, that I promise you.'

Comrade Lok watched him impassively. 'You'd better get the results I require, Colonel,' he said coldly, turning on his heel, 'and soon. We have no time to waste.'

Ti Rinpoche knew that his spirit was not long for the world and would soon be departing, leaving behind the broken husk that had been his body. He felt the intense pain of his crushed hand, but years of meditation and a sure confidence in his faith kept him calm and at peace in his heart. Instead of seeing the bestial hate in the eyes of the colonel, he concentrated on the brightening of the courtyard as the rays of the afternoon sun began to bathe the mountainside. The sky was clear and beautiful and he could hear, somewhere, above the grim sounds of torture and murder, a kind of music, perhaps birdsong. For most of his simple life from apprentice to master, this monastery had been the only home he had known. Here he had learned the wisdom of the world without having to see the world. Here too he had been spared the worst of mankind's stupidity and evildoing – until today.

Lu Yen awoke, shivering with cold, his robe damp from the mountain mist. Sitting up bewildered, he tried to remember if it was his turn to chime the morning gong and then wondered, perplexed, why he was outside instead of lying in his cot in the dormitory with the other apprentices.

Abruptly he gasped as the shocking memory of past events flooded back to him.

7

After Master Ti Rinpoche had instructed him to stay out of sight, he had hidden himself in an outcrop of large rocks and waited for his master to return, weeping with panic as he tried to block out the fearful sound of those dreadful screams with his cloak. The noise had carried so clearly up through the thin air, it was as if he had been in the midst of a battle raging with unseen warriors all around him.

Finally, faithful to his master's orders to do nothing, Lu Yen guessed he must have fallen asleep through exhaustion and nervous shock. Now, it was dawn and there was no sign of his master's return.

Shaking away the remnants of his fatigued stupor, the young apprentice got stiffly to his knees and peered over the rocks that had provided him with refuge. He saw that the mist surrounding the monastery appeared to lie much thicker than usual and, despite the dawn light, its familiar outline was obscured. With a growing horror, Lu Yen realized that what impeded his view was not fog, but thick, evil smoke.

Lu Yen needed all his courage as he approached his home. He could taste the acrid smell of burning rope, cloth and smouldering timber that stung the back of his throat. There was another, more overpowering, scent as he got nearer. It was similar to the aroma that emanated from the cooked pig and goats they had spit roasted in the hall ovens during the Monlam Festival, except it smelled as though it had been badly overcooked, even burned.

The place appeared deserted. Even with senses sharpened by adrenaline, the boy could hear no sound. He went tentatively through the large entrance to the monastery, now devoid of its wooden gates, and then stopped, frozen in horror by the sight that greeted him.

Bile rushed to his throat and made him gag as his empty stomach retched. All that remained of his fellow brothers, apprentices and new friends, the visiting nuns and monks, was a vast, scorched, blackened pile of unrecognizable grotesque forms.

There was no evidence of the wooden dormitory that had once stood opposite the great hall. The great hall itself was roofless and the thick timbers that had so proudly stretched across the low roof now lay across the floor, still burning and smoking. The meditation cells of the elder monks, formerly concealed within the mountainside beyond the hall, now lay exposed to the daylight like lifeless eye sockets.

Unable to utter a sound, Lu Yen ran across the courtyard, leaping over smouldering beams and piles of burning rubbish, towards the great hall. He had seen a familiar form and now he rushed towards it in the fierce grip of hope, offering prayers to heaven for the preservation of his beloved master.

Reaching the twisted form that lay motionless on the steps to the hall, Lu Yen dropped to his knees beside it.

'Master, master,' he gasped, pulling at the old man's slender, almost child-like body. The old patriarch's body rolled over easily beneath his touch, and Lu Yen could not prevent a cry at the sight of the beloved face broken almost beyond recognition, the eye sockets burned and sticky with a ghastly, bloody sap. The face and body were horribly blackened and charred: he had been set alight while still alive.

'Oh no, oh, my master,' whimpered the boy. He tried to hold the crushed hands, to rub life back into the scorched, limp body, but in his heart he knew it was useless. He began to wail, his fear of being heard by any remaining attackers forgotten, and rocked back and forth on his heels, cradling his master. Then, slowly, it seemed to him that, despite the tortured angle of the head and the mess of blood and gore, the holy man's lips were curved into the faintest smile, and his expression reflected peace.

PART ONE

Weaving the Web

One

EGYPT – MARCH 21ST, PRESENT DAY

Omar Al Kadeh felt blessed as he enjoyed the late-afternoon sun shimmering between the cinnamon-coloured mountains of the Sinai and the cool sapphire waters of the Red Sea. Soon, along with the pink smoky twilight, his beloved family would arrive, then later, under a clear night sky cluttered with countless twinkling stars, they would join together in great celebration.

Sipping hibiscus tea from the delicate porcelain cup that seemed so fragile between his large fleshy fingers, Al Kadeh considered how odd it was that his beautiful wife Fawzia, born and raised here in the quiet lee of the Tama Heights, preferred the hectic noise of Cairo, while he, brought up in the noise and squalor of the city, luxuriated in the tranquillity and peace of the countryside.

The immaculate robes of fine-blended linen and silk rustled as the rotund business sheik leaned back with an air of contentment.

'Perhaps every man seeks what is strange and new to him,' he mused. 'Perhaps each of us longs for what he does not have – silence when there is noise, and noise when there is silence.' Al Kadeh chuckled to himself. 'And with age comes the need to philosophize about life.'

Admittedly, the metropolis had served him well; the smells and excitement of the market-filled sidewalks had put the taste of commerce into his mouth, taught him his business and brought him the immense success that had allowed him to find sanctuary from its cluttered, raucous streets. But the city had changed. In the fifty-seven years of Al Kadeh's life, it had doubled in size from seven to almost fourteen million inhabitants. What

13

was a man to do to get peace these days? Or was that just another sign of age?

'Mind you, such an increase has been good for business,' Al Kadeh murmured to himself as he gently set down his empty cup. With a satisfied sigh, he lifted his bulky body from the over-cushioned deep willow couch and strolled to the centre of his balcony terrace. 'And now the merciful Allah has doubly blessed me.'

Resting the wide palms of his hands on the white stone balustrade, Al Kadeh gazed down at the complex of hotels and condominiums below and beyond to the great ships waiting to commence their passage through the Suez Canal, their massive holds full of valuable commodities bound for the west and north beyond the Mediterranean.

Everything he could see belonged to him. But – he allowed himself a small smile – it was almost as nothing compared to this, his latest triumph. He had reached the zenith of his career. How his father would have been proud of him! As would Brahia, his first wife. Both had been taken by cancer almost within weeks of each other. A cruel stroke of fate yet one which he, Omar Al Kadeh, readily accepted was in God's plans, Praise be to God.

That was almost thirty years ago and, over time, God had blessed him with two fine sons, and a daughter as beautiful as her mother, Fawzia. So God is truly great.

'Congratulations!'

Omar Al Kadeh turned swiftly at the unexpected voice that interrupted his thoughts. For a moment he was startled but then recognized the face of the tall, ebony-skinned man standing in front of him, impeccably dressed in a white linen suit. 'Ibrahim Qenawi! I am astonished. How did you get in here?'

'More to the point is why I am here,' responded the unexpected visitor.

An expression of bewilderment passed over Al Kadeh's face. 'You, of all people, have no business here on this day! Tonight is a private family occasion and, much as it distresses me not to offer you the kind of hospitality for which I am well known, I must insist that you leave.' He turned towards the doorway. 'Asam! Asam!' Where in the name of Allah was his servant? How dare he allow people to walk into his presence unannounced and without an appointment?

14

'Your servant can't hear you, which is as it should be.'

'What?' demanded Al Kadeh, his voice rising indignantly.

'Because we have important business to discuss that requires your urgent attention,' continued Qenawi so coldly that Al Kadeh experienced a slight shiver in his spine.

Al Kadeh recalled how he had taken an instant dislike to the man on the day they had met, at a reception for contractors bidding for the most exceptional business deal of all their lives. Al Kadeh Construction had only one competitor in the tender for the government contract, and Qenawi was their representative.

Al Kadeh was not sure what had repelled him about the other man – usually he respected his rivals, even while ensuring that he would eclipse them – but not this time. Perhaps it was because the prize was too great, too glittering, and because both men wanted it so desperately.

To be the constructor of the greatest building project in Egypt in modern times – that was the precious reward they both sought; to build the New Pyramids, a multi-billion-dollar town that would provide houses for over a million people, along with hospitals, schools and research centres. At first it was intended that the initiative to revive this formerly protected part of the Nile delta between Cairo and Alexandria would merely relieve the pressure of the already stretched infrastructure of Cairo, Africa's largest city. But the concept had evolved way beyond that. The two natural inlets of that part of the basin had inspired international architects to design a neo-ancient city redolent of the splendours of the pharaohs themselves that incorporated marinas, an airport, hotels and shopping malls. And dominating the skyline would be three pyramid commercial complexes, mirroring the Great Pyramids south of Cairo at Giza.

It was an impossible dream for Egypt without the support of its northern European neighbours – and, of course, America's commercial investment – and almost a lost dream owing to the Iraq War. But somehow it had stayed alive and now, with conditions imposed for housing, labour, infrastructure and building, the New Pyramids would be built, to stand as testament to a new Egypt: a glorious, pioneering construction that would ensure fame into posterity for all parties involved – and particularly, of course, for the successful contractors.

That very morning, Omar Al Kadeh had received the wonderful news. The company that he had founded thirty years earlier, Al Kadeh Construction, had been awarded the major portion of the infrastructure contract, worth over 500 million dollars. But more than the money was the glory of the award: the family name would live on for ever, inextricably linked to Egypt's greatest achievement of modern times.

As he observed his uninvited guest, Al Kadeh grew indignant. What audacity to come to his private home on such an important night!

'I have no business to discuss with you,' he snapped.

'That remains to be seen. I have a proposition for you to consider.' Qenawi's thick lips widened into a broad smile that did not reach his dark expressionless eyes. Omar Al Kadeh immediately guessed that this proposition must concern the contract. The final bidding had been close and he was convinced that Al Kadeh Construction had been successful in the tender because of its proven track record, experience and, importantly, because it was an Egyptian company. That was the decisive political factor.

Qenawi's company might be nominally Egyptian but Al Kadeh knew that its ownership had been traced to a subsidiary of the giant building and shipping conglomerate, Subedei Industries, based in Beijing. A Chinese-owned company. Even Qenawi himself, though he may have made Egypt his home and built up a successful business, was still Sudanese.

Al Kadeh eyed the intruder with great suspicion. There had been several occasions previously when Qenawi had approached Al Kadeh Construction and proposed coming to some alliance over the contract, which he, Omar Al Kadeh, as sole shareholder, had immediately refused. Why on earth the man should imagine that the situation would be any different now that the contract had been awarded, Al Kadeh could not think. He was growing irritated. 'I am not interested in any proposition you have to offer. Now please leave my home.'

Qenawi seemed unmoved by Al Kadeh's abruptness and said pleasantly, 'Come, let us be civilized. Is it not an old Arab custom to be gracious and hospitable with travellers, whether expected or not? I promise you that you will be most interested in what I have to say. It will be nothing along the lines of what you expect, I guarantee it.'

Al Kadeh's initial surprise at Qenawi's unexpected appearance had dissipated. He was still angry but also mildly curious. Perhaps there was no harm in listening to this offer, even though his answer would still be no. He was intrigued by what Qenawi could possibly think would tempt a man who had just won the contract for the New Pyramids.

He said, 'How can you expect me to be hospitable when you seem to have detained my servant? So forgive me for not offering you refreshment. However, I will allow you three minutes of my time. More than enough, I believe, for you to inform me as to how you think we may do business together.'

Qenawi made an exaggerated bow. 'You are indeed generous with your time, for which I profoundly thank you. And believe me, I did mean that congratulations were in order, because they are. No doubt you will be celebrating with your family and friends. Such a magnificent contract only comes once in a person's lifetime.'

'The opportunity to build a new wonder of the world is indeed gratifying for a humble servant of his country,' said Al Kadeh, and he bowed slightly. 'I thank you for your sentiments, though you will forgive me if I ask you, once again, to briefly state your proposition and then depart from my home. This evening is special and I must prepare for it.'

Qenawi smiled again. 'It is indeed good to be prepared in life. But how often are we truly prepared? How often are we ready for the unexpected in our lives? I know that you have no intention of accepting any business offer I could make you. But, I humbly submit, what if it is simply that you are unprepared? You have no idea of what I am about to say, and yet you are sure that you will refuse me. I ask you to prepare yourself to change your mind.'

'What are you getting at? What nonsense is this? Are you suggesting I don't know my own mind? You insult me.' Al Kadeh frowned, his thick, bushy eyebrows knitting above his dark-brown eyes. 'My patience is at its end. You refuse to speak sense and if you expect us to do business, you are wasting your time. We have already had that conversation and the answer I gave to you then remains firmly the same.'

'Well, you did make it very clear that you would not entertain my involvement,' returned Qenawi smoothly. 'However, you

17

may know that my company is a subsidiary of a much greater interest. My superior follows a very simple business philosophy and it is infallible. He has asked me to make you an offer, not for a piece of your contract, but for your entire company, for the whole of Al Kadeh Construction, and he is certain that you will want to consider it seriously. In fact, he knows without a doubt that you will accept it. Indeed, I too am sure that you will be only too willing to agree.'

'Such confidence is misplaced!' roared Omar Al Kadeh, anger flooding through him. 'The arrogance of your superior stuns me. How in the name of Allah can he know what I would or would not accept? And this extraordinary offer for my company is laughable. In the first place, he has no idea of the value of my business and, with the award of the New Pyramids contract, even I would not hazard to estimate the complete value of my company today. But let me tell you, even ignoring those factors, my business may as well be priceless since it's not for sale. Al Kadeh Construction will be an example of the *modern* Egypt's building prowess; it will be a shining gift to my sons and heirs, as well as an ornament to the nation.'

'Then, as I have been instructed to do so by my superior, I must offer you something that is priceless in return.' Qenawi moved leisurely across the plush carpeted room. When he reached the marble terraced balcony, he took a small pair of highly powerful binoculars from his pocket. With a lazy arrogance, he turned back to Al Kadeh and held out the field glasses. 'Please, at least do me the honour of surveying our offer and let me know what you think.'

'What foolishness is this?'

'If you would just be so kind as to focus on the large tanker that lies off the western bank.'

Warily, Al Kadeh accepted the binoculars, took a few steps away to distance himself from Qenawi, and raised them to his face. As he swept the device over the water that was just beginning to glow with the lowering sun, his eye soon caught a large ship. A slight adjustment to the focus was required.

'I have to tell you that I am not interested in more shipping.' Twisting the focus dial, Al Kadeh saw the tanker as if it were magically moored on the balustrade of his wide terrace. The

18

giant 195-metre supertanker had red insignias painted on the side that matched the flag flying on its stern.

'That is the *Temujin*,' said Qenawi. He had moved closer to Al Kadeh and spoke softly near to his ear. 'Magnificent, would you not agree? Immense power, yet so graceful.'

'The ship is big, I'll grant you that, but it is still a ship like any other of the hundreds that pass through this passage. In fact, it looks to me as though her size may risk grounding.'

'Ah, but it is not the ship itself – it is the cargo that I believe will be of greatest interest to you.'

'What cargo?'

'A priceless one.'

'How can I view the cargo from here? This is ridiculous.'

'Patience,' said Qenawi, almost in a whisper. 'Look at the area below the bridge. You should be able to see a cleaning platform attached halfway down the hull.'

Al Kadeh scanned the ship until he located the platform dangling, as Qenawi had said, against the massive grey hull of the tanker. On it he could see a number of people: three of them stood rock still, like statues sculpted upon stone plinths, while a further two moved freely around the frozen figures.

Zooming in with the powerful glasses, Al Kadeh felt as though iced water was being poured down his back, despite the sultry late-afternoon heat. Involuntarily tightening his grip on the binocular sides, he could now see why the three people were unable to move.

Their feet were encased in something. Something that was distinctly familiar to him. They were large cement sacks marked with AKC in black ink to indicate their manufacture by his own company. Slowly raising the binoculars to look at the faces, he gasped with horror.

There, filling the powerful lenses in front of his eyes, were the beloved faces of his wife Fawzia and his two sons. Al Kadeh felt as though his heart was being ripped from his chest. His terrified gasp informed Qenawi that the intended view had been seen.

'A priceless offer, wouldn't you agree? In fact, three priceless offers, though surely one would be enough to sign a sale agreement for your company. Am I not right?'

Still aghast with terror, the construction magnate seemed to shrivel into his bulky robes and his firm features sagged as he continued to gaze through the binoculars, not wanting to believe what he was seeing. His first words came out with a shudder. 'What are you doing? How can this be?'

Ignoring him, Ibrahim Qenawi took a mobile phone out of the pocket of his tailored suit. Without taking his eyes off Al Kadeh, he turned the phone deftly over in one hand, felt for a button and pressed it firmly. Within a few moments, a voice confirmed that the pre-programmed number dialled had connected successfully.

'What sort of monster are you to threaten a man with the death of his family?' rasped Al Kadeh in utter disbelief at what he was seeing.

Qenawi spoke slowly and deliberately, his voice cold as ice. 'Please listen to me carefully. Understand that I am very serious. The moment I break this connection, a member of your family will disappear. The water is deep at that point.'

'What are you saying?' demanded Al Kadeh, now totally disoriented with the shock of what was happening to him.

'I am saying that my superior wants to take over Al Kadeh Construction without delay. Your acceptance of his offer will allow for you, and your family to retire in luxury.'

'You're mad! This is a crazy bluff! You wouldn't dare!' cried Al Kadeh desperately, while once more raising the glasses to his eyes.

'Wrong answer. What a shame. And I had you down as such a family man. I am truly sorry you aren't more amenable to our reasonable request.' The cruel retort, emanating softly from between Qenawi's glinting white teeth, was whispered a few centimetres from Al Kadeh's ear. A thumb pressed down on the end button.

Al Kadeh screamed as the familiar long tresses of his wife's jet-black hair momentarily billowed upwards while her writhing, weighted body plunged into the depths of the sapphire water. The field glasses dropped to the floor as an uncontrollable spasm began to shake the whole of the distraught man's body. Al Kadeh's great bulk crumpled on to the marble terrace. His pleading eyes stared up at the tall man's hard ebony face. Qenawi quickly knelt down to push home his advantage before the other man went beyond reason. It was vital he agreed to the deal immediately.

'So you can see that the offer is a serious one! Is the price high enough or do you want me to call and raise it further?'

Breathing heavily, Al Kadeh grasped for control over himself and slowly nodded. 'Anything. Just give me my sons.'

Two

Ibrahim Qenawi rested his palms on the wide parapet of the marbled balcony of Al Kadeh's luxurious residence. He looked about him with appreciation. The fat little sheikh certainly knew how to live – this place was extremely impressive. Ibrahim had enjoyed the evening he had spent in these most salubrious surroundings, even if most of the time had been spent in complicated business transactions. Now all that was over, and Qenawi was able to savour the peace and satisfaction of a job well done.

He gazed out at the deep blue velvet of the sky. The multitude of stars above reminded him of the nights he had spent in the Sudan bush as commander in the rebel army. He had been young then, and the older rebels had inspired him with stories of how their ancestors had become immortal lights in the night sky in recognition of their glorious deeds. He had loved those nights of comradeship, of quiet talking round the campfire, of brotherhood and a sure sense of the cause that bound them together. All that was long gone now. When the purges had come fifteen years ago, Qenawi had made his escape by shedding his uniform and his weapon and mingling with the hundreds of other refugees fleeing into Egypt. He had even persuaded a starving young widow to pretend that she and her skeletal son were his wife and child in exchange for a few bowls of food on the journey. In that way he had crossed the border and begun life afresh, determining to make a place for himself in his new country. Over the years he had gone from a casual labourer to head of his own construction company – modest, perhaps, in comparison to the might of Al Kadeh Construction, but still successful, and completely his own. It provided him with wealth enough to live comfortably, and brought him some well-placed friends who had made sure of his Egyptian citizenship.

Then, last year, everything had changed when he had been approached by Subedei Industries. It had suddenly looked as though his company might be able to scale the heights and he himself could join the mighty players of Al Kadeh's mould. Qenawi had jumped at the chance to gain the financial backing that Subedei Industries had promised and he knew enough to realize that his new business partner was in a league of his own in every way. His instinct was proved right when, within weeks of selling his company interest to Subedei, a major contract had been won, despite the fact that the formal bid period had lapsed.

The coercion required of him came easily, although he made sure that he, personally, kept his hands clean. It was as easy as giving orders to his soldiers all those years ago and then leaving them to massacre villagers and burn their homes. And his old army instinct told him that his new chief would not tolerate failure.

That was why when he'd had to call Beijing with the news that the contract for the building of the New Pyramids had been awarded to Al Kadeh Construction rather than to Subedei Industries' newest acquisition, he had been beset with the kind of nerves he'd not felt since he was a boy. He had given the news as briefly and understatedly as possible, trying to conceal a tremor in his voice and the dryness of his mouth. His superior had listened and when Qenawi finished, there had been a chilling pause. Then, to his intense relief, the voice on the other end of the line told him that perhaps, after all, this was good news, as it now opened the door to the possibility of acquiring Al Kadeh Construction in its entirety.

Ibrahim Qenawi was to make an offer that could not be refused, the terms of which would be explained by someone arriving shortly from Hong Kong. As expected, the terms were ruthlessly simple. And he had followed orders to the letter, without hesitation. That was the way it had to be now – he understood that.

Qenawi tilted his head upwards and gazed at the glittering roof of stars above him. The day would come when his own descendants would hear stories of him and his exploits, making them proud of their warrior heritage.

The call he had put through a few minutes ago had been well received. Allowing for the time zone difference, Qenawi knew that his superior would be taking his usual working breakfast and would answer his private mobile immediately. The confirmation that the transfer of ownership of Al Kadeh Construction had been completed prompted a further instruction that all loose ends were to be tied up. Omar Al Kadeh had contacted a lawyer to conduct the legal aspects of the transfer, and the man had clearly been concerned and uneasy at the urgency of the deal. But the vast fee offered simply for transacting the documents sent electronically by Omar Al Kadeh had proved persuasive; full compliance to everything requested had been agreed.

It had been impossible to include the exact terms relating to the contract awarded for the New Pyramids because there were still some variables involved. Although the lawyer felt confident that the award would be transferred formally in due course, he wanted to include full liability disclaimers.

This had worried Qenawi – surely his superior would chafe at these provisos. After all, it was for the sake of that contract that all this was happening. But to his surprise, the disclaimers were of no concern to the man in Beijing, who apparently viewed the once-in-a-lifetime contract as simply a bonus if and when it was eventually ratified. This confused Qenawi, but he thought it prudent to keep his queries to himself.

At least the conditional terms relating to the New Pyramids had made the overall purchase contract very straightforward. The company assets and existing contracts were excellent, although it was a shame that the now-substantial family liquid assets would remain unclaimed in some untouchable account in Switzerland. But those were the orders of his superior and of course they would be obeyed without question. Qenawi's experiences in Sudan, under the command of his rebel chief, had taught him the kind of blind obedience required by a brutal warrior who was to be respected – and feared.

Ibrahim Qenawi reached for the harmless-looking cell phone that lay on the balustrade beside him. His right thumb pressed the call button while his left hand raised the binoculars to his eyes. Though dark, the electronic instrument captured the available light effectively enough for him just to make out the large bulky figure in its white robes positioned between two other, slightly smaller figures. All three were slumped through exhaustion brought on through hours of grief and fear for their lives.

Once more he looked up at the stars above him as the confirmatory voice on his cell phone acknowledged the connection.

Yes, such wealth would have done wonders in his Sudan. What good would it be now that there would be no one left to enjoy it? Millions rotting away untouched in the Al Kadeh account. Lowering the glasses, Qenawi decided that tomorrow he would confirm that all loose ends had been tied up, just as he had been instructed. Turning away from the terrace, he softly pressed his thumb on the button, terminating the call.

Nadir Bassein was transfixed. His heavy-lidded bulbous brown eyes were mesmerized by the consistent blinking of the silent cursor on the laptop screen. With drooping chin, a grey pallor and matching grey moustache, Bassein's hypnotic expression made him look like a zombie trapped in a zone of the living dead.

For hours he had been utterly engrossed in his work, his only movement the punching of the keys with two stubby index fingers. Now, with a clasping and stretching of his hands that made the knuckles crack in relief, he raised his chin and finally allowed himself to ease the tense muscles in his neck, and to smile.

Slowly shaking his head with incredulity, Nadir Bassein raised himself out of his chair and the position he had occupied since receiving the urgent instructions from Omar Al Kadeh, his eyes lingering a few moments more in awe at the display.

He had never imagined so much money could ever be his. Not that he was a poor man, far from it. He had lived comfortably for many years and had always thought carefully of the future, stashing away decent sums against his old age. But this – this would mean not just comfortable retirement. It would mean luxury for the rest of his days. It would mean his every wish could be fulfilled. He felt a shiver of excitement. Perhaps he could start collecting art, or cars, or racehorses, or pursue some other expensive, exclusive hobby. He could even take the time to find a wife. There would be plenty of women willing to help him spend his money, he was certain of that. Just for life in town, though. Nobody would be allowed to interfere with his sanctuary here. He needed to keep somewhere strictly for himself. He was accustomed to it after all these years alone.

Glancing at his watch, he saw that it had been three and a half hours since Al Kadeh's first call and confirmatory email, but he still had time for a late dinner. His client had been lucky to catch him. Or rather, he had been lucky to receive the call that had come through just after the heli-taxi dropped him off. Of course, such a massive interest as Al Kadeh Construction kept him constantly on his toes and he was used to taking calls at all hours from its chief executive. And as an experienced financial lawyer, he was careful to keep copies of all access codes, accounts and contract details in his safe here, so he had been doubly blessed. Speed had been the essence of the deal and he prided himself that he had done exactly as he had been asked as efficiently as it was possible to do it.

But, nevertheless, he was not entirely at ease.

He considered Omar Al Kadeh more of friend than a client, and had been astonished to learn that the intensely proud and stubborn man had decided to sell out to Subedei Industries. The actual amount of the offer had not been disclosed but Bassein had been able to discern that it was a magnificent sum, substantially more than the company was worth. The condition was that the offer was only on the table for one night.

Perhaps, despite his pride and his deep love for his family name, he had had a price after all, and all it took was for the right sum to be offered. In Nadir Bassein's opinion, this incredible offer had to be because of the New Pyramids tender that Al Kadeh Construction had just been awarded – there was simply no other explanation for it. He had felt it his duty to remind his old friend of how hard he had worked for this tender, of how he'd laughed at the very idea of ever sharing his company or its success with outsiders, especially Subedei Industries. He had felt obliged to point out that this sale was a complete volte-face, a reversal of everything Omar Al Kadeh had claimed to believe in: the honour of his family and the desire to bequeath something great to posterity. But, to be honest, his argument had not been too forceful and it was obvious that it fell on deaf ears. Al Kadeh would brook no opposition.

'I am sole owner!' he had declared. 'This is my decision, and mine alone. This is an opportunity which I am in no position to refuse. Do you understand?'

Nadir understood the power of money – who was immune

to it, after all? When Al Kadeh had offered him one thousand times the usual fee for conducting such a transaction, on condition that the deal was done that night, he had felt that power himself. Besides, if he did not do the deal, there were plenty of other lawyers who would, at a fraction of the price. What did he, Nadir Bassein, have to lose? His retainer from Al Kadeh Construction, which would no doubt cease on transfer of ownership, was paid many times over by this fee.

The transaction itself had been relatively easy. Subedei Industries would pay the sum agreed instantly into Al Kadeh's Swiss account on the signing of a contract that transferred a schedule of all agreements and company assets. The only difficulty was the New Pyramids contract, since the details had not been finalized and there could be some major liabilities – but back came the assurance required: the new owner would assume any and all liabilities involved.

On that basis, Nadir had prepared a simple contract with an attached schedule of all assets and current contracts attached to Al Kadeh Construction. The consideration sum was to be filled in by Omar Al Kadeh himself and he would be arranging the transfer.

In the meantime, Nadir Bassein was instructed to transfer a fee of sixteen million dollars to his own account. Who was he to argue? Omar Al Kadeh was the majority shareholder. He could do as he pleased, even if it was a flat contradiction of everything Nadir had understood about him. The fickleness of human nature, he thought. How the promise of wealth changed values. Omar had spoken of retirement, of moving to South Africa – it was so out of character, particularly as his boys were reaching maturity, taking an active part in the business.

Nadir shrugged to himself. The fee was conditional on there being no questions or issues whatsoever arising after the transaction was complete – but he ought to cover himself. Indeed, he must cover himself with some insurance, just in case. Walking towards the phone lying next to his computer, he examined his conscience and assured himself that he had behaved with perfect probity throughout this whole, strange affair. But still . . . something was niggling him. The decision made, Nadir Bassein picked up the phone to make the call.

Three

The pilot of the Bell Jet Ranger felt that his day was at last improving. Flying at 2000 metres between the towering, tawny Gebal peaks of Katherina and Shomar on the Sinai Peninsula was simply exhilarating.

Such a spectacular sight went some way to making up for the fact that his peaceful holiday had been so rudely interrupted. Admittedly, he hadn't *wanted* a peaceful holiday in the first place, and had in fact protested strongly against the whole idea until it was made clear to him that he really didn't have much choice. He was to get some peace and quiet, and that was an order. And once he'd reached the secluded lodge overlooking the Gulf of Aqaba, one hundred kilometres south of Nuweiba, he'd changed his mind at once. Now, this he could get used to. It was an undisturbed paradise of tranquillity and sophisticated luxury – the perfect place to recharge his batteries. And God knew he needed to replenish his energy, after everything that this job demanded of him.

The best thing of all was that nothing and nobody could reach him – there were no phones, faxes or computers and his mobile was kept firmly switched off. He was incommunicado and loving it. Until last night. But that was, he reminded himself wryly, entirely his own fault.

Feeling good and relaxed after stepping from a vigorous shower following a great day's diving, he had poured himself a pre-prandial malt whisky, sunk into the bubbling Jacuzzi on the canopied terrace, and switched on his phone to make a call. OK, so it was a stupid thing to do. He should have known better. He might have guessed that they'd reach him before he'd even realized that the damn thing had a signal. The instant the phone had chimed 'Scotland the Brave', he'd known the holiday was over.

Of course he had agreed to the request that he travel imme-diately to a remote wadi off the Nile, knowing that the call would not have been made lightly. His superiors would only have contacted him if there had been no realistic alternative. Delay in this kind of situation, as he well knew, simply wasn't an option. He'd set off at once, putting all thoughts of relaxing Jacuzzis far behind him. Irrespective of the errand, when he had said he would do something, his word was sacrosanct. *Passion with Integrity* was the family motto and he was not going to let his Scottish heritage down.

Setting off at dawn, he had driven the lodge's Jeep along the steep mountain road to the small military airbase at Nabi Salih, north of Mount Sinai. He'd had an instinct that he'd find exactly what he needed there, and sure enough, once again, the huge network of contacts he'd built up in his previous career worked to his advantage. The commanding officer of the base was one Wing Commander George Edward Maadi, who just happened to be his former training instructor.

The sight of the wing commander brought back a lot of memories. The Delhi-born officer had devoted his life to mili-tary service and had great faith in the strongest discipline. That, along with his bulldog stare and walrus moustache, had made him a figure to be feared by his students, except the few who'd learned to trust, respect and like their instructor.

'So it is you!' thundered Maadi, his back ramrod straight and his eyes flashing menacingly. 'Connor Brock. Up to no good again, eh? Tell me, does trouble still follow you or do you continue to follow trouble?'

The next moment, the tough façade had been dropped and he had grabbed Brock's hand, pummelling it with his familiar knuckle-crushing shake. 'It's been a long time. To what do I owe the honour of this visit? No – let me guess. You want a favour, eh? For one of your infamous sight-seeing excursions, no doubt? Well, to be honest, I didn't think you were interested in the state of my health.'

Brock had protested with a grin that he was delighted to see Maadi looking so robust and not a day older than when they had last met, but the wing commander brushed away the social niceties and demanded instead to know how he could help. When he had heard that Brock needed to borrow a helicopter, and fast, he had frowned and hesitated.

For a moment, Brock had thought he'd pushed the boundaries of friendship too far; then Maadi's face had cleared and, with a laugh, he had said he would risk it – but he insisted that his friend be accompanied by one Flight Sergeant Benerzat, his top student navigator, arguing that he could not otherwise justify the loan of one of Egypt's military aircraft, however old it was.

'Fine, old friend,' Brock said with a smile. 'Whatever it takes. If you think this sergeant is good, that's fine with me. Where is he? Can he leave immediately? I'm in a bit of a hurry.'

He should have known better than to make assumptions these days. Maadi had summoned Flight Sergeant Benerzat and there was no getting round it – she was gorgeous. She stood to attention in front of Maadi's desk, black-haired and olive-skinned, her dark eyes solemn and the flight fatigues she wore outlining her excellent figure beautifully.

'Flight Sergeant Benerzat is my insurance for your returning my machine in one piece,' said Maadi gruffly. 'You never could return the same way you left, could you, Connor? This way you'll have to make sure I get both my helicopter and my sergeant back. Unharmed. Understand?'

'Absolutely,' said Brock smoothly. 'I wouldn't dream of doing anything else. You know me, Wing Commander. I'm sure Flight Sergeant Benerzat will be an excellent asset to my little sightseeing trip. And you can be sure that she'll be safe with me.'

'Hmmm.' The wing commander stared up at him from under bristling eyebrows. 'You're a man of your word, Brock. I know that. I want everything back here at the base within twenty-four hours. Clear?'

Brock had smiled. 'Yes, sir.'

'Flight Sergeant –' Maadi addressed the young officer curtly – 'you are to navigate the flight to whatever destination Brock instructs you. Then get him back here. Obey his orders and make sure he doesn't do anything stupid with our aircraft. I'm quite fond of the old things, even if they are well past their retirement dates – and so is the government. Understand?'

'Yes, sir,' said Flight Sergeant Benerzat obediently, and her

30

dark eyes flicked quickly to Brock and then away again to the space over her commanding officer's head.

'Good. Off you go then. Have a good trip, Brock – and I'll see you tomorrow – at the latest.'

Yes, thought Brock, the view was certainly spectacular – inside the craft as well as out. Flight Sergeant Benerzat sat beside him, calculating the co-ordinates according to Brock's instructions. Her splendid eyes were shielded by dark glasses and her face was almost obscured by the earphones she was wearing, but there was no hiding the fact that she was an extremely beautiful woman.

Stop it, Brock scolded himself, and turned his gaze resolutely back to the golden scenery outside. Not only was this hardly the time or the place, but the last thing he should be thinking about was the attractiveness of a soldier under his protection. And he had to concentrate on the task in hand. He was grateful that the sergeant didn't appear to be the chatty type, but let him get on with piloting the helicopter in peace.

Feeling pleased with the way things were turning out, Brock guided the Bell Jet Ranger away from the receding Sinai Peninsula of creviced valleys, across the shadowy Red Sea towards the greying yellow horizon of the Eastern Desert.

The navigator was also pleased. Bored rigid doing menial tasks way below her capacity, Neusheen Benerzat had welcomed this unexpected flight. Gaining a first in physics from Brown University at Rhode Island had been the pinnacle of Neusheen's life and she'd been looking forward to pursuing her academic studies. But her father had insisted that she had to do her two years of national service. It was to serve his own political ambitions, she knew that, and despite her arguments that she could better serve her country as an international scientist, her father refused to allow it. Privileged and pampered Neusheen might be, but she had no way of resisting her father's wishes, only managing to wring the concession that she could return to her studies when her service was over.

Neusheen had applied herself to the task: she had quickly gained her navigational qualifications and won her wings. And those two years finished, at last, at the end of next week. She was looking forward to getting back to a culture where she wasn't treated as a second-class citizen simply because she was a woman.

Checking her co-ordinates, she confirmed their position. 'Just a few minutes from reaching your destination co-ordinates, sir,' she informed her pilot assertively.

'Thanks,' Brock acknowledged briefly. He didn't look at her but kept his searching gaze on the arid land below them.

Since leaving the fertile conurbations that sprawled the western shore of the Red Sea, the view, except for the occasional brown wadis or dried-up river beds, had become increasingly monotonous as the vast expanse of the Eastern Desert opened before them. Neusheen wondered if the pilot expected her to chat to him. She hoped not. She couldn't bear the kind of empty pleasantries that she usually associated with the boring, political types who thronged her father's house when he gave his cocktail parties.

She allowed herself to slide her gaze over the man beside her. She was curious about him, this tall, athletic, broad-shouldered stranger, dressed in weathered safari trousers and a blue denim shirt. After all, it was not every man who could walk in from nowhere and charm a helicopter out of Wing Commander Maadi. Neusheen was fairly sure that today was the first time she'd seen her CO even smile.

Apart from the quiet yet strong confidence the pilot exuded, the most compelling physical feature about him was his eyes. Azure in colour, they were full of a kind of sardonic humour, as though their owner found it hard to take life seriously, or concentrate on anything of importance, and yet she'd felt that they'd shrewdly assessed her in seconds. She put him at about fifteen years older than herself, though when he smiled the years seemed to fall off him and he appeared closer to her own age of twenty-four. But his dark hair was speckled with a little silver at the temples, so she guessed he had to be over thirty-five. Old, she thought, but still handsome.

A tanned strong face reflected a resilient and determined character. Despite the etched laughter lines, it had a remoteness and an occasional hard look whenever he appeared deep in thought. His professionalism in going rapidly through pre-flight procedure and confirming the flight co-ordinates had surprised and impressed her – he clearly knew what he was doing, this Connor Brock.

She hadn't meant to stare, but the man suddenly turned his

head to look straight at her, as though he could read her mind and knew what she was thinking. Embarrassed, she tried to cover it up by saying strongly, 'We are not far from the Nile here. It's about thirty kilometres distant. This is what you would call a stockbroker belt – big houses, rich owners, complete privacy, all a short ride from Cairo.'

Brock smiled. 'Good to know my navigator has all the specialist knowledge I require.'

From their height, the grooved wadis looked like tentacles searching blindly at the bottom of towering peaks for Mother Nile. In the distance a large tentacle seemed to spread out as Brock flew towards it. A large section of the wadi that wove between the deep barren valleys below actually contained water. Water must have been siphoned off from the distant Nile by pipe and then dammed to create an oasis of privacy.

Brock swept the Bell down the mountainous valley and a luxurious residence, complete with pool and helipad, came into view. Walls three metres high enclosed a lavish garden that contrasted with the rough, dry terrain surrounding the man-made oasis. Brock looked about for an appropriate place to set down, ignoring the obvious charms of the empty helipad. He never took the easy path if he could possibly help it. And it seemed that someone else thought the same way. As they circled the house, he caught sight of a grounded helicopter on the lower rear side of the residence, previously hidden by his flight path.

'Looks like we're not the only visitors,' commented Brock, as he throttled back and banked into a wide-turn descent.

Neusheen looked down at where Brock had indicated. Below them, a figure in flight overalls emerged from the parked heli-copter and stared upwards at them for a few moments before quickly running towards an entrance set in the high wall of the residence.

'Hmm, looks like another pilot,' commented Neusheen. 'Could it be the owner, perhaps? Or his personal pilot? Is your friend expecting you?'

Brock didn't reply and she suddenly realized she knew nothing about this mission. She'd assumed that they must be calling on whoever it was who owned this lavish place but, actually, there was no reason at all why she should make that assumption. She felt a prickle of curiosity as Brock banked round for another turn.

A moment later, the pilot reappeared accompanied a giant of a man built like a sumo wrestler and dressed incongruously in a too-tight suit, his long black hair tied back into a ponytail.

'Well, well. The entertainment's a touch on the heavy side, wouldn't you agree?' said Brock, watching as the huge man waddled a few steps forward and raised his hand to shield his eyes and stare up at the approaching helicopter.

'He's the size of a house!' exclaimed Neusheen. 'He must be a bodyguard. The rich guys often have them. Even my father has a couple – but none as big as that.' As she watched, the colossus gesticulated to his colleague before quickly turning and disappearing back through the doorway.

The smaller man began to walk briskly towards his machine, breaking into a slight run.

'They don't look overjoyed to see us, do they?' Brock grinned over at Neusheen. 'I've seen friendlier faces on a Welsh number eight. We seem to have put the wind up them – looks like the gruesome twosome are in a hurry to leave. Well, we'll just have to see what it is they're so anxious about, won't we?'

Turning the craft back for a final straight descent, he hid his frown from his navigator. There was no point in making her nervous but something did not seem right. His jaw clenched as he felt a familiar tingling sensation on the back of his neck. His intuition was throwing out warning signals of danger ahead. As soon as the runners of the helicopter touched the ground, he acted.

'Take over the controls now,' Brock commanded, without looking at the young flight sergeant sitting next to him. 'Drop me and then get back in the air immediately.'

'What?' said Neusheen, startled.

'Just do it. You have control – now!'

Brock was already out of his seat, leaving Neusheen to grab the joystick before it could enjoy its freedom. Dumbfounded, she allowed her training to take over.

Pulling the rescue flare pistol from its overhead casing, Brock thrust it into the map pocket of his safari trousers. He took off his flight headphones and immediately lost mike contact with Neusheen. 'Stay in the air until you see my signal,' he shouted over the roar of the engine and the thump of the blades turning above them.

'What?' she yelled back, unable to look at him while she wrestled with the controls.

'Wait for my flare!' Brock jumped to the ground and began to jog determinedly towards the other helicopter.

The pilot saw him coming. He had already fired up his machine and the blades were revolving increasingly fast. As Brock got closer, he could see confusion and uncertainty on the face of the pilot. He obviously had no idea what to do, and was considering if he should take off without his enormous friend. Reaching the aircraft, Brock was surprised to see the pilot suddenly vacate it by the other door, leaving the engine throbbing and the blades turning.

'Hey, what's the rush?' he called.

The man sped quickly around his machine, trying to avoid Brock, who immediately diverted course to intercept him.

Brock shouted again. 'There's no need to panic – I just want to talk. Friend!'

The two men stood warily facing each other at the side of the helicopter, the pilot's gaze slipping about nervously as though he were looking for an escape route, but Brock was ready for any move he might make. They stood facing each other for a moment, each swaying with their readiness to move, then the pilot made a sudden reach for something inside his jacket. Brock immediately tucked his head down and dived, hitting the pilot squarely in the chest, the force of his momentum making the other man stagger backwards, knocking the wind out of him and flinging his empty hand upwards.

Automatically following through the action, Brock brought his fist up to smash into the pilot's jaw. If someone appeared to be going to take a pot-shot at him, he always preferred to take decisive action. There would be plenty of time to ask questions, or, if necessary, proffer tender apologies later. Right now, things did not feel the way they should and in such circumstances Brock knew that action was always more important than words.

Despite being winded, the pilot anticipated Brock's follow-up blow and escaped it by swinging himself to one side like a monkey on a jungle vine.

A split second later, Brock's eye caught the dull glint of a weapon as it appeared in the pilot's hand. Without hesitation, he once more dived headlong at the man, chopping hard with his right hand against the wrist holding the small pistol that was inexorably being pointed towards his chest. A cry of infuriated pain escaped the pilot's throat as the weapon spun from his hand. Doggedly, he tried to twist for it, not noticing Brock's clenched right fist fly out to catch him full on the jaw. His eyes rolled into the back of his head as his body collapsed heavily to the ground.

Stepping around the unconscious body, Brock moved toward the machine. It would, he thought, be prudent to switch off the engine and stop the dangerous blades slicing through the air.

Climbing in, Brock settled himself in the pilot's seat and started going through the close-down procedure. Suddenly the whole machine rocked and Brock turned, startled, to see a pair of strong hands pulling violently at the other door, as though attempting to wrench it from its hinges. A moment later, the door was open and the pilot's vast colleague appeared. Brock saw a face with high prominent cheekbones and a wide forehead under thickly greased-back hair. Black eyes, on fire with pure malice, bored into him.

His huge body crammed into an expensive-looking designer suit that seemed totally out of place for the desert, the oriental man was slightly shorter than Brock but, as he had previously observed, the width of a sumo wrestler. In the moment they locked eyes, Brock realized that the Chinese man's intentions were murderous. Then, in an instant, the bulky form climbed with surprising agility into the cockpit.

There was no time to shut off the throttle as Brock rose quickly in defence, knocking the stick hard with his left leg and causing the throttle to scream louder and the machine to lurch. The unexpected movement unbalanced both Brock and the suited sumo. While Brock flung out his hand to grab the seat for support and stayed on his feet, his attacker crashed to the floor, once more rocking the helicopter.

Sweeping his right hand downwards to his map pocket, Brock grabbed the jutting handle of the flare pistol, intending to use it as a club to subdue the fallen man, but before he could, his mammoth assailant sprang back to his feet and kicked out viciously.

Brock's reactions were highly trained and he swiftly side-stepped the lethal kick, instantly grabbing his advantage and kicking out hard himself at the groin that was now vulnerable in front of him. The big man bellowed with pain but the blow seemed to enrage him more than hold him back. A huge fist pounded into his stomach like a sledgehammer. The pistol flew from his grasp and he was thrown backwards through the open door. As he fell, his leg caught in the overhang of the landing gear, making his body twist painfully and effectively anchoring him to the helicopter. He fought to free himself just as he realized that the unpiloted machine was beginning to move, bouncing forward as though eager to be airborne and dragging him along the stony ground. Caught like a snared animal in a hunter's trap, Brock urgently tried to catch the open door swinging above him: if he could grasp the handle, he would be able to shift his weight and pull himself free.

Seeing his enemy's struggles, the big man took up the advantage, snatching the fallen flare gun and standing himself in the open doorway above the helpless Brock. With one hand grasping the door jamb, he lifted the gun to shoot his victim, smiling as he did so.

The noise of the lethal blades as they sliced the surrounding air was deafening and the small stones thrown up by the vortex savagely stung Brock's face and arms. In a desperate bid for survival, he swung up his arm and punched the swinging door shut just as the pistol fired.

The expelled flare hit the slamming door and ricocheted back inside the small cockpit. Intense, blinding light burst out of the machine and a wave of panic engulfed Brock as he thrashed to escape from being trapped by a moving fireball.

Bracing himself for the worst, he realized that the ear-splitting roar had suddenly ceased. The engine stopped its straining and the runners dragging him over the uneven ground came to a stop. Brock jerked his leg free and lay prone, listening to the blades above him whisper through the air like scythes cutting wheat.

Trying to ignore the pain in his leg, Brock got back to his feet. The intense light of the flare had died away and it seemed eerily silent now that the grinding din of the engine had ceased. He paused for a moment and then opened the door to assess the situation inside the aircraft. The large man was slumped between the two front seats, lying on his left arm. His head lay at an odd angle by the throttle stick, his eyes closed in a face charred and blackened from the scorching projectile.

'Must have caught the full force of the flare right in the face,' said Brock out loud. 'Nasty business. But very thoughtful to use his neck to close the throttle. Selfless to the end.'

A quick search of the brute's pockets revealed a betting slip from Happy Valley Races in Hong Kong and a Chinese credit card. Both items went into Brock's own jacket.

Deftly, Brock removed the nylon cord from the seat map pockets, climbed down from the cockpit and limped back to where he had left the pilot he had earlier incapacitated. Less than ten minutes had passed since he had first jumped to the ground, and he searched the sky for the Bell Ranger helicopter as he walked.

'Just what the hell is happening here?'

'It's been a little more action-packed than I expected, I have to admit.' Brock glanced up at Neusheen seriously, then turned away to bind up the hands of the unconscious pilot with the nylon cord he'd taken from the other helicopter, while Neusheen fought for control over herself. He looked over at Neusheen's angry face and allowed her a wry smile. 'Look – I'm sorry. I certainly didn't mean to get you mixed up in this, which is why I wanted you well out of the way. Our chums here meant business and they wouldn't have stopped at a little beating, you can be sure of that.'

Neusheen opened her mouth to retort, but Brock cut her off. 'We'll talk about it later. Right now, I need you to stay here with the helicopter.' He stood up and made his way swiftly to the house, entering it through the door that his massive assailant had left open. A short corridor opened into a large study. In the centre of the floor strewn with books was a body.

With eyes bulging more than usual from the ligature that had been tightened around his neck with his own ornate letter opener, Nadir Bassein lay propped against his desk like a lifeless mannequin discarded from a window display.

Brock went to him immediately and checked for signs of life, though he knew it was futile. Those thugs outside had obviously been practised killers. This poor man hadn't had a chance. He stood up and scanned the room.

A sliding door torn from its hinges had been revealed by the large bookcase being thrown to the floor. Inside the hidden room was a mess of files and electronic equipment. The safe in the wall was empty except for a pile of bonds and some photographs. It had been thoroughly searched, that was clear. There was nothing of interest in here.

Brock turned back to the study. What had those assassins been after? He caught sight of a black calf-hide attaché case resting behind the door. *Bingo*, thought Brock. The sumo must have been intending to return for his prize and had left it neatly here for Brock to find. Going over to it, he flicked its latches open and saw that it contained a small laptop computer and a CD-ROM with sheaves of printed emails and schedules dated the previous night stuffed on top. In the side pocket were thick wads of 500-Euro notes and 100-dollar US bills, which Brock surmised had been recently removed from the safe. Probably a little fillip for the hired hands – any booty around to be theirs for the taking if they delivered what their bosses demanded.

As far as Brock could tell from a brief skim read, none of these messages had been copied to Zurich. Bassein must have contacted them by phone and had probably decided to wait until Brock arrived and hand over everything in person.

Brock looked grimly at the dead man. If he had arrived just a little earlier, Bassein would still be alive. Now, that's pointless thinking, Brock chided himself. He'd long ago resolved not to agonise over 'what ifs'. Life was unpredictable, chaotic and unfair, and to start thinking he had the power to change it or make it better for everyone was madness. He did what he could – that was all. And he was not the cause of this poor fellow's murder – that was the work of someone else, someone he would no doubt soon be closer to than was perhaps comfortable. Bringing about some kind of justice was the best he could do for the dead man now.

Thirty minutes had passed by the time Brock returned to the helipad and he could see that his young navigator was pacing up and down, warily watching the bound pilot.

'It's time we went,' said Brock as he approached.

'Oh,' replied Neusheen, feigning disappointment, 'haven't we

39

time to cause havoc somewhere else? Perhaps land on the Sphinx or maybe invade Sudan?'

Brock smiled, pleased to see that Neusheen retained her feisty spirit. Turning to the bound and somewhat dejected pilot he enquired, 'Well, does our guest speak English?' Receiving no reply from him he curtly continued, 'Not to worry. Come on, you're coming for a little ride with us.'

The man turned his face away with a look of scorn. Neusheen regarded him with distaste. 'Must we take him?'

'He doesn't have to come the whole way,' Brock said with a crooked smile. 'He might ask us to drop him off somewhere and I expect we'll be only too happy to oblige.'

With still no response, Brock grabbed the man by the scruff of his neck and pushed him towards the aircraft. The man struggled and looked at Neusheen frantically.

'Good idea,' she said, striding purposefully towards the heli-copter.

Four

'Alexander the Great. Caesar. Napoleon. Rommel. They all came here, these famous and infamous conquerors, seeking divine intervention at this lonely oasis sheltered from a timeless sea of sand by these same pink and white cliffs that rise before you.' The voice of the young woman rose, measured and clear, with the beautiful tone of a low bell. 'We can only imagine the answers they sought here, but all of them wanted to confirm their destiny, their greatness.'

Pausing for effect, the young woman raised her head slightly towards the mud-brick warren of jagged pinnacles that rose from the ancient hill of Aghurmi, their immediate destination.

She was striking to look at, with the large dark eyes, high cheekbones and sensual, proud mouth of a noble heritage. Such beauty, coupled with a perfectly modulated accent indicating an Oxford education, ensured the rapt attention of her audience. The two men were mesmerized by her and fascinated by the blend of myth and mystery in her words. She was enjoying the power she held over them as they stood in the clearing among the dense palm groves, gazing out over the ancient oracle temple and the old town.

'Behold!' she commanded dramatically, stretching out a slender arm towards the temple built into the hill, and turning her head in classic pharaoh profile, emphasizing her glossy straight black hair, curving eyebrows and long eyelashes. 'The temple of the Oracle of Ammon.'

The men turned obediently to look in the direction she indicated. For VIPs, they were remarkably docile.

Ayeesha Al Fahila laughed quietly to herself. She made a good tour guide, and she'd certainly brought a new lease of life to

41

the Supreme Council of Antiquities, where she had recently been appointed director. Until her arrival, it had been devoid of inspiration or money, as mummified as its relics. Her recently arranged appointment had changed that. Now, with the huge injection of commercial funds that she had been partly instrumental in arranging, new sites could finally be excavated, and everything had changed. The place had come to life. No wonder they had swallowed her ideas like hungry desert dogs scavenging on any morsel that would sustain their empty bellies.

'I never imagined that oases were spread out so,' said the taller of the two oil executives. Wearing an old baseball cap with newly bought khaki shirt and trousers, the slightly overweight Texan had the look of a man who had spent too much time in air-conditioned offices and long-haul planes. Despite his greyish-white pasty look, his bright blue eyes indicated the inner persistence that had built his business from a wildcat venture to a respected oil company.

John Ridge and his colleague had travelled almost 500 kilometres from Alexandria Airport by helicopter that morning, and he was still in awe at the immense area of green in the middle of the desert that had appeared like a mirage as they emerged from the ragged Qantarah Depression.

'Are they always like this?' he asked.

'Oases are natural depressions below sea level and can be of an immense size,' offered Ayeesha. 'Siwa Oasis is over one thousand square kilometres, though the southern half is covered by a sea of sand. It is eighteen metres below sea level and its water comes from Equatorial Africa, taking half a millennium to get here, passing through salty strata on its long journey north. That's what makes this the saltiest of the six large oases in Egypt. There are smaller ones but none is inhabited. The romantic image of desert life belongs to a forgotten past. Today the camels have gone, along with most of the tiny places that nomadic caravans stopped at for water.'

'Geez, will you look at the vegetation here? Who would have thought that all these fruit trees would grow in sea water?'

Matt Ferguson was shorter than his American colleague, but the tanned, red-headed Irishman, clad in weathered stone-coloured shirt and jeans, looked stocky and solid. He had exclaimed with surprise at the abundance of fig, olive, lemon

42

and pomegranate trees as they had walked through the groves to reach the clearing where they stood now.

Ayeesha looked over her shoulder as she led the way towards the hill. 'Being slightly salty from rock minerals does not turn fresh water into sea water. Later you will discover that the water has a distinctive taste but it is refreshing. All over this ancient oasis are natural wells, many of them big enough for bathing, where the water is so clear you can see bubbles of ancient trapped air still rising from twenty metres below.

'Come, follow me to the temple,' she added, 'we only have a short time before leaving for the Cambyses II exploration site.'

'Seems bizarre to drill for oil and strike gold, so to speak,' said Ridge, as the two men caught up with their beautiful guide and strode beside her. He was eager to turn the conversation towards the real purpose of their visit.

'We at the Supreme Council of Antiquities are delighted at this vindication of our decision to work in partnership with commercial interests. In the course of exploration for oil, all manner of artefacts, temples and tombs have been discovered and saved. The crowning glory is this magnificent find of the Lost Army, giving us a veritable treasure trove from the twenty-seventh dynasty.'

'What's puzzling me,' said the Texan in his slow soft drawl, 'is why you've named this site Cambyses the Second. Where's the first one?'

'You'll have to excuse my friend,' Ferguson said apologetically, as the woman's eyes sparkled with scorn. 'I don't think ancient history is really his thing. In fact, I have to admit that my own grasp on it isn't so hot. Cambyses was a king, wasn't he? Would you be kind enough to tell us the story?'

Ayeesha shot him a look of disdain but the Irishman's appealing green eyes softened her haughtiness. Perhaps she ought to look at it as educating these ignorant infidels in the glorious history of her country. 'Very well,' she said graciously.

The two men listened respectfully as she began. 'According to Herodotus – an historian of ancient times,' she added, fearing she could not rely on these barbarians to know even that – 'Cambyses II was a mad tyrannical despot. Having defeated the Egyptian Pharaoh Psamtek the Third in 525BC, he became the first pharaoh of a Persian dynasty that ruled for almost two hundred years, until Alexander the Great defeated Darius the Third and became King of Persia and Pharaoh of Egypt. Ironically, Cambyses's father was Cyrus the Great, the role model of Alexander the Great.'

'Why is that ironic?' asked Ridge. 'Don't all leaders have a role model, good or bad? Look at Saddam. We learned in the US that his hero was Stalin, another despot.'

'It is ironic because Cambyses sought out the Oracle of Ammon, some say to seek legitimization of his empire, as Alexander did two centuries later, although others believe Cambyses may have intended to destroy the oracle. What we do know is that he sent out a fully equipped fifty-thousand-strong army from Thebes, supported by a great caravan of pack animals.'

'Fifty thousand?' interrupted the Irishman. 'To attack this place? That's a hellava load of people to face down a hole in a cliff.'

'One of the largest armies of ancient Egypt – and it vanished.'

The Texan looked quizzical. 'How could an army just vanish? This sounds like a hoax to me – real Bermuda Triangle stuff.'

Ayeesha tried to remain patient. 'Crossing the desert is no mean feat,' she explained carefully, as though stating the obvious to very small children. 'The distance between this oasis and the nearest that could service such a multitude is at Bahriyah, three hundred and twenty-five kilometres away. That would have been at best a thirty-day trek in blistering heat.'

'So they just got lost and died of thirst then?' offered Ferguson. 'Hence the Lost Army, eh?'

'It is believed that a freak sandstorm of enormous magni-tude was the reason,' Ayeesha continued. The Irishman's charm, she thought, could be a little grating. 'Storms in the desert can be as dangerous as storms at sea. According to Herodotus, who spoke directly with Siwa Bedouins, the troops were finally nearing Siwa, having struggled for days through soft sand, and were taking a rest when a catastrophe came down on them without warning. A powerful and blindingly dense sandstorm came from the south and buried the whole army alive, along with all the support animals, chariots, armoury and a huge treasure. History records that there was not a trace of it left. Until now, perhaps, if we have found what we think we have.'

Ridge looked up at the sky with some concern. 'How often do storms like that happen?'

'Well, we don't get to hear of the truly fierce ones unless the people caught in them survive, but they certainly happen. The last major incident was when a caravan of two thousand people disappeared without trace in 1805.

'With radios and trucks, a journey that once took weeks is now only a seven-hour drive from Cairo. Yet, like the sea, the desert is a beast that has no mercy for the ill-prepared. Even Alexander, who departed from Siwa along the route Cambyses's army had travelled towards this oasis, ran out of water before his army reached Bahriyah, *en route* to Memphis on the Nile.

'And today, if you break down without sufficient water, as people are still stupid enough to do, the chances of survival are slim, particularly at this time of the year when sand and dust storms stirred up by the spring winds are prevalent.'

'But with mobile phones and satellite navigation—' protested Ferguson.

Ayeesha stopped him with a look and said, 'Though you might not get lost with satellite-directional on-board computers, storms can still be disorienting. I have heard stories where people go off into the desert with every modern navigational device available and yet still have to be found by a rescue party, if they are lucky.'

Ferguson was clearly not convinced. For people to get lost even with the benefit of satellite navigation was beyond him.

'Visitors to the desert,' Ayeesha said pointedly, 'have little conception of the size of the Sahara, which includes portions of eleven countries. It is a barren mass of desert stretching over an area that covers eight and a half million square kilometres.'

Ridge looked at Ferguson with a smile. He might not know about ancient history but he knew about facts and figures relating to the Sahara. 'Matt, my friend, you know as well as I do that you gotta respect the desert. No point in underestimating this baby, not if you're going to drill for oil and strike it lucky. This place is dripping with iron, copper, manganese, tin, nickel, chromium, zinc, lead, cobalt, silver, gold, platinum . . . you name it. Even thorium and uranium, if that's your bag. But without a bit of understanding of how this magnificent place works, you're gonna get nowhere fast, no matter how many machines and computers you got.'

Ayeesha looked mollified by this speech, and pressed forward towards the temple.

Ferguson followed her. Ridge was close behind, his expression grim now that their guide could no longer see his face. He was impatient with all this delay and having to pretend for politeness' sake that he was interested in some damn temple. It was gas and oil that interested him. Metallic minerals? Forget it. They were often tortuously inaccessible, making their recovery a waste of time and money. But gas and oil . . . that was different. They were viable and Ridge knew it and he was damned if he was going to get cut out of any deal when he'd been instrumental in bringing the whole thing about. He'd heard that some competitor had appeared on the scene, a shady outfit offering some under-the-counter political deal. Just who the hell was Ammon Oil anyway? He had never heard of them until they began building a refinery right next door to his own at Alexandria. Well, he was on his guard, and he didn't get to be head of his own successful oil company without being a formidable businessman. He was content to go along with this public-relations tour that had been laid on for him, but he wanted to get to the negotiating table at this Cambyses II. Hell, they needed his pipelines, didn't they?

They reached the entrance to the temple and turned to look out over the green expanse below. Ayeesha gestured out over the impressive view. 'They say this was a city of several hundred thousand people once, a city marked on ancient maps as Ammonium, because of the temple. Today it is just a village of ten thousand. Who knows? The exploration for oil and antiquity may bring prosperity to this area once more.' The woman looked suddenly rapturous. 'Today a new era is dawning, a new dynasty, perhaps. It is only thirty years since Egyptian sovereignty was restored to this soil, after a millennium and a half of colonial rule. But now our influence is growing great again, as great perhaps as that of antiquity, when Egypt was the guiding light of the world. Who knows what we are capable of? I don't, gentlemen. But perhaps the Oracle of Ammon does.'

As they stood at the threshold of the temple entrance, both men turned to look at the dark woman between them, drawn by the fervent way she had spoken of the past and future.

46

'What happened to Cambyses? Was he lost with his army?' asked Ferguson.

'No, he had stayed in Thebes. But the loss of his army was the beginning of the end for him. Having conquered Egypt with an army of mercenaries, he heard of trouble at home in Persia and decided to return. Passing through Syria on his journey, he learned that his younger brother Bardiya, supported by influential nobles, had seized power and taken the great throne of Cyrus. Upon hearing the news, he swiftly mounted his horse to finish the journey home and, in his haste, stupidly managed to stab himself in the thigh with his own dagger. Believing his fate was sealed, as prophesied by Egyptian priests, he awaited his death. Sure enough, the wound became gangrenous and he died. I'm sure few people mourned the passing of such a tyrant. You know he once had an enemy's sons murdered – their throats slit and their blood mixed with water and wine and drunk – in front of their father's very eyes.'

Ayeesha led the way towards the inner sanctum of the Ammon Temple. They halted in the darkness, their eyes adjusting to the cold gloom inside the murky stone cavern. She paused dramatically and then said, 'But here, exactly one hundred and ninety years after Cambyses's death, right where *you* stand *now*, stood Alexander the Great.'

'Holy mother of God, is that so?' whispered Ferguson.

The two men stood in reverence, aware that they were standing in the very footsteps of history.

'Yes, this is indeed only one of two rooms in existence that we know for certain Alexander stood in. The other is Cyrus the Great's tomb near the ancient Persian capital at Pasargade, or Paradise in English, where some say Alexander was directed to go by the oracle to retrieve something.'

Ferguson raised his eyebrows. 'Something? Don't we know what it was?'

'No. But what we do know is that Alexander was greeted here as the son of the god Ammon, or, as his scribe Callisthenes recorded, the son of Zeus. Indeed, the Greeks revered this Ammonium oracle with almost as much importance as the Zeus sanctuary at Delphi.'

'So they thought Alexander was the son of god. Well, little wonder they called him Great,' commented Ridge. 'And he must have had something powerful on his side. I heard he became master of the known world in less than half the time it's taken me to build my company.'

'Quite so,' continued Ayeesha, lifting one eyebrow at the Texan's guileless comparison of himself with the great conqueror. 'He was a phenomenon. Few exist today with the fortitude and dynastic vision of Pharaoh Alexander, despite the billions more that populate our planet. Many have dreams, but few choose to follow them.'

The three visitors to the Ammon sanctuary were silent as they entered the small inner sanctum that measured just three paces by six. Here, they knew, kings, pharaohs and emperors had stood, the only people ever to be allowed alone in this sacred room. Here, the mightiest on earth had asked their most secret questions of the god.

The three stood there, not looking at each other, as though considering what question they themselves would ask of the divine.

The next moment, both Ridge and Ferguson were lying on the floor unconscious.

Five

ZURICH

The board of ICE sat around a black glass table; four men, formal in sombre suits and ties, each with a console in front of him. Despite the haste in which the meeting had been convened, every board member was alert, calm and concentrating on the matter in hand.

The chairman, Sir Duncan Buchanan, a six-foot-tall Scotsman with a mop of greying red hair, glanced around the table at his colleagues. He raised one bushy eyebrow in a furrowed forehead.

'There are too many irregularities and unanswered questions here,' he said in his soft brogue. The gentle voice belied the iron will that had taken him from a tiny tooling garage in Rosyth, Scotland, to being the world's leading manufacturer of oil, shipping and construction equipment. 'There are too many roads that lead nowhere. What do you think, Paul?'

'I think this is looking exceptionally bad.' Dr Paul van Lederman, founder of ICE, gazed frankly at his old friend, his expression concerned. 'I don't think I've ever seen anything quite like this.' He looked round at the other two members of the board, Carl Honstrom, chief of field operations, and Jean Luc Cambriol, director of Interpol. 'Gentlemen, if we ever had a reason to be confident of our role in the world, it is now.'

ICE – or the Investigation of Corporate Espionage – was the brainchild of the tall, distinguished-looking Dutchman, whose quietly elegant dark-blue suits and crisp white shirts concealed a taste for risk and adventure. At twenty-one, he had defied his father's ambitions for him and joined the French Foreign Legion, a raw recruit motivated by romantic stories and a rebellious attitude. Five years in the hardest school he could

49

possibly have imagined had knocked that out of him and taught him discipline and realism. Once he had gained the rank of captain, he left to join the corporate world, moving to Zurich to work with a global insurance group, pulling himself up through the ranks with skill and determination, eventually becoming CEO. On retiring, he had accepted the invitation to bring his expertise on security and investment to the think tanks of the European Parliament – and that was when he had realized how wrong things were going.

First, it was the corporate governance scandals that rocked Europe, shaking faith in the probity of business to the core. Then the pension fund debacles began to hit and the stock market started to become as jumpy as a chained bear surrounded by barking dogs. Not only were van Lederman's retirement plans seriously affected by the chaos but there was an added ingredient, an unknown that undermined confidence in the markets throughout the world. Terrorism. Random acts of violence and hostility, with the aim of attacking Western economies, began to bite hard, and corporate bureaucracy was helpless in the face of it. Van Lederman knew he had to do something about it.

With the help of his friend, Sir Duncan Buchanan, van Lederman used his considerable network of knowledge and contacts to form ICE, a unit specifically created to investigate threats of terrorist sabotage or passive espionage against industry, and to provide early warning of anything that might jeopardize trade for developed and developing nations. The aim of ICE was to protect investment security and the economic future.

Industry was right behind them. Funding began to pour in from the major multi-national industries: pharmaceutical and chemical manufacturers; electronic, technological and communications companies; banking, insurance and energy. Once ICE had proved its integrity and effectiveness by investigating and halting potentially damaging corporate scandals and espionage, governments and intelligence agencies began to show an interest in forming alliances and sharing information with them. The European Parliament provided a substantial budget and offices were opened in Zurich, London and Washington, though the US had yet to be as eager to hand information back as it was to take it.

ICE enjoyed a substantial reputation for protecting the

50

interests of industry and guarding economic stability throughout the world; its advisory board was comprised of business chiefs of the greatest prominence and it had contacts at the highest government levels in the most powerful countries on earth.

But now, if van Lederman's instincts were correct, and they usually were, ICE was about to face its greatest challenge.

'Subedei Industries,' van Lederman stated, his gaze resting on each of his colleagues in turn. 'On the face of it, as you know, a respectable business group based in Beijing. It appears to be doing what a great many businesses are in the wake of the Iraq war, now that tensions are defusing and sanctions are being lifted – seeking development opportunities in the Middle East and North Africa. In the last year, Subedei has increased his interests at a meteoric rate in these areas. And most of these initiatives are good ones: good for stability and good for growth.

'Our concern is that among the wheat, the weeds are also springing up – unscrupulous groups taking advantage of the situation through organized crime or through the unsettled status quo. Subedei Industries is not necessarily in that category, but the reality is that an inordinate amount of contracts have been awarded to it recently. Far more than could possibly be legitimate in ordinary circumstances. Though the information available indicates that the transactions are legal and above board, warning lights are coming on.'

'How much information *is* available, Paul?' asked Sir Duncan, leaning back in his leather chair.

Van Lederman smiled ruefully. 'You won't be surprised to learn that there's very little. Lawyers are always quick to claim client confidentiality, as we all know, even when regulations demand transparency. That's why the situation has recently stepped up a notch in terms of urgency.' Van Lederman glanced down at his notes. 'When a lawyer actually volunteers information to us, I always get a nasty feeling.'

'But that's what we are here for, isn't it?' put in Carl Honstrom. 'To deal with those nasty feelings and find out what is behind them.'

'You're absolutely right, Carl.'

'What is it you've learned?' asked Jean Luc Cambriol, leaning forward with interest.

'Three days ago, we received a call from a lawyer, one Nadir

51

Bassein, acting for a major construction and shipping company in Egypt, Al Kadeh Construction. The company was sold without warning in a high-speed transaction to – you guessed it – Subedei Industries. The lawyer had misgivings about the deal that he himself negotiated, and contacted us. His suspicions have heightened the concerns we already had about Subedei.'

Honstrom said enthusiastically, 'But that's excellent news, isn't it? That is the break we've been waiting for, surely.'

Van Lederman returned his colleague's eager look with a grim one. 'Up to a point. Our investigator arrived to find the talkative lawyer would be saying very little more on the subject. He'd been murdered.'

Sir Duncan whistled lightly through his teeth and shook his head. 'A bad business,' he said. 'Very bad. Did the investigator find anything of use?'

'He did,' said a deep voice from the doorway, and the board members turned to see Connor Brock standing there.

Carl Honstrom rose to his feet. 'Connor! Impeccable timing as always.' He held out his hand to Brock, who came forward and shook it. 'Good to see you. I'm always happy when my director of special operations makes it back from the field.'

'I'm always happy to be back,' said Brock dryly, 'though my timing could be improved on, given recent events.' He looked over to van Lederman. 'Hello, Paul.'

Van Lederman smiled back quietly in Brock's direction. 'Connor. Sit down. We're just discussing the case and what we know about Subedei Industries.'

Brock took a seat at the table and leaned back easily in his chair. He seemed completely relaxed in the presence of the board and nodded a greeting at each of them. 'I hope that there'll be a lot more to add in a very short time. I arrived too late to save our contact's life, but I did manage to retrieve a laptop that his killers were evidently in the process of obtaining when I got there. I've handed it over to Pete Kenachi and he's working on gaining access to it right now. As soon as he has, he'll download to our consoles.'

Carl said, 'That's Pete's speciality. The computer doesn't exist he can't break into.' The Swedish man looked proud of his communications and data specialist.

'Sounds like some good work, Brock,' said van Lederman.

'With any luck, it'll provide us with some vital information. I'm only sorry we had to cut short your holiday in order to get it. You happened to be in the right place.'

'Considering you were the one who insisted I take a break . . .'

'I know. We'll make it up to you.'

'Promises, promises.' Brock sighed theatrically. 'I don't know – you make more promises than I can keep track of. Well, I've got a plan. I'm thinking of going somewhere so dull next time that there's no possibility I can be of any use to you.'

'Great idea.' Van Lederman's eyes twinkled with amusement. 'Except for one thing. Trouble follows *you*, remember? Not the other way around.'

Brock laughed. He had been van Lederman's recruit and there was an unmistakeable respect and affection between the two men. Van Lederman and Brock's father, Cameron, had known each other since their days in the Foreign Legion and had remained close friends. Paul van Lederman had watched Brock grow up and often thought of him as the son he would have wished for, if life had seen fit to give him children. He'd seen something special in the boy and now the man was living up to that promise, bringing his special abilities to the benefit of ICE.

'Delighted you can join us, Brock. We'll await Kenachi's finds with interest. Meanwhile, shall we continue?' asked Buchanan. 'Jean Luc, what can Interpol tell us about Subedei Industries?'

Cambriol, a thin, pallid man, looked about the table. His appointment to ICE was part of the package of being director of Interpol and he never quite felt a natural fit here. There was Brock, for example, obviously a favourite of the other board members, but too rash and trouble-prone for his own taste. He preferred method and considered thinking – some might even call him pedantic – and found all this dashing about and derring-do distasteful. Caution was his watchword and it served him well, even if he knew he was not exactly a beloved leader at the Interpol headquarters in Paris.

'Our colleagues in Beijing have kindly provided us with some information on Subedei Industries,' he began. His dark brown eyes below thin, black eyebrows darted to his notes as he delivered his prepared briefing. 'Currently it is one of the most successful, and certainly the largest, businesses in modern China, with major interests in the country's construction, shipping and energy. It is controlled, apparently very firmly, by Temujin Subedei, the founder and chairman of the group.'

'What do we know about him?' asked Sir Donald.

Jean Luc flicked an irritated glance at him. 'I am coming to that, of course. As with other Chinese entrepreneurs, very little is known about Subedei's early life. The official story states that he emigrated with his parents from Mongolia in 1949 in their bid to be part of a new and better life under the Republic promised by Mao Zedong.

'Within weeks of arriving in Beijing, both his parents, along with many other immigrants, were reportedly attacked and massacred by rioters blaming them for taking their jobs. The action, apparently led by supporters of the deposed Chiang Kai Shek, was condemned as against the People's Republic by Mao Zedong who promised to eliminate such factions.

'The nine-year-old orphaned Subedei managed to escape and raised himself on the streets of Beijing, running errands, cleaning fish barrels, basically doing whatever would earn him a bowl of rice.

'In time he owned his first fishing boat and a market outlet for his catch. This increased to a fleet and later he gained valuable harbour rights from the People's Republic of China. During the terms of Deng Xiaoping and Jiang Zemin, Subedei Industries went from strength to strength by gaining most of the building and shipping contracts in Shanghai and Guangzhou Provinces.'

'Rags to riches,' put in Buchanan.

'Quite,' said Cambriol, not pleased with the interruption. 'And now you could say that his political clout has struck oil for him, literally. Two years ago his group was granted government licences to explore for oil and there is talk that he is being quietly wooed for membership of the Chinese Politburo. He pipes his own oil to his own tankers and is now looking to gain access to US and European markets, building his own refineries with his own construction companies.

'My sources admit that the rise has been meteoric but insist that they absolutely cannot find anything untoward. He is a friend to governments and charities and patron to many cultural departments.'

Carl Honstrom nodded his head in agreement. 'I have heard

the same. In fact, I have just heard that a very generous donation has been made to the Supreme Council of Antiquities in
Egypt. They've been desperate for funds for years to keep excavating their lost treasures.'

'Yes,' said Cambriol through clenched teeth, 'I was coming
to that as well.'

Van Lederman raised his eyebrows. 'Another Egyptian connection. As well as the purchase of Al Kadeh Construction.
Interesting.'

'Subedei is famous for his philanthropic donations,' said
Cambriol. 'If more businesses followed such an example, just
think of the benefits to society.'

Brock had been glancing at the console in front of him. Now
he looked up.

'I don't know how you define philanthropy,' he said, 'but I
doubt if it includes murder.'

Six

'What do you know, Brock?' demanded Sir Duncan Buchanan sharply.

'I'll fill you in on that when you've had a chance to look at this. Kenachi has been even more speedily efficient than usual.' Brock inclined his head towards his console.

The faces of the other four turned towards their screens as the information successfully accessed by computer wizard Kenachi scrolled down in front of them.

The files before them related to contracts and transfers completed forty-eight hours previously and had last been accessed by the now-dead lawyer.

Buchanan read out aloud the section Brock had indicated. 'In consideration of the electronically transferred, undisclosed sum as agreed by the contracting parties, Subedei Industries forth-with takes full title of all contractual agreements and assets of Al Kadeh Construction and furthermore agrees to accept all declared and undeclared liabilities, whether agreed or contended, thereby dissolving the Vendor of all future disputes.'

'How can the agreed contractual sum be "undisclosed"?' questioned van Lederman. 'An amount of such magnitude, and for such a transferral, would surely have to be transparent?'

'If both parties agree and the actual consideration is elec-tronically transferred and confirmed simultaneously with the contractual parties exchanging, it can be done,' answered Buchanan. 'But you're right – it is highly irregular.'

'Irregular – but still legal from a contractual point of view,' put in Cambriol.

Brock looked over at him and said slowly, 'Possibly. But I'd be interested to know exactly how legal it is if the parties have been coerced into signing.'

'You don't know that!' sneered Cambriol. 'It is mere supposition.'

'No, I don't. But I do know that a fee of sixteen million dollars for processing a contract is pretty unusual; and you may think differently, but to me it looks distinctly as though someone, somewhere, was under duress. And the other person who had his doubts about this contract has ended up dead, so my gut tells me that I'm not far off the mark. If it's all above board, why take the trouble to silence the transacting lawyer?'

'This is all assumption,' declared the Frenchman. 'I want to discover the truth as much as anyone, but I'm disturbed by the way you are so eager to blame a businessman who, as far as we know, is a model of integrity. Why could this lawyer's death not be the unfortunate result of random burglary? Such crimes are not unknown in the environs of Cairo, you know. The timing might simply be coincidental.' Cambriol leaned back on his chair with a satisfied air.

Brock gazed at him for a moment, his expression impossible to read. Then he said lightly, 'Random burglars rarely have a US Sikorsky helicopter in my experience. Nor are the usual Cairo criminals Cantonese-speaking Chinese. But there is a simple way to find out whether or not this contract was signed under duress.' He looked over at van Lederman, who was observing the interplay between the director of Interpol and Brock. 'The obvious thing is to go straight to the man who signed the contract and ask him. Ask the owner of Al Kadeh Construction.'

Carl Honstrom shifted uncomfortably. 'There's a problem there, Brock. We can't locate Omar Al Kadeh or any of his family. We've been trying since Nadir Bassein first contacted us but our sources tell us that the whole family has apparently left Cairo, perhaps on vacation.'

'Vacation,' repeated Brock, lifting one eyebrow. 'So no one involved in this deal can be contacted?'

Cambriol tapped his pen lightly on the glass table. 'Forgive me,' he said in a voice heavy with sarcastic charm, 'but I have a theory that might explain this. We know that Al Kadeh Construction was awarded the government tender for the New Pyramids. Correct?'

'The most valuable and prestigious contract of recent times,' put in Sir Duncan.

'Exactly. But suppose Al Kadeh had been planning to sell out as soon as he had received confirmation of the award? That would explain his haste in pushing through the deal, before the government got wind of the plans and changed the tender contract, or even rescinded it, losing him a vast fortune.

'If that were the case, then little wonder Al Kadeh inserted a clause protecting them from all future liabilities. And surely it comes as no surprise that they did not want to disclose the sum. People would say that they sold out the biggest initiative of the country for personal fortune. That they cared more for their greed and gain than they did for the prestige of their nation. No doubt the Al Kadeh family have left the country to avoid the outcry when it is learned what they have done.'

Brock stared at Cambriol for a moment, his blue eyes steely. Then he said slowly, 'Interesting theory.'

Sensing the growing tension, van Lederman acted to defuse it. 'The truth is, we don't know anything for certain yet. We'll have to keep investigating the whereabouts of Al Kadeh – Carl, that's your brief, obviously – and studying these files that Brock has so kindly provided for us. Jean Luc –' he turned to the Frenchman – 'we'd like to hear any more you can add about the current status of Subedei Industries. Your input is, of course, invaluable.'

Cambriol looked mollified by van Lederman's praise and turned back to the notes in front of him.

'Besides his interests in Venezuela, Russia and the US, Subedei appears to be concentrating on growth in North Africa and the Middle East. As Carl quite rightly said earlier, generous donations to the Supreme Council of Antiquities have secured him friends in the Egyptian government. Recently he was granted rights for the exploration of oil in the Western Desert and won the dredging contract for the Suez Canal, for his subsidiary Khan Marine and Dredging. He also has permits to build new harbour facilities and a petroleum refinery west of Alexandria.'

'I can see the sense of investing in the US and Europe,' said Sir Duncan, leaning back in his chair and crossing his arms. 'But the reasons for his Egyptian portfolio, which is now formidable with the addition of Al Kadeh Construction, are much more opaque. The reserves of oil in Egypt are difficult to make profitable because of the problems with accessibility. And as far as we know, he hasn't discovered any new reserves anyway – so why build a refinery for it? It's simply bizarre.'

'Well, Temujin Subedei does have a reputation for being a magical entrepreneur as well as a philanthropist,' replied Cambriol. 'Now that the tension is defusing in the Arab world, he may consider it a major investment. We know that China would like to gain more global influence and Subedei – no doubt as a prospective candidate for an influential position within the emerging modern party leadership – could simply be doing his patriotic bit.

'Let's face it. The US has adopted a policy of reducing its overseas commitment – apart from the military – to sort out its own fiscal problems, so countries like Egypt are welcoming alternative investment with open arms. And such investment of course attracts further investment, which is probably why long-awaited initiatives like the New Pyramids are happening. Indeed, I do hope that we are not becoming some stifling party against such action.'

Van Lederman turned towards Cambriol, his eyes hardening. 'We are all for such investment as you quite rightly say, Jean Luc. It is the very seed-corn of future economic growth for the region. Our responsibility, as you are well aware, is not to stifle such actions. We are not some monopolies commission misguidedly impeding growth. Our responsibility is to ensure that good corporate governance is applied behind any investment. We are absolutely neutral and unbiased. We are never swayed by political considerations.

'My god, if I ever thought for a moment that we were not acting in line with our values and the interests on which we are founded, I would initiate an inquiry into ICE itself.'

The Interpol director tried to hold the ICE chief's gaze, knowing that his remark had been inappropriate. Then he dropped his eyes downwards and murmured, 'My apologies, Paul. I spoke without thinking.'

Buchanan coughed and said loudly, 'Thank you for your comprehensive report, Jean Luc. We appreciate your input.' He turned to the field operations chief. 'Anything to add, Carl?'

Honstrom leaned forward in his chair and rested his forearms on the table. 'Yes, three things.' He held up three fingers and knocked one down with every point he made. 'First, we have been trying to ascertain a schedule of recent acquisitions by Subedei Industries of European companies with major US

59

shareholding. This is in response to a request from our Washington office, though so far they've not been forthcoming about why they're suddenly interested in Subedei Industries. Naturally, I'm staying on the case and pressing for more information.'

'Interesting. And the second?' asked Buchanan.

'Well, this could be entirely unconnected. But our contact inside the Vatican has just sent us information which mentions Subedei. The timing is curious, so I thought I ought to mention it.'

Brock laughed, startling the others. 'Has Maria discovered that Subedei is thinking of converting to Catholicism? Then we'd really have to look at the extent of his ambitions – he might be aiming to become Pope.'

Honstrom shot him a glance. 'Very funny, Connor.' He turned to the rest of the table. 'Maria Zanoletti is the archive curator at the Vatican and has been one of our regular informants for some time. She has learned that a couple of weeks ago Temujin Subedei contacted the Vatican personally with a request for assistance in some research. As the request was accompanied by the offer of a very generous donation in return, the Monsignor in charge was only too happy to oblige. He has now asked Zanoletti to help with this research, which is how she came to know of it.' Honstrom shuffled through some papers in front of her. 'She's just emailed me to say that she has further information that may be of interest to us.'

'Excellent,' interjected Buchanan. 'It may not be much, but every little helps in building up a picture of Subedei and his interests. When can she send it?'

Honstrom swivelled in his chair towards Brock. 'Well, there is apparently a condition. Signorina Zanoletti will be delighted to pass on whatever she has – but only in person. To Connor Brock.'

Brock raised his hands in mock surrender. 'Don't look at me like that, Carl. You know as well as I do that part of Maria's recruitment deal was that she would only give sensitive information to me. The intrigue in that place where she works is hotter than hell. Her words, not mine.' He looked at the expectant faces around him. 'OK, I'll go to Rome tomorrow and see what Maria's discovered.'

'Good.' Sir Duncan turned back to the Swede. 'Now, Carl. Last thing.'

'Last, but perhaps most important.' Honstrom looked grave and ran a hand through his grey-blond crew cut. 'We've been following up on a report we received about an oil company that is involved in exploration in the Western Sahara.'

'Libya or Algeria?' asked Buchanan.

'Close but actually Western Egypt, though around the Libyan Desert, near the Siwa Oasis. In the past, oil exploration in the area has never been considered commercially viable and not permitted by the authorities anyway. But we've learned that an Egyptian company, Ammon Oil, has been given a licence to explore for oil in exchange for paying substantial royalties to the Supreme Council of Antiquities to fund its archaeological sites and museums.

'Ammon Oil came to our attention because a US oil company, South Western Oil, has been repeatedly refused permission to drill near Siwa, even though it already has a petroleum refinery and a pipeline in place that it uses for oil at its Libyan border reserves. South Western learned that permission was recently given to Ammon for an exploration strategy almost identical to South Western's. They complained of malpractice, so we looked into it.' Honstrom looked round the table, his expression sombre. 'And we've discovered that Ammon Oil is one hundred per cent owned by Subedei Industries.'

Sir Duncan drew in his breath sharply and glanced quickly at van Lederman, who murmured, 'This is getting serious.'

Honstrom went on. 'So we contacted Ammon Oil and arranged for a friendly visit to their site at Siwa by the chief executive and founder of South Western, a man called Ridge, accompanied by one of our investigators posing as a company director.'

'Who did we send?' asked van Lederman.

'One of our best, of course. Matt Ferguson.'

Brock broke into a grin. 'Good old Matt! Trust his Irish luck to get him an assignment to the same country where I have to pay for a vacation. When does he get back?'

'Well, I wish I was able to answer that,' said Carl, concern audible in his voice. 'The trouble is, both he and Ridge have disappeared without trace.'

Seven

Resembling a long slippery eel, the sleek black Mercedes swept out of the underground parking on to the wide Mythenquai fronting the still serenity of Lake Zurich, in one smooth motion. From the back seat Brock gazed meditatively across the misted dawn water reflecting the flickering lights dancing between the decorative arrays of geometrically gabled buildings that hugged the prestigious shoreline; each one nestling for position between grandiose office chateaux and steep church spires, while the faint horizon of snow-capped peaks stood resolutely on guard.

The last time he had made this early morning trip to the airport in an ICE Mercedes, Matt Ferguson had been with him.

'Connor, my pal, this sure beats the hell out of a cold jeep on the way to Sarajevo airport, doesn't it? Who would have thought that two rascals like you and me would end up with such a buttery smooth ride? My old ma would be beside herself if she could see me now. Her youngest boy, with his dirty knees and his mucky hair, being driven about in a motor like this, for all the world like I'm president of the old country.'

Brock remembered Matt Ferguson's joviality when he'd been recruited to join Brock as a member of ICE. The irrepressible Irishman had joked that no matter where Connor went, he, Matt, was bound to follow. 'Just think of me as your guardian angel,' Matt would grin, 'always on hand to get you out of trouble.'

He was closer to the truth than he knew, Brock reflected. Matt had no idea how much he had helped Brock through the roughest moments in his life. The two men had met twelve years earlier in the RAF, having been placed in the same unit after their joint COs had cooked up some war liaison game. The serious Scot and light-hearted Irishman had blended well together from the start, their complementary strengths making them a formidable duo. In the course of winning their war game, a firm friendship was formed along with a mutual respect that had deepened over the years. They'd both moved from general service into the Special Forces at the same time and had watched each other's backs in the various sorties they'd been sent on in their tours of duty. They had saved each other's lives more than once.

And besides the memories of knife-edge, life-and-death situations, Brock reminded himself, were the sweet ones. The happy times, like the day Brock had married the beautiful Heather McCoy. He remembered Heather coming into the kirk on the arm of her father John. He'd been overwhelmed with the sight of her, in her slim white dress, holding her bouquet of heather and roses, smiling that celestial smile of pure happiness. At that moment, Matt, his best man, had whispered, 'Hey, old man. She's too good for you, I always said it. Why don't you bow out now and let me take over? It's the least I could do for an old friend.'

Unable to take his eyes off the gorgeous woman walking towards him, ready to pledge her life to him, Brock muttered, 'Thanks but no thanks, Matt. This is one mission I'm happy to handle on my own.'

He knew that Matt had noticed how overwhelmed he was, and his friend was tugging him back to earth just enough to make sure he knew where he was and what he was doing. It was the kind of light, thoughtful touch that characterized Matt.

Brock grinned wryly to himself. Well . . . light and thoughtful couldn't really describe Matt after the ceremony. His speech had been just the right side of bawdy, and lively and funny enough to have the whole wedding party and all the guests in tears of laughter. If ever an Irishman had been given the gift of the gab, it was Matt. Only Brock knew how nervous his friend had been. After the speeches, the jokes and the affectionate toasts to the newly-weds, Matt had been able to relax and let his hair down, and he certainly had. Brock would never forget the sight of his ruddy-faced best man, a little the worse for some fine Scotch whisky, whirling the bride about in the ceilidh. He'd been just as enthusiastic with the bride's mother, and with her sister and, if Brock remembered correctly, the bride's startled grandmother.

Then, just fifteen months later, they were back at the same kirk. This time Heather had been in her coffin and Matt one of the pall-bearers carrying it down the aisle the young bride had walked down so recently. He hadn't tried to pull Brock back to earth that day. He'd sat with his friend until late in the night, pouring him whisky and listening to the distraught Brock railing against the horrific unfairness of life, and the anonymous driver who had stolen his wife from him in a few, devastating seconds when the car had hit her, sending her spiralling upwards into the air, and raced away almost before Heather's broken body had fallen back to the ground.

Matt had been there for him in those terrible days after Heather's death, and he would never forget it, even if he couldn't bring himself to speak of it.

And now it seemed as though his old friend was in trouble somewhere in the Sahara desert, perhaps involved in the same tangled business that had brought Nadir Bassein to his untimely end. Brock knew he had no option but to go to Matt's aid as quickly as possible. Rome and Maria Zanoletti could wait. He had said as much to van Lederman and Honstrom at dinner the night before.

'Matt comes first,' he'd said brusquely. 'If it looks like trouble out there, that's where I'm needed more.'

Van Lederman nodded his silver head thoughtfully. 'Of course, Connor. I wouldn't stand in your way. And my own instinct is that whatever is happening in Egypt at the moment is priority.'

'I agree.' Honstrom poured wine for them all from the ice bucket by the table. He had specifically directed the waiters to stay away so that the three of them could talk in peace. 'Matt has now missed two report-in calls and all attempts by South Western Oil to contact their CEO, the man Ridge, have proved useless. According to Ammon Oil, they're trying to locate Ridge and Ferguson as well, after they failed to make an agreed meeting at their Cambyses II site outside Siwa.'

'Do we trust them, now that we know they're owned by Subedei?' queried Brock, frowning.

Honstrom shrugged. 'You tell me. But somehow the media has got hold of the story of the missing businessmen, possibly lost in the desert, and Ammon's air and land rescue search is getting them a lot of good press.'

Van Lederman leaned forward, looking searchingly into his younger protégé's face. 'There's something else, isn't there,

Connor? Something you didn't mention in the briefing today. You were going to, and then you changed your mind. What is it?'

Brock pushed his plate away and looked up from under a heavy frown. He paused, as though considering what he should say next and then sighed heavily. 'Forgive me, Paul. I did hold something back. Cambriol was riling me – you could probably tell – and I suddenly felt that I didn't want to give everything away. There is something more.' Van Lederman and Honstrom listened expectantly, waiting for the Scotsman to find the words he was searching for. 'OK – you remember the Chinese assassins I discovered at Bassein's home, just too late to stop them from carrying out their mission. One, a great mountain of a man, I had to deal with there and then before he mushed me up into a pulp. The other was a weaselly little fellow. I took him with me on the return flight to the base and, I have to admit, I got more than a little pleasure in dangling him out of the door of the Bell Ranger at ten thousand feet.' Brock grinned lopsidedly at his chief. 'I don't usually enjoy that kind of thing, but he was a nasty piece of work.

'Anyway . . . our man screeched at me in Cantonese but found himself a bit of English when he was hanging, scared witless, with nothing but God's good air between him and the earth. He claimed to be nothing more than a bagman for his big mate, who went by the name of Wheng Zhu. Claimed to know nothing except a few names and places. He mentioned the name "Qenawi" – mean anything to you?' Brock directed his question at Honstrom, who shook his head. 'No. Me neither. He said this name, Qenawi, and he said that Wheng Zhu was just back from the Red Sea. I asked him who Wheng Zhu reported to. He pretended to know nothing at all. A few more swings over the landing gear refreshed his memory. He suddenly recalled something that Wheng Zhu had said.'

'Yes?' Van Lederman leaned in towards Brock, his eyes fierce with concentration.

'Apparently, he liked to declare, "I am Wheng Zhu, the hand of the Great Mongolian."'

'Subedei?'

'Sounds like it to me. Didn't Cambriol say that he emigrated to China from Mongolia with his parents?'

'Yes . . . but . . . Damn it!' Van Lederman slapped his hand on the white linen tablecloth. 'It's not quite enough. It's not the concrete identification we need.'

'Near enough, surely,' said Brock.

'But not the identification we need,' repeated van Lederman.

'Well, Paul, it's good enough for me,' said Honstrom. 'This is a step forward. And if it is Subedei who's killed Bassein, then it's a bad lookout for Al Kadeh.'

'Where's this Chinese man now?' Van Lederman turned back to Brock.

'I handed him over to the custody of Wing Commander Maadi, who I think was planning to pass him on to the authorities.'

'We should get hold of him if we can.'

'I doubt you'll find any more than I did. Maadi may have already handed him over. He's a dead end to my mind. A gofer, nothing more.'

'All right. If that's what you think.'

'I think it looks like your next stop is Western Egypt, Connor,' said Honstrom. 'I'll investigate this name – Qenawi. You get on with locating Matt. I think Maria will be able to hold on to what she's got for a day or two more.'

Van Lederman sipped at his wine and then said, 'I'm not altogether comfortable about you going in alone, Connor. You don't have any back-up.'

'Matt went in the front door, so to speak. My way will be the back door. You don't need to worry. And I've got a plan for a bit of support, so don't be too concerned about that. My flight to Alexandria is already booked.'

'It seems that Egypt holds the key to all this,' said van Lederman.

'Then that's where I should be,' said Brock. 'We need to get some answers. And fast.'

As Brock's car arrived at the flight departures terminal, he sensed that this investigation would be a demanding one. It was already more complex than he could have guessed at when he arrived at Nadir Bassein's residence just a few days earlier.

The questions were piling up: why had Matt gone missing? Who was Qenawi and where was Al Kadeh? Why had anyone bothered to silence Bassein?

As he checked in and made his way through the flight gates, Brock felt strongly that Subedei was the heart of the mystery.

What did this boundlessly rich businessman hope to achieve? He was clearly powerful and influential, and, by the looks of it, he was pursuing some kind of goal that made him ruthless, single-minded and deeply dangerous. Why else would someone like him on the one hand publicize his generous acts of patronage, and on the other, risk the kind of criminal activity – murder and kidnap, for example – that he appeared to be undertaking? Unless, of course, he knew that he was untouchable.

Whatever his plans were, it was certain that he knew that ICE would now be a thorn in his flesh. And Brock was right at the sharp end.

Eight

Matt Ferguson felt as if he had been rubbed down raw with sandpaper. He guessed that it must be at least fours hours since he had woken and discovered that he had been buried up to his neck in sand.

It had been weird coming round to consciousness in absolute pitch-black darkness and being unable to move. His first thought was that he was dead. His second was that he was paralysed. A confused panic at the thought of either situation caused him to struggle violently against his containment. The slight movement he gained and the sharp stab of pain that he felt at the back of his head reassured him that both scenarios were untrue.

Since then his parched mouth and throat were becoming increasingly uncomfortable, feeling as if they had progressed from the state of dried out leather to petrified wood.

A short time ago the hoarse whispers with Ridge, buried in a similar fashion, had ceased. Ferguson could not see the American's face as the two of them had been strategically buried back-to-back about a metre apart.

Initially, the worst hardship was being unable to ease the discomfort of grit-filled eyes. It reminded Ferguson of the time that he had been unable to scratch his plastered leg after he had broken it falling off his motorcycle. Holy Mary, the unbearable frustration of it! The only thing that took his mind off the desperate need to rub his eyes was cursing himself for not being more on his guard in the Temple of Ammon.

The pleasant public-relations trip afforded by Ammon Oil must have been a scam. He and Ridge had too easily allowed themselves to be distracted from their destination at the Cambyses II site. But what was the point? Surely their visit could not have been considered such a threat as to warrant attacking them and burying them up to the neck?

OK, South Western Oil had voiced some suspicions of malpractice, but only in the most diplomatic of language. And why would Ammon Oil agree to a meeting with a view to negotiating an alliance if they regarded their competitors with such hostility? What could they hope to gain from this? Neither he nor Ridge could understand what had befallen them or why.

'What the hell happened?' Ridge had numbly cried out earlier, his voice cracking into a muffled whisper.

'It appears we got sandbagged in the desert,' quipped Ferguson, trying to keep up his good humour. He could tell that the other man was in a state of shock.

A note of panic entered Ridge's strained voice. 'Where are we? The last thing I remember is standing in that inner sanctum. We must have been whacked good, if my achin' head is anything to go by.'

'I think that's about the size of it, but God alone only knows why the hell we're here. I was kind of hoping this was a dream but I'm quickly losing faith in the idea that I might wake up any minute.'

'We have to get out, call for help,' returned Ridge and began trying to yell, his cry echoing back from the dark walls of the cavernous tomb above them.

'Save your breath and conserve your strength as best you can,' counselled the Irishman. 'We don't know how long we're going to be here. Can you move at all?'

'Only my fingers.'

'Good. Me too, so we have not been tied up. Try to work them through the sand. See if you can manipulate your hands out. My feet feel as though they are placed on firm ground, maybe stone. Push with your hands and arms. Do what you can. Maybe the people who put us here are coming back, maybe not. But we must do something.'

'But what the hell is going on?' Ridge repeated. 'Is this a kidnap or something?' The back of his head began to throb painfully. He recalled how his office had continually warned him about such situations. They had insisted that a premium relating to ransom situations had been included in his key personal policies.

'Surely this can't be happening,' he said, more to himself than the man directly behind him, though the echoes of his words

69

were eerily repeated above him. 'What about that woman and Cambyses II? What about our meetings and schedules?' Ridge's voice croaked as he raised his voice. 'Where the hell are we? Christ Almighty, I need water! Who the hell is doing this to us?'

'Perhaps we'll know soon enough, but listen, John,' whispered Ferguson, trying to convey confidence in his voice to allay the other's rising panic, 'concentrate for the moment on freeing your hands. It'll take your mind off worrying about something we can't do anything about right now.'

'Well, whoever the sons-of-bitches are, why don't they give us a goddamn drink?'

Shortly afterwards, there was quiet from the Texan. It seemed that Ridge had passed out from exhaustion. Ferguson's hands, aching from exertion, were now almost level with his shoulders. Spurred on by the desire to rub his eyes as well as the primary motive of escape, the tough Irishman ignored the stress his body was under, forcing himself to continue while trying to keep down the waves of claustrophobic panic that periodically welled up in him.

If the idea was to imprison them psychologically as well as physically, they were doing a first-rate job, whoever the captors were. There was almost no light to speak of. Even though his eyes were now well accustomed to the dark, there was nothing Ferguson could make out. He had guessed from the way their words had eerily echoed as though others were whispering back at them that they were in a cavern. The dank musty smell, reminiscent of his pot-holing days in the army, confirmed this. Determined not to succumb to the claustrophobic fear that he recognized was trying to engulf him, he kept his mind on his immediate goal.

Focus, he thought. I need to stay focused. He remembered what his father had said so often: 'Think only about what you are doing. Don't be distracted from your efforts by worry, because worry is the interest on a payment not yet due.' Ferguson had learned the truth of it over the years.

Even as he struggled to work his hands upwards through the weight of the sand, he knew that he would pass out soon without water, his dehydration caused by his exertion rather than warmth. It was surprisingly cool where they were entombed, a complete contrast to the fierce desert heat they'd experienced earlier. How much earlier he couldn't even guess – he'd lost all track of time.

But I must have missed at least two report-in calls, Ferguson thought, searching for a scrap of comfort in the situation. Honstrom is bound to be on the alert by now. Help must be on the way.

The only thing was, he was not at all confident that they would be found. If he remembered correctly, their beautiful guide had said that numerous underground caverns existed under Siwa. What were the chances of a rescuer finding the right one? He thought about Ayeesha Al Fahila. How much did she have to do with all this? She wasn't here, so she must have been involved in the attack. Had she set them up? Why would she? What would the director of the Supreme Council of Antiquities have to gain from such an act of violence against foreign guests?

Now he thought about it, what did anyone have to gain from this? It had been clear from the outset of their prearranged trip that South Western Oil was simply interested in Ammon's operation with a view to having some part in it. Admittedly Ridge was not exactly happy that Ammon Oil had usurped his strategy and used its connections to win permission to explore for oil, but, as he had said, 'The oil business is the oil business, and if we can't have it all, then we'll have a bit. Hell, with our petroleum refinery and pipeline infrastructure at Alexandria, it's a perfect marriage for both of our companies.'

But that hadn't stopped him alerting ICE to possible fraud and corruption in the awarding of exploration rights to Ammon Oil, and readily agreeing to take Matt along with him in the guise of a South Western executive.

Ferguson took a rest from his exertions, knowing that the wet around his hands was not sweat but blood from the nails that had been dragged away from his fingers as he worked them through the sand. He was gathering his strength to continue when he heard footsteps scuffing the ground as they approached.

He quickly closed his eyes and slumped his head forward to feign sleep. A moment later, he experienced the combination of first pain, as large halogen lights were switched on, searing at his closed eyelids and making him screw up his face, then pleasure as a bucket of cool water was thrown over his head. Opening his mouth, the Irishman reached out his tongue thirstily for the life-saving liquid, savouring its ever-so-slightly salty taste.

'Good. You're awake.' The voice sounded harsh, distant, and it echoed in the darkness.

'Yes. Thanks for the shower. Now, what's for breakfast?' enquired Ferguson lightly, squinting into the brightness. The voice had thickly accented English – an Eastern European voice, if he were not mistaken. Russian? Czech? He needed to hear more to be sure.

'Excellent! I see that you are a man after my own heart. Courageous even in the face of adversity. No doubt some would say your joking is merely stupid bravado but, in my view, it is commendable.'

Ferguson heard the man walk round to where Ridge was buried, and repeat the bucket of water routine. There was a splutter as Ridge came round, waking to the same shower of precious liquid.

'What the hell do you want with us?' rasped John Ridge as soon as he could speak, unable to disguise the panic in his voice.

The man knelt down in front of the oil executive, the halogen light giving his face a ghostly white look as it reflected off the hard pock-marked features.

'What do I want? Hmm, let me see. Your refinery first, but while we're about it, the whole of South Western Oil would make a much tidier package, don't you think?'

Ferguson concentrated on trying to identify the man's accent, while Ridge drew in his breath.

'What do you mean? Is this a kidnap?'

'In a manner of speaking it is. No doubt you have insurance against such an event. It's just that the ransom, to put it simply, is your company.'

Ridge tried to look up into the face of the nightmare in front of him. 'Are you crazy? Did you just say what I think you said? OK, I've had enough. This is just not happening.'

'Do you think we could have that breakfast now?' enquired Ferguson. 'Then perhaps we can discuss the finer points of your request.'

'Yes, truly a man after my own heart!' Laughing, the thick-set man turned to unseen companions standing behind the lamps.

'Give them something to drink. We don't want them dying on us just yet. I shall return in a day or two.'

A day or two? thought Ferguson, his stomach sinking with despair. He didn't think he could last another hour or two in this frightful sand trap. Ridge obviously felt the same, for he shouted in a voice cracked by his parched throat, 'Hey! You can't just leave us here like this!'

Their captor turned back to gaze down on them. 'Why ever not? I don't think you are in a position to argue with me. I agree that it doesn't look very comfortable but, like you, I am a visitor to this country and I have learned that it is unwise to go against local custom. These natives seem to think that you are idolatrous infidels, which is why they have buried you up to your necks. Whatever you do, don't upset them or they may well insist on stoning the parts that are not buried.'

The man turned again, and walked away into the darkness, disappearing as soon as he was beyond the range of the halogen lights. Ferguson heard a murmur of voices: the accented man was obviously giving orders to whoever else was in the cavern. A moment later, two black-robed Bedouins emerged from the darkness, crouched beside the two men, and offered earthenware saucers of water to their eager mouths. As he slurped gratefully at the liquid, Ferguson tried to unravel the Arabic that the robed men muttered to each other. It was impossible to decipher anything – not that he knew much beyond a word or two anyway – but he could certainly tell that these two were not at all happy with the situation.

All too soon, the saucers were wrenched away, and the Bedouins disappeared into the darkness. A moment later, the light went out, leaving Ferguson and Ridge enveloped in thick blackness.

Ridge moaned softly. Ferguson strained his ears until he could no longer hear their footfalls and immediately resumed working his hand to the surface. The water and rest had slightly restored his energy and he urged on his trapped colleague.

'Force your hands out somehow. We have to escape before they return because there's no other way we are getting out of here alive.'

'They're mad. We came here to negotiate but they intend to kill us and take over my company! Did you ever hear anything so crazy? It's not even as though I can give them the goddamn thing – I'm only a shareholder now.'

'Details don't matter right now. Saving our skins does.'

Zarakov was impressed with the prisoners despite himself. They'd shown spirit even in the face of their desperate situation.

I wish there was more bravery in the cretinous fools that this country seems to spawn, he thought to himself as he left the cavern. Not to say intelligence. Hakim and Mohamed had been instructed to incapacitate the two foreigners, not to fracture their skulls and bury them up to their necks. Idiots.

The Siberian Russian was used to dealing with fanatics but the two Bedouins were really something. They'd been anointed as guardians of the Temple of Ammon and took their duties very seriously. The rewards that Zarakov had promised them had simply spurred them on their quest to protect the place against the infidel – they hadn't thought twice about disposing of the frail elder who protected the temple, stuffing his body into one of the many funerary urns to be found in the underground depths. Well, as long as they didn't take it into their heads to murder their prisoners before the order was given.

Reaching the fixed monorail that would take him out of the network of caverns, Zarakov got into the waiting trolley cart and pushed his key card into the slot on the slim white dash. As the cart began to glide down the illuminated tunnel, he looked at the woman beside him and smiled.

'That was a good job. Well done. You remind me of the spider enticing the fly into the web. By tomorrow, they will give us whatever we desire.'

Ayeesha Al Fahila smiled back. 'I'm glad to hear that, for your sake. You have taken such a risk to capture this important prey, I suppose you had better not fail.'

'That sounds like a threat,' scowled Zarakov, his thick black moustache and bushy eyebrows becoming even more pronounced.

'Not at all. It's just that I understand Subedei would not appreciate failure. Even I have to be careful not to anger him unnecessarily.'

'I see. And no doubt you take a keen interest in making sure he's fully informed.'

Ayeesha laughed. 'I know how to please him.'

'As all females like to please the male.'

'But don't forget – even the tiny female spider is the stronger than her mate.'

As the railcar sped towards its destination, Zarakov turned to look quizzically at his companion. The passing lights reflected like flickering flames in the woman's dark eyes. For all his training and hard-won experience, he shuddered involuntarily.

If, as he suspected, this devil-woman was Subedei's lover, he would have to watch his back. He was confident in the mutual loyalty that he and the Mongolian overlord had proved to each other over the years, though much of it was based on what each knew about the other. But there was no telling what influence a woman could wield, if she so chose and if the pull she had over a man was strong enough.

He didn't know much about this particular woman but he could tell that she sought power. She had likened herself to a spider and Zarakov knew what kind she meant: the deadly species that ate her lover after mating.

Nine

During the flight from Zurich to Alexandria, Brock studied a copy of the file Carl Honstrom had supplied to Ferguson. It had been important that Matt was completely up to speed on the situation with Ammon Oil and what South Western hoped to gain from approaching them, and Honstrom had prepared an in-depth analysis for him, including satellite pictures of all the relevant sites.

Brock flicked to them. The grainy black-and-white photographs were clear enough to make out South Western's petroleum refinery, and the new one being built near Alexandria by Subedei Industries, presumably for Ammon Oil's use. It seemed to Brock that the latter occupied a less strategic position in the new deep-water facilities that had recently been constructed on the western basin of Alexandria. Moreover, it looked more like a mausoleum than a facility associated with processing crude oil into petroleum. There were the giant cylindrical containers set into the ground but a distinct lack of the spaghetti pipes that crawled like geometric worms over the South Western placement.

Brock frowned. There was absolutely no need for two oil refineries. Half of Egypt's demand was already met from Port Said. Why build another?

Turning to a smaller-scale photo that revealed the larger surrounding area, Brock followed with his finger the two thin symmetrical contours that indicated a pipeline and rail track. They skirted the Ad Diffah Libyan Plateau leading west towards oilfields at Musaid; but only from South Western's refinery.

Outside Alexandria at Al Alamayn was a second pipeline that appeared to be close to truncating the first. The second lay in an almost straight line as it made its way across the Qattara Depression coming from the direction of Siwa.

Interesting, mused Brock. He gathered up the photographs and file information and put them back in their envelope. It seemed that the builders of the new pipeline knew something that no one else did. Well, it would be interesting to find out what that was. Perhaps Matt had already stumbled on something that shed some light on the whole thing – hence his sudden disappearance. Brock didn't fool himself that Matt and the other oilman had got lost in the desert – he'd seen his friend find his way out of some pretty tight situations in the past and knew that only being somehow forcibly restrained would stop the Irishman from reporting back to headquarters when he was expected to. That's what made Brock all the more eager to find him.

Within thirty minutes of landing at Alexandria Airport, Brock had passed through control, re-entered domestic departures, and was soon striding across the airport tarmac towards a green and blue South Western Oil helicopter. The pilot stood by the aircraft, neat in a tailored flight suit, formally awaiting the arrival of the passenger.

'Good afternoon, sir,' said the pilot courteously, as Brock approached.

'Afternoon, Sergeant,' grinned Brock, appreciating the pilot's slim legs and graceful posture. 'Ready for another sightseeing trip?'

'Of course. I'm just hoping that we're in for more of the same non-stop excitement.' Despite herself, Neusheen Benerzat's full lips curved upwards into a reluctant smile. 'I take it I have you to thank for this unexpected pleasure?'

'Why would you think that, Flight Sergeant?' teased Brock.

'Hmm, let me see.' Neusheen cast her eyes upwards speculatively. 'Perhaps because my wing commander told me that you'd specially requested me for secondment to this flight.'

'Maadi was only too pleased to let you go.'

'Considering I only have a week of service left, I'm surprised he couldn't wait to see the back of me.'

'Well, it's a fine view, if you don't mind my saying. Now, shall we board?'

As they climbed into the cockpit of the Jet Ranger, Neusheen said, 'What I don't understand is – why me?'

'Because you're professional, cool under pressure, and a good navigator and pilot. You speak four languages, and, so far, you've proved yourself lucky for both of us. That carries a bit of weight in my line of work.' It had been a simple task to arrange for the young navigator to be seconded to South Western for the last week of her two-year conscription. Edward Maadi had readily agreed – as had South Western Oil – to Carl Honstrom's request.

'If you put it like that – how could I refuse?' Neusheen put on her flight headphones and switched on her mike, preparing to fire up the engines.

'You couldn't. That's what gives me the advantage.' Brock buckled himself into his seat. 'OK, get clearance and let's get airborne. Make a heading across the Al Alamayn. I want to pick up a pipeline and follow it southwest across the Qattara Depression to Siwa.'

Neusheen turned to Brock and gave him a wide smile. 'I don't speak Siwan.'

Brock could not help but return her smile, though quizzically. 'Don't they speak Arabic or French there?'

'They do but with their own particular dialect that includes Greek.'

'Greek?'

'Yes, remember the Greeks ruled over Egypt for two hundred years and though the Arab occupation of our country lasted five times longer, the remote desert area of Siwa retained its ancient Greek base. There is no other language like it in the world.'

'Will you be able to get by in Arabic?'

Neusheen gave another of her winning smiles. 'Of course I will. Most of them speak Arabic as well.'

'Thanks for that little history lesson, Sergeant,' said Brock drily. 'Now – shall we be on our way?'

Twenty minutes later, they were above the outskirts of Al Alamayn. Surveying the area below him, Brock remembered what his father had told him. A devoted student of military history, Cameron Brock was an expert on all the decisive battles of the Second World War. I must have absorbed it all somehow over the years, thought Brock. Here at El Alamein, as the allies had referred to it, the British 8th Army led by General Harold

Alexander and Field Commander Montgomery succeeded in frustrating the efforts of the Axis forces, commanded by Field Marshal Rommel. Brock pointed at the area below.

'Looks peaceful and untouched, doesn't it? Yet, down there, in the region of two hundred and thirty thousand Allied soldiers battled with under half the number of Axis troops.'

'The numbers hardly seem fair,' replied Neusheen, her dark eyes glancing downwards at where Brock had indicated.

'War is never fair. And anyway, the Germans had the upper hand over us enough times. But this is where the British began the devastating attack that led to Rommel being forced out of Egypt, and prevented him from seizing the Suez Canal as he'd planned – which would have been utterly disastrous for Northern Africa and for Europe.'

'Really?' Neusheen looked interested. These events were so far beyond her lifetime that it was obvious she felt they had little relevance to her. But, looking down again at the desert below, she said, 'It's hard to imagine anyone caring much about that patch of sand. What made this area so important?'

For a moment before answering, Brock considered how like his father he was sounding, holding forth about battles long since consigned to history books. 'It doesn't look like much, does it? But the Qattara Depression descends to well over four hundred feet below sea level and contains salt lakes and marshes. Because it was impassable to military traffic, the depression formed a natural anchor at the southern end of the British defence line here at Al Alamayn against the final advance of Field Marshall Rommel. If he had got past here, there would have been no stopping him.'

Neusheen nodded slowly as she absorbed this.

Brock said almost apologetically, 'My turn for a history lesson.'

'Actually, it's fascinating. No one's cared much about this area for decades. But my father tells me that oil is beginning to draw people back here.'

'They discovered deposits on the northern parts of the depression in the late seventies. It's the age-old story: wealth. Buried treasure. The black gold. Wherever there's the hint of oil, there'll be people desperate to find it. And now, by the looks of things, it might have been located in the south. Look, there's our pipeline right on schedule.' Brock pointed at the large pumping station below them. Nearby were vast piles of huge pipes, resembling a series of timber poles stacked across a Canadian logging post. The mountains of pipes forged outwards in two or three directions before appearing to peter out into nothing. One pipeline, though, headed straight and clear into the distance.

'Look at that!' cried Neusheen indignantly. 'There must be scores of pipes there, just left unattended. Typical. People think they can treat our country any way they want, with no thought for the environmental effects – and the government does nothing to stop them! It only cares about money.'

'That doesn't make it so very different from other govern-ments,' replied Brock dryly. 'Those pipes may be links waiting to be added – do you see how that main line doesn't tie into the main system at the pumping station?'

'Yes, I see. It's not finished. So where is everybody? Why isn't anyone working on it?'

Brock had already registered that despite the fact that every-thing was in place for transporting the pipes there was a bizarre emptiness to the scene. He quickly checked once more the compass heading for Siwa.

'Follow that pipe,' he quipped. 'By lucky chance, it's heading in exactly the same direction as we are. The Siwa Oasis.'

Neusheen glanced over at her passenger. 'Could this be a good time to ask exactly where we're going and why? I'd appre-ciate being forewarned of any plans to take on a couple of homicidal maniacs this time. If that's all right with you.'

'Old Maadi didn't succeed in telling you just to follow orders then?'

Neusheen raised an eyebrow at him, shook her head and didn't reply. Instead she turned back to her instruments and concentrated on the flight.

As they followed the grey pipe that snaked on its high struts through the marshes, lakes, rocks and finally encroaching desert, Brock explained some of the mission to Neusheen, telling her about the disappearance of his colleague Matt Ferguson and the CEO of South Western Oil, John Ridge, but leaving out the possible involvement of Subedei Industries and Ammon Oil. There was no need to endanger her by handing over more infor-mation than was necessary. Neusheen absorbed everything without question. She was too well trained to start pestering for more detail than Brock was willing to give.

At midday they had arrived over Siwa. Leaving the trail of the pipeline, they headed towards a motley collection of buildings that served as a refuelling station, trading post and a form of motel for passing travellers. Neusheen brought the helicopter down on a patch of sand near the shabby buildings and they both enjoyed the quiet that followed the quelling of the engines.

'Come on,' said Brock. 'I don't know about you, but I could do with something to eat.'

'Are we flying on after lunch?' asked Neusheen, unbuckling herself.

'I don't think so. We'll carry on another way.'

They climbed out of the craft. The heat had been just about bearable inside the helicopter, but outside, the searing noon temperature almost took their breath away.

'If this is late spring I don't know how people can visit Egypt for a summer break,' exclaimed Brock. 'God knows how your countrymen cope.'

'Quite easily. They know a special secret,' returned Neusheen.

'Which is?'

Neusheen grinned. 'They don't visit the desert at midday.'

'Do you know what they say about mad dogs and Englishmen?'

Neusheen looked blank.

'Ah, well – let's just say, here's one Scot who's also mad enough to go out in the midday sun.'

Brock sent Neusheen off to make arrangements for leaving the helicopter while he found a place among the corrugated-iron shanty-town buildings where he could hire a Nissan pick-up truck. Meeting his pilot on the dusty road outside, he led the way to what passed for a restaurant in the halfdeserted pit stop. There, they sustained themselves with roasted lamb kebabs and watery couscous.

An hour later, their energy levels restored, they were roaring out of Siwa's desert service station, Brock behind the wheel of the Nissan truck, heading back towards the pipeline. With the air-conditioning whirring like a disturbed hornets' nest, and the wide wheels stirring the dust behind them, they bypassed the old hill-top town of Aghurmi and followed the road that weaved between the intermittent wells and sinks.

Soon they relocated the pipeline lying incongruously across the sea of sand like some deserted pier on ugly jutting stands. They followed it on for twenty minutes, before a dark shape loomed up on the horizon ahead of them.

'Bingo,' said Brock with satisfaction.

'What's that?' Neusheen squinted against the desert glare.

'That is Cambyses II – where someone is hoping to strike oil. That's where we're going.'

Ayeesha Al Fahila swirled the ice around in her glass as she listened to Zarakov make his daily report on the telephone. She tried to dampen down her irritation that it was the Russian on the phone to Subedei, and not her. Of course, she'd acceded to Subedei's insistence not to mix business with pleasure. He'd told her that no matter what kind of relationship they enjoyed in their private lives, his business would be kept strictly separate. She understood that, but she found it irksome. She wanted to know more about his plans, to share in them and be a part of his inevitable triumphs. She wanted them to be a team, a partnership.

She recognized that her driving force was power and control. It was why she had been attracted to the Mongolian in the first place. Well, there was nothing wrong with that. And no doubt her lover was attracted to her for the same reasons; he must have recognized her natural ability to lead, her urge to power, even her evident destiny for greatness. Like attracted like, after all.

There were twenty-five years between them but they were kindred spirits, Ayeesha knew that. Old souls. Cynical, world weary, ruthless. It was a shame that all that compatibility did not extend to the bedroom where, to be honest, Ayeesha found herself bored and underwhelmed, although some of the bizarre techniques and sexual aids her eastern lover insisted upon at least made her smile. But it was worth it, to share in his unstoppable determination to achieve his ambitions.

Nevertheless, she had power over him, she felt certain of it. He had been enthralled by her as soon as he had set eyes upon her, as most men that she chose to be in her life had been. And she had known how to use each and every one of them to climb from rung to rung, leaving them far behind when they were no longer useful. Only once had she almost succumbed to a man, when she'd thought for one ridiculous moment that she was in love with that fool of an American who wanted to marry her and continually fill her belly with babies.

She shuddered involuntarily.

Thank god she'd come to her senses in time. How could she have allowed herself to be weakened from her resolve by his expert love-making and persuasive tongue? True, he'd made her feel like no other man ever had. But she had stopped herself in time. Just as well too. For now, Ayeesha Al Fahila had a new opportunity opening up before her: to rule like a queen at the side of the most powerful man she'd ever known.

'Ayeesha is sitting opposite me now. Did you want to tell her yourself?'

At the sound of her name being spoken, Ayeesha's reverie was broken and she made to rise. She noticed Zarakov's eyes glitter sardonically.

'OK, I'll tell her. Goodbye.' The Russian put the phone down.

Ayeesha hid her flash of anger by continuing to rise smoothly, and she headed towards the side table where iced tea had been laid out for them, asking casually, 'Anything interesting to report?'

Zarakov smiled inwardly at the woman's adroitness. Years of interrogating prisoners had honed his observational powers to a point where he seldom missed anything. Her untouched glass hardly required a refill and putting the onus on him to report was a good ploy that he would play along with.

It would give her face.

Well, he thought, if she is one of Subedei's women, and I've rarely been wrong about who is sharing his bed, I will continue to be wary of her. This one has steel in her, anyone can see that. And I've seen too many friends and colleagues brought down through the insidious power of pillow talk.

He took a sip of his iced tea, watching Ayeesha's graceful form as she stood at the table. Then he said, 'Tomorrow I will return to Turkey to oversee the completion of our Caspian pipeline to the eastern Mediterranean facility at Ceyhan. I need to ensure that the scheduling of our port refineries is coordinated, so from there I will be going to Al Qantarah at Suez, before returning to control at Alexandria.'

A slight smile passed Zarakov's lips as he paused. 'It would be most helpful if you could personally handle all the arrangements for the *Pharaoh Queen*. Only the best will suffice for the floating banquet, and naturally all the dignitaries and invited guests must have the attention that only you are able to deliver. Subedei will be flying in next week.'

A haughty smile just touched the woman's lips, indicating that Zarakov had couched the request perfectly.

'Of course. I would expect nothing less than absolute perfection, as you well know.' Ayeesha felt her previous annoyance evaporate. It had been her suggestion to hold a spectacular event that would allow so many influential people to meet her powerful lover. A few were already within his patronage – or should she say, *their* patronage. But there would be many more prepared to fawn all over them in the hope that they could win favour with the mighty Subedei. And what could be better than a cruise of extraordinary luxury down the Nile to captivate an audience? It would be another opportunity to show Subedei how indispensable his Ayeesha was to him; and then he would take her completely into his confidence.

'And what of our other guests? The two oilmen?'

Zarakov answered comfortably, 'In good hands and being well looked after. They are no longer your concern. My brother Dimitri will attend to them in my absence.'

He had no real doubt that the two executives would end up dead. Assassination had been a part of both his and his younger brother's life for so long that it no longer seemed to have much meaning. As young men, they had been both humorous and enthusiastic about it: it was really the only way to cope with being a murderer on a daily basis. He stopped himself caring. He plugged up any places where empathy might escape and he built a mental wall against the fear that one day it would be him in that position, facing the barrel of the gun or the blade of the knife. The unexpected bullet was the kindest of all and if he ever met his end at the hand of another, then that's what Zarakov hoped for. The long-drawn-out, torturous death was what he closed his mind to. He'd inflicted that nightmare on others enough times to understand its particular horror.

Perhaps Dimitri was still able to embrace the killing eagerly but he, Zarakov, had become bored with it. It was necessary, of course, but it was now like brushing his teeth: routine, part of what was necessary to stay in good health. That was all.

That is why he had not been surprised to learn a few minutes ago from Subedei about Wheng Zhu.

Stupid.

His was a classic case of building a fearful reputation, then believing your own propaganda about the reputation you have built, and finally becoming complacent about it. The consequences were always disastrous.

Over the years the tautness of being always on your guard had taken its toll, but it had ensured Zarakov's survival on countless occasions. It was a bonus now therefore that Subedei had just forewarned him about the investigations by ICE. He had heard of them before and the name Brock. It had not meant anything at the time but now it came to mind. Last year he had heard how a former colleague who had built a seemingly-legitimate import-export business in antiquities, had been put out of business and lost his life in the sewers of Moscow in the process.

Zarakov already knew that his colleague not only provided bespoke museum Artefacts in return for business favours and profits – stolen Artefacts, of course, the old fool – but also that every outgoing shipment was a cover for sending human cargo in the form of young girls from Chechnya and Georgia intended for the streets of Western Europe. And every returning shipment was loaded with more goods *borrowed* from museum archives.

'Success encourages arrogance,' his hard mentor had told him. 'Look for arrogance first and you will find the source of their insecurity. When you have that, they are in your power and the first step to finding out what they know is easily done. The threat is more powerful than the action. Of course always be prepared to carry out whatever is required immediately and without thinking. But do so in the right order.'

That had been Zhu's downfall, Zarakov thought; he enjoyed the action and suffering he was able to impart because it made him feel successful.

Arrogant fool.

And so stupid.

The Egyptian woman is arrogant, but not stupid.

He would have to be careful, but by God he needed the

danger, the risk. His body was used to it, like a drug. Was that what they had made him become? A professional killing addict?

'One of them, the shorter of the two with the green eyes, is cute.' Ayeesha slowly crossed her legs, sliding one slim calf over the other as she held Zarakov's gaze.

He kept his eyes on her face. Was she teasing him?

'You must mean the humorous one. The one who makes jokes when he is in danger. Green eyes, eh? Interesting to hear that you got close enough to notice.'

Ayeesha smiled demurely. 'If you want to distract someone, put them off guard, you have to get close, don't you? At least, I find that works for me.'

Zarakov's face was unreadable. 'I'm sure it does, my dear. I'm sure it works very well indeed.' The Russian watched as the woman before him leaned forward attentively, this time revealing a tantalising amount of firm cleavage. 'Much as I enjoy your company, I must, unfortunately, be on my way.' He raised his glass. '*Nostrovia!*' He drank, replaced the glass and went to the door.

Ayeesha's smile faded as Zarakov left the room. 'How dare he call me *my dear*,' she murmured coldly to herself. 'Well, my *dear* Siberian friend, in due course when the opportunity presents itself, as it always does, I will turn my attention to you.'

Ten

The fierce afternoon sun beat down on Brock as he raised the small but powerful field glasses to his eyes. The sign on the gates of the enclosed facility was in Arabic and English: *Welcome to Cambyses II. Commerce and Heritage working together for Egypt's future. No unauthorized admittance.*

There were no security guards to be seen but it was clear that the gates were well secured against entry, whether welcome or unwelcome. There were small huts on either side of the gates and, beyond them, a large building resembling an aircraft hangar, its curved sides and roof constructed in a half-moon shape.

At the far end of the site was a series of cylindrical containers and drilling rigs. To the right of the hangar building were excavation vehicles poised on the edge of large rectangular holes that looked like archaeological digs. Brock glanced at his watch.

Two thirty.

Working hours varied in the desert. At this time of year, any work on excavation would start at first light, continue until midday and then stop until the next morning.

Any investigation of the morning's findings would take place inside, in a cool, temperature-controlled environment. Probably in the hangar, Brock surmised.

When they had got within viewing distance of Cambyses II, Brock had parked the Nissan to the side of the giant pipeline they'd followed from Siwa. With the engine off, he had heard the distinct sound of humming emanating from the pipe.

'It must be the pumps,' suggested Neusheen.

Brock frowned. 'Yes. Except – how can they be pumping oil through it when we know for a fact that at the moment there is only a dead end for the oil to go to?'

He climbed out of the truck, took the wheel wrench from

87

the Nissan and placed one end against the pipe and the other to his ear to conduct the sound more clearly.

'The vibration sounds more like a tram or rail line. I know that robotic welders, the kind often used in pipeline construction, run on a monorail, but the sound here is . . . well . . . as if something is approaching.' Brock looked thoughtful, his blue eyes serious as the noise level sharply rose and then quickly fell away again. 'Whatever it is that I can hear, it appears to be leaving the complex along this pipeline.'

He went back to the truck and collected his field glasses. Turning them back now towards the hangar, he could see that the pipe entered the building.

'Strange. You would have thought that an oil pipe would go directly to the supply containers. Not to a hangar.' His instinct was already telling him that this was probably not the straightforward oil exploration site it appeared to be – another reason for not simply announcing himself at the gate, or walking in as a guest as Matt must have done, if he'd ever made it here.

Brock turned to Neusheen, who was sitting patiently in the truck as he completed his survey.

'I'm going into the complex. You have the satellite phone. If I haven't returned within two hours, drive back to Siwa and wait by the helicopter. If you have not had contact from me within another hour, get airborne and press four on the sat-phone. That will patch you through to someone – tell them exactly what's happened and be prepared to take further instructions. Is that all clear?'

Neusheen looked at the set jaw and hard blue eyes of the man before her. 'You're doing it again, aren't you? Dashing off and leaving me suddenly in charge.'

Brock smiled, his face relaxing. He squinted through the desert light, his tan already more burnished by the Egyptian sun. 'Not at all. This time I am giving you plenty of notice before you have to take control of your aircraft.'

'Can't I go with you?'

'Nope. 'Fraid not.'

'I could be your back-up.' It was obvious the girl did not want to be left alone in the dull silence of the featureless land.

'You are my back-up – that's precisely why I need you right here.' Brock's smile was replaced with a determined seriousness as he turned, took a leather pouch from the glove compartment, strapped it to his belt and followed the pipe towards Cambyses II.

The security measures were not as high as he might have expected. And if everything were just as it seemed, there was no reason for them to be. Archaeological digs do not require high-level protection until their findings have been proved to be of value. And oil wells – if you discounted the terrorist threat, which didn't seem high out here in this peaceful landscape, then there wasn't much point in thronging the place with guards. It took more than a lone intruder to make off with gallons of oil.

So it went against everything Brock was sensing about this place that there was a distinct lack of alert security patrols. But that didn't mean he wasn't right, he reflected, as he removed the Leatherman tool from its pouch. It meant, if anything, that luck was on his side. He was here before he was expected.

He followed the pipe right up to its entry point through the wire mesh fence around the campus and quickly widened the gap around it with his pliers. He ignored the Arabic signs of *Danger – keep out*, illustrated with a bolt of lightning indicating high voltage. It was clear to see that the pseudo-electrified fencing was neither earthed nor connected in a series, and too many articles that would have immediately earthed any current had been carelessly pushed against the inside of the fence. The signs were there to distract opportunists who felt like a look around.

The wire came away easily beneath the pliers and, as soon as he had cut enough room, Brock slid quickly and easily along the cool concrete body of the pipe and found himself inside the perimeter of the fence. It was about fifty metres to the hangar and he had stealthily paced half the distance when an access door to the side of the hangar opened, and two men came out, talking loudly in English.

Brock dropped immediately into the shadow of a lorry parked nearby, and observed the men. They were both suntanned, dressed in khaki shorts and black T-shirts emblazoned with a logo that read *Ammon Oil.*

'There's no liaison,' said the heavier-set man in a voice shrill with complaint, placing the cigarette in his mouth that the second, leaner man had offered. 'Drill, don't drill, drill. They can't seem to make their minds up from one day to the next. Who are we working for anyway, these antiquity nerds or what? I thought we were oilmen.'

'It does seem to be a one-way bloody street of co-operation,' replied the leaner man gruffly in a south London accent, as he lit their cigarettes. 'I mean, they said in the contract that we had to assist those arckey-whatsits. It wasn't supposed to be what we did all bleeding day, was it? I'm used to prospecting for oil, not looking for stone-age bits and pieces. All we seem to be doing is using all our tools for excavating caverns.'

'It's not even as though we get to see anything afterwards. They lock those caves off the minute we've accessed them. I wouldn't mind seeing a bit of the stuff they're finding, whatever it is. But you try going anywhere near it! They're as twitchy as mice if I even wander nearby.' The first man talked round his cigarette, which bobbed up and down as he spoke.

'The point is—' His companion stopped suddenly. 'Hold up.' The sight of Brock walking casually towards them silenced him.

'Hi, guys,' began Brock, casual and confident. 'Thanks for all your efforts recently. I do hope we're not causing you too much aggravation.'

'Not at all, mate, we're . . . um . . . only too pleased to be of assistance.' The first man dragged deeply on his cigarette, eyed Brock sideways and spoke through clouds of smoke while his friend frowned at the stranger. 'So how long do you think it'll be now before you find what you're looking for?'

'Well,' offered Brock conspiratorially, 'between ourselves, we're almost there.'

The second man said, 'I haven't seen you about here before.'

'I mostly work offsite,' Brock explained. 'In Ammon head-quarters.'

'Oh, right.' The man's face cleared and he seemed satisfied.

The heavier-set man bent his head towards Brock. 'What is it you're trying to find exactly?' he enquired curiously.

'Sorry, mate – I can't say just yet, but you'll know soon enough.' Brock brightened his voice. 'Anyway, you'll have to excuse me for the moment, but once again, thanks for your assistance. I know I speak for my colleagues too.' He walked smoothly past them, opened the access door and entered the hangar before they could say any more.

The bitingly cold environment, generated by giant air-conditioned units, was a shock after the intense heat outside. Great arc lights provided a near-daylight effect, giving the enormous hangar the feeling of a floodlit football stadium.

Except here there were no stands packed with ecstatic fans. The place was weirdly empty, except for a collection of tables at the far end of the hangar, where some figures were bent over hard at work, absorbed in whatever it was in front of them.

Just a short distance to the right of where Brock found himself stood a row of electric carts, lined up in front of the mouth of the great pipe that Brock had followed across the desert.

Now, that was a mystery. Why build an oil pipe that is not for oil and place it nowhere going to nowhere?

You don't.

So it has to serve a purpose.

Brock walked confidently towards the table closest to him, wanting to appear as though he was on a specific errand, while, out of the corner of his eye, he counted the people who stood around the carts and pipe access.

Then he saw what was lying on the tables.

'Jesus!' He couldn't prevent the quiet exclamation at the sight. Row upon row of skulls, mostly in pieces, and human bones were arranged in an orderly fashion.

What was remarkable was the sheer number: there had to be thousands of them, covering surface after surface, all neatly arrayed so that the ones that had remained intact faced in the same direction, their hollow black eye sockets staring forward. Another set of tables across the hangar was spread with an array of spearheads and pitted swords.

Again, there were too many to count.

A voice in Arabic acknowledged him from a nearby table. Brock waved and walked confidently but with respectful deference towards the woman who had called him.

'Oh, I see you are European,' the woman said apologetically in English. 'Can I help you? I don't seem to recall seeing you here before.'

'Scottish, in fact,' replied Brock. 'From Aberdeen, to be precise. The cold northern home of oil.'

'I see – then you must be from the Ammon contingent.' Fatima Saeed looked relieved. As a personal assistant to the new marketing director of the Supreme Council of Antiquities, she was a little out of her depth here. Her boss had instructed her to take a look around and report anything that seemed out of the ordinary. But in this place, what was ordinary, and what was not?

To her, everything was out of the ordinary. Wonderful and fascinating, of course. But it was hardly the stuff of everyday to discover one of the greatest hoards of military antiquity in the history of their country.

Cambyses's Lost Army. It made her gasp and shake her head when she thought of it. It was almost unbelievable that, after all these centuries, the remains of the legendary mighty host should be seeing the light of day.

Yet all this cloak and dagger confused her.

However, rules were rules, and she said to the tall stranger, 'I'm sure you're aware that this area is out of bounds.'

'Of course. I've been sent over, though. We were just wondering if there was anything further you and your team required,' said Brock.

'I know it must be a nuisance but, as I just informed your colleagues, if you can be patient a little longer we hope to be out of your way soon.'

'Oh, it's going well then? You must be incredibly excited about your find. My god, I would love to see what you've discovered on site. The thrill must be like what we feel when an oil strike erupts.'

Charmed by the tanned, strong-looking oilman in front of her, Fatima didn't feel too uneasy about talking to him. He was one of the Ammon Oil people, after all, and as a marketing communications and liaison officer, it was her job to talk, wasn't it?

'You're right, it is exciting, though I have not even experienced it myself first-hand yet. My superior takes the shuttle every day to check on the progress at the dig itself. Unfortunately we leave later today, so I will probably miss out on the final push.'

Brock looked at the young woman with her smock and dark wide trousers. She had the appearance of an anxious schoolgirl trying to please, but her nervousness did not hide the fact that she was an intelligent and highly effective individual. He sensed that her reticence was part of her culture and he needed to try and take advantage of it.

'Would it be completely out of order to go down there? I need to check on what machine parts may be required in case we're suddenly expected to provide an emergency service. You know, it's a raw deal,' he added quickly, 'having to provide maintenance without parts, and you're leaving today, so why don't we take a quick look at what's going on? I'm stuck here for a further two weeks yet, incommunicado, so I'm hardly going to say anything to anyone. You have my word. And I certainly shan't be telling your colleagues that we went down there. What do you say?'

The woman looked hesitant. It obviously went against her training and personality to break the rules but then again, she was clearly strongly tempted. No doubt she knew that this would be her last chance to look at whatever was down there in situ, where history had left it.

She looked across anxiously at the empty carts parked in front of the pipe monorail. The light that indicated there was no incoming traffic glowed temptingly green. The curiosity she felt for what was down there was overwhelming. Turning back to look once more into the azure eyes, she relaxed, her decision made.

After all, she had not been ordered *not* to go; she had merely assumed she had to be given permission.

'A maintenance inspection would be in order, I believe, Mr . . . ?'

'Brock. Connor Brock at your service, ma'am.' Brock was acting, as his old mentor Sasanaka would say, in the manner of a swan. Serene and majestic, it glides effortlessly along the surface of the water, while, beneath the surface, unseen, its feet paddle furiously.

'The secret in communication is to be yourself,' his mentor would say. 'It may be the conditioned nature of man to add or subtract from the truth, but the closer he is to truth, the nearer he is to being himself. It is the nature of man to lie, but if he has to lie about his own name, he cheats himself.'

93

Saying his own name came naturally to Brock and such sincerity was necessary to convey the confidence required by the person in front of him. There was no reason at all for anyone at the facility to know who he was or why he was here, but he still breathed a mental sigh of relief when, instead of an unwanted flicker of anxious recognition, there was a smile of relaxed acknowledgement.

'Fatima Saeed, from the Supreme Council of Antiquities.' The woman smiled, and held out her hand to shake Brock's in the European manner. 'Now is as good a time as any. Let's go.'

The blinding arc light that had been moved to shine directly in front of him whipped harshly at Ferguson's eyes. But squeezing them tightly shut in an effort to maintain the darkness that had become the status quo only caused him greater pain.

'I trust you slept well?' enquired Zarakov.

'One of the best, thank you,' croaked Ferguson. 'Can't even remember turning over.'

The Russian laughed deeply. 'Ha! Very good. I like your jokes. How about you, Mr Ridge?'

The past twenty-four hours had taken a severe toll on the older oil executive. He looked as if his entombment had drained all his reserves, both physical and psychological.

Any hope of escape had disappeared when Ferguson, having finally freed his arm, had been caught in the act of trying to liberate the rest of his body. When the light had gone on unexpectedly, Ferguson had been caught like a bear in a trap. He had tried to resist with growls and his one free arm but had been immediately overpowered by the Bedouin guards, and reburied. Only this time his hands had been tied. The punishment had been no water.

Now the oilman had resigned himself to whatever fate lay before him. Nevertheless, his spirit was not broken. 'Go to hell, you son-of-a-bitch,' he whispered venomously. 'You think you can wrench my company from me? Go ahead, kill me. You still won't get it. The whole caboodle is in a foundation. I couldn't touch it even if I wanted to. The oil industry is not some Sunday afternoon tea party. Unwanted takeovers go with the territory, so I protect it from scheming bastards like you!'

'A commendable speech, Mr Ridge. It's just unfortunate that

94

the trustees of your foundation couldn't hear it. As from last night, they have already been persuaded that the foundation's interests in the US will be better protected by licensing the refinery at Alexandria to Ammon Oil for the foreseeable future. So we are no longer being too demanding. Just a simple licence will suffice.'

John Ridge widened his grit-filled eyes in surprise. 'They still need my seal as acting chief executive to ratify any such move.'

'Correct. That is what I have been led to understand, so I thank you for confirming that.' Zarakov knelt in front of Ridge, smoothing the oilman's bedraggled hair in an oddly tender gesture before continuing. 'I also understand that the seal is in your safe at the foundation and only you have the combination for it. Mr Ridge, we're not unreasonable. I already explained that it was my over-zealous colleagues who preferred to use their ancient methods of negotiation.' He motioned for one of the two Bedouins to bring water. 'I assure you that I prefer more civilized methods but right now I am under some pressure myself – deadlines and other incidentals, you know. Why don't you just agree to my simple request and you can be on your way?'

Ferguson broke in. 'Forgive me, but even though I have little movement I can still feel when I'm having my leg pulled,' he croaked. 'You hardly expect us to believe that you are going to let us go when you have what you want.'

'I can give you my word that I will not kill you or, for that matter, have you killed. I can't promise not to detain you for a while longer but, when the time is right, there is no reason why you should not be able to turn up somewhere in the desert safe and sound.' Zarakov paused a few moments while he stood up and slowly walked around them in a circle before continuing.

'No reason at all. After all, the reports of you missing in the desert have already been accepted by your colleagues and the media. Indeed, we ourselves were the ones who offered to organize the extensive search for you.'

'Which, of course, has been unsuccessful,' cut in Ferguson flatly.

'Not entirely so. We're getting some good media coverage for making our resources available to the brave rescue forces at no expense, and for assisting our friends at South Western Oil with up-to-date information.'

Zarakov paused while he took the saucer of water that the young Bedouin proffered begrudgingly, then knelt down and held it to Ridge's dry lips.

'However, we digress from the issue. What is your answer? Is your life worth one little licence or not?'

Ridge's throat hurt as he swallowed the water. All he could taste was dust. 'OK, it's a deal,' he breathed, silently cursing whichever one of the trustees had had the audacity to agree anything with these bandits. If he ever got out of here, a lot of people were going to be very sorry indeed. 'I'll sign the licence. Just let us go.'

'Excellent! You really have made a wise choice.'

Fifteen minutes later, Ferguson and Ridge were free of their sand prisons and lying on the floor. Their arms and legs felt as though a thousand pins and needles were being pushed into them as their joints, allowed at last to move freely, came back to full feeling.

Ferguson rubbed his eyes. 'It's the little things in life that are important, as my mother used to say,' he moaned with relief. 'They give us the most pleasure.'

'Talking of little things, may I have the combination, please, Mr Ridge?' asked Zarakov politely but with a firm edge to his voice. 'Then all you have to do is to relax here while the combination is checked out and the seal made available.'

For the first time Ferguson was able to take a good look at his captor. He recognized the air of a hardened professional. Zarakov's posture was a clear signal of tough military training. The erect carriage, wide shoulders and thick neck looked immensely powerful, and the observant but expressionless eyes never matched the wide smile emanating from the mouth.

The Russian turned suddenly to look directly at Ferguson, as though he had sensed that he was being appraised. They locked stares for a moment, and the Irishman was sure that he saw an almost imperceptible nod of acknowledgement. Ferguson knew that whatever cover he'd had was now non-existent.

Ridge repeated the combination a couple of times, and, having committed it to memory, Zarakov turned back to Ferguson. 'Perhaps you will explain *your* involvement in the oil business when I return.'

'I'll look forward to that,' said Ferguson lightly. 'Any excuse for a good long chat.'

Zarakov motioned to the two Bedouin guards to retie their prisoners' hands and left the cavern.

Brock did not suffer from claustrophobia but beetling along on the automated four-seat cart surrounded by air and water ducts was like being trapped inside a life-support machine. Knowing it was better for him to ask questions rather than provide answers, Brock continued to probe Fatima without giving away that he was utterly ignorant of what was going on or where they were heading.

The girl had become quite excitable since realizing that she would not be encountering any resistance in taking a cart and speeding towards the real Cambyses II site. The two people nearest the pipe mouth had not even looked up from the table they were engrossed in, and when she nervously slotted her pass card into the dash, the cart had whirred to life. She was now annoyed at herself for not realizing earlier that she obviously already had permission to visit the site.

Brock asked about the quantity of bones and artefacts, and let the woman recount the story of the Lost Army of Cambyses to him, though he already knew the tale well. It had been another of his father's favourites, and Herodotus was one of Cameron Brock's heroes.

When Fatima paused for breath, Brock said idly, 'So why are the caverns themselves so far from the site above ground? We've been going along this pipeline for some time already, haven't we?'

He instantly regretted his question as a look of consternation passed over the girl's face. She glanced anxiously at him.

'Well, you of all people should know that the complex was a fair distance from the actual caverns because they were so unstable. I heard that several of your people were severely injured, two even killed as a whole rig collapsed into the ground. It is shocking that even now, centuries later, the legend continues to take lives.'

'A disaster that was doubly felt by us all because they were friends, as well as colleagues,' said Brock, recovering smoothly. 'I meant that it's annoying we had to go so far back from where the caverns stop, because of the extra time involved for the council's work. Our geologists were emphatic about going further but we still have not started pumping. We would hate our colleagues' lives to have been lost in vain.' Brock held his breath as he watched her consider his words.

She relaxed and the pinched, nervous look faded.

'Hard to imagine, isn't it?' added Brock. 'Such a huge army sheltering in caverns, only to be trapped for eternity under a million tons of sand.'

'It would have been impossible to dig out from under five hundred feet of soft sand. Dr Suleiman Attallah is convinced that the soldiers must have survived for several months by resorting to cannibalism. I, for one, do not see how they could have lasted more than a few hours before going mad trapped in that terrible darkness.'

'You mustn't underestimate the human spirit,' Brock replied. 'People can withstand more than you'd think, when it comes to survival.'

At that moment, the track rapidly descended. From the angle of incline, Brock estimated that they had dropped several hundred feet. He thought it imprudent to mention that, at the surface, the pipe appeared to stay above ground, mounted on its struts. There were obviously two lines – one possibly for appearance, though probably for future oil, if drilling were ever commenced; the other for the purpose of providing access to the caverns. That was why the humming noise he had heard earlier had disappeared so quickly. There had to be a forked intersection.

The cart itself was running on an automatic program and there was no need for steering, or stopping for that matter. Brock assumed a cut-out switch would slow and stop the cart when it reached its destination.

'Suleiman Attallah?' Brock wanted to take this opportunity to learn everything he could. 'I don't think I know that name.'

'He's the Antiquities Council's director and curator at Cairo Museum. It was he who ratified the agreement for Ammon and us to work together on this project that will restore so much of Egypt's heritage. A brilliant man, though I have had not had the privilege of meeting him yet. I am bound to next week, of course, at the announcement of our magnificent find!'

'Here?'

'No!' Fatima laughed. 'We're hardly going to let people wander all over here, are we? And getting VIPs and reporters out to the middle of the desert would be impossible, even for a discovery of this magnitude. No, the occasion is to be held on the Nile aboard a yacht.'

'Now that's what I call style. I have no doubt that all the grandees will prefer that,' commented Brock.

'As will the all-important media, of course,' added Fatima. 'Yes, we are really lucky. The Supreme Council has always been stuffy in the past and would not even consider such extravagance. Nor would they have the funds. But our new patron is generously lending his magnificent yacht, the *Pharaoh Queen*, and covering all the expenses.' She glanced at him, her eyes sparkling. 'Can you imagine, I have lived in Egypt all my life and I have never yet experienced a cruise down the Nile? And now I have learned thirty minutes ago that not only am I going, but I am to leave this afternoon to start planning the event.'

The track levelled out and the cart slowed to a stop on a rotating circular platform, which then slid off to one side while another took its place.

'Look, here we are!'

Neat, thought Brock, as a red light above them flashed to green. Prevents collision from oncoming traffic and, more importantly, allows only one in and one out at a time. Another quick look at the dash showed that there did not appear to be any controls, not even an emergency stop. When they had got into the cart and it had registered the presence of a security pass, it had immediately started its pre-programmed trip.

Brock glanced at his watch. Their automatic cart run had taken less than five minutes. They had been moving at about twenty to twenty-five kilometres an hour, which, allowing for their downward descent, meant that they had probably travelled a distance of less than two kilometres. They must be close to the outskirts of Aghurmi with its warren of wells.

Brock frowned as he stepped out of the cart. Unless he was wrong and they had travelled in entirely the opposite direction, Ammon could never have drilled for oil here. Surely the facility Cambyses II was placed where it was in order to mislead onlookers. The rig disaster story was just that – a story.

Why? Why not just come clean?

It would not be the first time that oil exploration had revealed elements of archaeological interest, after all. And any drilling would have to take place some way from the caverns, so why delay, if finding oil was what they were interested in?

Imperceptibly shaking his head as he followed Fatima, Brock put the thoughts to the back of his mind.

The focus of attention had been to get in to the site. Now that he was here, his purpose was to locate Ferguson and Ridge. The final goal would be to get out again. Brock pursed his lips.

Now, that would be a challenge. Being down here was like being an insect trapped inside a bottle, with only a slim neck leading out. Above his head was a mass of sand and rock and there was no chance of getting through that. After all, a desperate army had been unable to manage it.

Escape would certainly take some focus, he thought. Still, he had walked in and he would cross each bridge as he came to it.

Eleven

The size of the cavern was unexpected. Shaped like a giant egg, laid on its side, it was as big as an ice rink and just as cold. It smelled of death, ancient death. The walls seemed to be composed of petrified wood, millions of years old, and limestone.

Along the sides were a series of entrances or exits. Just off-centre were stacks of what looked like two-wheeled chariots, huge mounds of bones; and an even greater stack of ancient armoury. It was like being transported back in time.

'She said it was like some ancient natural inlet created by the water erosion when this depression was once a sea,' Fatima's face was wide-eyed, her voice quiet.

'Who?' whispered back Brock as they moved further into the cavern.

'Ayeesha Al Fahila.'

A group of people stood at the far end of the cavern. They did not appear to shout but their words were as audible as if they had been standing right next to them.

'Is that you Ayeesha?' Fatima looked surprised. Brock's mind was taken back in an instant to the first time he had visited St Paul's Cathedral in London. In the whispering gallery you could hear your partner talking to you despite the fact that they were the opposite side of the great dome. Only the acoustics here were uncanny. You could hear the person's voice but be too far away to recognize their face.

Fatima waved hesitantly and began to move toward the group.

'If you wait here I will just explain why we are here.'

Brock smiled in acknowledgment and turned to the side as something caught his peripheral vision. Exiting one of the entrances was a heavy-set man walking purposefully towards him. Fatima had noticed him too and turned back to Brock.

'Miss Saeed,' smiled the man. 'What a surprise to see you here. I thought you would be leaving. Do you have a message for us?'

Though looking a little nervous, Fatima replied easily, 'No, sir, I just wanted to have a look myself before I left. I thought it would assist with the media marketing. It is in order for me to, isn't it?'

'I am sure that Madam Al Fahila will be pleased to learn of your dedication.' The heavily moustached man turned his eyes to Brock enquiringly.

Fatima noticed and immediately said, 'The opportunity presented itself because this gentleman thought it a good idea to check on possible maintenance requirements, and so we came together. Mr Brock, this is Mr Zarakov.'

'Good idea. How do you do, Mr Brock.' Zarakov did not miss a beat in the rhythm of the introduction. His expression did not register any flicker of recognition, concern or enquiry as he shook hands with Brock. 'Actually, now you mention it, I have noticed some possible malfunctioning in the air units. I'm glad you're here to check it over, Mr Brock. But forgive me, I must rush to another appointment, and I am already somewhat late.' He took a pace toward the turntable and the cart that had lined itself up in readiness for its next passengers. Then he paused and, as if forgetting something, turned back. 'Miss Saeed, by all means feel free to take a look around, though be careful to stay within the limits of this cavern. Some of these adjoining caves are like a maze and you could easily get lost. Mr Brock, could I bother you to take the brief trip back with me? I am in a rush, as I say, but I would like to discuss my own mainten-ance concerns. You can return immediately and do what you have to do before coming back with Miss Saeed.'

'Certainly. It would be my pleasure,' returned Brock smoothly, as relaxed as the Russian. Maintenance, my foot, he thought. He's a cool customer, though. And if I'm not mistaken, he recognized my name, although he hid it brilliantly. Brock sent a silent apology to his mentor and promised himself he would practice a convincing alias.

Zarakov ushered Brock towards the waiting cart as Fatima went to join the group at the far end of the cavern. The two men took their seats in the little car without speaking and, as it moved off, Brock gauged that there were about twenty metres before the tramway picked up speed to start its ascent and before the tunnel became dangerously cluttered with the vents and tubes that ran along its walls. He would have to act quickly. Brock leaned in toward Zarakov so as not to arise any suspicion of his intent.

'Quite right, Mr Brock,' remarked Zarakov, interpreting Brock's movement as one that would prevent him from being pushed out. 'One has to take great care travelling on these beetle bugs with their unreliable safety monitors. Regrettably, we had a colleague who fell off. It was not a nice sight. While the careless fool lay stunned, jammed by the rail, a following car crushed him. The trouble is, once they set off, they don't stop. It took ten minutes to make the turn around and by the time we returned, most of him had been chewed to mincemeat. Not nice, not nice at all.'

Zarakov smiled to himself as Brock moved in closer.

'It can't be easy to just fall out of these contraptions,' replied Brock, sounding concerned, while he swiftly monitored the approach of the oncoming slope. The cart's speed had almost reached its zenith when Brock hurled himself over the side. Within a split second, the cart had shot up the incline and away from him. He caught a glimpse of his companion's startled face staring back at him before the cart whisked away along the rail.

A jolt of pain raced up Brock's back. It had not been possible to land correctly in such an enclosed space, and his tail bone had collided with the rim of a welded pipe joint. Ignoring the jarring pain, Brock sprang to his feet and, gritting his teeth, ran swiftly back towards the turntable.

That gives me twelve minutes at most, he thought to himself. Zarakov will be unable to stop the cart and turn back. But I don't think he's going to be in a very good mood by the time he returns.

At the cavern entrance, Brock paused and assessed the situation. The group at the far end was now engrossed in showing Fatima the piles of archaeological treasure. Good. That would keep them busy. Using the cover of the stacks of bones, chariots and armoury, Brock made his way silently toward the dark mouth in the wall of the cavern where he was sure Zarakov had come from.

He quickly followed the dimly lit trail through the passage for thirty metres, when it widened and forked in two directions. Only one was lit but Brock could see that the rough sand of the unlit tunnel had been recently disturbed.

Then this will be the one I take, he decided. Ten paces, and if nothing comes to light, I'll turn back. Feeling along the clammy walls, he ventured forward carefully. At nine paces, the tunnel turned sharply and Brock could just discern a light much further away down the passage.

He continued pacing carefully and silently along the tunnel. After a further ten to fifteen metres, it widened again and Brock saw evidence of temporary and very basic habitation. Two bed rolls lay on wide hessian rugs that covered most of the floor. Two prayer mats were arranged to the side while in the centre, on the lid of a crate, a variety of dried fruits were laid out. Brock approached it quickly, removed the fruit and opened the crate. Inside he saw more provisions, several torches and packets of lamps and batteries. Excellent.

Grabbing one of the torches, Brock continued towards the light at the end of the tunnel. The humming of a small generator covered the sound of his footsteps as he approached the entrance of a harshly lit cavern. Brock knelt down and peered carefully through the entrance. From the interior, bright with two powerful halogen lamps, came the unmistakable growl of Matt Ferguson followed quickly by a series of expletives in Arabic barked in a harsh voice.

With his hands tied behind his back, Ferguson had hunched his shoulders and stood, legs apart, desperately trying to prevent one of his two robed wardens from pushing him back into the hole in the ground.

'Did you not hear your man?' roared the resilient Irishman. 'He said tie my hands, not bury me!'

The Bedouin nearest him clearly did not understand. Pulling a short curved dagger attached to the sash around his waist, he began to scream at Ferguson, while his companion made a grab for the weary-looking oil executive standing nearby.

Ferguson's attacker jumped at his tied prey, lunging viciously out with his blade. Ferguson feinted to the left, quickly swinging back to his right, causing the young Bedouin's strike to slice harmlessly through air. Intending to drive a kick into his assailant,

Ferguson swore as he lost his balance and crashed heavily on to his shoulder.

The Bedouin was upon the fallen man in a flash and raised his dagger. He turned to his brother in arms, jabbering in triumph, and then stopped in confusion as he saw his companion staring over his head.

Brock had darted forward and now sprang at the man pinning Ferguson to the ground, slamming a hard fist into his sternum. The Bedouin fell back, winded by the heavy solar plexus blow, gasping for breath. His companion screamed with outrage and slashed at the American he was holding, slicing his knife into Ridge's back and pushing him aside to turn his attentions on Brock.

Brock was taken by surprise at the agility of the robed man as he sprang forward and aimed his blade towards Brock's chest. With a lightning reflex, Brock turned sideways to avoid the knife, while simultaneously smashing the torch he was holding down on the other's outstretched wrist. Brock seized the advantage and threw him sideways, punching his closed fist into the man's throat. Both Bedouins were now choking and helpless on the floor.

'I can see they're as speechless as I am to see you!'

Brock smiled grimly at his friend's comment as he stood up. 'Good to see you too, Matt.'

'I was beginning to wonder what was taking you so long to get here,' said Matt chirpily. 'How hard can it be to locate an underground cavern in the desert?'

Deftly Brock removed the Leatherman from his belt and sliced through Ferguson's cords. 'Don't push it, Matt. We're not home and dry yet.' He turned to Ridge, who had sunk to his knees in pain. 'Are you all right, sir?'

The Texan raised his head. 'Damn fellow got me in the back with his knife, but it ain't so bad. I can stand it. Cut me free, can you?'

Brock obliged. 'Can you walk, Mr Ridge? I don't like to worry you but we've got less than ten minutes to get out of here.'

Ridge's eyes glittered with defiance. 'Hell, I can walk. And I'll take on anyone who tries to stop us.'

Ferguson was busy using his bonds to restrain the two Bedouins. He looked over to Brock. 'I take it that you are the sole member of our rescue team? And if you're acting true to form, you'll be making up the exit strategy as you'll be going along.'

'That's about the measure of it. But there are three of us now.' Brock shook the hand of the oilman. 'I don't think I've introduced myself, Mr Ridge. Pleased to meet you. I'm Connor Brock. Let's go.'

As Zarakov made the return journey to the cavern, he was furious with himself. Losing a captive within seconds of unexpectedly finding him and then being stuck on a one-way trip in a computerized trolley would have been amusing if it had been any other person than himself. Perhaps he was getting too old for this side of the business. He'd naturally been expecting something along the lines of Brock's sudden departure, but not quite as quickly as it had occurred. He had to admit that Brock's pretending to sit more tightly in the cart had been a good feint.

What was even more infuriating was that he didn't have time to deal with Brock's recapture himself.

'Do they have weapons?' asked the athletic military man seated beside him, holding a lethal-looking Glock pistol, its barrel extended by a silencer.

Zarakov glanced at his brother. 'I don't think so. Brock may have something about his person. The other two are unarmed, unless you count ancient swords. Yet the four of you must be on your full guard, Dimitri. If the man Brock has discovered his friends, which I've no doubt he has, then he will be formidable. Two of them are professional, perhaps former military. I think we can assume that they'll have made short work of those Bedouin idiots. But they are now trapped and we have the advantage. That will not make them any the less dangerous, however – if anything they will be more desperate.'

'You don't have to tell me how to deal with this, brother. It's completely straightforward as far as I can see. A walk in the park. It'll be my pleasure to deal with the intruders.'

Zarakov looked into the hard eyes that matched his own. It was like looking in the mirror except that his brother reflected back a younger version of himself. 'Remember Chechnya, Dimitri. Rats are at their most lethal when caught in a barrel.'

'Do you want them alive?' his brother asked calmly.

'Ridge, perhaps, though even he is not critical to us any more. Otherwise – whatever. Do not risk any of the relics, though. Understand?'

They reached the turntable platform and Dimitri climbed out of the cart. The sound of the second cart holding his team came closer.

'Good luck, brother,' said Zarakov, as the second cart pulled to behind him. 'I know I can trust you.' He reinserted his card into the dash, and began the return journey to the surface. He had wasted enough of his time already. Deadlines were closing fast.

Dimitri led the way into the vast cavern, his silent helpers trailing him expertly. Inside, a group of people were examining a pile of ancient armour. They looked up startled when Dimitri called to them.

'Hey, you lot! Get yourselves out of here, all right? Up to the surface, all of you. Those are orders. Come on. Move!'

Obediently, the group left the mound of objects and filed out towards the monorail.

'Is it a maintenance procedure?' quavered a nervous-looking young woman as she went past.

Dimitri shrugged. 'Yeah, yeah, that's right. Maintenance. Now get a move on.' He gestured to one of his men to accompany the group back to the turntable and make sure they all departed for the hangar.

As the cavern emptied, Dimitri walked purposefully towards the tunnel that his elder brother had exited twenty minutes earlier. His remaining colleagues swept around the stacks of ancient military relics quickly and professionally. Finding nothing suspicious, they joined Dimitri and they all advanced, covering each other every five paces.

Arriving at the fork in the passage, Dimitri smiled grimly.

'Good idea,' he said to himself, as he removed the powerful torch from his belt. All the lights in the previously lit tunnel had been smashed. 'I would have done that.'

Ferguson swigged happily on the cool water and then stuffed his mouth with dried figs. It was sheer heaven to feel his blood sugar levels rising, restoring his energy.

Meanwhile, Brock surveyed Ridge's wound. The blade had

been deflected from piercing a lung by the scapula, but it was a difficult cut to bind. Brock looked into the eyes of the oilman, gauging his pain threshold and his ability to move.

'It no doubt feels worse than it is and I bet it feels like hell.'

'Just bind it the best you can and let's get the hell out of here,' rasped Ridge. 'I'll make it. It's the least I can goddamn do for you since you've gone and rescued me.'

Brock quickly tore a strip from the bottom of his shirt, folded it into a wad and tied it tightly into place around the other man's torso with the leftover cord. 'That ought to hold you together until we can get you fixed up properly. Wait here, you two. I'll be back in a moment.'

With a glance at his watch, Brock made quickly for the entrance of the cavern and headed back towards the fork in the tunnel. Once he got there, he dashed down the lit tunnel that he'd previously ignored. Twenty paces later, the passage abruptly ended in a small hole that was just large enough for him to crawl through.

He bent down and pulled himself into the hole, edging his way through it using his elbows. It was about the length of a body, and he quickly eased himself free on the other side, coming out into a dark room. His torch revealed that it appeared to be almost perfectly square. His light fell on to something hewn into the wall at the far end. Moving closer, Brock came upon a man-size polished stone sarcophagus. From its sides sprang rows of thick curled horns made of some material he couldn't identify at this distance. He was curious to investigate but time and his survival instinct decreed otherwise.

A quick survey revealed that the only apparent way in and out of the room was the hole he had crawled through. Thinking of the wounded Ridge, he assessed the situation and made a decision.

As he re-exited the hole and raced back down the tunnel, he smashed the lighting. Rejoining the others, he saw that they had placed the now blindfolded and gagged Bedouins in the sand holes that had previously contained their prisoners. The two men were quietly whimpering round their gags.

Brock went to his friend. 'OK, Matt, do you remember how they brought you here?'

The Irishman shook his head ruefully. 'No, we were out cold.

One moment we were in the old temple at Aghurmi and the next we woke up here.'

'I estimate we're under Siwa, possibly even close to Aghurmi. There has to be another access from one of these caves or waterholes.' Brock glanced again at his watch. 'The fact is, we've run out of time. And unfortunately we don't have any weapons other than a couple of knives. We have to assume that they will have more sophisticated weapons than that, although they'll have to be careful when they use them.'

Matt raised an enquiring eyebrow. 'And why would that be? Do you think they care about us enough not to shoot us?'

'No.' Brock pointed his finger upwards. 'First, they won't want to take the risk of being buried under a thousand tons of sand through a cave-in. Second, I'll bet they're under orders to protect as much down here as they can. Now – there's only one way out that we know of, the way I came in. See that waterhole?' Brock gestured towards a dark well at the back of the cavern that had previously gone unnoticed. 'There are quite a few of those round here. If all these caves are linked, it stands to reason that the water must come up somewhere else. I think that there's a whole chain of caverns and tunnels here, and if I'm right, there must be some other access to the surface via a subterranean channel.'

'OK, let's say that's true. But if we're dealing with diving into water pools, then there's the difficulty of knowing how long we have to hold our breath before we reach an air pocket.' Ferguson looked at Ridge, who was sitting with his good side leaning against the wall, his face gaunt with pain and exhaustion. 'That's if we can make it.'

'Exactly. That's a last resort. So our main hope is subterfuge.' With a quick glance at the two restrained Bedouins, Brock lowered his voice as he shared the plan that he had now formulated in his mind.

Twelve

'**O**ur target is resourceful, Anton,' whispered Dimitri to the man nearest to him. 'Perhaps he has already found his way through Ammon. Stay here at the fork while we check it out.'

Leaving Anton at his post, the other two Russians crept silently along the tunnel, torches kept low in their left hands, their right hands hovering over the holstered handguns and knives in their belts.

Reaching the hole at the end of the once well-lit tunnel, Dimitri pointed two fingers at the hole and then to his eyes, motioning to his partner to wait for two minutes and stay alert for any escaping prey.

Silently the veteran assassin took five even paces to the left and immediately three to the right and stepped quietly into the square cave. Standing silently in the dark, he listened acutely for any sound.

Nothing.

Crouching down on one knee, he swung his torch round the empty room. The beam fell on the sarcophagus at the far end: it was closed. Another turn of his torch beam round the small room confirmed that it was empty.

Perhaps the fellow was not that resourceful after all, Dimitri thought to himself. He paced soundlessly over to the upright sarcophagus and swung open the horned front to make sure that it had not been entered.

Satisfied, he returned to where his team member waited and quickly whispered some instructions. As the man disappeared into the square room, Dimitri stealthily made his way back to the fork. He knew that, by now, all the remaining carts would have left the cavern. The fourth man in his team would be at the turntable station, awaiting the signal they had earlier agreed upon. Not even the other team members would be allowed past without it, and Dimitri had not divulged it to them.

As he and Anton made their way in the dark towards the cavern that contained the prisoners with their Bedouin guards, Dimitri's vigilance increased. Years of experience had honed his ability to sense danger – and he sensed it now.

Flat to the floor as he peered into the cavern, Dimitri could see that the arc lights had been placed on their sides so that they shone directly down the waterhole. He tensed as he made out two figures in the shadowy penumbra of the lights.

Both were robed and lay utterly still. Raising his hand to shield out the halogen brightness, Dimitri tried to focus on them. He could just make out the gagged and blindfolded face of one of the Bedouin guards. He was leaning against the wall and lying at his feet was his equally zealous brother-in-arms, also bound.

Nothing unexpected, Dimitri thought. He continued to scan the room, taking a full two minutes to do so before gazing back towards the arc lights. As head of security at the site, he had never been happy in using the undisciplined and clearly unhinged pair of buffoons, but his elder brother had been concerned that anyone other than Bedouins protecting the temple would draw unwanted attention. The only sound was the dull humming of the small generator lighting the halogens.

Dimitri was just about to stand up when the noise of a falling rock caused him to tense once more. The acoustics of the cave were deceptive but it sounded as though it had come from the waterhole. Staring hard at the dark area around the hole, he could just make out a rope. Realization began to dawn. The very stratum of Siwa Oasis was like a labyrinth. Why should there not be a possible exit through the maze of deep waterholes?

With his fingers drawing a circle behind his back, Dimitri motioned for Anton to enter the cave and follow the wall towards the waterhole. Anton nodded, carefully slid the torch into his belt and removed his pistol. With his left arm slightly over his right to protect his gun hand from being suddenly knocked, he stepped lightly forward, staying close to the perimeter of the cavern wall.

Brock could feel the slight vibration of approaching foot-steps. Keeping absolutely still, his ear and the side of his face lying in the dirt, he held his breath, every fibre of his being taut in readiness. Within seconds, the agitated muffled sounds from

111

the young Bedouin a few feet away confirmed the closeness of the approaching footsteps.

Ignoring the whimpered cries, the Russian continued towards the waterhole. Another sound seemed to reverberate upwards from it. He lay on his belly and inched towards the edge to peer over. Brock could see the thick end of a gun barrel glint in the halogen light and his jaw tightened as he recognized the silencer; this gun would dispatch the opposition with a quiet cough.

With the light shining down the hole, Anton could clearly see someone struggling further down. He motioned quickly to Dimitri that they had their targets. Dimitri, scuttling in a half-crouch, joined Anton immediately and together they looked down the waterhole. Twenty feet below, just above a dark water-line, the hole widened almost to six feet across. Someone was still attached to the rope, desperately reaching out at the rocky side of the well, trying to get under cover. Dimitri recognized the safari clothes that the Texan oil executive had been wearing when he was first brought down unconscious from the temple. He smiled grimly.

A short distance away, hidden by the Bedouin head cloth and robe, Brock watched as the men, peering down at their target, got up on their knees and aimed their weapons at the dangling puppet.

While the bound Bedouin beside him continued with his muffled pleading, frantically trying to draw their attention, Brock silently prepared himself to spring into action.

A few feet nearer to the well, directly behind the light, lay the prison pit that had earlier entombed Ferguson. Brock knew that though there could be no signal between them, the resilient Irishman was also ready. They trusted in each other to take action at exactly the right moment.

Dimitri was aiming his gun at the swinging figure of the oil executive below, when he sensed something approaching him from behind, at speed. In a split second, he realized that the now upturned face of the person dangling on the rope was not that of a pasty white oilman, but of a dark Bedouin. It was a set-up. He jumped to his feet and turned to see a robed figure tearing towards him.

Alerted by Dimitri's movement, Anton turned in the same

direction and, with lightning speed, levelled his gun and pulled the trigger.

It was a split second too late for him.

Ferguson's solid boot caught the side of his knee. Unable to keep his balance, the Russian toppled into the hole, bouncing off the sides twice before falling with full force against the gagged man swinging below.

Brock was not so lucky. Utterly focused on his own survival, Dimitri was completely unfazed as his partner began to fall. Instead he aimed his gun at the man running at him and, as Brock dived forwards, pulled the trigger. As Brock crashed into the heavy-set Russian an instant later, he felt as though the skin of his upper arm had been flayed by a white-hot poker. Despite the impact of Brock's full weight, the other man kept both his balance and the tight grip on his Glock pistol. In one deft motion, the Russian used the momentum of Brock's attack to dive in a rolling motion away from the edge of the hole. Without stopping to catch his breath, he raised his weapon and pointed it at Brock.

The sound of Ferguson racing round the waterhole to attack him from behind drew the Russian's fire, his gun spitting three times. As it did, Ferguson threw himself into a roll to avoid the shots, the bullets each missing his head, back and leg by inches. Instantly, Dimitri jumped back towards the edge of the water-hole and aimed directly at Ferguson, the gun quickly spitting once more before a savage kick by Brock caught the Russian's gun hand right on the middle knuckle and sent the weapon spinning.

Dimitri quickly side-stepped Brock, driving his bunched fist into the other man's exposed side, but before he could retrieve his gun, he felt Brock's knee drive with full force into his thigh, dead-legging it. Momentarily paralysed, he fell helplessly towards the hole, powerless to avoid it. He swung his arms in an instinctive windmill movement, desperate to keep his balance and for a moment he teetered on the edge, before gravity exerted its pull and, with a look of disbelief, he crashed downwards.

Brock winced from a sharp pain. The Russian's bullet had given him a raw flesh wound, exposed by the lightweight robe he still wore. Ferguson had been luckier.

'How come you never get hit?' Brock asked, pretending to be aggrieved. Actually, he was glad that one of them at least had remained unscathed.

'It's the luck of the Irish,' Ferguson whispered back. 'We have a knack for getting out of things. That, and being quick-witted.'

With the flashlights switched off, Brock led the way back through the passage while Ferguson helped along the wounded Ridge. The main cavern would be protected by more men, Brock guessed. And it wouldn't be too long before they started investigating what had happened to their colleagues. Speed was of the essence. They had to find a way out.

Arriving at the fork in the passage, Brock listened intently before switching on his torch and shining it along the ground. The sandy tunnel floor now bore the marks of heavy boots. Some headed off on the route to the small square room he had visited earlier.

Perhaps there was more to this room than met the eye, he thought. It could be worth another look. Clearly Zarakov's men had wanted to ensure that they had not entered it. He padded quickly down the passage to the dark mouth of the hole that led to the small room. Slowly and painfully, he crawled through and emerged in the darkness of the square cavern. He moved his torch beam over the smooth walls; the light fell on the sarcophagus at the far side. It was now wide open.

The tingling sensation that Brock felt at the back of his neck made him drop instantly to the floor. He heard the small cough at the same time as something shot by him so close it almost parted his hair. He threw his torch out in front of him and its light was instantly extinguished as another bullet shattered it in mid-air.

With the room in total blackness, Brock held his breath. Any moment he expected a powerful torch beam to light on him and guide a bullet to him. Grasping a handful of sand from the cavern floor, he threw it in the direction of the sarcophagus. The sound brought a bullet slamming into the ancient coffin and, while the gunman's attention was diverted, Brock pushed himself vigorously backwards through the hole behind him, feeling the spray of sand in his face as two more bullets spat into the ground.

Forcing himself backwards on his elbows, Brock slid out of

the tunnel and found himself back in the passage outside. Immediately a sound to his left made him race blindly back down the tunnel, but he quickly came to a halt and pressed himself against the wall, holding his breath and trying to remain absolutely silent. As he expected, a moment later, he felt more than heard something moving swiftly past him, heading towards Ferguson and Ridge. Instinctively, Brock slammed his fist into whatever it was. He heard a startled gasp of pain as the man he had hit doubled up. Brock went blindly for where he thought the man's gun would be, and the two men stumbled for a moment together before the gun coughed. Brock felt the other man tense and then fall back.

A moment later, the light from Ferguson's torch illuminated Brock nursing his hand. The man on the floor lay still.

'Is that the lot?' asked Ferguson, running the torch beam over the man's frozen features. 'Are there any more of his pals waiting to play with us?'

'That should be our quota for now,' Brock said. 'But there'll be more along, you'd better believe it. So we've got no time to lose. Now, there's something odd about this square room. While I've been squashing myself flat as a griddle cake to get in and out of it, our friend here came out fresh as daisy and twice as fast. I think there's another way in.'

Brock rose stiffly and reached for Matt's torch. He led the way back along the passage to the hole in the wall. Running the beam along the left-hand side of it, he followed the light with his hand, smoothing it along the stone.

'Aha. I was pretty sure there had to be another route. And one that's a bit saner than that sardine trap down there.' As he spoke, Brock vanished from sight.

'Hey, where are you?' cried Ferguson. 'Don't be leaving us here in the dark.'

Brock's face emerged, white and black in the shadows, seemingly from a solid stone wall. 'It's all a question of what you know. There's a hidden partition here and if you're familiar with the fancy footwork, you can slide right through. Come on.'

'Hey, would ya look at that?' said Ridge in wonder. 'He's found a secret passage.'

'Brock is the original canny Scot,' Ferguson said solemnly. 'And they haven't yet invented the place that can contain him.'

'Your friend's a real find.'

'You're not wrong. Though I taught him everything he knows.' Ferguson grinned. 'Come on now, let's be getting out of here.'

The two men followed Brock through the hidden partition into the square cave.

Ridge looked about nervously as Brock approached the opened sarcophagus with its jutting horns. He frowned as the Scotsman appeared to disappear into its depths. 'Kidnapped, buried alive, wounded and now walking into a tomb?' he murmured. 'Perhaps it is time to retire.'

Ahead of the other two, Brock made his way up the narrow passage that led from the interior of the sarcophagus. There were no steps. The path rose steeply, following a tight fissure in the rock. The air was thick and damp and getting warmer. Then, after rising for some way, the passage came to a sudden dead end of solid rock. Brock pushed at it from various angles in the hope that it might swing back on itself like a door, as the sarcophagus had done.

There was no movement at all.

'Damn!'

'Problem?' asked Ferguson, coming up behind him.

'We must have missed an opening,' Brock said as he pushed past the other two and paced back slowly the way they had come. Taking his time, he felt for any voids to his right or left as he went. An instant later, his left hand lost contact with the wall for a moment before touching it again.

'Hello, there – another of these clever partitions,' he said, and slid behind it, disappearing from view.

The other two followed him, and the three men found themselves in a small dark room carved into stone. A swing of the torch beam revealed five large stone urns, inlaid with a motif of curled horns like those on the sarcophagus below. Brock went over to them curiously. The sealed lids of the first three lay broken in pieces on the floor, as though they had been smashed with a sledgehammer. Brock shone his torch inside; the urns were empty.

A fourth still had part of its lid in place, and from what Brock could see, it appeared to contain ash. The fifth, also missing its lid, was filled with robes. Brock went to pull at the cloth and felt something cold and dry. A chill went down his spine as he recognized the shape of a human hand.

'It appears that this place has been ransacked and very recently at that,' Brock said grimly. 'And whoever tried to prevent it was murdered.' He shone the torch on to the contents of the urn. The others came forward to look.

Ferguson reached in and parted more of the cloth so that the corpse's face came into view. 'This fella looks like he was an easy target. Don't think he could have put up much resistance. He must have been getting on for a hundred and he's as light as feather. I could lift him with one hand.'

'Poor old chap. By the looks of things, he was in the wrong place at the wrong time. No doubt those two nutters downstairs who buried you had something to do with this.' Brock glanced at the luminous dial on his watch. It had been just over two hours since he had left Neusheen. She would be on her way back to Siwa in the truck. 'We've got to get a move on, lads.'

Ridge frowned as he looked round the dark room. 'You know, Matt, this place is almost identical to the inner sanctum of the Temple of Ammon.'

'You're right. I thought I recognized the smell.' Ferguson wrinkled his nose. 'Probably the stench of this poor old corpse.'

Brock scanned the room again and spotted a series of steep steps carved into the wall. At the top he found another dead end but he was no longer fazed by the apparent barriers in their way. Once more Ferguson and Ridge followed his zigzag movement.

'This is it!' cried Ridge, as they emerged. 'We're back in the temple on top of Aghurmi.'

'No wonder we were taken unawares,' said Ferguson. 'The room was empty as far as we could see. It's not until you stand right against these partitions that you realize they're false walls.'

'That would be how the priests would listen to their visitors and be able to give answers as though from an oracle!' said Ridge. His voice was light with relief at finding himself alive and somewhere he recognized. 'The whole oracle thing was nothing more than a scam. Imagine influencing all the conquering leaders for centuries.'

'People hear what they want to hear, and others will say what they know people want to hear,' said Brock. 'And if they say

the right things often enough they become legends, even oracles.'
He led the way back through the dark temple towards the bright
entrance.

'Come on,' he said. 'There's someone I want you both to
meet.'

Neusheen stared at the satellite phone anxiously, and then looked
again at her watch. This time, she was determined to obey
orders. She'd sat for two hours in the heat and dust of the desert
in the relative shelter of the pick-up. It had been strangely
exhausting to stare endlessly at the unchanging view of the giant
pipe stretching into the perimeter fence of the campus. At any
moment, she'd expected Brock to come running out, pursued
by security guards, shouting at her to start the engine. Either
that, or she'd be discovered by someone patrolling the area and,
without a weapon or any protection, she'd have to rely on her
ability to talk her way out of the situation. It was a strain to
remain alert and on edge minute after minute while absolutely
nothing happened.

The two hours seemed to crawl by until it became apparent
that Brock was not returning within the agreed time limit and
that she would have to drive off without him. Immediately time
sped up; she didn't want to leave without Brock, but his orders
had been clear. If he hadn't returned, she was to drive to Siwa.
Five minutes after the deadline, she said furiously, 'Where the
hell are you, Connor Brock? What are you doing, leaving me
here on my own?'

Then she fired up the pick-up truck, spun it round in the
sand and headed back towards the outpost where they'd left the
helicopter.

It hadn't taken long to get back there and, by the time she'd
returned the truck and got back to the helicopter, the last hour
was only part way through. The waiting was less hard now. She
was sure she wasn't going to see Brock. He must have been
captured at the Cambyses II site. As the hands of her watch
showed that the time was almost up, she climbed into the aircraft
and stared at the satellite phone.

'OK,' she said to herself. 'This is it. I'm making the call.'

She pushed four on the dial as Brock had ordered. After a
moment of quiet static on the line, it was answered.

'Honstrom,' said a terse voice on the other end.

Neusheen opened her mouth to reply when a firm hand attached to a tanned, muscled forearm in a bloodstained black robe reached in to take the phone.

Neusheen gasped and looked up to stare directly into the azure eyes of Connor Brock. He smiled at her as he said, 'Brock here, reporting in.'

She saw two men stumbling across the sand towards the helicopter. They were a dirty, ragged, motley pair: a stocky man holding up a taller, older figure stooping in pain.

'That's right, mission accomplished. We're on our way back and I'll give you a full briefing when I get back.' Brock cut the call and looked at Neusheen, his eyes exhausted but still sparkling with a touch of his sardonic humour. 'Glad to see you're finally learning how to take orders, Flight Sergeant. You've done an excellent job.'

'You pushed it right to the limit,' she said pertly. 'Another five minutes and I'd have gone.'

'My mother always told me it was rude to be early.'

'Well, hello there,' said Ferguson, coming up to the helicopter and grinning impishly at Neusheen. 'What a sight for sore eyes you are.'

'Neusheen – my colleague, Matt Ferguson. Ignore him, he thinks he's irresistible and it's never good to encourage him. And this is John Ridge, a little the worse for his recent trip.' Brock reached out to help support the weary oilman. 'Come on. Let's get you home.'

Brock and Ferguson strapped the wounded Ridge carefully into his seat while Neusheen prepared for take-off. Less than five minutes later, as they sped back towards Alexandria, Neusheen turned to Brock expectantly.

He was fast asleep.

Thirteen

Lucius Giovanni was trying very hard to maintain his impassive attitude and not show in his eyes his reaction to the angel who had just passed by.

Granted, it was made easier by the suit of mediaeval-style armour he wore, and the weight of the shining helmet adorned with feathers. He was a Swiss Guard, after all, entrusted with the security of the world's smallest independent country, and he would do nothing to bring his precious position into disrepute. Lucius's Swiss-Italian parents had used all their influence to get their son his post in the Vatican city and couldn't have been more proud than they were on the day he was enrolled into the Swiss Guards, the exclusive security force with the responsibility of ensuring the safety of the Pope himself, head of the vast Catholic family across the world.

Lucius had seen many marvels since he'd arrived in the Vatican. The thousand-roomed Palace of the Holy See was amazing enough, and his patrol had taken him through the government offices of the Roman Catholic Church, the papal apartments and the chapels. More recently he had looked in awe at the outstanding Gregorian museums of Egyptian and Etruscan art, and the magnificent library, with its priceless collection of ancient Greek and Latin manuscripts.

But then, standing on guard outside the offices of the Archivo Segreto Vaticano, he'd seen the greatest treasure of all. A beautiful woman, who had made his heart beat faster and his prized armour feel stifling, had floated past him on her way to the Secret Archives and Lucius had felt he might burst. Since then, he'd watched for her every time he was on guard, hoping he would see her again. It had been some time since she'd last passed by, and Lucius was beginning to give up hope of ever seeing her again, when the gentle clack-clack of her heels on the tiled floor had sent his pulse racing and turned his mouth dry.

A minute later and she was walking gracefully by, her silky smooth brown hair pulled back into a ponytail, her violet eyes thoughtful and preoccupied. Lucius held his breath as she walked past, hardly daring to let his gaze drop to the slim legs below the modest black skirt, even when she'd gone by. There was no way he would ever be able to speak to her: protocol forbade it. All he could hope was that one day she would look at him, meet his eye. Until then, he would go on dreaming about the beautiful angel who had no idea of his existence . . .

Maria Zanoletti felt burdened. She had recently returned from a trip to the fishing port of Pescara on the Adriatic coast to visit her mother, and the experience had left her tired and annoyed. Though she loved her mother, it was hard to bear the incessant complaints about all the ailments the old woman claimed to suffer. It meant that Maria returned from her holiday drained rather than restored. And then, immediately she had got back to work, the dreadful Eusebius had made her life even more difficult. He was Duty Monsignor, which meant he was effectively her boss, and he had wasted no time in issuing orders.

In her position as curator of the Secret Archives Maria knew that he, or any Monsignor for that matter, could only request, not order. Orders could only come directly from the Pope himself, although most of the Monsignors pretended that they acted on the Pope's own request. Yes, Maria knew that; and the Monsignors, in turn, knew that she knew; but she usually acceded to their requests so as not to antagonize them. They were flighty, difficult and sensitive creatures; it was best to indulge them as much as possible, for they could make her life uncomfortable if they wanted.

But this was different. This whole situation was causing her a lot of anxiety and had done since she had arrived back from her holiday three days before. She had come into the Vatican Archives office early, well before any of her staff, so that she would have time to catch up on whatever she'd missed. Waiting for her, already rubbing his hands in anticipation, was the rotund Monsignor in his tightly buttoned, long black robe, its red sash bound round his middle.

'Ah, Signorina, you are here, at last. I have a very important task for you. I must ask you to contact a most welcome and exceedingly honoured prospective patron without delay. Indeed, I believe that it would be His Holiness's very wish that you would do so immediately.'

'Good morning, Monsignor,' said Maria, calmly. She smiled politely. 'Whom does His Holiness wish me to contact?'

'Ah yes, good morning to you, Signorina Zanoletti.' The Monsignor frowned, impatient with the niceties of everyday life, his fleshy jowls nestling into his double chin. Maria bit her lip. He really did sometimes look like an old bullfrog waiting to catch flies, as her assistant, Sofia, had commented unkindly once.

'This man has suggested an extremely generous donation to us in return for some help researching material in the archives,' the bullfrog continued. 'A simple enough matter, I assume. I have left all the necessary details on your desk and I have every confidence that you will be able to deal with the matter. You, as curator, will of course be vital in assisting our new friend with whatever he wants to know. His Holiness is most interested in being kept apprised of the situation, so I will expect you to keep me fully informed as you proceed. Do not concern yourself with the financial details – I will be able to resolve those myself. Good day.'

Then, without waiting for Maria to reply or ask any further questions, Monsignor Eusebius departed, leaving behind him the odour of sweat mingled with the scent of an over-rich after-shave.

'Not concern myself with the financial details,' Maria repeated to herself. Her predecessor had quietly warned her that there were occasions when he had questioned the amounts moving through the archive accounts. There were often large deposits of cash, sometimes accompanied by slips written in Eusebius's hand. Maria had immediately installed a computer and insisted that all monies relating to the maintenance and development of the archives should be recorded on it, as well as by central accounting at the Vatican Bank.

Her action had made little difference, though. So much money moved about so frequently, it was impossible to keep track of all of it, and Maria had been told in no uncertain terms that her responsibilities as curator did not include the financial details of the archives.

Ignoring Eusebius's notes for the time being, Maria had sat down at her desk and switched on her computer to check her emails. Most of the inbox messages to her Vatican address had been dealt with by Sofia. Her personal inbox had been of more interest: her friends from Zurich had sent a routine request for information, this time asking for anything relating to a Chinese citizen, one Temujin Subedei, a known patron of the arts, or his company, Subedei Industries. The name meant nothing to her but she wrote it down carefully just in case. Then she returned to her messages and, a few minutes later, she heard her assistant Sofia arrive to begin the day.

By the time she had returned to Eusebius's notes, it was much later. As she started to read them, she was astonished and then, as she read on, incredulous.

Maria walked along the vast, arched corridors of the Vatican, hardly noticing the Swiss Guards she passed, or the great treasures that lined the halls. Familiarity had made her immune to the beauty that surrounded her every day. She left the building through a discreet side door and made her way along the curving cloisters of St Peter's Square, gazing up for a moment at the giant dome of the vast basilica. It was, she always felt, too big – too boasting and grandiose. She had made the mistake of saying as much to a Monsignor once, and the little man had almost fainted in horror.

'It is the most magnificent, the most holy building in the world,' he had declared. 'It is the earthly reflection of God's endless love for us. Are we to measure the size of His love and declare it too big? Never! No price is too great, no ornament too rich, if it reflects something so mighty.'

But, to Maria's mind, everything here was too large – it left too much room for secrets, for concealing things that people did not want discovered. And in the last three days, she had learned a great deal more about the mission Monsignor Eusebius expected her to carry out without question. She knew now why Monsignor was so reluctant to involve her in the financial aspects of the new patron's request. After making her own enquiries, she had drawn in her breath in amazement when she saw the size of the donation given by this new patron. It was one million Euros, at least five times the amount of even the richest bequests. No wonder that had got Eusebius leaping about like a frightened cat, making sure that this particular request was rushed through, oiling the usually slow works of the Vatican Archive Office. He was in every few hours, asking Maria how the work was progressing and how long it would be before their patron had some information.

What had startled her most, as she had started work on the research that Eusebius's new patron had requested, was that there were so many links that had quickly come together from unrelated paths. She'd already discovered documents relevant to the project and today she had unearthed more. It was making her both excited and scared.

As she walked briskly through St Peter's Square towards the Tiber, Maria reflected that what she was about to do might temporarily unburden her, but it could well make her life much more difficult.

Lucius felt elated. He had seen her again – it was enough to live off for days. She hadn't noticed him, of course. Why should she? It was reward enough for him to see her. As he replayed again and again the vision of his glossy-haired angel, he took no heed of the two bulky clerics dressed in matching black robes scuttling down the echoing corridor like two cockroaches.

Gianni Barracio smiled sardonically as he looked up at his companion's nervous face. Though a seasoned professional, Barracio could never resist goading what he referred to as the hired help.

'Now, just how difficult was that? Just like taking a prayerful walk to the bank, eh? And I'm sure you're used to that.'

Monsignor Eusebius wiped the thickening sheen of sweat from his brow and upper lip. Far be it from him to judge – and he had little experience of such things, he was glad to say – but he was convinced that the solid-looking client his new benefactor had politely but firmly requested be given entry was a Mafioso. He certainly did not have the look of an academic.

Curator Zanoletti had passed on the results of her day's work to Eusebius, and within an hour of his reporting what she had found, he had been told to expect an incognito visitor who would verify the findings; he was to give whatever assistance was required and in return, a separate donation would recognize his diligence.

Eusebius was no stranger to bribes, both giving and receiving them. Many times over the years, he had succumbed. But since last summer, when he had had to resort to having that promising young cleric wrongly accused of theft dismissed in order to direct the finger of blame elsewhere, he had promised himself it would be the last time. The problem was, the delightful money was too much for his weak will to refuse.

'This is the curator's office,' whispered the Monsignor, pulling the key out of his pocket. 'It is annexed to the Secret Archives department so you must be quick!'

As Barracio hurried in, he said, 'You'll be the first to know when I am done. I'll take as long as I need.'

'But you don't understand. There is an alarm. A central timer automatically activates it throughout the archives at eight o'clock.'

Barracio glanced at the heavy gold watch on his wrist. He had just over an hour. 'That won't be enough time. I'll just have to find what your curator has for us, locate the source and take that with me.'

'What do you mean? Are you saying you will take the source?' demanded the flustered Eusebius.

'Have you forgotten that our mutual client has generously paid for exclusivity? If the relevant sources remain, just how can that be exclusive?'

A rivulet of perspiration rolled down from Eusebius's temple to join other drops on his already glistening neck. 'For information – yes, of course. But we could never agree to sources going missing. I would get found out.'

Barracio looked unfazed. 'That's just a little problem you will have to sort out, isn't it? And, anyway, who said anything about sources going missing?'

Ignoring the sweating Eusebius, Barracio quickly removed the robe from his short body, revealing a dark suit stretched across a thick barrel chest and wide shoulders. He sat down in the curator's chair and switched on her computer. 'Password?'

'What do you mean?' enquired the Monsignor, standing nervously by his side.

'The password for the computer. To gain access.'

'Ah! Oh, we . . . um . . . we don't allow them.'

Barracio rolled his eyes. 'Very wise, I'm sure.' Despite his short fingers, he dexterously tapped at the keyboard, searching for the most recently opened and saved files.

Fourteen

Certain that she appeared to everyone around her like some treacherous spy, Maria tried to relax her grip on the brief-case she carried. To take her mind off its contents, she attempted to think instead of the meeting ahead, but her thoughts kept returning to the manuscript she had just removed from the Archivo Segreto Vaticano. As curator, she often took manuscripts home to study – it was a necessity if she were ever to get her work done. No one could ever accuse her of taking risks with any of the priceless collection of manuscripts or leather-bound volumes that made up the million sacrosanct volumes of the Vatican library. She treated every piece with the reverence and care it deserved. But the nature of the document she carried in her briefcase was sensitive to say the least. Most manuscripts belonged to the main library, inaugurated by Popes Nicholas V and Sixtus IV in the fifteenth century. The document Maria carried belonged to the Secret Archives, a collection only estab-lished in the twentieth century to preserve the most delicate and dangerous of manuscripts that would once have been destroyed. She had never dared remove anything from the Secret Archives before – only a papal decree could allow such a thing – and her nervousness showed in her darting eyes and white knuckles.

Maria had not told a soul of her intentions, not even Connor Brock. He had called from Zurich early yesterday morning to confirm their meeting and, for a moment, she'd been tempted to tell him everything. But she'd kept it in, not only because the phone lines were not safe, but because he would never agree to anything that might jeopardize her position or safety. So she had held her tongue and simply arranged to meet him at the Arco Tevere opposite her apartment in the Via Gregorio VII.

A brisk thirty-minute walk brought her into the bohemian quarter of Trastevere. Maria began to relax – she was now surely far enough away from the Vatican Palace to be confident that she was safe from prying eyes and ears. She thought of Brock, waiting for her in the Arco Tevere; it was a long time since she'd seen him but she still recalled vividly his imposing height and those azure eyes. She smiled to herself. Something about those eyes always made her a little self-conscious and, against her usually quiet, sober nature, flirtatious. Yes, she was looking forward to her evening with Connor Brock . . .

Trastevere was coming to life as the evening advanced. During the day, it was sleepy and quaint, peopled only by adventurous tourists prepared to stray off the beaten track. As night fell, the bars and trattorie came to life, filled with young Romans, students of all nationalities, and visitors to the city who knew that they would find good food, lively chat and a warm atmosphere. Older locals kept to the shabbier, less enticing bars, where they clutched their glasses of noxious-looking red or yellow liquid, scowling and watching the football on the television screens. Later, as the night progressed, quiet would fall again on Trastevere, as the students and tourists headed for the nightclubs of Testaccio, and the locals went home to bed.

Arriving at Arco Tevere, Maria scanned the tables expectantly. To her disappointment, Brock was not there. She glanced up and down the street but there was no sign of him, so she chose a table at the far end of the room where she could watch both the entrance and the door to her apartment across the street.

The elderly patron, busily polishing glasses behind the small bar, smiled in acknowledgement at his neighbour and regular customer. Maria smiled back.

'Your usual, Signorina?' he asked.

'Yes, thank you, Roberto. I'm waiting for a friend tonight. It seems he is late.'

She took her cell phone from her briefcase and put it on the table in front of her, tucking the case back down by her feet. When her espresso arrived, Maria drank it slowly, enjoying the bitter flavour on her tongue, and read the evening paper that Roberto brought her. Every few minutes she looked up, but Brock still did not arrive.

After half an hour of waiting, she was becoming concerned. Had she mistaken the time? She would wait longer, she decided. There were plenty of reasons why Brock could have been delayed – he would be there if he could, she knew that. She had just motioned to Roberto for another espresso, when her cell phone rang.

Snatching it up, Maria answered in English, assuming it was Brock on the line. 'Where are you?'

'Signorina Zanoletti?' It was an Italian voice.

'Yes, Monsignor,' returned Maria in her own language, quickly identifying the voice.

'Ah, good, it is you.' Eusebius sounded unexpectedly hurried and nervous. 'Are you at home?'

'Why?'

'You must return immediately,' ordered Eusebius, his voice now urgent.

Maria's heart missed a beat. How could he have discovered already that she had removed the manuscript?

'Monsignor, I have left the office for the evening,' she replied, forcing herself to be calm. 'And, furthermore, it is inconvenient to drop what I am doing right now. Can't it wait until tomorrow?'

'You are to come at once. You must leave home right now and return immediately. There's been a break-in!' Eusebius began to shout, his voice rising with panic. 'The archives have been ransacked, and someone has been severely injured!'

Maria sat stock still, stunned by the news. A break-in? Inside one of the most heavily guarded buildings in the world? How could this have happened? It had only been an hour since she had locked up the archives herself.

'I'm on my way,' she said, glancing at her watch. It was almost eight o'clock.

She hurried out of the bar and down the street to the taxi stand. She was relieved to see a taxi waiting and rushed up to it. Climbing in, she said, 'The Vatican, as quickly as you can.'

They reached the palace within fifteen minutes and Maria ran to the archives. She was unprepared for the sight that greeted her; her office was in chaos. Her computer lay smashed on the floor and the heavy shelves lining the walls had been emptied of their books, which were strewn everywhere. The neat files and boxes had been opened, their contents flung about like so much confetti.

With growing horror, she rushed through the entrance to the

129

Secret Archives. Normally the door would have time-locked shut by now, but Maria immediately saw Monsignor Eusebius and several Swiss Guards grouped around something. They moved aside as they heard the curator enter and Maria could see that one of the Swiss Guards lay prone on the floor. Two paramedics were carefully ministering to him.

Maria went forward; the face was vaguely familiar but she did not know who he was. The young Swiss Guard opened his eyes and gazed directly at her. A beatific smile crossed his face, then he closed his eyes again.

Maria knelt down next to one of the paramedics. 'Is he going to be all right?' she whispered.

'He'll live. But his injuries are serious,' answered the paramedic in a similar low tone, with a look to indicate that he did not wish to say more.

Maria got up to her feet and went over to Monsignor Eusebius, who had moved away from the group of guards.

'Monsignor, what is going on?' Maria's voice rose from the shock of what had happened. 'This is outrageous. Nothing like this has happened before. The place has been ransacked. Who would do such a thing? And how? It's only been an hour since I locked up.'

'So you *did* lock up?' said the sweating Eusebius querulously.

Maria was indignant. 'What do you mean? Of course I did!'

'Like you, I merely wonder how this happened. Pity you were not here until the time lock activated. Perhaps we will have to change that.'

Maria felt fury rising in her. 'Even if I had not locked up – which I most certainly did – there is still the question of how anyone managed to get inside the palace in the first place!' she retorted. 'Perhaps you should turn your attention to that.'

The black-robed priest licked his lips nervously. 'That is, of course, a matter of great concern.'

Maria looked about, frowning. 'Who discovered this?'

'The guards, of course. They disturbed the criminals at their work. There was a struggle but unfortunately they got away, after inflicting severe injury on young Lucius Giovanni. When the fracas was over, the guards summoned me immediately.'

Maria looked back at the Monsignor. 'And you were nearby?'

'I do not have to account for my movements to you,' he

snapped. 'But, as a matter of fact, I was researching in the library. His Holiness had a special request for me.

'Anyway,' he continued, after a momentary pause, 'it was lucky that I was here. Someone had to take charge.'

'Where are the police?'

The Monsignor looked horrified. 'Police? You should know very well that the police have no jurisdiction within the Holy See. Our own officials and guards can take care of this more than adequately.'

Maria looked around at the devastation. 'But this is a serious crime! We need more than *adequate* here. Surely we should have some investigating officers or scenes-of-crime professionals. One of our guards is badly hurt, and as for the damage . . . ! And what has been taken? What were they after? It will take hours of sifting through everything to discover what is missing.'

'Then who better than our own team to assess the situation? This is no place for outsiders.'

Maria's eyes sparkled with anger. 'Monsignor, you do not seem to realize that there has been a serious crime here. And as for assessing the situation – it will take us weeks to sort out this mess. I have no idea when we will be able to work out what has been taken. Getting everything into its rightful place is a huge task.'

'Well, there's nothing new there then,' he said quietly.

Maria was sure she detected a hint of menace in his voice. 'What do you mean, exactly?' She saw a look of annoyance pass over the priest's face, and a thought occurred to her. 'Are you saying things here were not in the rightful place?' she asked slowly.

'Well, we'll never know now, will we?' countered Eusebius. 'If you will excuse me, I have to inform His Holiness of what has happened. No doubt he will be deeply concerned and order an inquiry into how this could possibly have happened.'

Maria watched as Eusebius picked his way to the door through the books and files that cluttered the floor. What had he meant? Had he been alluding to the manuscript she had removed? She felt certain that he had . . . A moment of panic hit her. Where was her briefcase? She looked around the room. Had she had it with her when she'd returned? When she'd knelt down? For a moment, she couldn't think straight.

Think.

Calm down and think.

When did you last have it? she asked herself. She pictured herself arriving, getting out of the taxi.

She must have left it in the taxi!

No – she had paid with the notes in her purse. She felt the large side pockets of her loose jacket. There was her purse and her phone.

Wait. She remembered now. She had not had the case with her when she got into the taxi. Maria saw it in her mind's eye. It was down on the floor by the side of the table in the Arco Tevere, where she had put it just before her phone rang. She remembered taking the phone out of the briefcase and putting it on the table. The call had taken her by such surprise that she had rushed out of the bar without remembering to pick up the case.

Relief flooded through her – she knew where it was. But instantly her relief was replaced by new panic. What if the case had been stolen?

Her thoughts were interrupted by a cry of 'Holy Mother, what has happened?' and she turned to see her assistant Sofia standing in the doorway, staring with appalled wonder at the mess inside the archive offices. She turned to Maria, too stunned to say more.

Maria was glad to see that someone had summoned her assistant; she trusted her competence and good sense. She marched over to her and clasped her arm.

'Sofia,' she said firmly, 'the archives have been robbed. You can see what they have done here. I need you to take over for the moment and co-ordinate any investigation, if one is ordered.'

'Investigation?' replied Sofia, in a daze. 'Tonight?'

'I've no doubt we will be asked to start as soon as possible. But I have other business I must attend to, just as urgent as this. Can you stand in for me for a while?'

Sofia nodded.

'Good. The Vatican Inspector will be here shortly, I'm sure. When he asks for me, tell him I'll be back as soon as I can.' She gazed at her assistant earnestly. 'Thank you, Sofia. I know I can rely on you.'

*   *   *

132

As she left, Maria saw that the museum complex was already being sealed off, the full complement of Swiss Guards at their posts. To her relief, she saw a police car from the Municipal Station of Rome pull up outside – someone had obviously persuaded the pig-headed Monsignor that it would be wise to alert the authorities.

Hurrying back to the Arco Tevere, Maria went over in her mind what had happened in the past hour. The break-in had been a terrible shock; now that she had calmed down a little, she began to make connections. Could it be a coincidence that she had stumbled on the important information she had found on the very day someone ransacked the archive? The more she thought about it, the more it seemed to fit together.

The Arco Tevere was full. She pushed through the crowd to the back of the restaurant and the table where she'd been sitting earlier. Two men were sitting there in front of empty plates, drinking from tall glasses of beer. As Maria approached, they looked at her with interest, watching as she inspected the floor around their feet.

Maria's heart sank.

The briefcase was not there.

'Can we help you, Signorina?' asked one politely.

'Excuse me,' said Maria. 'I'm sorry to disturb you. I'm looking for my briefcase – I left it here on the floor. Have you seen it?'

Both men looked down and scanned the floor.

'I think I saw someone picking up something from here just as we made our way to the table,' offered the second man. 'I'm sorry if it has been taken.'

Crestfallen, Maria mumbled her thanks. She made her way back through the crowd to the bar where the patron was making up bills.

'Roberto!' she called above the hubbub of the evening drinkers. 'Roberto – have you seen my briefcase? I left it at my table.'

Roberto looked up from his bills, smiled a greeting at her and then frowned as he considered her question. 'A black brief-case?'

Maria's hopes rose. 'Yes, that's it.'

'After you left, a man sat at your table but he left suddenly a few moments later, before I had time to take his order. Now I think about it, I'm sure he was carrying a briefcase. But I can't be certain, I'm afraid. You know what it's like here, Signorina – people come and go all the time.'

'Oh no. Someone took it?' Maria's heart sank. She tried to push down her rising panic. 'Did you see what he looked like?'

Roberto looked at her reproachfully. 'I could not possibly recall what all my customers look like. I'm sorry if your case has been stolen. You know what it's like round here. There's not much I can do about it. I'll tell you what – we'll forget about the coffee, eh?'

'I forgot to pay? I'm sorry, Roberto, I was in a mad rush.'

The patron shrugged and smiled. He could spare a pretty woman an espresso.

Numb and confused, Maria made her way back through the drinkers out of the bar and crossed the road towards her apartment building. She could not be surprised – theft in this area was rife because of all the tourists and students with their currency-rich wallets. Anything that wasn't bolted down would disappear in a moment. She should have expected the case would be gone. But even now, it was difficult to believe her terrible luck.

She barely noticed that the street door was slightly ajar. The lift took her to the third floor and she walked down the corridor to her apartment. As she took out her keys, she saw slivers of painted wood lying on the dark carpet at her feet. Then she realized that the lock was broken. Her door had been forced open.

She didn't believe this was happening. Now she had been burgled.

Cautiously, she pushed open the door. It swung forward without resistance, showing the dark hall beyond. Gasping, Maria saw that the contents of her hall bookcase were scattered all over the floor. There was no sound at all coming from within. Her heart beat faster as she stepped into the apartment.

'Hello?' she called, her voice high and trembling. She was poised and ready to run if she heard a single sound, but there was nothing. 'Hello?'

It was probably foolhardy, she knew, but she couldn't stop herself. She advanced carefully down the hall until she came to the doorway to the sitting room. Then she froze with horror. In the half-light, she could see something or someone stretched out across her sofa.

Fifteen

Brock shifted from one side of the chair to the other, trying to get comfortable but it was no good – his entire body ached. Being poked awake with an antique metal hatstand hadn't helped. His whole body felt covered in bruises. Groaning, he rubbed the back of his head where he could feel a lump already rising.

'What the hell are you doing here, Connor?' demanded Maria, furiously. She was sitting opposite him, perched uneasily on a chair, the hatstand still clutched in one hand. 'You frightened me out of my wits!'

'I'm sorry if you got a scare,' said Brock ruefully. He winced. 'Still, I'd recommend that over a sharp blow to the head any day.' He looked over at the woman opposite. Her violet eyes were wide with fear.

'You were supposed to meet me in the Arco. I waited half an hour! Where were you? Why didn't you call?'

'Delayed at the airport. But I came as quickly as I could. To be honest, I thought I'd made good time, so I didn't bother to call. You can imagine I was surprised to find you'd left already. The old barman told me you'd suddenly dashed out without a word. I sat down to wait for you to come back – and found the briefcase I gave you, right there on the floor. Not like you to be so careless, Maria.'

'You found it?' she gasped. 'So you were the one who stole it?'

'Stole it?' Brock looked hurt. 'You mean, rescued it.'

'Do you have it now?'

'It should be where I left it. I waited in the bar for twenty minutes – incidentally, I called you several times but your phone was off by then. You'll find messages from me, if you don't believe me. Then I thought I'd try your apartment, in case you'd come back here. It was obvious it wasn't exactly as you'd left it.

135

The door was forced and your cleaner had been a bit sloppy, to say the least.' He gestured around at the room. Like the archives, it had been turned upside down. 'So I concealed the case in some of the chaos your visitor had already created and crept in to see what he was up to.'

'And he caught you?' said Maria, in disbelief.

'Your faith in me is touching,' replied Brock. 'But I'm only human. As I was heading quietly to the sitting room, someone was coming up very sneakily behind me. I seem to remember coming in here and then – boom. I wake up to the very warm welcome of a hatstand in the vitals.'

'I didn't know it was you!' cried Maria hotly. 'I thought you could be the burglar!'

'All right, it's OK.'

'If you knew what's happened tonight! What I've been through!' She brought a shaky hand up over her eyes.

'Hey, hey. Maria, it's all right. Tell me what's happened.' Brock leaned forward, putting a large but gentle hand on her arm. 'Come on, now. It's OK. I'm here.'

Maria pulled herself together with an obvious effort. 'I've been trying so hard to be strong,' she explained, her voice soft. 'But tonight has been so difficult. First, I take a huge risk and remove a precious document from the archives. Then you don't show up, and the next thing I hear is that the office has been ransacked. Monsignor insists I return immediately and back at the Vatican I find utter chaos and a poor young Guard who has been almost murdered. Then it seems my case has been stolen, my apartment burgled and a strange man is dead on my sofa. You can see why I'm feeling a little fragile.'

'An average day in my line of work,' offered Brock with a grin. 'That is rough. And more than a little worrying. It doesn't take a genius to see that all this is connected. You say the archives have been robbed?'

'I don't know yet if anything has been taken. But someone seemed to be searching for something.'

'And they've had a good old rummage round here as well.' Brock looked suddenly serious. 'First things first – we'd better make sure our friend didn't find your case.'

To Maria's intense relief, the briefcase was where Brock had left it. He held it up for her.

136

'Nice to see you treasure the little things I give you,' he said. 'I'm not happy about us staying here, especially with the door lock bust. Come on, we'll go to a hotel and you can tell me everything.'

Brock booked adjoining rooms at the Hotel Verdicchio. They went up to his room, Maria clutching the briefcase tightly to her chest.

Once they were settled, with a room-service order delivered, Brock opened the bottle of wine he'd requested and poured a glass each for himself and Maria.

'Here.' He handed the wine to her. 'How are you feeling?'

'Better.' She smiled at him, her face losing its worried lines to show her fine-boned features and the classical shape of her red lips. She took the wine and sipped at the ruby liquid.

'Glad to hear it. Want something to eat?' Brock gestured to the plates of sandwiches he'd ordered.

Maria shook her head. 'I don't know why, but my appetite has completely vanished.'

The lilt of her accent was almost as pretty as Maria herself, Brock reflected as he pulled the briefcase on to his knees. 'Let's see what you've found, then.' He clicked the catches open and lifted the leather lid. Taking out two documents, one yellow and brittle with age and one on modern paper, he put them carefully on the table in front of him. He stared at them for several minutes before glancing up at Maria, who was waiting patiently for his reaction.

'Sorry, Maria. Ancient Greek and Egyptian hieroglyphics were never my strong point. What am I looking at?'

Maria made a graceful gesture towards the ancient paper. 'That is the document I found in the Secret Archives today. The other is the reference material sent to me by Eusebius's new patron.'

'Temujin Subedei.'

'Exactly.'

'What was his request?'

'You see that his document has a series of symbols and hieroglyphics on it – he wanted us to find sources that contain the same ones.'

'That sounds like a hell of a job. How many papers with these squiggles have you got in the archives?'

'The Vatican isn't still in the dark ages, Connor, whatever you may think,' replied Maria touchily. 'I've spent a lot of time and effort getting computers installed, as it happens. And I've commissioned a software programme specifically for cross-referencing and deciphering hieroglyphics.'

'Very impressive. I apologize.' Brock made a contrite expression. 'I always knew you'd be a superb curator.'

Maria looked mollified. 'Thank you. When I first received the material from Subedei, I scanned in the symbols in order to find matching references, if any, throughout the archives. Literally hundreds came up because of one symbol –' she pointed to it on the page – 'a head with horns.'

Brock examined it. 'I've seen this one before – in fact, I've been coming across a lot of horns like that recently. What does it symbolize? Is it a devil?'

'Close.' Maria smiled. 'Depending on your point of view, I suppose. 'No, it symbolizes Alexander the Great, depicting him as the son of Ammon. But even today, in certain eastern provinces of his former empire, he is referred to as the devil. You know – used as a threat to keep the children quiet when they're being naughty. This horned symbol for Alexander became popular after his death. In fact, during the reign of Lysimachus, one of Alexander's Macedonian successors, the gem-cutter Protogenes engraved that image on the coinage. So from fifty years after Alexander's death until the introduction of the euro, this symbol was on the drachma.' Her eyes sparkled with enthusiasm. 'Amazing, isn't it?'

Brock shook his head thoughtfully. 'It puts a little perspective on things, certainly. So this symbol must reoccur quite a lot in the archives.'

Maria laughed drily. 'Oh, yes. Alexander was a king, emperor, pharaoh and god. There are countless references to him. Thousands in our archives alone. The task is enormous – without computers, it would take several lifetimes. But with the help of technology, I was able to cross-reference the symbols several at a time, to see what came up. Even this proved too wide a search – all the symbols are widely used and each combination seemed to bring up hundreds of references. Except when I added two.' Maria paused and pointed at the page in front of Brock. 'That one there.'

Brock followed Maria's forefinger as she pointed out the symbol of a sword set in a stone.

'And that one there beside it.'

The other symbol was the same-shaped stone, except the centre of it this time contained an eye with lines emanating from it like the sun's rays.

Maria said, 'Only two records came up that contained both of these symbols. One of the records is this manuscript, which you see also contains the image of Alexander depicted as the god Ammon.'

Brock leaned forward, attentive. 'And the other?'

'The other isn't a manuscript. It's a statue taken from Egypt, carved with the hieroglyphic autobiography of an Egyptian priest.'

'OK. So this manuscript is clearly something Subedei is interested in.' Brock looked again at the neat lines of black images on the yellow paper. 'Apart from a statue, it's the only thing in the archives to match with his reference material.'

'As I said,' Maria replied, a little curtly.

'Just getting my facts straight. I'm not an expert like you are. What can you tell me about this paper?'

Maria leaned back in her chair, stretching out her legs. She gazed down into her wine glass and seemed to be gathering her strength. She looked up again. 'This is a copy of a much more ancient manuscript. It was made here in the thirteenth century – we know this because the scribe followed Vatican procedure faithfully, carefully crediting and dating his copy. The original was discovered not long after a final decisive battle between the Mamluks and the Mongols.'

Brock raised his eyebrows. 'The Mongols, eh?'

'You've heard of the fearsome Mongolian horde, I assume.'

'Genghis Khan, of course. Everyone knows that,' said Brock. He pretended to think hard. 'Hmm, let me see. He had a moustache and he liked to cut the ears off his enemies, if my schoolboy history serves me correctly.'

She rolled her eyes. 'I'm sure he did. Along with other bits of them. Better leave the historical detail to me.' Maria shook her head, smiling. 'Well, once the Mongols had devastated Persia and sent marauding armies to Syria and Egypt, they were finally defeated at the Battle of Ayn Jalut in Syria in 1260 by the fierce

139

Mamluks. Many Mongolian records were left behind in the hasty retreat east. A lot of those records ended up here, in the Vatican, part of the Pope's search for evidence to justify the crusades that had taken place in previous centuries.

'Many were lost, destroyed or forgotten until the Vatican library was formally established in the fifteenth century. This is one of the documents that survived, but as it refers to a son of god, it has been hidden away ever since. That is the fate of any document that refers to a god, or son of god, that is not in line with Christian beliefs.'

'So there is a reference to the son of god here – in this case, Alexander the Great in his guise as son of Ammon. What else? Have you translated this manuscript?'

Maria shook her head. 'There hasn't been time. I've simply isolated the symbols that were of interest to the client. And as far as I understand it, this one –' she pointed again to the symbol of the sword set in a stone – 'refers to the God Sword. The weapon of Alexander the Great himself. According to legend, it contained a mystic stone that was the source of Alexander's power.'

Brock frowned. 'Sounds like a fairytale to me. What about the statue? What does it add to what we know?'

Maria looked excited as she leaned forward to share what she had discovered. 'The hieroglyphics carved on the statue *have* been translated. This symbol, the one of the eye in the stone, refers to a mystic seeing stone taken from the Zoroastrians by Cyrus the Great and placed in his sword to give him great power. Legend holds that his son took the sword from his father's tomb and used it to invade Egypt. He wanted to gain the endorsement of the god Ammon while taking over the city of Ammonium, but the huge army he sent to do his bidding was lost without trace.'

'Was this son Cambyses II, by any chance?' interjected Brock.

Maria looked at him in surprise. 'Why, yes, as a matter of fact. How did you know that, Connor?'

'It's not just Genghis Khan's moustache that I know about. You'd be surprised.' Brock grinned.

Maria laughed. 'That's what I like about you – you are full of the unexpected. In fact, the statue is mostly concerned with Cambyses' reign as Pharaoh, and only refers to Cyrus the Great and the seeing stone in passing. The Egyptian priest who engraved it, Udjahorresnet, was an advisor to Cambyses II.'

'So we've got two stones set in two swords, both supposedly extremely powerful for whoever wields them.'

Maria nodded. 'The statue tells us of the seeing stone contained in the sword of Cyrus the Great, believed to belong to the Oracle of Ammon. The manuscript describes a much later version – the mystic stone within Alexander's God Sword.'

'Could they be the same thing?'

'Of course, that is a reasonable question.' Maria looked thoughtful. 'We can only deduce, naturally. There is no proof. Cyrus founded the great Archaemenian dynasty that lasted until Darius the Third lost his kingdom to Alexander. Alexander certainly made a point of visiting Cyrus's tomb, where his sword was last heard of. According to Callisthenes, his personal scribe, it was Alexander's burning ambition to see the grave of his hero.' She paused, and swirled her wine around the glass, watching the dark liquid glint in the light. 'The stones could be one and the same. It is certainly a possibility – if they are more than simply a myth to explain great military might.'

Brock sighed. 'This is all very well, but what I don't understand is why Subedei should be interested in all this. What is the link? These old stories have been swirling round for centuries.' He leaned back in his chair. 'Who cares about Alexander the Great's sword anyway? It would be just a piece of rusting metal by now, if that.'

Maria almost quivered in her eagerness to tell him her thoughts. 'But that is the most exciting part of all! You see, the whole point about Alexander's sword – apart from the fact that it endowed him with almost superhuman powers – is that it was buried with him. According to history, after Alexander died – poisoned, some believe – his funeral party was returning the body to Macedonia when it was waylaid by his loyal general Ptolemy, who buried his friend in a great mausoleum he had specifically built in Alexandria, and used the sword himself. He founded the last of the great pharaonic dynasties, the Ptolemaic. On his death, the sword was returned to Alexander's tomb.'

'So . . .'

'So find the sword, and you find one of the greatest historical treasures in the world – the tomb of Alexander the Great.'

'Wait, you said that Ptolemy built a giant mausoleum. This just vanished, did it?'

'We don't know.' Maria looked solemn. 'All the records were destroyed when the great library of Alexandria burned down. One of the most tragic events of human history. When I think of the treasures that were lost, I want to weep . . .'

'I'd heard that the blaze was down to the Christians, ridding the world of heretical texts that contradicted their version of events,' said Brock mischievously.

Maria shrugged. 'Christians were certainly convenient scapegoats. They were not popular at the time. But there is a school of thought that believes thieves were seeking information on the whereabouts of Alexander's tomb, and the library was destroyed in the process. The trouble is that there are too many schools of thought. What we do know is that the location of Alexander's tomb mysteriously disappeared soon after that date. The search goes on for it, of course, but over the centuries the treasure that it contains has no doubt been exaggerated. What interests me, though, is the legend that whoever discovers Alexander's tomb will gain god-like power.'

Brock laughed loudly but stopped himself when he saw Maria's hurt face. 'Sorry . . . it's just . . . does anyone seriously believe these stories? God-like power? Come on, now.'

Maria looked a little sulky. Then her pout lifted and she smiled back. 'I agree. It sounds ludicrous. But the prospect of finding Alexander's tomb is not. I'm not exaggerating, it would be the most sensational find you could imagine. Archaeologists have been searching for it for centuries. It would be . . . incredible. It would ensure lasting fame for whoever discovered it.'

'Now we're getting somewhere.' Brock looked interested again, his eyes bright. 'Subedei has already linked himself with archaeology and the history of ancient Egypt. He makes donations to the Antiquities Council, and his team seem to have stumbled on quite a find in the caverns under Siwa Oasis. Perhaps he's after the tomb.'

'That,' said Maria slowly, 'is a conclusion I was coming to myself. And there's something more – something that is perhaps wild conjecture on my part. But I'm beginning to believe that I may be right.'

'Yes?' Brock's face took on a serious aspect. 'In my experience, hunches are often closer to the truth than anything else.'

'This reference material that Subedei sent – it puzzled me. Where did he get it from? What is it exactly? So I started to analyse it. At first, it seemed to be a series of symbols in no particular order. As if it related to part of another document, perhaps removed and jumbled in order to confuse the meaning. Sure enough, the computer appeared to agree with my instinct that these symbols were originally part of an organized script – the programme suggested replacements for missing symbols in order to make sense of it.

Maria paused, and took a quick, nervous gulp of wine before she continued.

'Connor, the computer analysis provided a startling hypothesis. Some of the suggestions were nonsensical but one appeared to make sense – a strange, incredible sense, but still sense. It offered the idea that these two symbols – the seeing stone of Cyrus and the God Sword stone of Alexander – were most certainly combined on some master document that would indicate the location of Alexander's tomb.'

Brock frowned while he absorbed this. 'Like directions in a treasure hunt?'

'It's a possibility.'

'That ties in with our suspicion that Subedei is seeking Alexander's grave.'

Maria nodded slowly. 'And it suggests the remote chance that, perhaps, he already knows where it is.'

Brock was startled. 'What? How?'

'It depends whether he removed the missing symbols from the reference material. If he did, it would be to stop us from coming to the conclusion that he was in possession of this amazing knowledge.'

'If he already knows where the tomb is, why send you hunting through the archives at all? Why not just get on with it? It seems madness to involve the Vatican.'

Maria shrugged. 'I don't know. He may not. It's just a theory.'

'The other question, of course, that immediately comes to mind is how did he come by it?'

'Exactly my thinking too. I've no idea.'

Brock leapt to his feet and ran a hand through his hair, sighing. 'This is something else, it really is. I think we need a change of scene.' He indicated the now unappetizing plate of sandwiches. 'I don't know about you, but I'm hungry. How about we go out for something decent to eat and let all this talk of kings and tombs and swords settle for a moment?'

A bright smile illuminated Maria's face. 'Sounds good to me,' she said.

Sixteen

They walked out into the cool night of a late Roman spring. The bars and restaurants were still open, welcoming in customers, and they passed many brightly lit, crowded places as they strolled down the narrow paved streets, enjoying the fresh air.

'I know somewhere we can go,' said Maria. 'A quiet trattoria with excellent food.'

'Wonderful. Lead the way.'

She took him along dark passageways to a small piazza dominated by a pretty fountain, and over to a low, ancient building with a tatty blue canopy over the old, iron-studded wooden door. It didn't look much, but inside, the atmosphere became warm, perhaps with the radiated heat of the old open oven, and tantalizing with the smell of roasting meat. The low buzz of conversation filled the air and white-coated, bow-tied waiters wove expertly between the tables, carrying plates of delicious-looking food.

'Ah, Signorina, we are always delighted to see you!' An effusive, red-cheeked host stepped forward to greet them, holding big black menus. 'Your favourite table is ready for you, as always.'

Brock raised his eyebrows at Maria as they were led through the large room to a table near the window. 'You must come here often. They seem to know you well.'

Maria flushed slightly. 'It's just talk. I don't have a favourite table – they show me to a different one each time.'

'If you say so . . .'

They took their places and read the menus. Once they had ordered and the waiter had filled their glasses with a fine Tuscan wine that glowed the colour of blood in the candlelight, there was an almost awkward pause. Maria stared down at the white linen tablecloth and traced a pattern over it. Then she looked up at the tall man opposite.

145

'It has been a long time, Connor,' she said quietly. 'It is good to see you.'

'You too, Maria. You're lovelier than ever.' His eyes softened as he looked at her, appreciating the magnolia colour of her fine skin and her wide violet eyes.

'Thank you.'

'How are you?'

'Everything is fine with me. My job – well, you know all about that. There are frustrations, of course. The Vatican is a slow, ungainly machine, held back by its history and its size and the people who belong to it. But the work is fascinating and what I dreamed of doing when I was a student. If I'd known then that I'd be working with – handling, touching – the most precious of manuscripts, the world's heritage . . . I would never have believed it.'

'I'm glad you're happy in your work,' Brock said sincerely. She realized that he looked older than she remembered. His dark hair was sprinkled with grey and there were more lines on that strong tanned face. Still, if anyone could make experience look distinguished and attractive, it was Connor Brock. Maria had been bowled over by his charisma the moment she had met him – and she had believed herself immune to the outer charms of most men. She'd been leered at and pursued by handsome and ugly fellows alike since she'd turned sixteen and her face and figure had blossomed. It had made her suspicious of them. Brock was different, she'd sensed that at once.

'And how are other things in your life?' he asked gently.

She shrugged. 'There is no one special in my personal life, if that is what you mean. I'm far too busy for all of that and my workplace hardly brings me into contact with likely candidates.' She laughed lightly with only a tiny trace of bitterness. 'Every man I meet has taken a vow of celibacy! I may as well be in a convent. As for my family . . . my mother is still on her deathbed – or so she claims. She seems perfectly fit and well to us. I see her every few weeks. My brother is very happy, his little family is growing up fast. I still miss my father, of course . . .'

'Naturally. You'll never be free of the sadness, I can promise you that, even if it hurts less with time.'

She looked at him quickly, watching his lips harden slightly. 'And you, Connor . . . how are you?' It was always a delicate

146

operation to ask Connor Brock about himself. It was a subject he was not eager to discuss, but Maria felt she could not let the moment pass.

'I'm well. Hale and hearty.'

'I can see that. I meant . . . in yourself . . . ?'

He shifted a little awkwardly and drank from his glass. When he'd put it back, he said in a softer voice than his normal one, 'Oh, Maria. In myself? I try not to think about what's inside too much. You know that.'

'It is five years now since Heather . . .' She stopped.

'Since she was killed. It feels like five minutes. It's still so raw. I couldn't even bear to think of it for the first three years at least. To be honest, I try not to think about it at all, if I can possibly help it. Nothing will change what's happened.'

'I understand how the hurt remains, how all you can do is learn to live with it. But . . . are you . . . coming to terms with it now?' Maria tried to hold a neutral tone in her voice. She didn't want to pry into a man's pain.

Brock laughed roughly. 'What does that mean? Maria, I'm sorry, but I just can't talk about it. Forgive me.'

Once you could, she thought. She remembered a long night with Brock in her arms, as he whispered all his hurt and grief and despair into her soft hair. 'Of course,' she said gently. 'But – may I ask . . . about Kathy?'

Brock's eyes hardened; the lids became hooded like iron shutters. 'I'll never speak of her,' he said abruptly. 'And nor will you. Understand?'

She was frightened by his severity. He had stiffened and everything about him was suddenly harsh. 'I'm sorry, Connor, of course. Forgive me . . .'

'Signor! Signora! Your first course – allow me.' The cheerful waiter bustled up with their pasta: creamy coils of spaghetti con le vongole for Maria and a rich mound of spicy tagliatelle for Brock.

Maria was grateful for the interruption. 'He thinks we are married,' she said with a laugh, as the waiter left, and then looked down at her food, embarrassed. 'Very silly of him,' she murmured.

'Maria . . .' She looked up and his eyes were amused, twinkling at her. 'Do you know how sweet you are?'

147

'Sweet! Now, Connor, I allow a lot of things from you but patronizing me isn't one of them,' she said hotly.

He laughed loudly. 'That's more like it! That's the fiery Italian I know. Now, tell me about these absurd fellows in the Vatican, I want to hear more.'

They savoured their meal: the guinea fowl braised in the Roman fashion and served with soft cheese, and the lamb grilled to succulent sweetness on the open fire. It was a pleasure to be together, gossiping and laughing, enjoying each other's company. Maria could not remember when she'd had such a pleasant evening.

They had finished a delicious ricotta cake and were lingering over their espressos when Brock turned the subject back to the matter in hand.

'This investigation is an unusual one,' he said, interlocking his fingers on the table in front of him. 'We usually deal in straight corporate threats – fraud or sabotage. Mismanagement, greed, insider dealing – that kind of thing. This seems to be on a different scale altogether, involving a whole raft of different people, businesses and concerns. There are a huge number of unanswered questions.'

'And they all seem to lead back to Temujin Subedei?'

'Precisely.'

'That was my instinct.' Maria bent down and picked up the bag at her feet. 'Once it seemed that he had strayed on to my territory – the pursuit of the past – I did some research myself. I have the results here.'

'You're an excellent addition to ICE, did you know that?'

'Of course. Now, listen for a moment.' She looked down at her notes, frowning a little. 'Ah, yes, here we are. First, Temujin is the name of the greatest political leader ever known. Most experts agree that he was responsible for establishing the largest land empire in human history, in the process overcoming the most advanced civilizations of the era, despite overwhelming odds.

'Who? I don't know that name. Are you saying this man ruled an empire bigger than Alexander's or the Caesars'? Surely I would have heard of him.'

'In terms of land mass, this empire was the largest ever seen.

Historians refer to this man as Chingus Khan or, the more western version, Genghis Khan.'

Brock's face cleared. 'Oh, well – my old pal Genghis. Why didn't you say so? Of course, that makes sense. But his empire hardly matches the others. He was an ignorant barbarian, wasn't he? A butcher. Nothing more.'

'What is that old saying? History is written by the victors? We don't like to acknowledge that Temujin was much more than a tribal chief who happened to get lucky in a few battles. Most of the conquerors of the Asian steppes may have been motivated by greed for riches but Temujin was driven by a soaring political ambition matched with a brilliant mind for advanced planning. He alone brought all the warring tribes together in a unity that has never been witnessed before or since. With the support of his foremost generals, nicknamed the four dogs of war, the Mongol Yuen dynasty of China was founded. Alongside that, all the principalities and tribes in Russia were subjugated and unified within one empire.'

'All right. Impressive stuff. I take my hat off to the man. So it appears that the megalomaniacal head of Subedei Industries has bestowed greatness on himself by naming himself after Genghis Khan.' Brock whistled softly through his teeth. 'Nothing like setting yourself a challenge.'

'Yes. Some might call it hubris. But only part of his name is tribute to Genghis. The rest is more interesting. Temujin's four generals were Chepe, Jelme, Kublai and the greatest was – you guessed it – Subedei. He won the complete victory over Russia, attacked Eastern Europe and wiped out within weeks all the large armies that tried to confront him, including several hundred thousand of Europe's greatest warriors. *The Secret History of The Mongols* describes all the princes of blood as the "succours of Subedei".'

'So, our friend does not go for half measures. Puts a new slant on the phrase "what's in a name", doesn't it?'

'Well, his namesake, Subedei, planned to conquer Western Europe all the way to the Atlantic, a strategy that had been devised years before by Temujin. But when he heard the news that Temujin's son and first successor, Ogedei, had died leaving the position of Great Khan vacant, Subedei, the Khan's last remaining general, was forced by Mongol custom to return home in order to face the political situation and elect a new Khan. A fateful decision for him and certainly one that was beneficial for Europe.'

'Why?'

'Because if Subedei had not chosen to follow tradition, and continued with his campaign, there would have been no European army left to halt him.' Maria glanced up with a bright smile. 'Here is where I began to be a little startled by the coincidences I was turning up. Ready for this? Before he returned home, Subedei commissioned a battalion of his bravest and fiercest warriors to track down a seeing stone.'

Brock raised his eyebrows. '*Another* seeing stone? That's the third one tonight. This is getting interesting.'

'I know.' Maria looked pleased. 'It's starting to make sense, isn't it? This stone could be the one from Cyrus's sword, or from Alexander's sword. Or all three could be one and the same. We have to assume that Genghis Khan and General Subedei would have heard mention of the legends surrounding both the former great emperors.

'And, more importantly, such a stone would have tied in with their spiritual tradition. Our records turned up that the Mongolian god, Duua, was known as the One-Eyed. Myth relates to it being a third eye, similar to the third eye of Shiva in the Hindu religion.' Maria shuffled through her notes and pulled out a page that she passed to Brock. 'Here is a quick sketch I made of Duua.'

Brock looked at the drawing, recognizing the eye-shaped symbol in the centre of the god's forehead that he had already seen on both the manuscript and Subedei's material.

'Almost identical,' he commented.

'Mythology has always stated that a cyclopean eye, when removed, turns to stone, often a precious one, usually a ruby. Such stones were prized by shaman druids and priests for the powers they bestowed on their holder. They had great talismanic properties and rulers would often take them by force to harness their magical powers. General Subedei obviously wanted that power either for himself or as a gift for his ruling Khan.'

'And our modern Subedei appears to be on the same mission. Did the general's battalion find the stone?'

'I don't know. Subedei died fourteen years before the battle

150

of Ayn Jalut in 1260, when the manuscript relating to the seeing stone was found. It doesn't reveal what happened.'

A waiter coughed behind them politely. They jumped and looked around. The restaurant had emptied; they were the last people remaining in the room.

'Excuse me, Signor, is there anything more you require?'

'My apologies,' said Brock smoothly, in Italian. 'The bill, please.'

He paid the bill and they left the restaurant. It was late. Silence descended on them as they made their way back to the hotel and up the stairs to their rooms.

'I want to check everything is all right,' said Brock as Maria unlocked the door to her room. 'I'll just scan round quickly.'

She opened the door and let him in, saying, 'You really think there might be danger?'

He moved swiftly about the room, checking the access points and any places where someone might conceal themself or something else. Maria shut the door and took off her coat, watching him with concern.

Brock finished his surveillance. 'It all seems fine. I don't want to take chances though – we'll leave the adjoining door open.'

'You honestly think I'm at risk?'

He walked towards her. 'Maria – your office and your home have been ransacked tonight. Someone is trying to locate something and they clearly think you have it. As you happen to be carrying a unique and priceless document around with you, one that contains the only match with Subedei's material in the entire archives, I think we can safely say that it could be what they're after. Don't you think?'

Maria's eyes widened in fear and her hands went to her mouth. 'Oh my god,' she whispered. 'Of course you're right. It is the Mongolian document they want.'

'We have to assume it's extremely important. Someone wants it very badly, anyway.'

Maria only half-listened to Brock. Her thoughts had already rushed back to the scene at the archives and her computer. It had been torn apart. None of the computer's records of the symbols had been backed up. It had been her office that had been the target, and then her flat. Now it was her.

'It is because of me that the archives have been devastated – so much awful damage! Irreparable harm . . . That poor boy nearly killed! And now it is me that they want. Oh no . . .' She closed her eyes. 'That man is dangerous – that Subedei. I don't want his curse anywhere near me!'

Brock went over to her without replying and wrapped her in his strong arms. She leaned her head forward on to his shoulder and sighed. A small sniff indicated that she was crying.

'Maria, don't . . .' he said gently. He lifted her chin with a finger so that her face tilted up to him. Her eyes were glittering with tears, her mouth trembling slightly. They both felt it at that instant: the tension that had been building between them over the last few hours burst into life and they were pulled together with irresistible force.

He dropped his mouth on to hers and they were caught up in a fierce kiss. Its strength possessed them both and they were soon lost. Brock picked her up, unable to remove his mouth from hers for an instant, and carried her to the bed. Oblivious to everything else about them, they were engulfed by their mutual passion, unable to resist each other. Their bodies intertwined as their frantic embraces led them at last to a wild, almost primitive release.

PART TWO

A Strategy of 'Accidents'

Seventeen

The circular palace, occupying the whole of a towering top floor, slowly turned six revolutions every twenty-four hours. The panorama showed a commercial fiefdom encompassing giant tankers, deep-water harbour facilities, oil and gas refineries, steel and concrete industries, and a score of giant factories. All of them, including the countless blocks of tiny apartments over-flowing with the essential human fuel to operate them, seemed to pay homage to Beijing's tallest building and its owner, Temujin Subedei.

From the black windows to the pointed domed roof, a thousand yards of fine linen and silk were draped like the sumptuous tent of an Indian Maharajah. Priceless hand-woven carpets of Chinese silk, Persian flax and Egyptian cotton lay thickly on the floor, much of their beauty hidden from view by the exquisite furniture, statuary and antique objets d'art that would make the world's leading fine-art auctioneers salivate with envy.

Few were allowed admittance to this rich sanctuary. Two broad Orientals, dressed magnificently in the lamellar neck-to-elbow and lower-leg armour of medieval Mongolian warriors, stood at the bottom of the wide staircase; their expressions were rigid as stone, their shining, razor-sharp scimitars ready to prevent any curious sightseers venturing up from the executive office suites and communication centre below.

Temujin Subedei rose from behind an enormous ebony desk, his black eyes burning with anger, like almond-shaped coals in a deep fire.

He was furious, almost quivering with rage. He stalked out from behind the desk and began to pace the floor in front of it in an effort to control himself.

Though in his early sixties, Subedei's broad shoulders and lean muscular body belied his real age. The only sign of it was the very slight greying in his straight black hair, and the few lines that marked the high-cheekboned face. There were faint scars, relics of street fights in his youth, but otherwise the gaunt cheeks were smooth and hairless. Under the flat-bridged nose, the thin mouth rarely moved into a smile. The only place to read Subedei's emotions was in his black eyes. Inside them was the fire of intense self-possession and confident invulnerability. His personal entourage knew those eyes only too well: one glance could inspire courage and loyalty, or instil bone-chilling fear.

Subedei enjoyed the familiar feeling of renewed energy and power that his anger always gave him. It had been the same throughout his life. Ever since the day he had helplessly watched his parents trampled to death by a rioting mob, he had sought to channel his frustration and anger into power and control. He knew that it was the secret of his extraordinary success, the thing that had protected him when he'd lived on the streets. When the gang members and Triad youths had attempted to rile him, tease him, goad him to anger, he'd stayed cool and impassive, outwardly acquiescent and calm. Later, his cold anger would have its revenge: anyone who ever crossed him, or tried to humiliate him, had lost his life.

It was his destiny, he knew that. Destiny had guided him every step of the way. What was it that had brought him to the helpless Chang Lok, if not that? He had seen the man, beaten and incapable in the gutter, left to die by a gang of assailants who had robbed him; he had gone to him and aided him. That was destiny. Chang Lok was a very important man, an influential member of the government of the People's Republic of China. Their paths had crossed for a reason, that was obvious. Chang Lok had been so grateful to his rescuer that eventually he had adopted him, the scrappy young street urchin, the Mongol member of the Borjigin tribe. He had been transformed into Te Su Lok, his adopted father's right-hand man, trained in the family business of finding, preserving and trading in historical artefacts.

Six years later, and Te Su Lok was well established. He'd learned how to negotiate his way through the delicate matter of winning contract licences within the corrupt government departments. He had been made first a representative, then later departmental head of the Protectorate of Historical Artefacts. As Comrade Te Su Lok, he had built an international network of wealthy collectors. None questioned where the priceless relics they wanted so badly came from. The fortunes they readily gave him were quietly used to gain valuable options and licences, and to lubricate the winning of essential contracts.

Chang Lok never knew the extent of his adopted son's success. He was the director responsible for issuing and overseeing the government licences for construction, shipping and energy, and he never suspected that his most trusted son was behind the intricate web of contractors that tendered for them. One foolish, ambitious contractor had threatened to alert Chang Lok to his son's business practices, unless Comrade Te Su made it worth his while not to. Te Su had pretended that it would be his pleasure – and then had the contractor and his entire family killed. That was the young Wheng Zhu's first mission for him. The first of many. Soon afterwards, Chang Lok had died and with him the risk of his ever discovering the truth about his son. It was only natural that Comrade Te Su Lok should offer to step temporarily into his father's shoes as director for government licences, until a proper successor should be found. Even more natural that, after his father's directorship was passed on to someone else, Comrade Te Su Lok should seek permission to leave the Republic and go to America; he had his father's international business to run, after all. And that was the last anyone heard of young Te Su.

But a new and more interesting figure took his place. An unknown entrepreneur appeared called Temujin Subedei, head of the already large conglomerate, Subedei Industries. This vital young businessman soon established himself as a shining jewel in the new party leader Deng Xiaoping's vision for China as a superpower.

Destiny, you see, thought Subedei. Destiny was everything. His guide. His lodestone. It was inescapable.

As Subedei Industries grew into a global concern, Subedei had gained increasing political power. When agreements were made with Russia for extracting oil and gas, Subedei was the natural choice to take on the contracts. Heavy industrial organizations seeking to

157

invest in China would be directed towards Subedei Industries. They carried the endorsement of the Communist Party of China and within the party, Subedei wielded enormous influence.

His temper flared up again, intense and hot at the thought that all he had achieved could be under threat. For now, just as he had commenced the operational plan that would fulfil his real destiny of greatness, some western upstart agency had dared to interfere.

Subedei returned to the monitor on his desk and reread the information displayed there.

> Connor McCoy Brock – born in Inverness, Scotland. Brought up, Kinloss, Moray
>
> Father: Cameron Brock, pilot, American Scot from Boston, Massachusetts.
>
> Mother: Isabel Ross, teacher. Married Cameron Brock during his three-year tour of duty as a squadron leader at the Nimrod aircraft base, RAF Kinloss.

A dialogue box appeared in the top right-hand corner of his screen, distracting him. It was his personal assistant, her face impassive in the tiny frame.

'I beg your forgiveness for the interruption, My Lord. You wanted me to inform you immediately Ibrahim Qenawi returned your call.'

'Keep him on hold,' replied Subedei, as he continued to skim through the information on Connor Brock.

'Very well. My Lord, your noon appointment has arrived.'

'Entertain him appropriately. I will signal you.'

'Yes, My Lord.' The dialogue box disappeared.

> Gained joint honours degree at Edinburgh University in History and French. Excelled in Athletics.
>
> Joined Royal Air Force after university, rising to rank of Flight Lieutenant during Gulf War.
>
> Active member of Special Forces in Bosnia, achieving rank of Squadron Leader. Decorated with DSO.
>
> Married Heather McCoy, Scottish, daughter of local banker John McCoy.
>
> Departed RAF after the death of his wife Heather in unsolved car accident.
>
> Disappeared for two years, believed to have been

studying at a Zen temple in Japan.

Upon return to Europe employed as special investigator for global reinsurance company.

Recruited by Dr Paul van Lederman, co-founder of ICE, Investigation of Corporate Espionage, to head-up special operations.

Fluent in English, French, Italian and Japanese.

Homes in London and Zurich.

Subedei leaned back thoughtfully into his chair, flicking his thumb against a switch built into the console of the chair's wide armrest.

'So, Ibrahim, my friend, what is your news?' he said to the ebony face that came instantly into view on the screen.

'Only good news for your ears, Lord Subedei,' replied Qenawi with a relaxed smile, using the formal title that he knew his superior preferred. He was accustomed to revering his Sudan rebel overlords in the same manner, and he was comfortable with the form of address.

When the successful takeover of Al Kadeh Construction had proved Qenawi's worth, Subedei had taken him further into his confidence and explained some of his future plans. They made Qenawi's former ambitions pale into insignificance and increased his loyalty to his new master a hundredfold.

'I assume, therefore, that you are on schedule.' Subedei smiled expectantly.

'We are now fully operational here at Al Qantarah and are already producing in excess of the quotas we calculated. We have surplus of fifty tons of the MM120 a day, in fact.'

'Good. And storage?'

'We are loading directly on to our recently acquired dredging barges. They will be placed in position when required.'

Subedei's expression remained unreadable. 'You have assured yourself that there can be no possibility of accidents so close to the water? It is imperative that there are no leaks.'

'I have made it my number one priority,' replied Qenawi. 'AKC's cement-sacking process has been modified to provide inner and outer layers of plastic. Every load of fifty MM120 sacks carries a receiver that will immediately indicate any trace of water so that our divers can isolate and re-tarpaulin the load. The receiver also operates as an activator, of course.'

'And our shipping? I include the Al Kadeh fleet.'

'Again, on schedule, My Lord. All employed on filling our refineries at Port Said and Alexandria.'

'Excellent, Ibrahim. You have done well. Anything else you have to tell me?'

Qenawi felt the sweat break out on the back of his neck. He was certain that Subedei already knew what he was going to say. 'There is something else, My Lord. It concerns the contract for the New Pyramids. It would appear that, with the change in ownership of Al Kadeh Construction, certain political opposition leaders are insisting that the infrastructure contract returns to formal tender—'

'No doubt wanting the bidding opportunity for their own preferred companies,' interrupted Subedei.

'I'm certain you are correct, My Lord,' said Qenawi, relieved at the seemingly relaxed view that Subedei was taking.

Subedei thought for an instant and then said, 'My instruction is for you not to bid for it. Moreover, I want you to release a statement, saying that, as new operator of AKC, you are withdrawing from everything in relation to the New Pyramids.'

The ebony face on the screen looked shocked. 'But, Lord Subedei, we could fight the request. After all, the contract is worth half a billion dollars to us . . .'

A cold stare from Subedei made Qenawi's voice fade into silence.

Subedei said quietly, 'It is good to be gracious and generous. Consider how no one will be able to point a finger at us for taking over Al Kadeh Construction just to win the tender you had previously lost. You will be perceived as being patriotic, even ethical, by withdrawing. Let another bid win. What does it matter to us? The labour used will have to be local, as, of course, will the cement, concrete and steel. Do you think that they will import it or buy it from existing factories? Having won the contract, whoever it is will have to come to AKC to provide the materials. The Americans like to win contracts, run the show and take the applause. We will let them. All liability in construction will be theirs. All profit in materials will be ours.'

'Yes, Lord Subedei.'

'And we can focus on more important matters that require our unflagging attention. You, of course, will be too occupied with such attentions to join me on the *Pharaoh Queen* for my little reception.'

Subedei terminated the call and resumed reading the screen, allowing himself one of his rare smiles.

> ICE represents an alliance between European Union countries, major intelligence agencies and leading multinational industries to probe into possible threats that jeopardize economic growth and ethical governance in developed or developing nations.

What a strategist Sun Tzu was, Subedei thought. Know your enemy, understand their motives, and befriend them.

'Mi Ling,' he said to his secretary as her face appeared in the dialogue box in response to his call. 'You can show Monsieur Cambriol up to my office now.'

As the screen before him went abruptly blank Qenawi's jaw tightened like chiselled ebony. He felt concern that he was already being punished for daring to question the Mongolian. The plan to introduce him as new CEO of Subedei Industries (Egypt) while announcing the recent takeover of Al Kadeh Construction to all the invited dignitaries aboard the *Pharaoh Queen* had been Subedei's own.

'The man is not that shallow,' Qenawi said aloud to himself, leaning back in his chair while resting his elbows on the chair's arms and pressing the fingers of both hands together in a steeple action. 'Yet he stings me where I am most sensitive,' he admitted to himself, accepting his need for recognition by a new peer group.

Qenawi's mind flashed back to a young girl with the grace of a gazelle and the eyes of a dove. By rights she had been his prize. He had led his small band of young guerrillas into the village and spared her. She was to serve the young commander however he desired. But his dream had been thwarted by the platoon's ambitious leader. Jealous of Qenawi's daring success, he had stung him where he could hurt him the most. Returning from a scouting errand that the platoon leader had sent him on, Qenawi learned that the girl had been first raped and then had her arms severed with a machete. The girl bled to death.

'The she-devil attempted escape and had to serve as an

161

example to those who try to defy our revolution,' had been the reason. In time Qenawi had acquired another slave but he always felt that he was being laughed at behind his back.

But that was twenty years ago, and living in the past is an old man's pursuit. He was in his prime and a leader and the Mongolian would have had good reason. But the image of the girl's eyes continued to haunt him whenever he felt vulnerable.

So many ghosts, Qenawi thought as his office door opened and the large white face of the chief engineer of the plant, Michael Maynard, peered into the room. Born and bred in Leeds in the north of England, the gruff Yorkshireman was a specialist in port construction, dredging harbours to entertain deep-draught tankers and cruise ships. His claim to fame had been the new Liverpool docks. But such fame turned to infamy when, through trying to avoid bankruptcy in the early nineties, he had been involved in the illegal deconstruction of ports with a view to winning new marina complex tenders.

Charged under the terrorism act of holding explosives with intent to cause wilful damage, Maynard departed the UK while on bail. Though permanently on the list of sought after-terrorist suspects, he was in fact a brilliant marine-construction engineer. Funded by a cartel of Greek shipping magnates, he had recently developed a new form of marine cement he had coined MM120. Through the cartel, Subedei had learned of the material, taken over the research and Maynard.

Maynard, whose other passion was continually eating, sat his obese body into the chair opposite Qenawi without first being asked. Qenawi looked at him. The cultural differences were so vast between himself and this whale of a man who was sweating in front of him that he maintained a polite tone to overcome any offence he might feel or give off.

Maynard sighed as he mopped his brow. 'This bloody heat. It would be a bloody sight more convenient if you could put an air-conditioned passage between my bloody building and this bloody building.'

'Couldn't agree more, though it was your own recommendation to keep them separate from a pressurization perspective, wasn't it?'

'What is it I can do for you?' asked Maynard, pushing his thinning red hair back from his forehead with his handkerchief.

'First I wanted to thank you for increasing production to in excess of fifty tons a day.'

Maynard nodded, unimpressed at the praise.

'Second I wanted to clarify the quantities. Ultimately it is I, not you, who will be responsible for any errors,' added Qenawi more seriously. 'You have double-checked your calculations relating to tonnage and exposure?'

Maynard looked at the black man opposite him without hiding his obvious disdain.

'Look, lad, I would not have bloody given 'em to you unless they were correct.'

'So, by the last day of the month we will have all the material in place?'

'By tomorrow I will have delivered all the material required,' returned Maynard bluntly. 'But I will not be held accountable for it being in place. As you quite rightly say, that is your responsibility. My contract is to develop, produce and advise on location. Any delay on positioning on site is nowt to do with me. Understood?'

Qenawi raised his eyebrows. 'Not be held accountable? I suppose history will be the judge of that, Mr Maynard. Who knows, this may be just what you will be remembered for.'

Eighteen

Jean Luc Cambriol savoured the delicate lemon and vanilla taste of the vintage Ruinart champagne that had been ceremoniously poured into a crystal flute by the demure Chinese girl. When she had curtseyed as she proffered the glass, he had seen the firm, creamy thigh unexpectedly exposed by the high-cut slit of her silk cheongsam. Another pleasure to enjoy, along with the exquisite morsels of truffle and foie gras. The Frenchman warmed towards his host. He was evidently a man of great refinement.

'My favourite champagne,' Cambriol commented with satisfaction, smacking his lips, 'though I have to admit it seems odd to be enjoying such fine French delights here in Beijing.'

'There is much the world can learn from the French, particularly about *la mode de vie*,' replied Subedei, pleased that the information about the Interpol chief's tastes had been accurate. 'Almost as much as the west can learn from the east, which means to say that for lunch, I have arranged some more colloquial delights for you to experience.'

'I feel you honour me too much.' Cambriol looked across the room at the sumptuous feast being discreetly laid out by stunning girls. Each moved gracefully and silently in her shimmering silk cheongsam.

'I assure you, the honour is mine,' answered Subedei. He bowed his head politely at his guest. 'When I contacted Interpol for assistance, I did not expect to meet with the director himself.'

Cambriol shifted in his seat. 'Your request could not have been timelier as it happens. My particular focus is on Europe. I am often tied to Paris and so I always welcome the opportunity to travel. This is my first trip to Beijing.'

'Then I feel privileged to welcome you here by offering you some of the hospitality that is so regularly bestowed on me

164

when I am in Paris.' Subedei stood up, gesturing towards the extraordinary banquet laid out on the table. 'Please, allow me to introduce you to some culinary delights that will, I hope, serve as a memorable souvenir for a connoisseur.'

While the two men enjoyed the selection of dim sum, soft-shell crab, exotic soups and delicate noodles, Subedei gestured at the view, pointing out the different parts of Beijing he had developed to provide employment and stimulate economic growth.

'It is a passion of mine to provide a living for the thousands of migrating rural peasants seeking opportunity in our growing cities,' said Subedei sincerely. 'And now, under our new leadership, with its many reforms, so many dreams are becoming possible. I believe that those of us in China with influence must use it to build a greater future, a greater world.

'Of course, there are elements determined to keep China from growing, particularly towards globalization. Some of the hardliners in our government consider that globalization is simply another term for Americanization. There are some that also feel antagonistic towards Europe.'

Cambriol smiled inwardly. His host was turning the conversation towards the real purpose for his invitation and this excellent meal. 'How would this relate to your request for assistance from Interpol?' he asked.

'It has come to my attention that many of my company's activities in Europe and the Middle East are being investigated,' replied Subedei. 'Indeed, I understand that Interpol has carried out some information-gathering here in Beijing.'

'It is not unusual, Monsieur, for any conglomerate to attract our attention, particularly when there is such meteoric expansion through mergers and acquisitions.'

'I was not aware that Interpol interested itself in such mundane business activities, though I welcome the opportunity to have an esteemed organization such as yours to investigate us.'

'A refreshing perspective,' said Cambriol, surprised. 'Though we at Interpol are very discreet, our enquiries can, nevertheless, be damaging to a business's reputation, even when nothing untoward is discovered. People tend to believe the English expression: no smoke without fire. To welcome our intrusion is . . . unusual.'

165

Subedei leaned forward in his chair, reaching for the paper-thin porcelain cup that had been quietly filled with green tea by one of the silken cheongsam maidens. 'On the contrary, I believe that when the world stops taking an interest in a business, the business has ceased to make a difference. I view your efforts as positive because they have no doubt shown that we have nothing to hide.

'Total transparency is, I understand, essential for any candidate conglomerate aspiring to qualify for associate membership of ICE. I will come straight to the point. In addition to Interpol locating the whereabouts of Omar Al Kadeh and his family, I would like you, in your capacity as a director of ICE, to broker my application for membership.'

The Frenchman looked at Subedei in astonishment. The three things he had least expected in the course of this meeting were references to the Egyptian company that Subedei Industries had acquired, Cambriol's own involvement in ICE, and a request for membership.

He kept his expression neutral and quickly regained his composure. 'I would have imagined that you would have a clearer idea of where Al Kadeh was than Interpol.'

'Unfortunately, no,' returned Subedei, his face worried, as though the whole problem weighed heavily on him. 'In fact, because of this worrying disappearance, I have decided not to pursue a major contract that Omar Al Kadeh had personally committed his company to fulfil. It's true we are investing heavily into the Middle East, and particularly Egypt, but it would be wrong both politically and morally to continue with a contract intended to help Egyptian business rather than foreign interests.'

'And why would Al Kadeh's presence make a difference?'

'Because an integral part of the buy-out was that he and his sons would oversee the fruition of the New Pyramids contract. Now, no sooner has the deal been finalized and monies paid than he has reneged on our agreement.'

Cambriol felt elated. His suspicions that Al Kadeh had taken the money and run were correct.

'With my future plans,' continued Subedei, 'I consider that it would be prudent to support ICE in their mission towards positive economic growth and ethical governance. Naturally, for my part, I would benefit from protecting my organization's investments from scurrilous people like Al Kadeh. More importantly, of course, as a representative of the People's Republic of China entrusted with promoting foreign growth, I am eager for further strong links between Europe and China. It is a relationship which I know our government places a lot of value in securing.'

Cambriol quickly saw the implications. He imagined the faces of Buchanan and van Lederman when they learned that he had secured not only the Chinese government as a partner, but also a huge injection of funds for ICE to expand throughout Asia.

'This is all fascinating. I think I can safely say that what you've requested is entirely reasonable. In my Interpol capacity, I undertake to keep you apprised of any information concerning the whereabouts of Al Kadeh or any family members. In my ICE capacity, I can see no problems with brokering your application for membership. I can make no promises, of course, but I will do what I can. Will your application be on behalf of Subedei Industries or the Chinese government?'

'You could say we enjoy an almost symbiotic relationship.' Subedei smiled. 'The new president is committed to our nation having greater influence in world affairs, a responsibility that a rapidly evolving superpower should take seriously, of course. He has personally made me an ambassador for China's economic and commercial growth, particularly in the essential area of energy. You can expect that whatever contribution is agreed for my own organization's membership will be matched by my government.'

Cambriol could not believe his ears. A government endorsement of ICE and financial contribution were exactly what his co-directors at ICE would insist on. Industry and government working together was vital to stimulate economic investment. 'In that case, I can say with some confidence that my colleagues at ICE will be contacting you.'

As he rose to shake his host's outstretched hand, Cambriol relished the idea of his triumph. What a coup for him to net Subedei Industries and the People's Republic of China! It would prove him a man of substance.

Nineteen

Zarakov tried to imagine the once-beautiful plains of cypresses and wheat that bounded the natural harbour of the Gulf of Alexandretta on the furthest eastern tip of the Mediterranean Sea. Yet looking down over the modern bridge that crossed the river Payas below him all he could see were ugly sprawling factories intent on spewing out their pollution and dust. The view he had been directed to see was obstructed by a web of power lines and a superhighway with access roads cutting up the historic bank.

He tried to imagine the two great armies tearing into each other across the river bed. It was nigh impossible for him. All he could see externally were examples of how man fulfilled his frenzy for energy. All he could see internally was the broken body of his brother Dimitri. He shook his head to clear it.

'And just to the left of the oil terminal you can see the ancient mound of Issus where Darius stopped to mutilate Alexander's wounded troops. It was to serve as a warning to the Greeks, but had the reverse effect. Down there on the river bank Alexander's small band routed the much bigger Persian Army. Darius escaped, leaving his whole family and great wealth behind and Alexander became King of the great Persian Empire.'

'Fascinating story, and place,' replied Zarakov politely, yet unenthusiastically. He had heard the story already from Subedei. But he was beginning to become frustrated at how the Mongolian's obsession with Alexander the Great seemed to dog his own footsteps.

'One of strategic interest too, of course, as I am sure you are aware. The main routes from Anatolia to Syria and Egypt still come through here and all the recently-opened pipelines from Iraq come here, as of course our own pipeline does from the Caspian.'

'And that of course does interest me.'

Zarakov turned from the window towards his compatriot.

'You are on schedule? I do not want to learn that there are technical hitches at the last moment. After spending two billion dollars we do not want to lose our race to the western initiative led by the British.'

Nicolai Starobnya, born and raised in Georgia, was fiercely patriotic and proud of Russia's future with its more capitalistic outlook. Admittedly life in the south was not as harsh as the north, but he did not take kindly to the abrupt manner of his Siberian comrade, who seemed even more disillusioned and cynical than usual.

His own father had owned a profitable farm in Georgia and, helped by perestroika, had been able to afford an excellent education for his son. After attending university in St Petersburg, Starobnya had been sent to the US and excelled in engineering at Berkley. With almost perfect timing major oil deposits had been discovered around the Caspian soon after he had graduated and he had immediately gained employment constructing the Caspian consortium pipeline from Tengiz in Kazakhstan to Novorossiysk on the eastern Georgian banks of the Black Sea.

As soon as his own responsibilities had been completed, he and the whole team he had put together were headhunted by Subedei Industries. It had not only been the money that had motivated him. It had been the opportunity to have full decision-making over the contract.

He had suggested that they take a more northerly route than the western consortium pipe, through Georgia rather than Azerbaijan. Licences had somehow been effortlessly acquired by Subedei Industries at a political level and they had saved weeks and millions of dollars in costs. They were streets ahead of the British and ahead of schedule. Starobnya felt the back of his neck burn. How dare his professionalism be questioned?

'One billion dollars less than the British-led consortium and ahead of schedule is no mean feat, comrade,' replied the Georgian cuttingly. 'More importantly there will be no last-minute hitches. We are ready to pump at the first of next month.'

Zarakov held the younger man's indignant gaze. The eyes

reminded him of his younger brother. The hair was a lighter brown but the light blue-grey eyes were almost the same colour. He reached up, placing a hand on the taller man's shoulder.

'You have done exceedingly well, Nicolai. You must not mind the cynicism of an old dog like me. And it is fitting that this town will witness the success of another great strategic enterprise to compare with Alexander.'

Zarakov turned back to the window. 'Now, tell me more of this great battle, and then let us go through in detail the plan and shipping schedule.'

As a much calmer Nicolai Starobnya began to point out where the Macedonian phalanx had crossed the river in order to circle the Persian Army, Zarakov tuned out. The young man had exceeded expectations. But what his reward would be remained to be seen. As a young man he too had been filled with enthusiasm and had done well on countless missions for his country. Yet his reward had been two years in the salt mines. He had done well for Subedei and so had Dimitri and what was the reward? His brother dead, while that Egyptian whore gleefully calls to inform Subedei. At least his suspicions about that woman had been confirmed.

Zarakov retuned to what was being said and tried once more to imagine the carnage that ended the great Archaemenian Empire that had lasted 200 years. He remembered how that woman had explained to him how it had begun with the father of Cambyses II. Nothing changes, he mused to himself. Power, greed and revenge were still the motivators of killing. He had no care for the first two. But his brother's death would be avenged.

The white corridors were crowded with a sea of people hurrying about their business. No one cared about the insignificant man who quietly limped past them. There were far more serious cases to attend to.

Sure of his way, the man went silently and purposefully to the third floor. He trod noiselessly past the staff room, the clinical consultation office, the pharmaceutical store and the intensive care unit. When he reached the four private rooms on the far ward, he scanned the corridor. It was empty, as he'd known it would be.

A minor explosion just off the central station forty minutes earlier had sent the Alexandria Hospital into panic mode. All hands were needed, and that included the guard who had been sitting here throughout the morning.

The man opened the door of the room he had identified earlier and went in.

John Ridge was in the deep sleep brought on by heavy sedation. His knife wound had proved more serious than anyone had realized and during a routine cleaning and stitching, he'd collapsed through blood loss, exhaustion and dehydration. The doctors had insisted on his admission, and now his body was being helped to rest so that it could begin to heal, while a drip attached to his forearm restored the vital fluids.

He was not aware that anyone had entered his room.

The quiet man removed the drip with clinical dexterity, inserted a syringe in its place and injected a solution. It was done in seconds. Replacing the drip, he calmly left the room.

Twenty

Brock strode through Arrivals at Zurich airport. As usual, he was travelling light, with just a battered holdall as luggage. In his casual moleskin trousers and well-cut leather jacket, he looked as though he could be a weekend visitor to the city or a resident returning home. What set him apart from his fellow passengers was his height and his air of seriousness, along with the vivid blue eyes on constant alert.

'Hey there! Connor!'

Brock looked over to the gaggle of people waiting for the arrivals. Next to a cab driver holding up a cardboard sign was a familiar figure. Brock smiled heartily and went over to his friend.

'Welcome back.' A wide grin split Matt Ferguson's face. His red hair was a mess as usual and his cheeks were ruddy.

You can take the boy out of Ireland . . . thought Brock. Matt was never going to look at home among the polished folk of Switzerland. 'Matt. Good to see you.' They shook hands heartily. 'You look a lot better than you did last time I saw you.'

'I was in it up to my neck,' quipped Matt. 'I'm all the better for a bit less of the sun and sand.' He led Brock out of the terminal towards the car. 'What about you, though? How was Rome?'

Brock looked noncommittal. 'There were high points and low points. You know me, I don't like things too simple. I got slugged by something heavy – and it wasn't a drink.'

'Running true to form. You'd better tell me all about it. How was the lovely Maria?' asked Matt cheekily. 'By golly, she's a peach, isn't she?'

Brock didn't reply for a moment, then said, 'Maria's fine. We've had to arrange protection for her, though. I'll tell you more in the car. But what are you doing here? I wasn't expecting you. I thought you'd taken a few days' leave.'

'Van Lederman suggested I should but, hell, as I said to him – people pay fortunes at health clubs to be buried up to their necks in mud. Like them, all I needed was some real food afterwards.'

They climbed into the sleek ICE Mercedes, and Ferguson drove them smoothly out of the airport and on to the autoroute towards Zurich. As they travelled, Brock related the key details of his Rome trip. It was a quick, to-the-point debriefing, the kind Brock and Ferguson had often shared during their military service. Ferguson listened intently until Brock had finished. 'So you think that Subedei was behind the ransacking of the Vatican Secret Archives?'

'Has to be,' replied Brock. 'It's too much of a coincidence otherwise. Maria locates a specific source and almost immediately someone breaks in, searching for something. They're not to know she's removed it, but nonetheless, they take the precaution of turning over her flat just in case.'

'But why bother with the danger and trouble of breaking into the Vatican when they were going to get the information anyway?'

'Exactly. Either they simply couldn't wait or there's a more interesting reason. Perhaps it wasn't ever needed,' answered Brock flatly. 'If Subedei has already found what he wants, then he may be trying to remove all the information that exists that could lead others to whatever it is. First thing this morning I called Pete Kenachi and asked him to contact the leading museums and archives in the world. He called me back just before my flight to confirm that Subedei had already approached all of them with offers of generous patronage if his enquiries can be met. Even if they aren't keen on divulging client details, Pete has his own inimitable way of finding out.'

'Don't suppose the British Library or Museum would be too happy to learn his methods.'

'They would if we could prevent the senseless damage that the Vatican has just experienced.'

'You're right.' Ferguson frowned. 'But I still can't see why Subedei would go to all this trouble. What's the likelihood of someone else being interested in this obscure treasure hunt?'

'Well, from what I understand, locating Alexander's tomb would be on a par with tracking down the Holy Grail. Very big stuff indeed. A lot of people would be very keen to be the first

173

one there. And, from what I learned from Maria, it would seem that Subedei is a megalomaniac with delusions of grandeur and a crazy belief that if he finds this tomb, he'll be endowed with limitless power. Naturally he wants to protect that from any other would-be Genghis Khans.'

Ferguson laughed as they entered the underpass towards Mythenquai. 'This Subedei must have a screw loose if he believes all that malarkey. I thought he was supposed to be a world-respected businessman, not a fool taken up with crystal balls and the power of the pyramids.' He peered towards the road works they were approaching, and slowed the car down. 'And what a lot of hassle to go to, just in case of the unlikely event that whatever it is will be discovered by someone else.'

Brock shrugged. 'What may be irrational to us could seem perfectly rational to Subedei. When you're gripped by the delusion that you're the next best thing to Alexander the Great, you probably think you're above the consequences of your actions. Look out!'

The spiked bucket attached to the hydraulic steel arm of a JCB digger swung with alarming speed from the trench it was stationed over, right into the path of the oncoming ICE Mercedes. Ferguson slammed his foot down hard on the brake pedal and wrenched the steering wheel to the right in a desperate bid to avoid collision.

Too late.

The colossal metal fist smashed into the front of the car, bringing the two-ton vehicle to an abrupt halt and levering the back end high into the air. As airbags exploded in front of them, Ferguson and Brock reacted with lightning speed, lunging for their doors.

Brock pushed at his door. It had jammed. At the same instant he saw the hydraulic arm rise, swinging back its metal-toothed bucket for another assault, this time aimed directly at the front seats. Anticipating the crushing blow at any moment, Brock threw the weight of his shoulder against the heavy door. It shuddered and then burst open, and he dived for the road, hearing the sickening crunch of metal and glass behind him.

Dazed with the shock of how suddenly it had all happened, Brock lay motionless on the asphalt for a moment, then his adrenaline kicked in and he rolled swiftly over, leaping smoothly to his feet and out of range of the car. Poised for action, he assessed the situation with a swift, practiced eye. The car was destroyed, its entire front caved in to a mangled mess of twisted metal and broken glass. They were lucky to get out of that alive. The bucket on the end of the JCB's arm was wedged firmly into the front seats, like the bait swallowed by a fish that now dangled on the end of the rod.

Brock saw Ferguson limping towards the trench in an attempt to reach the earth mover, but Brock could see that the driver's cab was empty.

'No one here,' said Ferguson, as Brock joined him at the digger.

'Surprise, surprise,' said Brock grimly.

'What do you think? An accident?'

'Oh yes. That's why he came back for a second crack at us when the first one didn't do the job.'

'No sign of the driver.'

'Poor bloke is probably lying in a ditch somewhere – the real driver, I mean. Whoever did this has obviously skedaddled.'

Brock looked back at the line of cars building behind their crumpled Mercedes, the disciplined Swiss patiently waiting in their cars as if they were at a red traffic light.

'A little different to Rome and Siwa,' said Brock, 'except for the fact that we keep getting bushwhacked.'

Paul van Lederman looked grave as Brock and Ferguson walked into his office.

'Do you think he knows about the car?' muttered Matt from the corner of his mouth. 'I've written off a few now – Paul's getting cross.'

Van Lederman came forward. 'I've got bad news,' he said at once, not waiting for any greetings. 'I'm sorry to tell you both this, but John Ridge is dead.'

Brock felt his friend tense beside him. He saw Matt's face darken.

'What?' Matt said, disbelieving. 'Come on now. That's not possible. He's in the hospital, and he was fine when we left him. How on earth can he be dead?'

'A massive coronary. Apparently, there was a history of heart problems and the recent stress he was exposed to took its toll.'

'Bullshit!' rasped Ferguson, his soft voice unusually harsh.

'When did it happen?' enquired Brock.

'According to the hospital, about an hour ago. They called us at once.' Van Lederman gestured to them to sit down. Brock took a seat but Ferguson started pacing back and forth.

Brock said, 'No doubt he was on his own when this happened?'

'I know where you're going, Connor,' said van Lederman, 'and my own suspicions are high. But there's no evidence of foul play as yet. We can request a post-mortem if we wish to, but my own feeling is that any tracks will have been well and truly covered.'

Ferguson stopped pacing and said angrily, 'And as sure as the Pope is Catholic, Ammon Oil will be receiving a licence to use South Western's pipeline and refinery.'

'I know you're angry, Matt, but we have to keep cool.' Van Lederman returned to his desk and took his seat. 'We are not going to let up on our investigations for a moment, not least because there's been a development in an unexpected direction.'

'Another ruthless takeover by Subedei?' asked Brock.

'Not this time. The People's Republic of China has approached us with a view to joining ICE.'

Brock raised his eyebrows.

'I know,' said van Lederman. 'I was surprised, too.'

'Let me guess.' Brock tapped the leather arm of his chair. 'The application is commercially backed by Subedei Industries.'

'The very same. Subedei Industries is considered the flagship of the PRC. It would match any government funds.'

Brock laughed sardonically. 'I bet it would! A small price to pay, I would have thought, to get a voice on our board. I bet Subedei can't wait to start advising us on what company acquisitions, of *competitors*, should be investigated.' He shook his head. 'You have to hand it to Subedei. The bare-faced cheek of the man . . . This is his strategy to terminate our investigations.'

'At the very least,' replied van Lederman. 'We can assume his strategy is as multi-faceted as the man himself. But ICE cannot be bought. And he has given us an opportunity to investigate areas where we might not previously have had access. As an applicant member, Subedei Industries must allow us to study all transactions and operating records as a matter of course.'

176

'So while he thinks he is getting closer to us, we are in fact getting closer to him,' put in Ferguson.

Van Lederman allowed himself a small smile. 'Well, he can't really complain, can he?'

'How did this come about? Did the Chinese government or Subedei approach ICE?' asked Brock.

'Jean Luc Cambriol was asked to broker the deal. He is convinced that Subedei is on the level. Apparently, Subedei has requested that Interpol search for the missing Al Kadeh family.'

Brock and Ferguson looked at each other disbelievingly.

'He's got gall, I'll give him that,' said Ferguson.

'And meanwhile, we have permission to get close to Subedei.'

Van Lederman looked at Brock. 'Sir Duncan and I have been invited to attend a reception on board Subedei's yacht on the Nile the day after tomorrow. Unfortunately, both of us have prior engagements that we cannot cancel.'

'And we get to go in your place?' Ferguson smiled.

'No. Connor gets to go. Matt, I want you as back-up. Subedei's people may recognize you as John Ridge's colleague.'

'Well, hold on a second. A few of them might recognize Connor!' protested Ferguson.

'Most of the people who saw me won't be doing much talking,' said Brock. 'And the Russian who did . . . well, I'm sure they know by now that I'm a member of ICE. They'll be expecting to see me at some point. But if they're under the impression that Matt is not ICE but South Western Oil . . . wouldn't that be interesting, to say the least?'

Van Lederman frowned, considering. 'They'll know that Matt has at least some inkling of their aims.'

Ferguson said eagerly, 'Come on, take a chance, Paul! Let's see what they do about it.'

Van Lederman leaned back in his chair thoughtfully. 'Well, it might stir up a hornets' nest.'

'Isn't that what special operations is about?' said Brock.

'I had a fascinating tour last time I was in Egypt,' Ferguson added brightly. 'Wouldn't mind meeting the guide again actually. I'm sure we've got lots to talk about.'

Van Lederman shot him a quizzical look but before he could say anything, the intercom light flashed on his desk phone. He rose at once and headed towards the doors that led into the boardroom.

'You can fill me in on whatever you mean by that later. Right now, there's someone I want you to meet.'

Twenty-One

Brock recognized one of the two people standing at the far end of the room as Kurt Williams, the American Director of ICE. The other, a woman with blonde shoulder-length hair wearing a designer business suit, he did not. The woman's pale-blue eyes set in the strong and uncompromising Teutonic features of broad forehead, firm chin and aquiline nose turned directly towards Brock, instantly appraising him.

Brock blatantly returned the assessing look, guessing she was in her mid-forties yet appeared much younger, mostly because she clearly kept herself in shape, though the obvious finesse of coiffure, make-up and expensive clothes assisted.

Without waiting for a formal introduction the woman asserted herself; crossing the room with outstretched hand, smiling pleasantly to reveal even white teeth.

'Connor Brock, I've heard so much about you from my predecessor, Dieter Schmidt.

Instantly Brock guessed who she was as he took the firm grip of the proffered hand.

'All of it underestimated,' interrupted Van Lederman, looking slightly amused. 'But allow me to introduce you both. Connor, this is Carina Reisner.'

'The new CEO of UnitedRe,' cut in Brock.

'Good. Well, it seems you both have heard of each other,' continued Van Lederman.

'Forgive me, Paul, but you can imagine how much I was looking forward to meeting our elite former troubleshooter who I understand you were so fortunate as to lure away from us.'

Brock noticed the look of annoyance that momentarily crossed the disciplined Van Lederman's face. It had been just one of the bickering points between him and Dieter Schmidt, and now it looked as though Schmidt's replacement might be intending to carry the mantle, as the German female's sentence sweetly snookered him into an apologetic position.

But the seasoned ICE founder responded with a pot black. Brock smiled as his boss gently smoothed one side of his moustache, an idiosyncrasy that preceded his straight-to-the-point retorts.

'Ensuring that the global interests of founder members, such as UnitedRe, remain well protected without *infringing* corporate governance and risking any further embarrassment.'

Acutely aware of the bickering during Schmidt's term, Kurt Williams interrupted, acknowledging his own presence by grabbing Brock's and Ferguson's hands in quick succession; giving each quick hearty shakes. 'Good to see you, Connor – Matt.'

Built with the physique of a retired football player, the baggy dark suit and open yellow polo shirts he favoured did not set off his figure well; but his preference was for relaxed comfort. His wide smile, hazel eyes and brown schoolboy haircut delivered an easy charm.

'Though does it always have to be so cold here?' he added as he began to refill a coffee cup to the side of him.

'Welcome to ICE headquarters,' quipped back Matt.

'All right,' cut in van Lederman firmly. 'Let's sit down. We need to get down to business. Get yourselves coffee or water, or whatever you want, and take your places.' He took his own seat at the head of the table and tapped his entry information into the personal console at his place. The others quickly took their seats and waited expectantly.

Van Lederman looked at each of his colleagues in turn. 'You know what and who our current target is. Over the past forty-eight hours, we have compiled a ton of information about Subedei Industries, on both sides of the pond.' He shot a look at his American counterpart. 'The challenge was to trace all the holdings within the conglomerate – a mighty undertaking, as you might imagine. It has, though, been made a great deal easier by Subedei's application to join ICE. Carl Honstrom is currently on his way to Beijing with a team of auditors, in the odd position of being invited by Subedei to inspect everything.

'It would be nice to think that we could involve the Chinese government in our enterprise, but all signs point to the fact that the access gate is Subedei Industries and that means that it's a non-starter. However, we must, of course, be seen to go through all the motions diligently. There is little point saying anything further about that until we have received Carl's report.'

Van Lederman smiled warmly at Carina, his good humour restored. 'Carina – the floor is yours.'

The new CEO of the world's largest reinsurance group did not look at the notes laid out in front of her. Reisner had trained her focus to such a degree that she could quickly memorize the information her team of specialists had compiled for her.

'Thank you, Paul. The situation is simple. Over the past few years, the insurance market has been exposed to the increased potential of risk. That, in turn, has affected the reinsurance market that, as you know, insures the risks of those insurance companies. UnitedRe alone has been exposed to over two billion dollars in liabilities in the last five years, due to terrorism and the destruction of commercial enterprise. In addition, the unreliability of markets, the downward trend of shares and the non-viability of pension funds has caused UnitedRe, and those competitors that have followed our lead, to return to the basics of increased premiums and the safety net of underwriting for growth and risk-sharing.' Carina looked coolly at her colleagues. 'So far, so simple.

'Not surprisingly, a number of affluent Asian and Chinese corporations and individuals have taken the opportunity to become underwriters of UnitedRe. The returns can be high and, irrespective of whether losses are incurred, any committed sums will attract full tax relief. What will be of interest to you gentlemen is that Temujin Subedei, as from the end of last year, is one of our biggest underwriters.'

The others considered this for a moment.

Brock leaned forward, frowning. 'Are your underwriters able to choose the risks UnitedRe elects to reinsure?'

Carina held his gaze steadily. 'Yes. Since the Lloyds debacle over fifteen years ago, many underwriters insist that they be given choice and full undisclosed information.'

'And no doubt there's a pattern to Subedei's underwriting.'

Carina's face remained serious but her eyes glittered with the hint of a smile. 'There certainly is. All the risks that Subedei has chosen to underwrite are energy-related.'

'And none include either shipping or construction?' pressed Brock. 'Subedei's core industries?'

181

'Subedei Industries have underwritten twelve risks with UnitedRe. All relate to either oil and gas refineries or pipelines in Turkey, Azerbaijan, Armenia, Georgia, Kazakhstan, Iraq, Iran, Libya and Egypt. Most of the risk is across the Georgian border at Chechnya, where there is more potential for terrorist damage than accidental, although under current reinsurance terms we no longer cover such terrorism.'

'And I believe you have found links between these places and Subedei, in addition to his underwriting?' prompted van Lederman. The consoles at each seat flickered into life, showing a map of Europe and the Middle East, detailing the positions of oil sites, pipelines and refineries.

'Yes, thank you, Paul. Please look at your screen.' Carina paused for a moment and then continued. 'This map depicts the movement of oil from the major producing countries, either by pipeline or shipping. By far the biggest producer is, of course, Saudi Arabia, sitting on the world's largest proven reserves of two hundred and sixty-five billion barrels or twenty-five per cent of known supplies to date. Much of the oil Saudi exports to Europe and the US is carried by tanker either through the Suez Canal, or Sumed, the pipeline they funded in 1981. Sumed carries some eighty million tons annually from the Red Sea to Alexandria. Demand for oil in Europe and the US continues to increase and this has assured the viability of the major new pipelines you see emanating out from Iraq and the Caspian.

'The Caspian, though land-locked, has some proven one hundred billion barrels of reserves which will shortly be flowing through these pipelines. Similarly in Egypt, recent discoveries of large reserves close to the Libyan border are in the process of being piped to Alexandria.'

Brock narrowed his eyes as he concentrated on the illuminated map. 'The reserves appear to be at Siwa Oasis.'

'Yes. But that hasn't been officially announced yet.' Carina indicated her console. 'The yellow dots at Alexandria and Port Said, Ceyhan in Turkey, and around the Caspian represent Subedei's underwriting interests. They also include companies that are either directly or indirectly linked by ownership to Subedei Industries.'

'But there was no sign of oil at Siwa,' put in Brock flatly.

Van Lederman pressed his fingertips together and looked over at Brock. 'You'll be interested to know that the grand reception you are going to aboard Subedei's yacht is intended to officially announce the discovery of oil of Siwa, along with a major archaeological find. Thank you, Carina. Kurt – any comments?'

'Yes. Thanks, Carina. That was most enlightening.' William spoke in a leisurely, almost unconcerned manner. 'From a US perspective, we're interested in Subedei's activities in Venezuela. He appears to be behind the build-up of similar oil-production projects. And as we in the US import almost twelve million barrels a day, fifty-five per cent of our consumption, anything from a strike in Venezuela to unrest in the Gulf costs us heavy on our economic pocketbook.'

'How is the US's self-sufficiency strategy coming along?' asked van Lederman lightly, with a trace of sarcasm.

Williams laughed. 'All right. We call it the new American Dream. Despite Bush Senior's statement during the first Iraq War, that America must not be dependent on resources from countries that don't care for America, I'm afraid we still are. Nothing new there. Nixon said the same about being self suffi-cient over thirty years ago, and Carter promised to reduce dependency on foreign oil. Just twenty years ago, Reagan vowed that the American people and economy would never again be held hostage by the whim of any country or cartel.

'Yet here we are, with this guy seemingly building up a legit-imate cartel right on his own. However, for the moment it's not an urgent matter. Most of our imports come from Saudi Arabia and Subedei has no interest there. Couldn't have, either, with the existing royal cartel. Nevertheless, we're concerned, and I would sure like to know how this Subedei has managed to build up the interests he has.'

Brock continued to study the map. There had to be some pattern, he was sure of it. These were not just security invest-ments. His instinct told him that there was more to the situa-tion, and that the answer lay in the nature of the man he was investigating.

Carina said, 'With the Caspian reserves and the increase in Iraqi oil flowing to the west, the whole region is benefiting.' She shrugged. 'We must, of course, investigate Subedei's methods but we can't deny that his business acumen is right on target. From our perspective, it makes sound sense for him to invest his profits back into reinsuring the risk that his own insurers are covering.'

Brock looked at Williams. 'Kurt, how much of an economic stimulus to the US is the increasing supply of oil and its corresponding price reduction?'

Williams leaned back in his chair. 'Big. A drop of ten dollars a barrel is equivalent to receiving an annual fifty-billion-dollar tax cut.'

'Would you happen to know or estimate how much of the US dependency is on the Persian Gulf supplies?' asked Brock.

Kurt paused while he considered for a moment. 'In the vicinity of twenty-five per cent of our imports, to round up the figure. Why?'

'Well, just hypothetically speaking, if that twenty-five per cent were taken away overnight, without any warning at all, how would it affect the United States?'

'It would hurt us real bad but, hey, never mind the States, buddy – it would affect Europe just as much. Sure, we would have to get our oil elsewhere, probably from the Stans and the Caspian reserves, but the price would sky-rocket for everyone. Remember back in '82 when the price spiked up to over fifty dollars a barrel.'

'According to the International Monetary Fund's estimates, a ten-dollar hike in prices cuts world economic growth by one per cent. Literally hundreds of billions,' put in Reisner.

'Then,' said van Lederman, 'the effect of dramatically increasing the barrel price would be to seriously damage global growth and hold western countries to ransom.'

'And there would be another war,' replied the American flatly.

'But against whom this time?' asked Brock. 'There's no dictator providing a convenient excuse. The only war would be an economic one – and that requires legitimacy. The legalities could be questioned through the courts for months, years, even. The west wouldn't have an option – they'd have to pay the ransom.'

Williams nodded seriously. 'Yes, but in reality, it works both ways. The Persian Gulf needs us as much as we need them.'

'Unless they found their market elsewhere, from another

superpower. Say . . . China?' Brock looked questioningly at his colleagues. 'Just a thought.'

There was an uncomfortable shift around the table. Williams considered the question, a worried frown on his boyish features. 'OK, China would jump at the chance. Most of their crude oil comes by pipeline from Russia and the Stans. But the supplies are limited due to Russia's state pipeline monopoly, Transneft, which has already cut back flow to its shipping port at Primorsk in the Gulf of Finland to meet the increasing demands of neighbouring Estonia and Latvia. If Transneft were to cut back flow from Kazakhstan and Tajikistan, bordering China, China's own production would not be in any way sufficient for its needs.'

'So if Saudi could not deliver the oil to the west, they would have no option but to tie up with China, which could soon become a permanent relationship,' said Brock emphatically.

Williams looked solemn. 'I have to admit that many quarters believe that Saudi and the US tolerate each other because of their mutually useful economic relationship. Given half the chance, the Saudis would probably relish the opportunity to have a new bed partner who's less critical of their fundamentalism, and doesn't make it an evangelical goal to westernize or Americanize the Arabic Muslim world.'

'And, in turn, China would jump at the opportunity to have an oil-rich partner with no concerns over China's human rights policy,' added van Lederman.

'The foundation for a good "live and let live" relationship then?' said Brock, a sharp edge to his voice.

'A nightmare scenario. But only a hypothetical one, I'm glad to say.' Williams leaned forward, an uncomfortable look on his usually cheery face.

Brock's expression was serious. 'Looking at the pattern of Subedei's interests, and assuming he's a good chess player, I would say that the hypothetical is closer to becoming the actual than we might like. Look.'

They all turned to their screens as Brock drew electronically on the map on his own screen. He connected the rich oil wells numerously dotted around the Persian Gulf with a fictional pipeline that only had to cross neighbouring Iran before it could connect into the vast existing pipeline network that traversed the Stans direct to China and Russia. Brock then drew a thick line across the very thin gap of the Suez Canal.

'Jesus, Connor, you can't be serious,' said Williams, his voice rising a key. 'No one in their right mind would dare cut that economic umbilical cord. The Egyptian government relies heavily on the revenue it receives from us – it would never allow it. Not only that, but many commercial heavyweights are dependent on the passage of the Suez Canal. There would be hell to pay.'

Brock said, 'It was the Egyptian government that closed it the last time back in the sixties after the Israeli War. I seem to remember that scenario gave the US a bad case of oil indigestion right up into the seventies.'

Williams pursed his lips and ran a hand through his hair.

Van Lederman got to his feet and began to pace at the head of the table. 'All very interesting, but the state of the global economy today is vastly different to that of thirty years ago. Let's look at all this carefully. If your theory is correct, Brock, and the aim is to shut off the Suez Canal, then, from a European perspective, that simple event could well act as a catalyst to split the European and the US economies from the whole of Asia.'

'And as Asia becomes more self-sufficient, the west becomes more dependent on it,' added Brock. 'Dependent on an energy cartel run by Subedei.'

Williams folded his arms, not wanting to be convinced. 'There is still the Sumed pipeline. He'd have to cut that off too.'

Carina Reisner coughed. 'Er – interesting you should say that. We actually took out reinsurance for the new Red Sea to Alexandria pipeline intended to update Sumed. The ownership is Egyptian, but the licence to operate it has been granted to Subedei Industries. I've just noticed that it is not marked on the map as it should be. It runs parallel to Sumed.'

'OK,' said Williams seriously, 'that does place a sharper angle of concern on things. But, frankly, I can't see it happening.'

Van Lederman turned to face his American colleague. 'I'm beginning to fall in with Brock's line of conjecture. It's starting to make good sense – and it's the only scenario that does. As you very well know, Kurt, relations between America and those countries that perceive her as imposing alien cultural values on them have never been worse. Think of it from an Arabic point of view – if there was the chance not to be beholden to the

US, not to be forced to accept terms or risk American military might, and to receive equal wealth and technical support from another rising superpower, one that does not view Americanization as the definition of globalization . . . well, don't you think that would seem attractive? If not irresistible?

'As I understand Connor's hypothesis, we have a situation that is like a game of chess where the active player has been placing his strategic moves for some time and the other has not even realized the game has started. Suez may seem an isolated pawn but its strategic blockage puts Europe in check.'

Van Lederman motioned at all the yellow dots depicting Subedei's interests. 'All these other pieces control the field to the west. The only loose piece – the Saudi Kingdom – will seek refuge in the east by default.'

Reisner stared at her screen, her blue eyes reflecting the colours of the map she was appraising. 'My god,' she breathed. 'It's a win-win situation for Subedei. China gets the resources for growth. He can legitimately maintain high oil prices which eventually have to be accepted by the west. Egypt makes money from the oil reserves now available in Siwa, which he also controls and, when Suez reopens, there'll be a nice new status quo – a tight relationship between Asia and the Middle East. No wonder he has underwritten his own interests. Maintaining their operations is too big a risk . . .'

'. . . for an empire that encompasses most of Asia and controls the west,' finished Brock grimly.

Ferguson whistled lightly through his teeth. 'Geez – no wonder we're beginning to get hot under the collar about Subedei.'

Reisner's eyes shone with excitement. 'You have to admire Subedei's audacity,' she burst out. 'What a coup, to swing power and influence from the US and Western Europe towards Asia and China.'

After the experience of the last ninety-six hours, culminating in almost being squashed like a sardine in a can, the last thing Brock wanted to hear was praise for Subedei and his ruthless methods. His jaw tight, he growled, 'Like a modern Attila the Hun, storming imperialism at the gates of a complacent Rome, eh? I don't believe that the people who've paid for it with their lives would share your sentiments, Carina.'

Reisner stared back at him, her eyes momentarily frightened.

She obviously hadn't expected such a strong response. She regained control quickly, and turned her gaze downwards. 'Forgive me, Connor, if I gave the impression that I'm endorsing Subedei. That really is the last thing I mean to do.'

Brock's anger left him and he relaxed. Perhaps he was over-reacting a little. After all, Carina had only said what a lot of people would think when they saw the extent of Subedei's achievements. He let it pass. 'Could you give me a schedule of all of Subedei's interests that you know about? I'm particularly interested in the areas of shipping and construction.'

'You'll have it today.' Carina made a quick note to herself, scrawling on a pad with her Mont Blanc pen, and glanced up again at Brock, as though checking to see if she was forgiven. She risked a small smile and he returned it.

Brock turned to Van Lederman. 'Paul, I'll be returning to the Sinai Peninsula tomorrow.'

Van Lederman frowned. He had seen the tiredness and strain in his director of special operations. 'Is that a good idea?'

Brock laughed. 'Don't worry, the last thing on my mind is taking leave. This time I intend visiting the western side of the peninsula: the Gulf of Suez. Perhaps a trip through the canal itself might be just what is needed prior to our invitation to sojourn the Nile around Alexandria.'

Matt Ferguson turned towards Brock. 'What about me?'

'You're steering.'

Twenty-Two

'Connor, *mon ami*, good to hear your voice!' Ahmed Amuyani had been in his office just five minutes when the phone rang. 'As ever you catch me right between lectures.'

The Iranian professor sat back in his chair, a broad grin on his face. It was always a pleasure to hear from Connor, though it happened all too rarely these days. How long was it since they used to spend their evenings in dark Parisian bars and cafes, locked in deep discussion? They debated politics, history, morals, religion . . . anything that crossed their minds or seemed of relevance to them. Now Amuyani thought about it, it was more than twenty years ago. He had been rescued from Tehran back in 1979 by Cameron Brock, just in time to avoid the death sentence. The Ayatollah Khomeini did not take kindly to outspoken academics criticizing his regime, it turned out. Brock had brought Amuyani to his own flat in Paris and installed him there while the professor considered his future. During his stay, he had made the acquaintance of Cameron's son, Connor, a dark, brooding boy who had just left school and was spending a summer in Paris before going up to Edinburgh University. He'd been a surprisingly mature boy, and Amuyani had been impressed by his breadth of knowledge and grasp of world affairs. He'd always thought it a shame that Connor did not pursue an academic career, as he himself had, gaining a tenure at the Sorbonne as a professor of history. To Amuyani's thinking, a military career meant the waste of a fine mind. When Connor Brock had joined the air force, Amuyani had deemed it a sad day. Nevertheless, he was glad to have remained his firm friend.

'Between lectures?' Brock's voice was amused. 'How far apart are they these days?'

'Connor, I'm a very hard-working man. In my own way.'

'Hmm. Your own inimitable way of making hard work take a very long time indeed.'

'Ah, but what is time if not the slave of man?' returned the jovial professor. 'If man cannot master his time, how can he be master of his life?'

'By making the hours work for him instead of working for hours?' suggested Brock.

'Ah, yes! Good to see that you have not forgotten. But students today never remember. And so I must constantly remind them that it is not the hours they put in that count, it is what they put in the hours. And by doing so, I break my own rules and waste my time, but such is life. Practice and theory will never be bedfellows.' Amuyani guffawed with laughter, which was followed by a coughing fit. When he got his breath back, he said ruefully, 'And for all that time is my slave, it seems to be gaining an advantage over me. I'm feeling my years a bit, Connor. You'd better come and visit me quick, or it may be too late. I'm just a little wheezing, balding old man these days.'

'Come on now, Ahmed. I don't believe that for a second. And your mind is as sharp as it ever was. Now – the reason for my call, besides saying hello, is to ask you a very small favour.'

'Is it one that I will enjoy?' asked the professor mischievously.

'Cyrus the Great, Alexander the Great, Genghis Khan, Temujin Subedei. I would have thought those names would set you salivating right away.'

'Music to my ears. But I thought you said it was small . . . nothing about those men is small.'

'For your resourceful mind it is.'

'You flatterer. Just like my students, you want to take up the precious time that's left to me! Ah! Still, sounds interesting. How, specifically, do you want me to help?'

'I'm going to email you some documents. They contain information in relation to a specific artefact, or artefacts. I would like your creative thoughts on them and also any details that might relate them to a book called *The Secret History of the Mongols*.'

'Ah, the Mongols! A perfectly fearless and nomadic culture! One that influenced and shook the world, only to be brought down by the very tribal fighting that made it great when brought together under the Khan and his generals.'

'That's the one. All right if I call you in a couple of days?'

'I fear that once again you have become master of my time, *mon ami*,' said Ahmed dolefully.

'OK, now I feel guilty,' conceded Brock.

'Wonderful.' The professor was jovial again. 'The time you spend on being so will be part recompense for a poor professor squandering his, immersed in research.'

Amuyani could hear Brock's unsuppressed chuckle on the line.

'Ahmed, you will never change. By the way, this one is for ICE, so of course there is the usual fee.'

The professor stayed silent.

'And naturally I will bring you a bottle of Lagavulin malt the next time I am in Paris, though you know I would anyway.'

'Ah, my time is blessed with good friends and interesting things to do. Talking of which I must go. Send me those documents and I will get started right away. *Au revoir, mon ami.*'

When Brock put the phone down, he was smiling. The professor always had the ability to cheer him up. But he had to get back to business, fast. His next call was to ICE's techno-guru Pete Kenachi, asking him to send the necessary documents over to Amuyani.

'Sure.' Kenachi paused and Brock could hear the rhythmic chewing of gum down the line. 'What do you want me to do with this manuscript?'

'We'll have to scan it and send it electronically. We can't risk exposing a document as old as that to much light, so try and get it right the first time, if you can. Then it will have to be heavily encoded – it's important that it can't be picked up by anyone other than the people we want. Can you do that?'

'Er, yeah,' replied Kenachi idly. 'Of course.'

Brock had known he could. Kenachi was a wizard, everyone knew that. An American Japanese whose name appeared on the 'most wanted hackers' list at Langley, he was insouciantly brilliant.

'Great. Thanks, Pete. As well as sending it to Professor Amuyani, hide copies in the files of all those museums you discovered had received enquires from Subedei. Then put it in our vault until I can return it.'

'I thought you didn't want copies floating about.'

191

'I don't. But with the kind of money that Subedei is offering, they are going to keep looking for anything he wants and if people start turning up more copies of this thing, it will keep Subedei quiet trying to track them down, and take the heat off Maria Zanoletti in Rome.'

'Gotcha. Clear as day. But this is the guy who ordered the Vatican break-in, isn't it? Aren't you worried he'll do the same at other museums?'

'Not at all,' replied Brock comfortably.

'How can you be so sure?'

'Simply because I intend to tell Subedei beforehand.'

Despite all the time he had spent living in Switzerland, which, over the years, must add up to quite a lot, Brock never considered himself a resident. The very fact that he had insisted on a houseboat on Lake Zee rather than a flat in town or a chalet in the mountains seemed to reinforce his lack of permanency. Even his home was ready to be on the move at a moment's notice.

Actually, he'd always loved being near the water. Growing up in Kinloss in Scotland, he'd spent hours gazing out over the sea at Findhorn Bay, watching the water change from slate-grey through mineral-green to an almost lavender-pink as it reflected the colours of the Scottish sky. Now he could never bear to be too far away from it. As part of his recruitment package to ICE, he'd insisted on a home similar to the houseboat he owned on the Thames in London. Van Lederman had agreed without argument.

'Won't you be a bit isolated?' was Paul's only comment.

'Just the way I like it, Paul, you know that.'

Van Lederman had come up trumps with the converted Dutch barge. Brock wasn't exactly a homebody but over the years he'd made it cosy and welcoming, somewhere he could find a bit of peace and quiet, enjoy a couple of his favourite malt whiskies, listen to blues high priestess, Nina Simone, and sink into a book.

He treasured that moment now, as he relished a little bit of time on his own. He padded about the sitting room on the barge, getting himself a drink. The boat was a long, flat vessel, much larger than it appeared from the outside. It boasted almost lavish accommodation, with a thirty-foot sitting room, a kitchen, two double bedrooms with en suite bathrooms, and a box room, which Brock had set up as a high-tech study. The riveted steel exterior was harsh and industrial but inside he had banished anything that might connect the place with its old role of moving quantities of freight about the waterways of Europe. The floor was soft with thick Persian rugs; a Russian-style wood-burning stove kept the place warm and homely; the furniture was a mixture of battered antiques and a comfortable new sofa. Paintings – many of the stunning Moray landscape of his home – brightened the walls, and a state-of-the-art stereo let calming music float out into the room.

Armed with his whisky, Brock slumped into his favourite armchair. He'd been looking forward to this moment. The last few days had taken it out of him, in more ways than one. Not only had he been fighting for his life more times than he felt comfortable with, but his night with Maria – though a delightful experience, of course – had robbed him of several hours of precious sleep.

'Connor Brock!' he said to himself, laughing. 'What have you come to if a night of passion with a beautiful Italian woman makes you regret a bit of lost sleep! You are getting old, my friend.'

As he settled into his chair his cell phone played its familiar melody.

He was tempted to leave it, but the habits of a lifetime forced him to answer. 'Brock,' he said.

'Connor. Hello.' The woman's voice had a soft Scottish lilt.

'Myrna!' Brock smiled broadly. 'How are you?'

'I'm fine – and so is Andy. But we're wondering why we haven't heard from you for a while.'

Brock stretched out his legs and stared at the flickering flames inside the stove. 'I was ordered on leave and now I'm back on operations. I'm sorry, Myrna. I should have called before.'

'Kathy's been asking after you.'

Brock's stomach clenched and his fist tightened around the phone. He said nothing and the dead air between Zurich and Scotland crackled faintly.

'Connor?'

'I'm still here.'

193

'You usually call at least once a month. She's been wondering when you're going to ring her.'

Brock heard the mild tone of accusation in his sister-in-law's voice.

'How is she?' he said, at last.

'Oh, Connor, she's adorable. Beautiful. I've emailed you some photos – have you got them?'

'I haven't logged in today.'

'Well, they're waiting for you. And she and Lucy are closer than ever, like twins. You should see them together.'

'Where is she now?'

'It's late here, Connor. She's in bed.' Myrna hesitated and then said, 'To be honest, I wasn't sure whether to call you at all. I know you prefer me to wait to hear from you. But it's been so long . . . I was beginning to get worried.'

'I'm fine,' Brock said gruffly. 'I'm sorry. I'll call again, when she's awake.'

'And will we be seeing you any time soon?'

'I can't say. I'm caught up in something big at the moment. I'm travelling again tomorrow and don't know when I'll be back.'

There was a gentle sigh down the phone.

'Myrna . . .'

'I know, I know. Just don't let too long go by. You don't know what you're missing.'

'I do,' Brock said sadly. 'I promise you, I do.'

When Myrna had filled him in on the family news and said goodbye, Brock sat for a moment in contemplation. Then he went to the study and logged in to his email. He printed out the schedule from Carina Reisner and folded and stuffed it into his top pocket before turning to open the attachment on Myrna's message that was waiting for him.

The screen was filled with a beaming face: bright azure eyes, like his own, soft round cheeks, a smiling mouth revealing perfect, tiny white teeth. White blonde hair was pulled into two pigtails that curled down to a pink collar, a fringe swept the brow.

'Kathy,' whispered Brock. She was the image of Heather. It was painful to look at her.

He downloaded the other pictures: Kathy with her pet rabbit, almost as big as she was; Kathy and Lucy giggling into the camera, their arms round each other's waists; Kathy caught in a moment of wistful thoughtfulness. His own wistful memories came.

Ever since the death of Heather he had cut all ties that reminded him of a homely situation. His daughter Kathy had known no other family than that of Heather's sister, Myrna, who had brought the child up as her own and a sister to her own daughter of the same age. Brock played the part of an adoring godfather and uncle to his own daughter.

He had never been fully persuaded that her mother's death had been an accident, yet whatever the truth of the matter, Brock had insisted that, with the nature of his work and lifestyle, it was vital to keep the fact that he had a daughter secret. His sister-in-law had agreed only on the condition that the truth was explained to Kathy by Connor when she became old enough to understand.

'It is what Heather would have wanted,' she had argued. 'She would want her daughter to carry the name of the man she loved.'

Brock smiled as he raised himself from his chair and walked over towards the wide picture widow. He recalled the words of his wife's twin sister. Myrna McCoy Adams was just as strong-willed and stubborn as Heather, and her own husband, local banker, Andy, had been persuaded to take on the name of McCoy, double-barrelling his name. Similarly Brock had to readily agree when Heather had asked him.

'I love you and I'll be proud to carry your name, but out of love for my father and respect to his heritage I will carry his too.'

John McCoy was the last male descendant of his line after his younger brother had been killed in action in the Falklands in 1982. The McCoy's of Inverness were renowned as sound patriots both of Scotland and Inverness, and he had been delighted when both Brock and Adams had included his daughter's maiden name in their own.

Brock frowned as a black Mercedes cruising along the Mythenquai diverted his reverie to the earlier attempt on his and Matt's life. He knew it could be no accident simply because it was too coincidental. But the timing of it meant that someone was following their every move. And to make it look like an accident involved a creative logistical planner. One thing was certain; he could count on there being more.

'Then the best line of defence is one of attack,' said Brock quietly to himself as he pulled out the schedule that Carina Reisner had emailed him. 'In which case, you must know your enemy.'

Twenty-Three

Captain Raoul Thamad felt as though something of the spirit of the Suez Canal was in his blood. Not only had he spent his whole life working on it, from the time he was a young boy, but his father and grandfather and their ancestors for six generations had been operating as master dredgers on the greatest man-made river in the world.

Captain Thamad made it a point of pride to know everything about Suez. He devoted his spare time to learning its history and making sure his son, Ali, knew it too. He was known for his ability to summon up any obscure fact about the canal and its construction. 'This thing is a marvel!' he would say to anyone who would listen. 'A wonder of the world.'

He liked to gather an audience about him and relate the history of the canal. He would tell them that the concept of linking the Mediterranean and Red Seas dated back over forty centuries to the reign of Amenhotep I, but the idea had not become reality until 150 years later, in 1874 BCE, under the rule of Snosert III.

'Imagine that!' Captain Raoul would say. 'The greatest marine engineering feat that the ancient world ever witnessed! All the digging was done by hand, with picks and baskets, using slave labour. An amazing achievement, a great one. The first man-made canal.'

After that, during the next 1,200 years, the canal went through a cycle of silting up and being reopened. The captain would shake his head over the waterway's long history of decay and resurrection. 'Depending on who was in power, this thing was considered a marvel and a necessity – or a threat to be got rid of. Darius had it cleared because the Isthmus of Suez was of great importance to Persia; Ptolemy II kept it going and extended it. But then it was allowed to fall into disrepair, neglected by everyone until the Romans came along in 98AD, re-dug it and rechristened it Trajan's Canal, after their emperor.' The captain would sniff scornfully. 'Typical Romans, claiming everything for their own.'

The captain knew well enough the rest of the history of the canal – how it declined along with the Roman Empire and silted up under Byzantine rule, to be revived following the Ottoman conquest of Egypt in 642AD until Caliph Abu Ja' far al-Mansour ordered it filled in, lest it provide a supply route for the rebels threatening his rule. But it was the modern history of the canal that he preferred, for that was when his own family began to play their part in the illustrious story of the great waterway.

'It was the French who started it,' he would declare. 'And the Venetians. So I suppose they were, after all, good for something, though all they really wanted was to get their greedy hands on the East Indian trade. A route from the Mediterranean to the Indian Ocean would break the monopoly of the Portuguese, the Dutch and the English. But their schemes came to nothing until Napoleon came here – that puffed-up Corsican with the idea of being the new Alexander! He had his eyes on Egypt and he had his eyes on India, and he was clever enough to see that this ancient canal might help him. He ordered a survey but his engineer miscalculated the height of the Red Sea – he thought it was ten metres above the Mediterranean and that a series of locks would be needed. So it all came to nothing again and it wasn't until fifty years of negotiation and surveys had passed that further progress was made.

'This,' he would announce proudly, 'is where the Thamad family have their vital role. When Sa'id Pasha, viceroy of Egypt, gave permission to the French Suez Canal Company in 1859 to excavate the old route, digging commenced in the same way it had some four thousand years before. Peasants dug by hand with picks and baskets.

'But it was no good – they needed to move almost one hundred million cubic metres of sediment. So they brought in European labour, with their dredgers and steam shovels. Dredging was cheaper than dry excavation, you see, so they flooded the terrain artificially and then dredged it wherever they could.

'Dredging became a sought-after occupation and some of the harder-working local peasants were offered the opportunity to become master dredgers. The first Egyptian dredger was a man called Raoul Thamad – my direct ancestor. He operated here, on the Tur'at as-Suways al Hulway, meaning Sweet Water Canal. The Suez, of course.' The captain would look at his audience, his chest puffing with pride. 'He was a hero. Do you know why? In 1865, there was a winter flood and under the pressure of the water, the alluvium barricades collapsed and the entire settlement below, where all the workers lived, was threatened with utter destruction and the loss of many lives. So Thamad drove his eighty-ton boat into the barricade and filled the gap, giving the settlement the precious time they needed to evacuate. After the flood, there was a terrible cholera epidemic and it was sixteen weeks before they recovered his dredging boat. His decomposing body was found still clutching the wheel. They gave him a medal for it, a posthumous award for his bravery and courage. And his son Ali took over the recovered boat and continued in his father's profession.'

Everybody would react well to this tale, gasping at the self-sacrifice of the captain's ancestor and congratulating him on his noble forebear. So that when the captain told them of the magnificent ceremony four years later, with all the sovereign families of Europe attending, when the royal ship *Al Mahrousa* sailed through the canal, followed by a convoy of 777 other ships carrying almost 10,000 invited guests, it was as though the splendour of the achievement was the Thamad family's alone.

Since then, the Thamads had continued their work as dredgers, maintaining the canal by clearing the constant build-up of silt that would otherwise ground the vessels as they passed on their way from the Mediterranean to the Red Sea and back.

Captain Raoul Thamad stood now on the deck of his dredger, watching with a jaded eye the fantastic array of colour that the rising sun reflected off the Great Bitter Lake. He took an aggressive swig of the very strong and sweet coffee that the first mate, his son Ali, had delivered to him while he contemplated the dawn of another frustrating day.

'Hey, Captain! Another day on this Great Bitter Lake, eh? They named it well, didn't they?'

Thamad looked up, his face pinched with bad humour. The speaker was his son, Ali, a thin and muscular young man, with large brown eyes and a crop of black hair, which continuously sought escape from a grimy white hat matching the colour of his T-shirt and loose trousers. He had recognized his father's mood and was trying to lift it.

Thamad smiled at his son. His heavy, swarthy face, exposed to a lifetime of salt, hot sun and the pollution of ten thousand tankers, looked more like tough leather than human skin, cracked into a delta of deep lines.

'I wish I could tell you with sweet words that we are able to move north. But we're stuck here. It's madness. The work deepening the navigation channels from here to the Kabrit Bypass is done, yet still we wait here, while the channel through from El Kab to Al Qantarah silts up – as it always does this time of year. Your grandfather always said to me, "It's not the deepening that counts, Raoul, it's the maintaining. Be vigilant. Nature is always at work, undoing your efforts." But will anyone listen to me? For six months we break our backs deepening the south, while the north gets shallower every day!'

Ali came up to join his father on the forward deck. 'I thought that the new satellite readings and depth-sounding equipment installed at Al Qantarah confirmed there was no problem.'

'Pah! We have become the slave of technology. My nose tells me when something smells fresh or rotten, and right now something is rotten.'

Ali leaned against the rail. 'In that case, Captain, I'm with you. This is the flagship of the fleet. You are the captain. Let's just return north anyway. What's to stop us? We've done our work, after all, and finished it ahead of time.'

Captain Thamad eyed his son with pride. 'You are a real Thamad, my boy. You're like your grandfather – you have his independent spirit.'

Ali took the compliment gracefully and said politely, 'As did our forefather, your namesake, Captain. Perhaps if he'd not acted as he had, our family name would not be so respected today.'

The boy had touched on something that was fermenting in his own mind. Thamad had already been seriously considering returning, irrespective of orders. Listening to his son made him reach a decision. He straightened up, feeling his authority for the first time in weeks. 'Prepare to depart by noon. That way we'll be in good time to be first through tomorrow.'

* * *

200

The agency girl breathed a sigh of relief as her boss finally left his desk. She'd delivered yet another espresso to his office only five minutes ago and it seemed to have done its work. The director of Interpol sauntered past her desk, heading for the corridor.

'I will be back in a moment,' said Jean Luc Cambriol briefly, hardly looking at his temporary secretary as he went past.

She smiled back, her Eurasian features demure and innocent. As soon as the door to the corridor closed behind him, she got up from her desk. Hearing her own heart beating, she quickly entered his office and sat down in front of the open laptop that lay running on the desk. She entered the internet address and saw the dialogue box appear requesting its password.

She had been lucky. Three weeks earlier, on only her third day filling in for Cambriol's regular secretary, the opportunity to memorize the necessary five digits had presented itself. It had been so easy. The Frenchman was just a typical man, after all, and her timing had been perfect. Just as he had gained access to the site and was about to enter his code, she'd walked in with a pile of papers and dropped them, scattering the contents everywhere. She'd bent to collect them, and gazed up quickly to see the Frenchman staring straight down her gaping shirt, just as she'd intended.

He'd been so discomfitted that he'd entered his code clearly before her eyes, his distraction making him slower and more deliberate. She'd memorized the keys. Mission accomplished.

With the secure ICE intranet page open, the girl quickly located the information she sought, copied it and emailed it to the usual destination. The file was much larger than usual because of the director's trip to Beijing, and, as the extra few seconds ticked by, she felt a film of cold sweat form on the back of her neck.

With rising panic, she exited the site, deleted the record from the sent box and returned the screen to its former view. She was sitting back down at her desk just as the Interpol director entered the room. Her relief turned to panic as she realized that she had not erased the record stored in the delete box.

'I thought you'd said we'd be sailing up the Suez! What happened to our pleasure cruise on a felucca?' moaned Ferguson, sweating despite the cold night air, as he swerved the yellow van to avoid another oncoming lorry. 'Is it me or don't they know how to drive here?'

Brock looked up from the map he was studying. 'A little bit of both, I'd say,' he said with a smile. 'As for the felucca – sorry, Matt, I changed my mind. We'll be joining the main road at Faqus in a few kilometres. From there, it's a straight run to Al Qantarah passing right under the Suez Canal. According to the schedule I received from UnitedRe, Subedei has three known interests directly on the canal, all acquired within the last six months. There's the new pipeline from Suez to Alexandria running alongside Sumed; Khan Marine and Dredging, also under former government licence; and the Al Kadeh cement-making facility at Al Qantarah.'

Brock had taken careful steps to make sure that he and Ferguson would shake off any parties interested in their where-abouts. They'd originally been scheduled to travel Egyptian Air to Alexandria that morning, but a call to a pilot friend who flew DHL transport planes had ensured that he and Ferguson made an unregistered night flight to Cairo. They borrowed a DHL van to transport themselves and their equipment along local roads, as far as Faqus. Brock was certain that no one had been able to trace them. After the incident in the Zurich underpass, he didn't want to take any chances.

'There's the turn-off,' directed Brock. 'According to the satellite image and this map, I would guess that this portion of the Suez Canal is the most strategic. It's equidistant from the alluvium lakes either side of it and the main road access to the eastern Med. It also happens to be the former core facility of Al Kadeh Construction.'

'Is that our main aim on this mission? To find out why Subedei was so intent on acquiring the business?'

'Yes. Particularly as he has so magnanimously relinquished his legal interest in the New Pyramids, if Cambriol's information is correct. It puts a whole new slant on the thing. What on earth could his motive be for getting his hands on an Egyptian construction company that's successful enough but surely small fry for someone like Subedei?'

'Your hunch is that he plans to close Suez, right?'

Brock looked back at the map. 'Well, the Al Kadeh facility lies exactly on the canal's most vulnerable place. It's the only ten-kilometre section of the canal with no passing bays and a maximum allowable draft of sixteen metres. Even that can be reduced very quickly with alluvium build-up.'

Ferguson looked both amused and cynical. 'So what's the plan? Shall we bowl up to the facility and see if anyone feels like telling us what their boss is planning? Is that it?'

'In a manner of speaking,' answered Brock.

'Meaning nice and early, so that we don't disturb them, eh?'

An hour later, just before the first light of dawn, they parked the van on the canal side in a position that afforded a complete view of the Al Kadeh facility. As Ferguson prepared the scuba equipment they had brought with them, Brock scanned the area.

Hugging the concrete quay were three large buildings. The first had open doors and appeared to be a semi-enclosed storing bay for gravel and alluvium. The second was enclosed, fronted with wide hangar access doors. The third, joined to the second by an access bridge at first-floor level, seemed to be a suite of offices.

Ten minutes later, Brock, wearing a torso wetsuit, slid into the warm murky water. His full-face mask allowed him to speak as well as receive from a separate dive radio, the close-fitted ear sockets and wireless microphone taped to his chin. His buoyancy jacket had a powerful thin-beam halogen torch and his Leatherman attached to it. Strapped above his dive watch on his left wrist was a depth gauge and directional compass, and on his right leg, a dive knife.

'Now, remember,' he heard Ferguson say in his earpiece radio, 'twenty thousand bloody great ships pass by here every year. By my reckoning, that's fifty during daylight hours, so this is not the ideal place for a dive.'

Brock had already calculated that, according to the timetable, there was another full hour before the first convoy arrived at Al Qantarah. 'I've enough air for less than an hour so I'll be out long before the first ship passes through.'

Staying just below the surface, Brock swam the 200 metres towards the deserted-looking plant. He dropped a further metre to bypass the security netting and came up under the loading jetty close to a metal ladder leading up to the concrete platform. Standing on a rung, he quickly removed his aqualung, face mask and flippers, hooking them on the first steel rung above the water level, and smoothly climbed the ladder.

There were two small dredgers moored to the pier, both lying heavy in the water. Brock moved stealthily through the loading cranes that filled the yard towards the looming warehouse doors of the centre building. Trying the handle of the side entrance door, Brock felt it open. Stepping inside, he heard a television and saw its light coming from one of the prefabricated offices built on the steel-framed mezzanine floor of the warehouse. To the side of the office was the access bridge.

'Five-minute report, Connor,' came Ferguson's tinny voice through Brock's earpiece. 'All OK?'

Brock scanned the floor of the warehouse. 'The place is just full of cement, there must be thousands of sacks of it.'

'Well, now, that's strange, isn't it? What are they doing in a cement-making factory?'

'OK, wise guy. Just concentrate on keeping a look out.'

Silently, Brock climbed the steps to the first floor and made his way to the access bridge at the far end of the mezzanine level. He dropped low and scuttled quickly past the watchman's office, opened the bridge door and in twenty seconds had crossed into a newly decorated hall that led to a series of extravagant offices overlooking the canal.

The first two doors were both unlocked and revealed nothing untoward. The third proved to be locked. A cursory glance indicated that the lock was a sub-standard latch that gave way quickly under pressure from Brock. Allowing his intuition to guide him towards anything out of the ordinary, he scanned the room.

'Looks like the morning shift will be arriving soon, Connor.' Ferguson's voice buzzed tinnily in his ear. 'Two truck-loads of people heading your way.'

'Understood.'

Calculating the risk, Brock flicked the switch by the door and a sumptuous-looking office, far too grand for a construction-material facility, was bathed in light. He moved decisively towards the marble-topped desk with a view to searching the drawers. As he did so, he glanced at the doodled drawing on the notepad by the phone.

'Gates opening. You have no more than five. Watch yourself.'

Brock glanced at his watch. 'Understood.'

The drawers were locked. Brock snatched up the doodle, returned to the door, switched off the light and exited. He sped down the adjacent stairs to the ground floor.

To his immediate right was a further short enclosed passageway, which, by the look of the green and red buttons to the side of the door, was pressurized. Brock pressed the green button; there was a short whirring sound and the door opened. At the end of the passage was another door with similar buttons. Unlike all the other signs about the place, which were in Arabic, it was in English: *M. Maynard – Strictly No Admittance.*

Brock smiled as he pressed the green button to open the door. The arrogance of the English, he thought to himself. So many of them were still under the illusion that former colonies did what they were told and everyone in them understood English.

Considerably colder than the other offices owing to great air-cooling units, in addition to the overhead air-conditioning, this room extended across a wide expanse. Most of the space had been devoted to a chemistry laboratory with testing areas. The part that had been reserved as an office looked like a pigsty, with cartons of fast food lying where they had been thrown. A large plan on the wall behind the desk caught his eye; it looked familiar. After a moment, he realized that it was a detailed plan of the doodle he had in his pocket. For a whole minute, Brock studied it.

Despite the urgency of the situation, Ferguson's voice was calm and professional. 'Exit time, lights are going on all over the place.'

'Exiting now.'

Brock opened the lock on one of the wide sliding windows directly behind the desk, jumped to the ground and closed the window behind him. He padded quickly across the jetty towards the ladder and climbed down below the level of the platform just as the warehouse doors opened and a team of five workers moved towards the first dredger.

Hooking his mask and flippers on to his buoyancy vest, Brock stood with both feet on the ladder to replace his aqualung; then he sank into the canal with hardly a ripple. He rose directly under the pier, where, safely hidden from view, he strapped on his face mask, connected his breathing apparatus and replaced his flippers. A roaring noise suddenly erupted a few metres to his right.

He heard Ferguson. 'Hold it where you are, it looks like the first dredger is underway already.'

'Understood.'

While Brock waited, he recalled the drawing he had studied: a cylindrical object lying beneath a cage-like structure that, in turn, was covered in something.

'OK. Clear,' said Ferguson. 'No. Wait. The first dredger is stopping.'

From his own viewpoint, Brock could see the hull of the dredger begin to turn, its propellers making the water look as if it were boiling as its engines stirred it up.

'Moving your way,' said Brock, before slipping beneath the surface and retracing his entry path.

From his vantage point, Ferguson was able to train his field glasses on a level with the boat. He readjusted the focus. 'The dredger is almost directly in line – it's turned ninety degrees to lie against the canal. It's strange – maybe it's a trick of the light but its tarpaulin appears to be flattening out. No, I'm right. The damn thing looks like it's dumping its load directly through its hull. I can't see how else it can be doing it from my sight line.'

Brock swam nearer to it, carefully breaking the surface just ten metres from the dredger. 'I'm taking a closer look, Matt.'

Ferguson sounded doubtful. 'Not a good idea.'

'Don't worry, from the other side. This section is the narrowest of the canal and I need to verify the depth, particularly if they're dumping instead of dredging.'

'OK, but traffic will start in two zero minutes. You must be clear by then.'

After a quick glance at his compass to confirm the direction, Brock dropped three metres below the surface before kicking out towards the other side of the canal some sixty metres away. With visibility at just four metres, he swam steadily until he encountered the canal's concrete shelving. Then he dropped down until he reached the bottom of the canal. He was surprised to find that the depth was just nineteen metres – he had expected it to be more, having calculated that he would need two short stops on his way back to the surface, even after such a short dive, to avoid depression sickness. The canal was meant to be around thirty metres deep; a depth of only nineteen was danger-ously close to the maximum allowable draught of sixteen metres required by some of the huge cargo and supertankers to pass through.

With visibility down to just one metre, Brock stayed close to the bottom and felt his way towards the same datum line he had calculated the dredger occupied on the other side. Suddenly the poor visibility descended into complete darkness. He looked up swiftly to see what was blocking the light.

Immediately above him was a large black object. Not able to make out what it was, he switched on the high-powered halogen spot pencil torch and tentatively made his way towards the surface. Within two metres, he came to an abrupt stop as his fingers felt the rough edges of a steel mesh. The material his fingers touched beyond the mesh seemed like plastic or thick polythene. He scanned it with the torch but it revealed nothing. He began to feel his way along the mesh, trying to find the end of it.

'Dredger number two is making a course for the other side, directly opposite the first.' Ferguson's voice sounded faint and remote.

Brock kept quiet to indicate that he was not receiving clearly. Perhaps, he thought, the steel mesh is interfering.

'Connor, you are definitely in the wrong place. Dredger number two intends to dump.'

'Understood,' Brock replied automatically, as he continued to feel his way in the dark. He felt as though he were moving at a snail's pace, as he slid along the mesh. He calculated that he had pulled himself along ten metres when he came to the edge of the mesh, but any hope of swimming past it vanished as he realized that this side of it curved directly into the canal bottom, forming a semi-cave. The picture of the doodle came unbidden into his mind and he realized suddenly how it fitted into his current predicament. His positioning must be right above the Al Qantarah underpass – that was the cylindrical object, and this mesh was the cage placed directly over it. If he recalled correctly, the cage construction was semi-circular in shape, as if surrounding the lower cylindrical object. But somehow he had gained direct access.

He heard Ferguson again, now even fainter. He strained to make out his friend's voice.

'Number two dredger has stopped directly in line with the one on your side of the canal. You had better not be where I think you are.'

'Timing is everything,' replied Brock, as he swiftly turned and began blindly retracing his route. He knew he had only moments before a deluge of alluvium poured down and blocked it permanently. Twenty seconds later, Brock could just make out where the entrance was but, as he neared it, he realized that the area was already impassable. I must have missed where I came in, only by a few metres, he thought. Turning back, he moved cautiously, hand over hand, along the steel mesh and plastic wall.

His right hand pushed through open water before the light on his left revealed the entrance. Visibility was restored, though only to one metre. Brock realized with relief that he had gained freedom before the alluvium had been dumped.

Before he could swim through the entrance, a solid object dropped on to him, knocking his shoulder. As Brock instinctively recoiled, another object caught him on the side of his head, forcing his face mask down to his throat and pulling the air valve away from the mask, so that the oxygen from his breathing apparatus escaped and bubbled away. As the added momentum knocked Brock back, an army of falling objects identical to the preceding ones pounded into the area around him. The disturbed sediment stole all visibility and, within seconds, Brock was plunged into complete watery blackness without air to breathe.

Twenty Four

Ferguson felt his chest tighten as he witnessed the tarpaulin on the second dredger sinking slowly down. In the same way air-traffic controllers are trained always to speak even more slowly and precisely to instil calm and confidence into a pilot disoriented by a severe storm, the Irishman kept his voice reassuring and precise. There would be plenty of time for 'I told you so' remonstrations later.

But there was no reply. Just an ominous silence.

Immediately his mask had been knocked away, Brock had calmly swung his right hand in an anti-clockwise motion behind him, located the hanging valve and reattached it to his mask. Tilting his head back and squeezing down, he had blown the water out of the mask with the incoming air. Then he calmly rested on his knees, forcing his breathing to be slow and steady, then lifted his hand to his ear. As he'd suspected, the small electronic transmitter had been lost in the jarring blow.

Brock did not feel overly concerned by the loss of radio contact. He knew that Ferguson would already be donning his own gear to search for him, and the luminous dial on his wrist displayed twenty-five minutes' dive time remaining. Allowing five minutes to stop on the way to the surface to avoid the bends, he still had a good twenty minutes to escape.

Brock and Ferguson's numerous training sessions as dive buddies followed certain guidelines; one was to stay in the vicinity unless it was absolutely impossible to do so. Brock shone the torch at the wall that now blocked his path. The plastic coverings of a small mountain of sacks reflected back to him. He couldn't be certain, but, by the size of the sacks, he estimated that the barricade must be at least two metres thick. Even if it were less than that, the mountain would be impossible to push through.

Brock moved.

He knew that Ferguson would be heading towards the other side of the canal, but he decided to follow the entire length of the caged tunnel that imprisoned him, in the hope that there was another opening. With the air he had available, there was little point in staying where he was. A fleeting thought that he might not make it rose in his mind. Brock quickly pushed it away, scolding himself. Focus on what you can do, don't think about what if.

After he had slowly crawled twenty metres, closely checking for any exits, the sediment cleared, improving the visibility afforded by the torch light. Brock could see that the steel mesh was firmly held in place by the heavy sacks lying against it. The only open area must have been the portion he had inadvertently swum through – which had just been sealed with a load of sacks.

Why, he wondered. Why dump a load of sacks? But he pushed the question out of his mind. He had only sixteen minutes' dive time remaining. He had to concentrate on survival now.

Eight minutes later, after he had crawled a further ten metres, Brock's hopes rose. As he swept the area with his torch, he noticed a place that did not reflect back the greyness of the sacks and plastic sheeting. There was definitely a hole. Quickly, he kicked towards it, only to have his hand hit the steel mesh. Several of the sacks had slipped away, forcing the mesh down, but it had not broken and, although the way was tantalizingly open beyond the cage, the steel mesh would have to be cut.

Brock felt for the Leatherman tool strapped to his jacket and began to work away at the mesh. The small pliers were tough and sharp but the thick steel was resistant and after two minutes Brock had only cut three strands. Jamming his torch into one of the diamond-shaped holes of the mesh, he continued to work at the steel cage. He knew that in just over five minutes the last of his air would run out but he continued to work away with the Leatherman.

Three minutes later, the now-blunted Leatherman had cut and bent back enough strands for Brock to get his head through. With another ten, he estimated that he might be able to get his body through but already the tell-tale signs in his breathing warned that his tank was almost empty.

During his air-force training, he had undergone situations where he had been starved of oxygen and nearly drowned. The first began with disorientation; the second with the feeling that his chest, followed by his head, was going to explode. With both, the pain was numbing, surely a terrible way to die. But Brock would not allow himself the fearful panic that usually accompanied the sensation of drowning. Switching his mind from the tightening pain in his chest as his lungs began to burst for want of air, he squeezed with all his remaining strength on the strand he was working on. Almost in a drunken stupor of pain, he watched as the light he had heard people say came to greet them at a moment close to death approached. Slowly, the light revealed a one-eyed face that snaked towards him.

Ferguson rammed the buddy mouthpiece through the hole towards Brock. Brock stared at it for what seemed aeons to Ferguson, before he deftly grabbed it, tore off his face mask and placed the life-saving valve hungrily into his mouth.

Ferguson had been startled to encounter a barricade of sacks below the surface. Sweeping down past them on the way to the bottom of the canal, he had spotted the light from Brock's torch as easily as he would a golf ball on a smooth green. As he swam towards it and entered a small tunnel of sacks and plastic, he had immediately noticed that there were no tell-tale air bubbles coming from Brock's tank. He had acted fast.

Brock felt the sheer ecstasy of receiving air after being starved of it. With his eyes tightly shut, he breathed in and recalled a pharmaceutical report he'd once read that argued that oxygen was the best drug available, guaranteed to make the human brain respond by releasing its natural chemical high, dopamine. He could confirm that, he thought, as the beautiful rush of air flooded his lungs.

He began to regain his faculties as he pulled on the dive mask that Ferguson passed him. For ten seconds he breathed steadily, then looked into Ferguson's concerned eyes, sending grateful thanks with his own. Pointing towards the mesh with a scissors movement, Brock returned to the task of cutting the wire, this time with Ferguson's help. Each of them worked closely on a strand until they had painstakingly cut a hole large enough for Brock to squeeze through.

As soon as Brock was through, both men kicked out for the swim back. Ferguson's flipper struck one of the sacks as he kicked, dislodging it and sending it floating downwards. As it descended, it snagged on the jagged prongs of the mesh hole and punctured. Expecting it to cloud the area, Brock and Ferguson watched in astonishment as the seeping material turned into viscous glue, filling the small tunnel like cold molten lava.

The escape hole Brock had passed through closed; it disappeared in a grey, clay-like mass that floated in the water like bubbly seaweed. Ferguson tentatively kicked at it with his flipper but, rather than pushing it away as they expected, the glue surrounded Ferguson's foot and he was stuck fast. Brock quickly turned to prise the substance off the flipper, only to realize with shock that his hand had become stuck to it. Pulling with their combined strength had only the effect of stretching the material, but not breaking it.

Brock slashed at it with the blade of the Leatherman but the tool simply became stuck. Ferguson went to remove his flipper but Brock motioned for him to ascend. The material travelled with them without breaking.

At six metres from the surface, while resting for three minutes to allow decompression, Brock continued to work at freeing his hand before continuing their ascent. Grabbing his dive knife, he prised and wrenched his hand away, tearing the skin off his forefinger. With blood clouding the water from his torn skin, he ascended to the surface.

'What the hell kind of stuff is that?' gasped Ferguson as they broke the surface.

'It sure isn't alluvium,' replied Brock, sucking in great gulps of air.

'Well, don't expect me to check it out,' Matt said, trying to look down at his ankle, where he could feel from the weight that the material was still stuck to his flipper.

'No time like the present,' shouted Brock, as he looked straight into the wide bow of the iron-and-steel barge bearing down on them.

Brock and Ferguson simultaneously dived, kicking furiously to avoid the flat-nosed behemoth. They missed it by inches as the water vortex turned them over and over, carrying them along the barge's keel and whirling them inexorably towards the massive turning propellers that mercilessly waited to slice them limb from limb.

Twenty-Five

If any of the sturgeon fishermen disturbed by the supersonic boom had bothered to raise their eyes, they might have caught a glimpse of a blood-coloured outline streaking over the El Burz mountain range, above the rich waters of the Caspian sea. Looking like a deadly arrow piercing the large cotton-wool clouds that dotted the sky, the aeroplane smoothly outran the sound barrier on its flight path towards Egypt.

Neither the fishermen below nor the occupant of the privately owned Concorde jet savouring another spoonful of caviar guessed at the link between them, and if they had, it would perhaps have amused the humble fish catchers to know that the sky-high gourmet paid a royal sum for the prized sturgeon eggs that they enjoyed for free.

Subedei's only motivation in securing a Concorde, soon after their removal from commercial operation, had been that it would cut his flight time from Beijing by half. His offer to purchase one from British Airways had been refused but Air France had readily agreed to sell, for a sum considerably more than the cost incurred in their maintenance and the bureaucracy of keeping them grounded.

The fact that the plane had the prestige of sheer luxury had been a bonus, and Subedei had successfully used it many times to ensnare ambitious politicians and beguile chief executive officers. They revelled in the opulence and exclusivity of the aircraft, relishing their proximity to the Mongol's power, and feeling gratifyingly important. As a result, they were beholden to Subedei for his generosity, and later found that their puffed-up self-importance was replaced by a strange sense of fearfulness.

The sleek jet had been completely overhauled, its interior transformed into the kind of state-room luxury that would beggar the world's finest yachts. The jet engines had been updated

213

with Rolls-Royce's latest supersonic turbines, which had cost more than three times the price of the liner itself.

Subedei's cold eyes swept over the bruised breasts of the naked Mi Ling lying next to him as she tentatively offered another spoonful of the black-grey oily beluga. It amused him to know that her husband, sitting in the forward saloon, would have easily heard his wife's cries of pain had she not forced herself to stifle them.

Subedei had noticed the beautiful girl working in his office two years earlier and he had quickly had her moved to train as his personal assistant because he liked to be surrounded by gorgeous things. There had been no thought of physical desire, until she had introduced her future husband to him. Observing the love that flowed from her eyes towards her fiancé, he had immediately decided he would steal it. It had been the work of a moment to entangle the young man in a disreputable financial muddle. Just as he had hoped, Mi Ling had come to him begging for help, allowing him to make his bargain with her. He would extricate her husband if she agreed to his terms. The distraught young woman had been horrified at what her employer wanted from her.

'You said you would do anything to save your husband. Never offer what you are not willing to lose,' Subedei remembered telling her afterwards. 'A great man will not be persuaded by meaningless promises, only by genuine commitment.'

He had then employed the husband as his other personal assistant at a generous salary, on the basis that Mi Ling's special services were continued at his convenience. Of course, the woman had no choice. She was clever enough to see that a refusal would not go unpunished.

Mi Ling looked at the cold eyes surveying her nakedness and tried to prevent a shudder. She knew from experience that the more she tried to dissuade the brutal Mongolian, the more fierce he became. Recently, the pain of her acquiesced rapes had become almost too much to bear but they had to be endured, and with as little show of the despair they engendered in her as possible. At this moment, she could tell that he was gearing himself up to take her again, and knew that if she showed the slightest sign of dreading the pain, he would tear into her already sore body even more viciously. Smiling, she lay back as though to offer herself. Subedei immediately seemed to lose interest.

'Do not be greedy. You have enough already to hide from your husband,' he said sharply. 'Get out and tell him to bring me the guest list for tomorrow.'

Mi Ling got up and made her way towards the mirrored bathroom. 'Right away, My Lord.'

'Then call my beautiful Ayeesha. We will no doubt be starting our descent soon.'

In the privacy of the bathroom, the young woman inspected her body. She was used to his cruelty by now but still felt a sting of horror to see what injuries had been inflicted on her. Streaks of fresh blood came from the tops of her thighs and between her legs where her master's rough nails had gouged into the soft flesh. Around her torso was a tattoo of yellow and purple discoloration, evidence of his earlier work. She stared at the bruises and the fresh blood, her eyes bright and hard, unable to shed a tear.

This life of sexual humiliation that her employer had forced upon her had destroyed almost all her self-respect. She hated herself, and no longer loved her husband or even life. Yet there was no escape that she could see – while she wouldn't mind dying herself, she knew that Subedei would kill her husband as well if she ever resisted him, and she could not be the instrument of that. Feeling like a prisoner locked into a dungeon of hell, she tidied her pale face, slipped on the silk cheongsam that revealed only her outer thighs, which Subedei always carefully avoided, and went through to the saloon. Her calm face was now an inscrutable mask, impenetrable to the outside world.

Just as Captain Raoul Thamad had planned, he had been the first allowed through the canal. As one of the main dredgers, well known to the convoy pilots, he had been permitted through ahead of the waiting tankers. Although his orders had been to delay his passage until the day after next, it was clear to him that the company's new owners did not understand how seriously he took his work. He had finished his job here and would now return northwards, slipping unnoticed into the Khan Marine and Dredging Quay just north of Al Qantarah. And even if he was noticed, it wouldn't make any difference. If they wanted him here in the Bitter Lakes, they could damn well tell him why.

Fancy sonar sounding equipment or not, he was still a captain and should be treated with respect.

In the growing daylight, he spied two of the fleet's smaller dredgers ahead of him, each operating on either side of the canal. Infuriated that his own patch was being usurped by these two minnows, he revved the engines slightly faster than was really permitted and rapidly cruised the next 200 metres.

The first mate, Ali, peered ahead, his eyes sharper than his father's. 'They seem to be about to moor at the quay of the concrete facility, Captain.'

'To do what, I'd like to know!' exclaimed Thamad. 'I can't see any scooping derricks on deck, so they can't be dredging.'

'Perhaps they're just sounding out the bottom,' offered his son. Thamad flashed a glance at Ali and was about to make a caustic reply when there was a change in the note of the ship's engines. A look of consternation flashed across the captain's face, and he immediately checked the instrument panel. It indicated no change in speed.

The noise of the engine suddenly rose from a low grinding groan to a shrieking scream of distress. Instantly, Thamad cut the power. Ali looked at his father in bewilderment and then, in the next moment, he was thrown to the floor as the old steel steering wheel he was holding swung downwards, turning the dredger directly towards the smaller vessel moored alongside the quay.

Thamad desperately restarted the engines, slamming them into reverse, realizing that, with the increased momentum born of the higher-than-usual speed, impact was only a minute away. The engines started without protest but apart from the high-pitched spinning sound, there was nothing else. No control and no effect.

'By the prophet, what's happening?' he shouted. He had never experienced anything like this before. Sure, engines had stopped or conked out, but he'd never had one screaming like this, without warning, and so impotently. 'The screws must have caught on something and jammed solid!'

'The wheel won't move, Father!' shouted Ali, in shock. He had leapt up and grappled with the steering wheel, desperately pulling on it with all of his strength, ignoring the blood trickling down his face from a wound inflicted by one of the spinning metal spindles moments earlier.

As if in answer, a series of giant knocks began to thunder against the iron hull, causing the whole vessel to shudder like a boiling can on a hot fire. The noise alerted the crew of the smaller dredger that now lay directly in the path of the larger, oncoming steel battering ram. They saw at once that, although the speed of the larger vessel was not great, the momentum behind its 22,000 tons would smash both them and the pier behind them into pieces. They began to flee their boat in panic, screaming and pointing as they went.

Captain Thamad and his son stood frozen, watching in disbelief as the collision became inevitable. They came out of their spell just in time to brace themselves against the impact, but it made little difference. Father and son were thrown against the wooden-framed wheelhouse as the thick flat hull ploughed into the smaller dredger, crushing it as easily as a man's fist could a tin can.

As the small vessel disappeared under the might of the bigger dredger, Thamad's proud ship continued to gnaw away effortlessly at the solid pier until the reinforced concrete stanchions resisted its further demolition, forcing the behemoth to tear along the jetty's side towards the other dredger. As its crew frantically deserted, the smaller boat was, like its companion, smothered without trace by the flagship of the fleet, its propellerless drive shafts still screaming in outrage as it finally came to a halt.

'Well, that's not something you see every day,' remarked Ferguson, kicking with his one remaining flipper towards the canal side. 'Now, we didn't cause that, did we?'

Brock breathed deeply, still enjoying the sensation of air in his lungs. He reached an inspection ladder at the side of the canal and climbed up, then helped Ferguson up behind him. They stood for a moment to survey the scene of destruction in front of them, and the great beached body of the enormous dredger that now listed helplessly against the canal side.

'We just missed being minced by that thing,' remarked Brock, as they gazed at it. 'An inch or two closer and you and I would be feeling half the men we are at the moment.'

'At the very least,' rejoined Matt. 'But what a mess! How on earth did it happen? That big monster just seemed to plough into the little fellas without so much as putting on the brake.'

'Your flipper did it, with a little help from Ariadne's thread.'

'Ariadne's what?'

'The magic unbreakable thread that Ariadne gave to Theseus to guide him through the labyrinth, so he could kill the Minotaur.'

The Irishman shot Brock a quizzical look. 'You'll be all right in a few minutes. Too much or too little oxygen has a way of doing funny things to the mind.'

Brock grinned. 'Mythology was never your strong subject, was it? I thought even you would know that story. But the point is, that substance puts me in mind of an unbreakable thread. Remember how we couldn't get rid of it? It stayed with us right to the surface no matter what we tried to do to get free. We were only lucky that your flipper was dragged off as we kicked away from the hull, leaving the stuff sticking to that great beast. It must have somehow got entangled in the rudder and the screws, which in turn must have reeled in the whole sack-load from the bottom, crippling it.'

Ferguson looked stunned, and he turned back to the cata-strophic damage in the water. 'Geez, I've never heard of anything that can do that. We only touched it for an instant, too. We've got to get some, Connor. It has to be analysed.' He glanced at Brock's torn hand. 'I'd better go down and get one of those sacks.'

'My guess is that the substance chemically reacts with water, which would explain the heavy plastic sheeting. If one sack can do the damage we have just witnessed, it makes sense to approach it very carefully indeed – preferably somewhere dry.'

The two men looked towards the commotion that was now going on along the half-demolished jetty. An obese-looking white man in khaki shorts and T-shirt, with thinning red hair, stood out amongst his darker-skinned colleagues. Amid the noise and shouting, the white man's obscenities rose in clearly distinguishable English.

Brock said, 'And I know just the place to get some.'

Raoul Thamad could not believe his eyes. He had been able to step directly from the bow of his ship on to what remained of the quay.

From there he could see that the stern had risen out of the water, revealing twin empty drive shafts. Only one of the two massive-bladed screw propellers remained attached, though now at an awkward angle. The other was jammed into the hull under a congealed grey-white mass that looked like a giant had stuck his discarded chewing gum there.

'You imbeciles!' snarled Maynard. 'Do you have any idea what your stupidity has done? Months of planning could be ruined! Why the hell can't you follow simple instructions? And don't give me any of your will-of-Allah nonsense. You'll need more than that to keep you from being skinned alive for this!'

Not speaking a word of English, Thamad had no idea what the fat, red-faced man was screaming. It was all he could do to comprehend that his pride and joy was lying wrecked in the canal – how, he had no idea. Fifteen minutes later everyone was still shouting, too involved in assessing the damage and apportioning blame to notice the tall man, his left hand wrapped in a handkerchief, leave the office he had exited before, just one hour earlier. In his good hand, he carried a plastic lunch box.

Subedei leaned back on the fur-covered bed, the sheer silk robe falling open as he replaced the in-flight telephone, and smiled at his reflection in the mirrored interior of his master suite. Ayeesha had confirmed that all members of his cartel would be at the arranged meeting in Alexandria. From there he would go directly to his Nile residence in time for his private meeting with the Egyptian president.

What better than to follow that immediately with his intended announcement on board the *Pharaoh Queen*? Perhaps he should persuade the president himself to make the announcement on his behalf – that would be more fitting.

Watching his reflection smile back at him, he focused on the faded tribal tattoo exposed on his upper chest just below the right shoulder. The day he had received it – his fourth birthday – was his first distinct memory.

He had promised his mother that he would not cry, and he'd kept his word, although it took all his effort to hold back the tears of pain. His father had looked on with pride at his son's silent courage. The boy knew that to bear pain without complaint was honourable – his mother had instilled that in him, and often punished him harshly to test his ability to withstand suffering. She always made light of his efforts. 'No man knows how to bear pain,' she would say scornfully. 'Nothing he has experienced can be like the pain of a woman giving birth. Our pain comes from man's pleasure, and it is the price demanded for a child.'

On the same day, as the ceremony commenced, his father had recounted his heritage with pride: how he was of the Borjigin Tribe directly descended from the tribal Khan, born and named Temujin who was later the great Chingus, the Father and Founder of the Mongol Nation, conqueror of the Tatars, the Naimans, the Merkits, the Jadirat, the Dorbet, the Katagin and Seljiut and later the Kirghiz. Then he quelled the three kingdoms of China: Chin, whose capital was Peking, Tangut in the north, and Sung in the South; he subdued the Uigar tribe whose written language the Mongols adopted, and then later, with the sword arm of Subedei, he became the defeater of the Shah's Persian armies, the annihilator of the Georgians of the Caspian, and the emperor of all of the Russian tribes. His Mongol Yuen dynasty ruled over all China for over one hundred years.

Throughout the whole time the small boy was being tattooed, his father continued to recite his tribal heritage. It seemed to him that the pain he felt increased when his father quietly related the changes in Mongol fortune, beginning with their defeat by the Egyptian Mamluks at Ayn Jalut. Then, as the ceremony ended, he told of the decline of the Mongol nation, its spirit softened by the passive teachings of Tibetan monks. His father said that, one day, another Khan from the tribe of Borjigin would rise and rebuild the greatness of the Mongols.

Subedei remembered how much he had wished he could be that man. He had hated the Egyptians and Tibetans for destroying the Mongolian heritage and he had promised himself that somehow he would bring retribution upon them.

Subedei touched his tattoo lightly with his fingers. The sword signified Mongolian courage, while the round eye behind it with lines emanating from the centre like a dazzling sun related to the god Duua and signified the spiritual principles that had been the foundation of Chingus Khan's rule.

It had been his destiny to be sent to Tibet by his adopted father all those years ago. At the time, he'd seen himself as a tool to wreak revenge on those spineless monks whose religion had destroyed his ancestors. But who can second-guess the hand of destiny, he mused. It had turned out to be much more than that.

The path of his fate had led him to the golden artefact, the repository of his destiny. To ensure its safety, he'd had to make sure that Colonel Quan, the only other person who knew of it, met with an unfortunate accident. Still, who would miss that good-for-nothing whoreson? And then – Subedei smiled to remember it – disaster! He'd dropped his precious treasure and broken it. He had been horrified, appalled by his clumsiness – until he'd seen that a new, more interesting treasure had been revealed. At the time the papyrus scroll had meant nothing, but the other item, wrapped inside a stretched section of human tattooed skin, meant everything to him. It seemed to stretch across the ages, the generations, and reach out to him. For it was the very zenith of his father's tribal stories manifested there, before his eyes.

It was impossible to go against destiny and both items had set him directly on a providential path. He would be Khan; a Khan recognized by the economy-driven forces of the twenty-first century. It was only a matter of perfect timing; timing which nobody could either anticipate or prevent.

Twenty-Six

From his dining table in the Montazeh Palace Hotel in Alexandria, Brock gazed thoughtfully out of the window across the chaotic but enticingly exotic city below, home to some three million souls.

In the distance, he could see the eastern harbour and imagine how the Pharos lighthouse, the last of the seven wonders of the ancient world to fall, would have dominated the skyline like an ancient Statue of Liberty, sending out its reflected fire from Archimedes' mirror. But it had been allowed to decay, finally collapsing into the turquoise-and-green waters from which it once rose so majestically to beckon the merchant ships to Alexander's great city.

Alexander had been twenty-five when he'd ordered this city to be built on top of the ancient settlement of Rhakotis. He had seen that, with the Nile connected to the Red Sea by a canal, such a city could serve as a gateway to the Indian Ocean. It would be a fitting tribute to himself and his monumental achievements. Eager to continue with his plans to vanquish Persia, Central Asia and India, Alexander stopped only long enough personally to mark out the city walls before continuing on his journey to consult the Oracle of Ammon at Siwa Oasis. He left the task of designing the city to the Greek architect, Dinocrates, and the new capital was born on April 7th 331BCE. Alexander never saw a single building of the city that immortalized his name. He returned only in death.

I've been a little luckier than that, Brock mused, looking down at his injured hand. He and Matt had stopped at Faqus to find a doctor who would tend his hand, then, after refuelling the van, they'd made it back to Alexandria by midday.

Food had been their main priority. They were both starving. Brock had led the way to the hotel. Its kitchen was renowned for its traditional delicacies and they'd feasted on an appetizer of a green soup known as mulukhia, followed by hamam mahshi, which was pigeon stuffed with strong spices and accompanied by the aubergine dip called baba ghannoush. With all this, and with tahini salad and the rice and lentil mix called kushari on the side, they were both finally sated, and leaned back in their chairs, satisfied. It was a stark contrast to the dry cheese sandwiches they'd had for breakfast. And their lunch box was now full of the substance that Ferguson had coined 'Ariadne's Surprise'.

'That feels a hell of a lot better.' Matt patted his stomach. 'Not bad at all, considering it was foreign stuff.'

'I'd have thought living and working abroad all these years would have broadened your palate a bit by now,' said Brock.

'Ah, begorrah, there's nothing like Irish stew and Guinness,' said Matt, affecting a strong brogue. He enjoyed playing the simple Irish lad occasionally. 'Oh dear, don't let me mention the black stuff. It's makin' me homesick, so it is.'

'It's a while since you've been home, isn't it? Your mother will think you've forgotten all about her.'

Matt shot him a look. 'I was back at Christmas, Connor. Saw the whole crowd of them then. How long is it since you've been back to Scotland?'

Brock frowned.

'Now, don't get cross with me, old friend. It's not escaped my notice that you've not seen that girl of yours in too long.'

'Matt . . .' said Brock, warningly.

Ferguson took a deep breath. 'Well, I wasn't going to say anything but as we're on the subject, I'm not going to keep it in. Connor, what do you think Heather would say if she knew you couldn't face seeing your own daughter, her precious child?'

Brock said nothing, and Matt, emboldened, continued, 'I know you've been mourning that girl for years, but some time you've got to get on with your life, and you can't neglect Kathy because the sight of her is too painful. Heather's gone. The child's the one who needs you now. She's the one who needs the love you can give her. And if you don't, you'll be punishing the both of you. And believe me, Kathy won't thank you for it later.' Matt paused for breath and glanced nervously at his friend. 'I'm only saying it because I think you're making a mistake.'

223

Brock's face worked as he tried to master his emotions. Anger and guilt passed over his face before it settled into a more impassive expression. 'I'm going to speak about this once, Matt, and then I don't want to discuss it any more. Understand? Now, are you listening?' His voice was rough and cold. 'I love that girl. That's why I keep my distance. That's why she doesn't have my surname, and that's why she doesn't know I'm her father. Not because I don't care about her, for God's sake, but because I'd crucify myself if anything happened to her because of me. Heather's death . . .' He stopped and stared hard at the table, before looking up with an icy azure gaze. 'It didn't add up for me. I've always thought that it was more than a random hit and run, you know that. And if it was, then whoever did it was after me – either they meant to kill me, or punish me by killing her. If they knew about Kathy, if anyone else whose murderous path I cross in this crazy job knew about Kathy, her life would be in danger.

'I know it seems unnatural to you, and to Myrna, but it's the only way I can see to keep her safe. I have to keep my distance from her, though it nearly breaks me in two to do it. If people think I'm Kathy's godfather, her devoted uncle, then that's one more degree of separation between us, and one more chance that she'll be left alone if anyone did take it into their mind to attack me. I've no idea what the future holds – I'll cross that bridge when I come to it. I'll take my chances that she'll understand one day, when I can explain it all to her. Maybe you're right and she'll hate me for this, but at least she'll be hating me and alive, rather than carrying my name, and dead.'

Matt flushed and looked downwards. After a moment he said, 'Connor, I'm sorry—'

Brock broke in. 'Let's say no more about it, Matt. Let's just not talk about it. OK?'

'OK.'

They sat and looked out over the harbour in silence until Matt broke it. 'Did he marry her?'

'Who?'

'The fella that killed the Minotaur.'

Brock shot Ferguson a bemused look. His ability to lighten the subject or get on with the job at hand, shutting out the trials and tribulations, made him a first-class ally. There was no other

Brock would trust to watch his back, yet the rails his friend's train of thought ran on never ceased to surprise him.

'No, as a matter of fact Theseus deserted Ariadne on an island named Dia, now known as Naxos, while she was sleeping.'

'Well, there's gratitude for you!'

'The gods had a hand in it; within a few days she married Dionysus, a son of Zeus, and went on to bear him many sons while her merry new husband, the god of wine, continued to wreak havoc among the mortals who worshipped him. Talking of which, I need to make some calls regarding another son of Zeus.'

'The one that founded this city. The son of Ammon.'

Brock raised his eyebrows 'So you know more about mythology than you let on.'

'Only what a pseudo-Cleopatra told me. Talking of which, I must go and courier 'Ariadne's Surprise' to Zurich and check out the *Pharaoh Queen*, as we discussed earlier.'

After Matt had gone, Brock left the cool, air-conditioned restaurant and headed outside into the tumultuous streets. The heat was already oppressive, even now in the spring, and his light linen trousers and loose shirt felt heavy and clammy within minutes. He walked decisively down several streets and then, after a quick turn down a side street, made another fast turn to the right and doubled back on himself until he came to a quieter area. He found a small café and took a seat at a table shaded far back under the front awning. Taking out his phone, he dialled a number in Paris.

'Ah, an interesting puzzle that you have sent me, *mon ami*. This little riddle has completely absorbed me,' chirped Amuyani, as soon as he heard Brock's voice.

'Any ideas?'

'Yes, yes – lots of ideas. Having ideas is not my problem – I'm just not certain that any of them will lead to a solution for you! However, you can be the judge.'

'I'm all ears.'

'Excellent. That is how I like it, Connor. Now pay attention. I began with Alexander the Great. Naturally, in order to get anywhere, I had to make some historical assumptions.'

'Understandable, bearing in mind the period concerned,' said Brock.

225

'The challenge was to link what we know from recognized source material with the new evidence you have provided. To begin with, I took at face value the interesting material that the delightful and respected Maria brought to your attention. I assumed that the God Sword – that is, a sword containing a mystic stone that belonged either to Alexander or to Cyrus or both – truly exists, and is not just the myth it has been thought until now.

'Second, as the manuscript related to both the God Sword and Alexander's tomb, I worked on the assumption that the two were connected – in other words, that the sword was buried with Alexander's body. This brought me into that controversial subject of the site of Alexander's tomb. But, much as I'd prefer to keep well away from that squabble, there was no avoiding it – your puzzle concerns it intimately.

'We know that the recorder Diodorus Siculus wrote that the body was embalmed in Babylon, where the conqueror died aged almost thirty-three, in June 323BCE and that, after a delay of two years, it finally started on the long journey to Egypt. But we don't know for sure if the final destination was to be Siwa, where the oracle had confirmed his divine lineage. Most scholars suspect that his Macedonian friend, Ptolemy Lagos, wanted the body to be buried in Alexandria so that a prophecy of Alexander's soothsayer, Aristander, could be proved true.'

'What prophecy was that?'

'That the country in which Alexander would be buried would be the most prosperous in the world. Certainly, as Pharaoh of Egypt and the founder of the Ptolemaic dynasty, Ptolemy had a vested interest but he could have been following what he thought would have been Alexander's wish.'

'Well, I can understand that,' said Brock. 'I suppose I know a little about the promises brothers in arms make to each other – they're pretty binding. But do you think that's what Alexander had instructed?'

Brock heard the rustle of papers on the other end of the line.

'What do I think?' The professor giggled. 'I have no idea, my friend. But there is some evidence to indicate that he wished to be buried at the deity's oracle and certainly his followers incorporated the horn of Ammon into iconography of their deceased king. But, whatever the motive, we do know that Perdiccas, the first appointed regent for Alexander's unborn son and his mentally deficient half-brother, Arrhidaeus, sent an army headed by his general Ptolemon to intercept the funeral procession and divert it to Macedonia.'

'Alexander's homeland.'

'Yes, so it would seem that burying him there was not unreasonable. After all, his father, Philip II, was buried there. In fact, his tomb was discovered at Vergina in Macedonia in 1977.' The professor paused to consult his notes and then said, 'So, the battle over Alexander's remains took place in Syria and many dignitaries from the funeral procession were killed. Centuries later, in 1886, a white pentelic marble sarcophagus was discovered at Sidon, just south of Beirut, and at first was believed to be Alexander's. In the event, it was proved to be Ptolemon's. He was killed during the battle. Incidentally, you can visit it if you like. It's now exhibited in Constantinople.'

'I'll remember the next time I'm in Istanbul,' said Brock drily.

The professor giggled again. 'Yes, of course. Istanbul. Sorry, I can't keep up with these modern names. I'm too busy studying old maps, I suppose. Now, where was I? Oh, yes! According to Diodorus, the funeral carriage reached Alexandria via Memphis. Ancient authors including Plutarch, Strabo and Pausanias mention that it was deposited within a gold sarcophagus in a grand mausoleum along with a great display of wealth appropriate for such a deified hero in the very heart of his eponymous city. How wonderful it must have looked! But apparently, two hundred years later, Ptolemy the Tenth exchanged the gold sarcophagus for a glass one.'

'Nice deal.'

'Money troubles, I expect. Naturally the dynasty was in decline by that time – all that inbreeding. Ptolemy argued that people wanted to gaze on the great man's body but I shouldn't think that fooled anyone. And it was all downhill from there. The last ruling descendent of Ptolemy was the famous Cleopatra, who married her two brothers, and was the lover of Julius Caesar and Mark Anthony. They all gazed on the body of Alexander before Cleopatra looted the tomb's remaining golden wealth in a moment of financial difficulty.'

Brock felt a pang of disappointment. 'It was all going so well.

Bad news for the survival of this God Sword, then.'

'That is why I worked on the assumption that it was buried actually *with* him or within his sarcophagus, to keep the two together. Otherwise the sword spins off into darkness. Even so, there is not a great deal more light that can be shed on the matter. Now we do know from Dion Cassius, the historian and consul of Africa writing two hundred years after Cleopatra, that the emperor Caracalla requested to see the body, and actually touched the nose, doing some damage. Horrified at what he had done, he then ordered the return of the body into a solid sarcophagus.'

'Hiding the evidence?' suggested Brock.

'Very likely. Like so many later generals and emperors, he was obsessed with Alexander and adopted clothes, weapons and behaviour as well as campaign plans in a bid to emulate him.'

'Alexander has a lot to answer for,' remarked Brock. 'He's the face that launched a thousand bloody dictators. Do we know what happened to this new sarcophagus?'

The professor sounded suddenly sad. 'A period of darkness falls, unfortunately. There were recorded rumours in the early part of the fifth century that the tomb had been located. This was during the time of Roman Patriarch Theophilus, shortly after the remaining portion of the great Alexandria library was burned to the ground in 391CE. We can only assume that the body had been secreted away, because neither tomb nor treasure has since been located.

'However, having said that . . .' Amuyani paused for dramatic effect.

Brock was unable to resist. 'Yes?'

'There are two other items that have come to light. First, a Greek archaeologist is convinced that she has located the tomb at Siwa Oasis. But, very strangely, she has been blocked from further archaeological work and her permit to enter Egypt has been revoked. Those are details you can check out yourself. Now, the second thing may interest you more, as it relates to the material you sent me, and this is the part that excites me. If I am correct, then the tomb must have been discovered and removed by the Ottomans during their occupation of Egypt.'

Brock raised an eyebrow as he looked out over the busy street. He smiled to himself. He'd been pretty sure that Amuyani would stumble over something that others had missed. 'Enlighten me.'

'When the Arabs took over occupation of Egypt from Rome, we know that Caliph Omar commanded the establishment of another capital, Al Fostat. Over the next thousand years Alexandria, with its four thousand palaces, fell into decline. The great Pharos lighthouse was allowed to sink to the sea floor, along with its sculptures, palaces and temples. But I believe that any icons of value would have been removed early on and Alexander's body would certainly come into that category. No Arab caliph would risk a non-Muslim deity's remains being used as a talisman against him in any future uprising. It makes sense to defuse its power by removing it. I would think it a reasonable assumption that Alexander was removed to rest in a place of the Caliph's choosing, wouldn't you?'

'Sounds very plausible. Where does it lead us?'

'Well, part of this manuscript found at Ayn Jalut infers that Alexander rests beneath the Nile palace of Amr. But we don't know where that is.'

'You get my hopes up and then dash them down,' said Brock with a laugh. A waiter came up to him and, with a gesture, he ordered a mint tea. 'Sounds like one needle leads to another haystack.'

'Ah, my very sentiments indeed, Connor. But don't despair. A little more research uncovered another needle for us.'

'You found the location of Amr Palace?'

'Not exactly. Now, just a moment.' Brock once more distinguished the sound of rustling papers over the line. 'I must get this right. Now, the palace was constructed for one Amr Ibn-el-Aas, and became the official residence for Ottoman governors until an earthquake in 1348 finally destroyed it. No records remain of its exact location.'

'Oh.' Brock was disappointed. He'd expected more.

'But this is the interesting bit. Now we take a diversion and join Temujin, or the Genghis Khan, as we call him, and his general Subedei.'

Brock felt a prickle over his skin. 'That name . . . I was waiting for it to come up.'

'You already know that Subedei was responsible for subjugating Eastern Europe and Russia. According to *The Secret History of the Mongols*, written at this time, Subedei continued to drive his horde west for twenty years after the death of Temujin Khan, serving under his son Ogedei. When Ogedei died, Subedei had to return to Mongolia to help choose the next Khan.

'During his campaigns, he had heard the legend of a seeing stone of Persia belonging first to Cyrus the Great and later taken by Alexander. He searched for it, as you know, and sent out a band of warriors to locate it, but died disappointed. The *Secret History*, though, records in poetic form that Subedei entrusted Hulagu, grandson of Temujin and brother of Kublai Khan, with the search for the stone, stressing its importance for the continued growth and protection of the Mongolian dynasty.

'Ten years after Subedei's death in 1256, Hulagu travelled west and overcame the Persian Ismailis. He mercilessly stormed Baghdad two years later, plundering and burning the cultural accumulation of five centuries and slaughtering almost a million men, women and children in the streets.'

'This Hulagu sounds like he was another nasty piece of work,' commented Brock flatly.

'He certainly was. His actions are remembered today as the holocaust of Persia. His ferocity was truly awesome, on a scale only equalled in modern times. Every mosque, library, monument and palace was reduced to ashes. Community after community was wantonly destroyed. His calling card was a hideous tower of skulls.'

'Charming.'

'He was probably emulating his grandfather a little more zealously than perhaps he needed to. But his methods worked – the fact is that most of central Asia was under Hulagu's control by this time.

'Also at this time it is recorded that Hulagu sent out scouting squadrons across Persia, Egypt and Syria to hunt for the stone and Subedei's original band of warriors, the ones he sent out who never returned. Then, upon hearing of the ruling Khan's death, his brother Mongke, Hulagu was forced to return home with most of his army, as Subedei had done years earlier. A year later in 1260 his remaining depleted army was severely defeated by the slave army of Mamluks at Ayn Jalut.'

'The battle site where the manuscript was found, then given to the Vatican,' said Brock.

'Absolutely, and now here is the part I know will most greatly

230

interest you. First, *The Secret History of the Mongols* refers to one of Subedei's chosen nameless warriors returning the seeing stone of the Mongolian deity Duua to Hulagu.'

'What? Wait, they claim to have found the stone?'

'My assumption is that it is the same stone, so yes, they must have found it.'

'And if we follow your previous assumption that the stone was in the sword and the sword was with Alexander . . .' Brock gripped the phone more tightly. 'Then it follows that a Mongolian warrior discovered Alexander's tomb. Right?'

'Correct, my friend,' chirped the professor, enjoying Brock's excitement. 'And the manuscript seems to tell us how they got their hands on the stone. Listen.' Amuyani cleared his throat and read. '*The Ashes of Ammon surrendered our stone in the name of Mongke Khan, brother to Hulagu, by the command of Subedei.*' The professor paused. 'From which we may assume, Connor, that they found the stone by *burning* the body of Alexander to retrieve it.'

'I don't believe it. They burned Alexander the Great?' whispered Brock.

'I think we can tell from their track record that the Mongolians weren't overly concerned with the preservation of the traditions and cultures of their enemies. So yes, it looks as though they burned the great conqueror's body, though he probably didn't mind. Most Macedonian kings were cremated. But what is exciting is that his instruction to his friend Ptolemy to bury the stone with him was taken literally.'

'I can't believe no one has spotted this before.'

'Well, your friend Maria's manuscript is not well known and not well translated – except by me, of course. And even if it had been translated properly, it takes a certain interpretation to come to this conclusion. But it is what I believe we can understand the writer to mean.'

'The way you've put it makes it sound very plausible. But what about this sword? The God Sword? Surely they didn't put that inside Alexander as well?'

'I can't help you much there. Who knows what became of it, or even if it existed? Icons will often be given a variety of names by different cultures. The symbol of the sword is favoured more in western mythology, whereas the mystic object is closer to eastern cultures. However, if we assume, as the engraved statue in the Vatican tells us, that Cyrus was given or took the stone from the Zoroastrian Magi, it may be that he carried an eastern icon within his sword, thus spawning the legend of the God Sword that so enthralled Alexander. But these are only guesses.'

'But the manuscript from Ayn Jalut does refer to a God Sword, doesn't it? As well as a stone?'

'Perhaps the stone had to be prised out of a sword. Or the sword could refer to Alexander himself. As I say, without firm evidence we can only guess. Though, from a psychological perspective, it may not be satisfying to your modern-day Temujin Subedei.'

'Why do you say that?'

'Simply because the evidence he holds refers to a God Sword. He is probably looking for an actual weapon. Perhaps that's why he contacted the Vatican in the first place, hoping they could shed light on the matter.'

Brock thought hard. 'OK – so let me see if we have this straight. The last rumoured location of Alexander's tomb was the Amr Palace; we are now assuming that the body was discovered by a Mongolian warrior sent out by Subedei, who then either burned the body himself, or took it to Hulagu, and he burned it. Either way, they found the stone inside the body. Do we have any word of what happened to it next?'

'There is nothing. But my own instinct is that they did return home with the stone, and that Hulagu gave it to his brother, the Kublai Khan, who immediately defeated Ariq-boeke, his rival for the throne. Interestingly, he became known as the Great Khan.'

'And you think that the stone made him great?'

'Such is the purpose of iconic talismans. And, of course, we never hear of the failures. But Cyrus, Alexander, Kublai Khan . . . these names are great ones and each is linked with the possession of the stone. Perhaps it truly carries mystical powers.'

'And in modern terms, Subedei is following a path to greatness. Subedei Industries has enjoyed a meteoric rise. Perhaps he already has the stone. To a man like Subedei, open to mysticism, owning a stone that he thought had the power to confer greatness would give him the boundless confidence actually to achieve his dreams.' Brock sighed and shook his head. 'But where would he have found it?'

Amuyani's voice came distantly down the line. 'There are theories . . . my hypothesis is that the stone most likely ended up in a Tibetan monastery.'

'Really? Why?'

'Because with the decline of the strength of the Mongols came the rise in Tibetan Buddhism. Control by the Tibetan Lamas increased over the centuries until the Mongolian Tibetan Church itself was proclaimed the Khan of all Mongolia. The pinnacle of this was when Altan Khan, a descendant of Kublai Khan, linked state and church in the sixteenth century, firstly by inviting a prelate who had claims to the primacy in Tibet, but also rivals, and proclaimed him Dalai Lama; then by conveniently finding a son of the line of Genghis Khan to be a first reincarnation of the prelate's line.

'Then in the eighteenth century when the Manchu dynasty controlled Mongolia they ruled that no man of the lineage of Genghis Khan could be "discovered" to be a reincarnation or living Buddha; that they must in future always be discovered in Tibet. Such a sanction split apart the church and state, weakening even further Mongolia, which had already reverted to nomadic tribes. At this time, all icons and religious artefacts of value were vested in Tibetan monasteries. If the stone was revered, as it must surely have been, then it would have been one of the first things to go.'

'Professor, you're a genius.'

Amuyani chuckled. 'Well, perhaps I am. Has this been of help?'

'It most certainly has.' Brock stared out over the busy street, not seeing the bustle in front of him. His mind had moved miles away to Temujin Subedei. How much of all this did he know?

'Now, may I ask a question?' said the professor. 'This man you are interested in, this captain of industry. Why do you think this stone matters so much to him? He is certainly going to a great deal of effort because of it.'

'He's Mongolian,' said Brock. 'My hunch is that he is seeking some kind of modern empire on a par with Genghis Khan's ancient military conquests.'

'Oh! Then he has delusions of grandeur, surely.'

'Every great man has had them – the difference between him and the lunatic is that he makes his delusions come true.'

233

'You are right, my friend. But if he wishes to found a new Mongolian empire, he is living in a dream world. Times have changed. Pan-Mongolism, the desire to reunite politically all the Mongols and rule an empire, was always more of a romantic idea than a practical one.'

'But stellar success in the business world would restore a sense of that empire, wouldn't it? There isn't a man alive who wouldn't relish achieving those heights.' Brock closed his eyes and thought for a moment. His friend waited patiently on the other end of the line. Then Brock said, 'He believes in his destiny, in his greatness. That's his greatest strength. Subedei is just that kind of man – like Genghis and Hulagu and Kublai and all of them – I can sense it. He is utterly ruthless where his ambition is concerned, because he believes it is his fate, that everything he does is justified because it is his destiny. It's why he's so dangerous. He thinks that no matter what he does, the great end will justify the means.'

Twenty-Seven

Subedei's face was expressionless as his black eyes darted to each member of the cartel. In his flickering glance, he gauged their body language as they conversed with each other while being entertained by Mi Ling. None of the four was aware they were being studied as they waited for their host. The highly polished mirror that obscured him appeared to be part of the elaborate decor.

Each of the four was entirely different. The only thing they shared, apart from their interests in the oil industry, was an avarice for priceless relics of antiquity, regardless of their provenance. These two traits made them ripe for Subedei's exploitation. He had gathered them here, in the opulent throne room concealed within the Alexandrian refinery, once before. Now they were here again, as he had commanded.

Subedei's successful manipulations had followed the principle of divide and conquer. All of them had been clients of his stolen antiquity network; each eager to acquire pieces without concern as to their true ownership. He knew all of their idiosyncrasies; their strengths and weaknesses. They neither knew his nor wanted to. So long as he delivered.

Listening to his guests' idle chatter, Subedei sensed that the initial conversational pleasantries were drying up. He got up from his gilded chair and made his way towards the throne room.

A few seconds later, Natasha Berentsky, a tall elegant woman in her sixties, noticed Subedei enter. She rose gracefully to her feet, her white, almost translucent skin sharply accentuated by the sleeveless knee-length black dress she wore. Her sparkling eyes and thin, heavily lipsticked mouth matched the high-carat diamonds and rubies that covered her fingers. She seemed to glide across the floor, raising her arms in the anticipation of a welcoming embrace. 'Temujin,' she said throatily, in a voice hoarsened by cigarettes. *'Moi dorogoi,* how marvellous to see you.'

Subedei returned the smile. She was, after all, the most dangerous of the four. Recently appointed head of Kazakhstan's most powerful oil barons, she had ultimate control over the Caspian Consortium pipeline.

'Always an honour and a privilege to see you,' he replied, embracing her.

A loud voice interrupted them. 'Stupid question, I suppose, but this is authentic, I assume?' William Somers, English lord, overweight gourmet, renowned collector of antiquity and wine, and defender of the English Right to Hunt, indicated the horn-headed statue of the Egyptian God of Thebes they had been grouped around discussing. 'Oh, good to see you, by the way.'

'Middle Kingdom, twelfth dynasty: the time when the God Ammon became prominent. And, to answer your next question, no, it is not available, but my warm welcome to you is, of course, William.'

'It's in jolly good nick for four thousand years old,' replied the Englishman, his crestfallen jowl, sullen brown eyes bordering a long nose and light-brown greying hair giving him the appearance of one of his own hunting beagles, sniffing dejectedly after losing its prey.

'Better even than some of us,' snorted Guillermo Nicaros. The Venezuelan oil baron seemed tired and haughty. It was obvious that he did not have much time for the other members of Subedei's exclusive cartel. His swarthy face beneath carefully lacquered black hair was in sharp relief to his pristine ivory-coloured linen suit and white shoes. 'We are on schedule, I trust?' he added, as he proffered a manicured hand to Subedei.

'Your lovely wife is enjoying the Columbian throat clasp, I trust,' replied Subedei pleasantly, ignoring the question. The Venezuelan's casual rudeness annoyed him but he concealed it well, with only the slightest edge of ice in his voice. 'Good to see you, my friend.'

Only those standing close to Nicaros could notice his slightly uncomfortable swallow. 'You too, my friend.'

Standing apart from the others, elbows bent and hands held firmly together, stood Walid Abd al Rahwan. Dressed in the ankle-length white robe, black jerkin, dextrously folded turban and silken cords that befitted his high office of a Shi'ite Mullah of Iran, Abd al Rahwan's intense eyes and severe-looking mouth, bordered by thick grey moustache and beard, sprang into a smile when Subedei turned towards him.

'May the peace of Allah be with you, Walid. It is good to see you again. Thank you for coming.'

'And may Allah grant you long life, my brother,' replied Abd al Rahwan earnestly, as he clasped Subedei's hand with both of his.

'Please, if you will be seated, we will begin immediately,' commanded Subedei. 'There is much to discuss.'

Obediently, the four guests returned to their seats. Subedei took his place among them and paused for a moment to make sure they were all attentive. Then he began.

'First and foremost, despite some unforeseen delays, we are on schedule.'

Lord Somers broke in at once, looking anxious. 'Hold hard – what kind of *unforeseen* delays?'

'Just a legality and a minor technicality. Both have already been resolved.'

'Concerning?' persisted Somers.

Subedei's eyes narrowed. 'Not concerning *you*, William, with all due respect. All such factors are within my responsibility. I do not have to account for every minor mishap.'

Somers relaxed slightly but his frown remained. 'Humph. So long as nothing involves our names being bandied around. I, for one, cannot afford to risk that.'

'I promised you immunity in name and impunity from action. I am not aware of any risk that involves you. I only know what reward you will be entitled to. Of course, should you no longer wish to share in that, you are free to go.'

Somers' already ruddy face, weather-beaten from years of riding to hounds, turned a deeper colour of crimson. 'Sorry, old man. Don't mean to be rude. I just get a little nervous sometimes, that's all. Please continue.'

Subedei smiled patiently. 'Thank you. I'm delighted that you have invested so much emotion into our project. Your concern is appreciated. The technicality was simply that one of our own dredgers became snagged up on our compound MM120. Fortunately, it happened just after the final load had been delivered. And, as is always the case, there were advantages. For one thing, we were given a first-class demonstration of the effectiveness of MM120. In fact, it proved itself considerably more powerful than we originally calculated.'

'Bravo, Temujin! For my part, I'm delighted to learn of yet another success, and one that will benefit us all,' declared Berentsky, her hard eyes swivelling around to glower at the Englishman. 'On schedule – and with a confirmation of an effective catalyst in our strategy,' she added. 'Let me be the first to congratulate you.'

'Thank you, Natasha. Now, the main purpose in calling you together is to hear first-hand from you that your own arrangements are on schedule. As you all know, there can be no disappointments.'

Abd al Rahwan spread his hands across the table, the palms facing upwards. 'Our pipeline has been ready these past three weeks now. In fact, our regime is becoming somewhat impatient for everything to begin, although I have reminded them that June is the date agreed. Our preliminary negotiations have proceeded magnificently with all of the Emirates. Both the Saudi kingdom and Kuwait have expressed interest in our proposals although they say that they see no future in them at the moment. The Yemen, with their Shi'ite government, will be more than happy to deal with us, as will Iraq. Their own pipeline to Turkey is continually targeted and damaged, which they find frustrating, to say the least.'

'Your strategy of using your Shi'ite friends to sabotage the main pipelines and then blame the former regime's resisting militia has worked splendidly,' purred Berentsky. 'And our new pipeline to China is more than sufficient to carry the flow from the Gulf, Iran and Iraq via the Caspian. And, of course, we can increase or decrease flow as we choose, allowing Iraqi oil to flow either west to Ceyhan or to the east.'

'Though it will not flow until the Saudis are persuaded not to send their supertankers around the Cape,' replied Abd al Rahwan. 'We are agreed on that, are we not?'

Subedei looked at Nicaros, who leaned back in his chair, surveying the large Havana cigar that he had just removed from its leather pocket before speaking.

'It will not benefit them even if they do,' said the Venezuelan.

'For the past year, under cover of the excuse of strikes and unrest, we have been stockpiling sufficient quantities to meet the Saudi supply to the US for three months. The US only cries foul when their oil is cut off, not when it flows more freely. For two weeks the barrel price will reduce dramatically with the increased supply, then, when Saudi oil no longer flows to them, the cost of our supply will rise significantly.'

'But how can we be certain that the Saudis will not continue to export to them?' questioned the mullah. 'Our countries may both be Arab Muslim lands, but their majority Sunni populace have proved in the past that they prefer dealing with the US before Iran. For that matter, so do Oman and Egypt.'

Subedei smiled confidently at the Iranian. 'In the event that Saudi oil does continue to be shipped to the US, I can assure you that it will only be for a period of months. After that, they will be forced to send it eastward. Remember, there is a whole network of inactive pipelines heading towards Iran that were built during the Arab Israeli tensions. It will only be a policy decision to switch routes. No additional investment will be required. There need be no concerns for Egypt either. I am negotiating with them personally.' Subedei's black eyes bore into Lord Somers. 'What about the UK, William?'

Lord Somers coughed. 'Yes, quite. Well, as you know, I head up the UK government policy committee for energy. One of our key agenda points is how to extricate ourselves from the mood swings of OPEC. The whims of the oil-exporting countries had an infuriating effect on our economy. To get round this, our own major oil companies have become the prime sponsors of the new pipeline that is fed from the rich Caspian fields. Though there will be political pressure to follow suit with the US in respect of protecting the flow of Gulf Oil, in reality we will support the flow from the Caspian and North Africa. It's best for our economy, you see.'

'But when the price per barrel is doubled?' enquired the Russian woman. 'What then?'

'Grin and bear it, I'm afraid, just like we did with OPEC.'

Nicaros sneered at the Englishman. 'And meanwhile you feather your nest very nicely, eh?'

'We all make a penny or two, don't we, my dear Guillermo? And as for my nest – it could do with a new roof and some

239

serious upkeep. The downside of a family estate going back centuries.'

The conference continued as they all ran through the schedule of operations. After an hour Mi Ling re entered leading a group of cheongsam-clad Chinese girls carrying trays of exotic dim sum delicacies, smoked sturgeon and caviar, sweet breads, spicy meats and honeyed morsels. An ebony box tray was placed before each guest.

'My dear colleagues,' said Subedei silkily. 'Much as I would delight further in your company, I must leave you. I have a meeting with the Egyptian president and then a reception on board my yacht – the importance of which you all fully appreciate.'

'The work ahead of you is vital to our cause,' murmured Abd al Rahwan. 'May your words this evening be guided by Allah.'

Subedei smiled at the mullah in acknowledgement. 'You already know, of course, how much I regret that we cannot be seen in public together at this critical time, so please do accept my humble hospitality here. When you are ready to leave, Mi Ling will direct you to your cars. They're waiting to take you to your respective jets.'

Subedei raised the glass of ice-cold Siberian Stolichnaya Mi Ling had surreptitiously placed by him. 'Natasha, gentlemen – a toast to our cartel, our project, our mutual objectives. To Operation Genghis Khan!'

The chorused reply rang with the clinking glasses.

'Operation Genghis Khan.'

It was the flash of red hair – so incongruous among the milling afternoon crowds – that caught his eye. Despite numerous cups of strong sweet Arabic coffee intended to keep him vigilant, the boredom of waiting and the strain of constantly studying faces to match the image from a memorized photograph, had dulled his reactions. But a second later, as the significance of that flash of red sunk in, Barracio became fully alert.

The Italian's jaw tightened as Ferguson came fully into view. After the first botched attempt in a Zurich underpass, he had waited in growing frustration at the airport for his targets to arrive. But they had never shown up. The schedule he had been given was incorrect.

It wasn't fair that he had been reprimanded for failing in his mission, for being unprofessional, when the information they had provided him with was wrong. What was he supposed to do about that? He could only work according to instructions. The onus of getting him the correct information was theirs, not his.

How dare they question him?

He had travelled immediately on to Alexandria, taking one of the only two seats left on the next flight. His instinct had been to stay in the area of the quay, close to the *Pharaoh Queen*. He was sure that one or the other, if not both, of his targets would come here before long to check out the vessel before tonight's reception. And his initiative had paid off.

He watched the red-haired man carefully, tracking his every move.

'Now, that's a yacht!' muttered Ferguson, impressed. The splendid vessel in front of him stretched ninety-nine metres along the quayside and blended the elegance of a bygone age with the latest modern technology. It was clearly lavish, from the swimming pool stretching along the lower deck to the helipad visible on the top deck. If the outside were anything to go by, then the inside would be the height of luxury, with opulent state rooms and gyms and cinemas and goodness only knew what else.

Not bad at all, thought Matt, wandering along the yacht's hull, trying to look as though he weren't particularly interested in it. Then he suddenly froze on the spot.

Standing on the prow of the teak-decked yacht stood a strikingly beautiful woman gazing serenely down the Nile. He knew that elegant profile and the sleek curtain of black hair.

'Well, hello. If it isn't our friendly guide,' breathed Ferguson. 'I wonder what web you're weaving this time.'

For a moment the Irishman enjoyed watching her. She was undoubtedly a gorgeous woman and Matt felt the stirring of desire as he looked at her slim form. Then the face of John Ridge came into his mind, igniting a determined resolve within him.

'You are to cast-off at eight o'clock precisely. Understand? Even if some of the guests are late. I want no excuses. Those are my orders.' Ayeesha stared at the crew imperiously. 'We are collecting the guest of honour, the president, and His Excellency Subedei from his estate at exactly eight thirty. On no account will we be a minute later.'

Ayeesha turned to her assistant, her eyebrows raised as if daring her to disagree.

Fatima said breathlessly, 'Alexandrian guests have been requested to arrive early, and all flights carrying our guests from abroad are on time. Their cars are already waiting, so we should not encounter any problem.'

'*Should not?*' Ayeesha tossed her head. 'Are those not ears either side of your head? There will be *no* problem.' Turning to the captain, she added, 'I repeat, you will depart at eight and not a moment later.'

Fatima Saeed looked visibly deflated at the reception her comments had received. Her cheeks reddened and she cast her eyes downwards.

'I am leaving now and will rejoin you later with Lord Subedei and our honoured guests,' Ayeesha continued. 'If there are any questions, ask them now, for there will be absolutely no allowance for mistakes. A team of our own security people will be boarding soon and they are to be allowed access anywhere on the yacht. Some of them will arrive incognito and, if they choose to, will make themselves known to you. Captain, you are responsible for the crew and the majority of the guests, but the security team is responsible for our host and the president.'

Captain Antonis Stanotopoulos, stocky, friendly, clean-shaven and looking younger than his fifty-two years, nodded politely. After twenty-five years of catering to the naïve arrogance of wealthy travellers on cruise ships and rich yacht owners, he was a veteran at how to handle them. He said smoothly, 'I speak for all the crew when I say we are utterly confident of our instructions. You and Miss Saeed have been highly competent and nothing has been left to chance. You have my personal assurance, Ms Al Fahila, that everything will go exactly as you have so thoughtfully and professionally planned.'

Ayeesha glowed with pleasure at the praise. 'Thank you for that, Captain. I appreciate your understanding, and I know my assistant here values your support.' She turned towards the gangway and stalked down to the waiting limousine, an anxious Fatima following closely at her heels.

*   *   *

Ferguson sipped the cold beer he had ordered from the quay café. He spent a good twenty minutes committing to memory all the essential details of the *Pharaoh Queen*, noting that the extended marquee constructed across the wide-open stern indicated that the reception would be partly on deck.

A movement drew his attention and he saw the beautiful guide from Siwa marching down the gangway, attended by a fluttering, anxious-looking girl. Both climbed into the waiting limousine and were driven smoothly away.

'Bye, bye, my little spider,' murmured Ferguson. 'I'll see you later.'

He continued to monitor the yacht. Five minutes later, a Mercedes van drove up and a group of heavy-looking men got out, unloaded bags of equipment, swung them over their shoulders, then boarded the *Pharaoh Queen*, some with an aggressive swagger, some with a loose, confident gait. Ferguson counted eight.

'These'll be our hired heavies. No prizes for guessing what's inside those bags,' he muttered. He finished his drink, got up, put some coins on the table and began to walk casually back in the direction of the Montazeh Palace Hotel. He was unaware that he was being followed.

Twenty-Eight

Signalling the cooling of the day's heat, the reddening sun descended slowly and majestically through the evening sky to sink beyond the palmed bank of the Nile.

Its disappearance brought welcome relief from the heat of the day for the guests on board the *Pharaoh Queen*. The throng of people – the women in sparkling evening dress, the men in dinner jackets or ankle-length robes with ceremonial silk turbans and cords – were eager for the trip to get underway.

The sea clock struck eight and immediately the fore and aft lines were released. There was an audible sigh of relief from the nervous young woman standing by the retracting silver gangway. She had been studying the guest list anxiously when the ringing sound of patent leather shoes coming up the gangway had made her look up.

She said happily, 'Good evening! Welcome aboard, Sir Duncan Buchanan and Dr Paul van . . .' She stopped in surprise. 'Oh!'

Brock smiled disarmingly as he handed her two invitations. 'Our office did confirm a change in delegate details, Fatima. Your list should have our names on it. I am Connor Brock, you remember. My colleague here is Matt Ferguson.'

'Pleased to meet you,' grinned the Irishman. He'd brushed up well for the occasion, looking almost presentable with a green silk bow tie and matching cummerbund.

Fatima shook their proffered hands automatically, her anxious expression changing to one of suspicion. 'But wait a moment – you're with Ammon Oil, aren't you? Not a representative of ICE,' she whispered, trying not to attract the attention of the security man standing a discreet two metres away. The last thing she wanted was a scene.

Brock had noticed the man immediately. That loose jacket

was a fairly penetrable disguise. He was packing some metal underneath it.

'Working with Mr Subedei's various companies does have its challenges,' he whispered back conspiratorially. 'But he insisted on us being here, hence the invitation change. All part of his strict security requirement.'

Brock flicked a glance to Ferguson and nodded almost imperceptibly towards the security. Immediately, Ferguson moved affably towards the guard, introducing himself and striking up a conversation.

Brock turned his attention back to Fatima. 'Our colleagues are being both discreet and supportive, I hope?'

Relief crossed Fatima's face. She obviously had regained her confidence in him. 'Oh, of course, I see now. Ms Al Fahila told me that the special security people would make themselves individually known to me. I'm sorry for being so wary.'

Brock smiled. 'Don't be. In fact, I will make a point of commending your vigilance to Ms Al Fahila herself.'

'But just a moment, Mr Brock,' called Fatima, as he moved into the yacht. 'Don't forget your headset.' Then she lowered her voice and said in a slightly embarrassed whisper, 'You probably have your own concealed one.'

Brock raised an eyebrow. 'Headset?'

'For the president's speech,' replied Fatima, handing him two tiny radios. 'He insists on only making them in his country's language.'

'Of course he does.'

'You can keep them. It will work as a normal radio as well. A gift from the marketing department, sponsored by our host, of course!'

'Generous of him,' grinned Brock. 'I'll treasure it.'

Short, stocky, with thinning silver hair, a large bent nose and almost unblinking hooded eyes, President Mohamed Jumair had not been swept to power on the basis of his looks. Rather, it had been his charismatic style and oratory skills, bordering on the fervent, that had won him the support of the minority of the Egyptian populace who had turned out to vote for him. That, and his promise of economic revival. He had vowed to put domestic policies and the good of the Egyptian people first.

Too many of his predecessors had been overly concerned with foreign policy. The only sort of foreign policy the new president was interested in was the overseas investment that would bring wealth to his people and his country.

Timing is everything in politics and Jumair knew that his could not have been more perfect. After three years of low tourism – one of Egypt's main industries – and conflict in the Arabic territories to the east, a complete turnabout had been realized. Within six months of taking office, Jumair had seen investment for the New Pyramids confirmed, solving almost at a stroke the unemployment endemic in the Cairo suburbs; a giant new desalination project to irrigate the eastern desert from the Red Sea had been announced; and now major oil reserves had been discovered, along with new archaeological treasures that promised a reawakening of interest in ancient Egypt and a corresponding increase in visitors. So – more investment, more hotels and more tourism would follow, and with it the economic growth so essential for political stability.

Feeling as content as a politician could, Jumair spoke in pronounced English, his sonorous voice reflecting his pleasure. 'My country's gratitude to the People's Republic of China is impossible to measure for what it has so generously done for Egypt. As its humble servant, I can only add my personal thanks to you, my friend, for your enormous efforts, investment brokerage and generous donations.'

'It is you who are the generous one, Mr President,' replied Subedei, his whole demeanour humble. 'I am not worthy of such praise.'

'You must allow me to be the judge of that. Our discussions over the last hour have only served to confirm my assessment.'

'Then I accept your thanks because we are friends.'

Jumair smiled broadly as he leaned back in his chair and sipped the postprandial sweet fig liqueur that had been so thoughtfully provided for him. He was impressed – few knew about his particular liking for it. 'Are you certain you want me to make the announcements on board the *Pharaoh Queen* tonight? I feel like I am somewhat stealing the credit you so richly deserve for all the risks you have taken, my friend.'

Subedei raised his eyebrows and held up his palms in mock

severity. 'Not at all, Mr President. It is you who are the representative of your country – you are the face of its people. Not
Subedei Industries or Ammon Oil. Without your foresight and
vision, none of what we are about to announce when we join
the yacht would have come to pass.'

'I have to admit that I am eager to see the look on the face
of Benerzat,' laughed Jumair. 'As they say in my country, he will
have the look of the hungry merchant who has saved the best
figs for himself, only to discover that they are sour.'

Subedei laughed politely. 'Well said. Benerzat's policy of
western favouritism could only have led to a reaction of distaste
from your people. And you will have your triumph. I personally ensured that the opposition leader was invited. He will be
waiting for us when we board the yacht tonight.'

Jumair looked across the low table at Subedei, his eyes mischie-
vous. 'It is good that you continue to stay in contact with him.
Good for business. Though perhaps not quite as good as your
contact with me. That lucrative dredging contract you were so
fortunate to capture soon after my inauguration would not have
been forthcoming if Benerzat had taken office.'

Subedei's eyes revealed nothing as he said, 'Our investment
decisions and loyalty remain firm, irrespective of short-term
contractual gains, or any unexpected rewards that may come
about through our friendship. In China, we believe it is important to get as close to the enemies of our friends as it is to our
friends. For when our friends are threatened, so are we.'

'Well answered, my friend,' replied Jumair, setting his glass
down on the table. 'And again let me personally assure you that
while I hold office, neither your loyalty nor our good relations
could be more highly valued. My only worry is that Benerzat is
undermining our futures through his demands for more inte-
gration with Europe. It is frustrating when prosperity is so close
at hand.'

Subedei smiled, his thin lips curving upwards. 'Then let me
assure you, Mr President, that following your announcement,
your rival and his policies will be soon forgotten.'

Casually sipping from his fluted glass of champagne, Brock
pretended to enjoy the tranquil view of the feluccas as they
moored up for the evening along the banks of the Nile.

247

Meanwhile, he surreptitiously observed the forty or so guests who had boarded at Alexandria.

At the centre of one circle was a distinguished-looking silver-haired gentleman. He was clearly someone of influence and the people around him – Europeans for the most part – seemed to be hanging on his every word. At his side was a striking young woman. She wore a black, full-length evening dress in shimmering silk, her creamy arms and shoulders only faintly visible through the veil that covered them. Her dark hair was piled on top of her head into a smooth, elegant style; her almond-shaped eyes were emphasized by kohl and her lips gleamed red. She was truly elegant: restrained and yet full of promise.

Brock shook his head slowly from side to side in surprise, as the young woman caught his eye, smiled, excused herself from her partner and made her way directly towards him.

He raised an eyebrow. 'Well, well, Flight Sergeant. Every time I meet you is more pleasant than the last. You look exceptionally beautiful this evening.'

Neusheen Benerzat smiled. 'Thank you, Connor. You look like a half-decent gentleman yourself, an improvement on the grimy individual I saw last. Incidentally, you disappeared without a word.'

Brock gave her an appealing look. 'Sorry, Neusheen. When I'm working, social niceties seem to go out of the window.'

'You don't say . . .'

'I promise I won't do it again. But what on earth are you doing at this bash?'

'I should be asking you that question. I didn't see your name on the guest list I requested,' replied Neusheen. She looked over her shoulder to the group she had come from. 'I'm here with my father.'

'Which one is he?'

She smiled and said cheekily, 'He is Imran Benerzat, leader of the opposition.' She laughed at Brock's obvious astonishment.

'You didn't tell me that,' he said, with mock reproach.

'Mr Brock – you never asked.'

'You're full of surprises, Neusheen.'

'I like to keep people guessing. And you could have worked it out, actually. You knew my surname. But then – most people outside Egypt wouldn't even be able to name the president, let alone the leader of the opposition. I suppose I can't be too hard on you for that.' Neusheen paused as she put her arm through Brock's and gave him her wide infectious smile. 'Now, come and let me introduce you to my father.'

Brock allowed himself to be led through the group to where Imran Benerzat, having caught his daughter's eye, closed the conversation with the person engaging him in the smooth way of an experienced politician, and turned to greet them.

'Papa, this is Connor Brock. Connor, this is my father, Imran Benerzat.' Neusheen performed the introduction elegantly as the two men shook hands.

'My daughter has told me a lot about you, Mr Brock, and your commendable organization, ICE,' Benerzat said. His eyes were warm and he smiled broadly.

'Thank you, sir, though you have me at a disadvantage. All I know is that your daughter holds you in the highest regard.'

Benerzat beamed warmly, reminding Brock of Neusheen's infectious smile. 'Praise for a politician and a father in one sentence, eh? Have you ever considered entering either profession? Both are rewarding.'

'So successful representatives of both have repeatedly informed me,' answered Brock. 'Though I freely admit that politics is a game I neither understand nor play well. Protecting corporate governance is more my line.'

Benerzat's eyes turned downwards. 'It is a game indeed,' he sighed, 'and sadly too often involving players who put their own interests before those of their team, supporters, and country.' The tinge of bitterness in Benerzat's metaphor was clear to detect.

'The world is full of self-serving men,' agreed Brock. 'Talking of whom, I've not seen our host this evening. Is he here?'

'He is boarding with the president shortly. Something to do with security precautions, I think,' said Neusheen.

Her father gave Brock a cynical look. 'Jumair likes to make an entrance. No doubt we will be treated to a long speech about how well Egypt is doing under his presidency. It's his favourite topic. I'll have to stand here and endure it, I suppose.'

'May I ask, sir, why you accepted this invitation?'

Benerzat smiled. 'Why do you think? Mr Subedei is extremely

249

influential. I really couldn't refuse and be taken seriously in the political world. It's the rules of the game, Mr Brock; if we are not in the game, how could we possibly hope to win politically?'

Fatima had continued to cast concerned glances at Brock, but she was comforted by his warm reception from such an important guest.

For the tenth time in as many minutes, she glanced at her watch and felt further relieved as she glimpsed the palace Subedei had made his Egyptian home come into view. They were right on schedule.

Observing the *Pharaoh Queen* glide nearer to the quay, Brock excused himself from the Benerzats and made his way towards the entrance of the salon. Right on cue, Ferguson slipped back in and joined Brock at the side of the room. Brock picked up two fresh flutes of champagne from the tray of a passing waiter and he and Matt stood casually, sipping at them while they talked in low voices.

'How did it go?' Brock asked.

'Like clockwork. These heavies are everywhere but they're meatheads, luckily. Subedei's stateroom revealed nothing untoward, apart from a selection of interesting toys that you don't want to hear about. No computer or communications equipment, other than a built-in video. And not even a doodle left lying around, before you ask.'

'Thanks, Matt. I suppose it's to be expected but I'd had a sneaking hope we'd find something.'

They were interrupted by the slightly wavering voice of Fatima, coming over the public address system, first in Arabic, then in French and finally in English.

'Ladies and gentlemen, in a few minutes we will be arriving at the recently discovered Temple of Ammon that you will see we are approaching on the eastern bank. As ancient Egypt's most revered god, Ammon had many temples built to honour him along the Nile, the most famous being at Karnak north of Luxor on the lower Nile.

'Our host, Mr Temujin Subedei, also patron of our country's Antiquities Council, has brilliantly rebuilt the ancient palace that formerly adjoined the temple, making a small part of it his Egyptian residence and generously gifting the rest to our esteemed president as a country home. I am pleased to announce that our guest of honour, President Jumair, and our host, Mr Subedei, are to board as soon as we dock.'

Ferguson looked at Brock and grinned. 'It's the man himself. I bet you can't wait.'

Brock ignored him. Instead, the knuckles of his hand whitened as he gripped his glass more tightly. 'Of course! It's obvious,' he breathed.

Matt gave him a quizzical look. 'Now, that'll be a look I know well crossing your face. You've lit up like a light bulb. What's up?'

'It was the Palace of Ammon,' explained Brock, an excited glimmer in his eyes. '*Ammon*, not Amr. Subedei *did* already know the location.'

Twenty-Nine

Within less than ten minutes of the *Pharaoh Queen*'s lines being secured, a further ninety guests who had been waiting under a marquee erected for their convenience had eagerly boarded. Two minutes later Ayeesha Al Fahila, flanked by six heavy-looking officials, followed. Her chin slightly aloof, she made directly for the podium at the end of the stern that had been placed in readiness; while the six security men directed the guests standing closest to the red-carpeted walkway to move back.

Standing unseen at the back of the crowd, Ferguson did not have to understand the language to recognize the royal tone that addressed the audience; enthralled as though they were gazing upon the face of Queen Nefertiti, her very name meaning 'the beautiful one'.

Within seconds of her introduction, both President Jumair and Subedei – closely surrounded by a further entourage of bodyguards that had remained part and parcel of the presidency since the assassination of Anwar Sadat – moved smoothly along the red carpet leading from the waterside palace entrance directly across the lowered walkway on to the waiting yacht.

Full of smiles, the veteran politician expertly shook all the hands of waiting well-wishers, before taking his place behind the raised lectern. Stretching his arms outwards as if to embrace the crowd, the slightly stooping insignificant lawyer seemed to grow in stature; starting his address as if he were officiating at his own wedding.

'My dear friends and respected colleagues, I feel deeply privileged to be your guest of honour this evening. All of us present here today are part of a generation that has experienced Egypt's return to its own sovereignty. But after enduring twenty-five centuries of abusive colonialism, the road back to greatness through our own independence has been fraught with difficulty. An arduous experience for our country but one which has only strengthened our peoples' resolve.

'The wealth contained within our heritage – a heritage that most of the world can only envy – together with the wealth of our natural resources has been sought and removed; a crime that caused my own administration, as well as those of my predecessors, immense frustration. But today as masters once more of our own destiny we are able to maximize such heritage and resources for our own benefit.

'Admittedly, however, we are still not strong enough to be able to optimize and develop our country without investment or support. This has been a personal burden for me as I have promised the Egyptian people positive improvements in education, employment and of course recognition and reward.

'For this reason I was determined to seek out allies who would prove to hold genuine commitment in our country's future, allowing us to determine it without the obligation of iniquitous contracts, one-sided agreements and impeding political ties.

'An impossible task many declared, and I freely confess that I quickly became of similar mind after so many false relationships. It was therefore with understandable cynicism that I first viewed an unsolicited approach I received from the People's Republic of China.

'Yet I am now able to stand before you on this day and announce that with their generous support on both commercial and altruistic ventures, Egypt has found within her womb new life that promises to realize her dormant potential. The world is about to witness the birth of a new Egypt. And it is only fitting that you as loyal citizens and supportive friends should be the first to hear the news of such an event.

'First from an archaeological perspective, so essential to our tourism and cultural heritage, the Lost Army of Cambyses II, appropriately the first overlord who deceitfully subjugated Egypt, has been discovered. Our very own Curator of the Supreme Council of Antiquities, Suleiman Attallah, heading his team of international experts, has confirmed that it is indeed a fortuitous discovery. Indeed it is the only archaeological find in our great history relating to a complete army. Now that we have a policy of tying in our cultural heritage with commercial tourism, we can expect great investment and revenue.'

President Jumair paused, allowing the applause to subside, beaming at the receptive audience.

'Secondly it is my pleasure to announce that reserves amounting to an estimated fifty billion barrels have been located, making Egypt one of the richest oil nations in the world.'

For a moment there was an absolute stunned silence as the full import of their president's words sank in. Then rapturous applause and cheers spontaneously broke out from the crowd. Members of the press invited to record the live announcement for later transmission; robed and suited business tycoons; lawyers and accountants representing wealthy clients all looked desperate to use their mobile phones, salivating like Pavlovian dogs at the news.

Jumair looked directly at the face of his opposing party's figurehead, Benerzat, and munificently beamed like a contented cat that had licked the only available cream; inwardly feeling slightly annoyed when the only reaction he saw cross his opponent's face was one of genuine pleasure. Again he royally raised his hand to quell the impromptu outburst.

'Neither of these great opportunities for Egypt would have been possible without the loyal commitment of the man who brokered the relationship with The People's Republic of China; a man whose generous patronage has rekindled our antiquities council, so weighed down under its budget constraints received from my predecessor's administration; a man whose welcomed investment into many of our planned developments will ensure their successful fruition.

'Indeed, I have learned just this evening directly from him that though one of his recently acquired companies had been granted the major construction contract relating to the New Pyramids, our flagship that will signal future developments, he has relinquished the contract. Why? Because he has insisted that fully-owned Egyptian companies be allowed to bid for it, acutely recognizing the importance of local ownership. But in addition to this and to ensure that the New Pyramids will not be delayed in any way, he has personally promised ten million dollars in construction materials to the project.'

The president paused as he directed the crowd's attention to the man standing just off the podium.

'My dear friends, my dear respected colleagues, please join me in extending Egypt's gratitude to Temujin Subedei.'

Subedei humbly acknowledged the warm applause, declining the calls for a response. Inside he could not be more content. Jumair had performed exactly as planned, taking the limelight while being directed from behind the scenes like a stringed puppet.

For the next fifteen minutes everyone wanted to come and shake the president's and Subedei's hand before returning in groups to discuss excitedly the news just announced. Jumair happily obliged reporters desperate to guide him towards another photo session while bombarding him with questions. For a moment Subedei was alone, enjoying the inner glory that the president's announcement had personally given him.

'You're very generous with Al Kadeh's money. Perhaps you could donate some more of it to the Vatican? You see, they didn't know involvement with you was going to cost them so much, as neither of course did Al Kadeh.'

Subedei's head jerked up at the rugged tanned features of the man who stood a foot taller than him; the azure eyes, as deep and cold as the ocean, penetrating his own.

The moment of being caught off-guard was fleeting as he instantly recognized the face. 'Mr Brock, how good of you to come in person.'

'Good of you to invite me,' replied Brock, inwardly impressed at Subedei's cool recovery.

'Well the invitation was really extended to your superiors, not their hired underlings, though I did count a little on you coming.'

'Speaking of underlings, you really ought to review your own. To bungle simple jobs at Siwa and Rome is one thing. But to leave sacks around for any passing dredger to get caught up on is just plain irresponsible. What are the job requirements? Keeping their eyes, ears and mouth shut like the three Chinese monkeys while they do your perverted bidding?'

Subedei's controlled demeanour momentarily evaporated once more; his malicious eyes narrowing menacingly as his face darkened with rage. Brock readied himself to receive the assault he had provoked. It was not forthcoming. Learning that the near disaster to his plans at Al Qantarah had been no accident had shocked Subedei to the core and he fought to maintain his self-control, his rational mind telling him this was neither the time nor place to be antagonized.

'You are without doubt an interesting man, Mr Brock. Yours is a commendable organization, an organization indeed that has been founded in the interests of economic relations, and one that I have been approached to join. So why is it you persist in trying to attach malpractice to mine? And don't think I am not aware of your actions. The reason that I have ignored them is that to do anything else would only be to place importance on your unsustainable allegations.'

'You're ice-cool; I'll give you that, which is the closest you'll ever get to taking over my organization.'

'Famous last words is the saying you quote in the west under such circumstances isn't it? Think on the bright side. When you are no longer with them you will be able to start a hobby.'

Brock grinned broadly. 'You know, maybe you're right, that's not such a bad idea. Now let's see what could I do that would absorb me. Perhaps I could direct my efforts to revealing the known location of the God Sword to all the museums in the world. Or, on second thoughts, I could give lectures on how to block canals and vital arterial auto routes at the same time. No, such lectures would only interest a limited audience. I know I could publish a paper on the merits of Mongolian Chinese domination won through discounted oil. I wonder what your namesakes Genghis Khan and Subedei, even the merciless Hulagu, would think of your strategy. After all, yours is certainly a transparent enough operation for even the primitive mind to see through.'

As Subedei's jaw wordlessly opened and shut, Brock realized that the few relevant pieces of information he had intuitively connected had struck home.

The pulsating vein on the side of his face was the only discernible movement from Subedei. His mind filled with rage and screamed questions at him. How could this man know the location? Why did he connect the term he used with the operation unless he knew? How could he possibly know about the underpass? There must be a traitor within his organization, or the cartel.

He was conscious of a hand resting on his arm.

'So, my dear, are you going to introduce us?' interrupted Ayeesha sweetly. She had noticed the mood her lover had entered, a mood she had not seen in public before. It disturbed her.

'Allow me, Ms Fahila,' offered Ferguson, who appeared at Brock's side. 'And afterwards perhaps you would allow me the opportunity to share with you the answer I received from the Oracle of Ammon. You were quite right, I wasn't expecting it. This is my colleague, Connor Brock; Connor, this is the delightful Ayeesha I told you about.'

The colour from Ayeesha's face drained as she looked into the green eyes of the Irishman.

'Well, we've done it again, Matt,' sighed Brock. 'Gone and flabbergasted our hosts with tactless charm and dress sense. I told you we should have brought a bottle.'

'You're a dead man, Mr Brock,' breathed Subedei.

Brock's voice was granite, his piercing eyes as sharp as flint. 'Well, thank you for that opinion. Personally I never felt better. The secret is to clean scum like you off my shoes on a regular basis.'

'You'll have to excuse my friend's frustration, Ayeesha,' added Ferguson as they turned. 'You see, he doesn't have the benefit of the bondage tools you both enjoy to release yours.'

Ayeesha's large eyes looked as though they were on stalks as she involuntarily blushed. No one had ever caused her to lose the famous composure of which she was so proud.

Feeling her arm drop she turned to see Subedei making his way determinedly towards two of his armed lieutenants. After one minute of rapid instruction she observed him stride over to President Jumair, smiling broadly.

Neusheen's eyes had stayed on Brock, while pretending to listen to guests animatedly asking her father for his comments on the announcement.

'Well whatever you said did not go down well,' she mused when Brock and Ferguson rejoined them.

'Just complimenting our hosts on how much we liked their style,' answered Brock innocently.

Ferguson raised his eyebrows. 'Is that really yourself, Neusheen? Or did I dream that you flew me to safety a few days ago?'

Neusheen gave the Irishman one of her genuinely warm smiles. 'And you are as charming as ever, Matt.'

'I don't think the lady over there would altogether agree with you,' argued Matt before adding to Brock, 'Well, I assume the plan was to rile them up a little, was it?'

'Something like that, though I don't know what good it's done apart from getting it off our chest. Subedei's as impossible to read as a closed book. A couple of calculated guesses seemed to hit home but that's a long way from any leads as to what he has planned, or evidence as to what he has already done. The next stop is to take a look at the Palace of Ammon. I believe that we might find some answers in there.'

'Well it's too late for that,' said Matt. 'We've just pulled away from the shore.'

Neusheen looked puzzled. 'That's odd; the president is still on board. He was to make his announcement and leave before the evening cruise with entertainment continued.'

'Well, no one else has left either. Perhaps he's changed his mind,' suggested Brock.

Neusheen rolled her eyes. 'If either of you had bothered to read the invitation properly you would have known that every guest had to agree to stay on board until the announcement had been formally transmitted tonight at ten o'clock. No phones are allowed either.'

'Hence the jamming device that exists on all incoming and outgoing calls,' put in Benerzat, who, having extricated himself once more, joined their conversation.

'Infernal nuisance for all of us, though I have no doubt that Subedei and Jumair have already taken advantage with their planned announcement coming on a Thursday evening.'

'Friday being our holy day,' added Neusheen.

'Conveniently planned,' sighed Benerzat. 'While our president pontificates about what he is doing for our people, his personal coffers continue to grow; using restricted knowledge to gain advantage with the foreign-based companies which he purports to denigrate, hiding any evidence of his own involvement in them.'

'Sorry to sound cynical, but doesn't that go with the territory?' enquired Brock flatly. 'Give me a politician, or for that matter a CEO, who mentions how he loves the people or values his employees in *every* sentence, and I'll show you a person who puts their own interest first and takes a bonus while ordering redundancies.'

'I would agree with you, Mr Brock, or may I call you Connor, though in our case we have compiled some evidence which we believe proves that our law-trained president is linked to numerous investment companies including Subedei Industries.'

Ferguson saw them first. Two stocky individuals in black tuxedos were converging on Brock from different angles in a classic pincer movement.

'Incoming,' he warned Brock as he turned to confront the one nearest to him.

Brock spun round, but too late. Knowing he was wrong-footed by the powerful-looking man blocking his way, he tensed his stomach to receive the expected body blow.

But it never came. The heavy face, with St Bernard eyes and thick trimmed moustache, politely leaned towards Brock's ear as if to whisper something. Brock shrugged and leaned forward in a corresponding angle to listen to what it was, assuming he was about to be asked to leave quietly. A moment later he felt the snub end of a small pistol against his stomach.

Unable to see what was happening since they were standing behind the security man's back, neither Neusheen nor her father had any idea why Brock seemed to be raising his hands slowly.

A moment later a bullet tore straight through the security man's jacket, hitting Neusheen's father directly in the chest.

Immediately a second bullet ripped through the gunman's own shoulder. Without the least concern for what he had done to himself, the gunman firmly pushed the assassination weapon directly into Brock's hand, and he reactively gripped his fingers around it.

Momentarily staring into Brock's face without a flicker of emotion, the gunman clutched out at the falling opposition leader. As he feigned to use his own body as a shield to protect the shot politician from more bullets, they both crashed to the floor.

His anguished cries while pointing at Brock bought chaos from the surrounding alarmed guests, who frantically ran for cover repeating the gunman's warning cry.

In the same second as he heard a piercing scream emit from Neusheen's throat, the breath was completely knocked out of

Brock as half a ton of security sentinels bulldozed into him from all directions, pounding the assassin they had caught into oblivion.

President Jumair, his face suddenly drained of all colour, stood close to Subedei, both tightly surrounded by government agents who had immediately reacted to the situation. Unable to see or even move beyond the screened protective circle, Subedei caught a brief glimpse of Jumair's expression.

What just happened? the president's frightened eyes silently demanded.

Subedei's whisper was barely audible. 'It seems we have both conveniently rid ourselves of our frustrations, Mr President.'

Not catching what Subedei had said, President Jumair gave him a questioning look in expectation of the comment being repeated.

'It seems there has been an assassination, Mr President.' Subedei smiled inwardly. 'Just as planned,' he added quietly.

PART THREE

Oil, Oil everywhere and every drop to sink

Thirty

David Bearne's brown eyes moved away from his *Financial Times* to contemplate the plate of eggs that had just arrived. How did Claridge's consistently poach them so perfectly, he wondered. He knew from experience that the two his waiter had just removed from one of the polished silver tureens adorning the linen-covered table of the Friday-morning breakfast buffet, were the same as the two dozen or more that remained. Not too soft so that they ran all over your plate, and not too hard to feel sticky on the palate. Just perfect and a perfect way to start the day in the far-from-perfect world in which he operated.

Though regularly advised by his field officers to alter his routine, the head of British Intelligence had refused to give up the one luxury he allowed himself. Since being divorced ten years earlier and not being able to cook for himself, let alone boil an egg, he had developed the preference. It was a time he could hold what he termed as his informal meetings. He knew that the expense account picked up by the tax payer on a monthly basis was still considerably less than those of some of his departmental subordinates.

He looked over the top of new frameless titanium spectacles that he had recently had to start wearing for reading, as his breakfast partner for the day wove his way confidently through the dining room's laden tables towards him.

'Good, glad you started without me, couldn't get a damn taxi. How are you, David?'

'Well, thank you, Sir Duncan, though as ever you are right on the dot. I just like to start a little earlier. Read the papers, that sort of thing.'

Buchanan delivered his order to the approaching waiter as he sat down. 'Orange Juice, smoked kippers, and tea. Oh, and brown toast, please. Appreciate you seeing me at short notice.'

'Always happy to see you, Sir Duncan, though let me say from the outset that I don't think there is much we can do to help you with this Subedei business.'

'Straight to the point as ever, eh? Look, David, you've seen our report. We both know that Subedei is behind a cartel that could cause an economic headache, and a political one, I might add, that would be worse than even the 1970s.'

'Possibly, yet I'm afraid your evidence is somewhat circumstantial and, I might add, a little hypothetical at the moment.'

'Perhaps a little, but you have always asked us to provide you with information that we believe is threatening to Her Majesty's interests. On the three occasions we have, all of them have been proved genuine. Admittedly you acted on them, but the delay on Moscow last year almost cost one of our investigators his life, you will of course recall.'

The lines of Bearne's furrowed brow and the crow's feet around his eyes joined as he screwed up his face into the familiar frowning grimace his colleagues had termed his Rumpelstiltskin look; an expression of blended patient dog-tiredness with an 'I do understand but guess what I have to do about it' look.

'Yes, of course I recall; and how your operative succeeded where ours didn't. But that is partly the point. The cold war is no longer in existence. These days we can't just go in and stop people from doing what we think they're going to do. And as for anything to do with Suez, we're still carrying the political embarrassment, and the political consequences.'

'All the more reason to do something before it is too late then,' retorted Buchanan, raising his eyebrows as the pair of grilled kippers, covered in melting butter, was presented to him on a pristine plate stamped with the Claridge's coat of arms. 'Excellent. Thank you.'

'I wish it was that simple. That damn canal has brought us headache after headache – and worse for those who have supported us. A hundred years ago, the Egyptian Premier Butros Ghali was assassinated by a Muslim extremist for supporting Britain's request to extend the concession on the canal. Fifty years ago, British control was lost when Nasser nationalized the Suez Canal Company. And don't forget that just over twenty years ago, Anwar Sadat was assassinated by a Muslim radical who thought his views too westernized. It's true that the closure of the canal in the seventies seemed like a blessing in disguise as it forced us to be less dependent on it. But it's burned an awful lot of political fingers. Whitehall doesn't like it. No one likes it.'

Buchanan looked frustrated. 'This is because we've consistently looked after our short-term interests instead of thinking about the future. But, David, this is not just about Suez. The issue here is that we believe Subedei is planning to hold the west to ransom through oil. Suez is just one of his pawns in the game.'

Bearne nodded and solemnly buttered a piece of toast. 'I read your report. If he's successful in restricting the oil supply, the price will rocket up. Basic economics. But what isn't clear is why he would want to do so in the first place. He's a businessman – clever, as I understand. Ruthless, I admit, but very clever. Cutting off our oil does not sound like a good strategy. And you forget the ties we have with the Emirates and Saudi. Kuwait is hardly going to stop sending us oil, is it?'

'It will not be a matter of what Kuwait wants, though. It will be a matter of can't.'

Bearne swallowed his last mouthful of egg and wiped his mouth with his napkin. 'That still doesn't answer the fundamental question: why? Look, I'm sorry, Sir Duncan, but I'll need a little more concrete evidence before I can take any action on this. I am prepared, though, to courier a copy of your report to the appropriate MP. These days I do need backing for anything that affects Britain's commercial interests.'

'This doesn't concern only commercial interests, David. If our assumptions are correct, and I do acknowledge that there is a big if involved, then lives will be lost.'

'That may or may not be the case, but you have my answer.'

Buchanan sighed. 'Very well, David. Thank you for that anyway. Which minister will you send it to? Beaverton?'

'So you can lobby him direct, eh, my friend? Sorry, but he no longer sanctions us. No, in this case, the report will be forwarded to the head of the policy committee for energy, Lord Somers.'

Buchanan looked thoughtful. 'Yes, I've met him a couple of

times. Well, let me know what he says and I'll keep you apprised of future events.'

'Good. Her Majesty's government would really not want anything to disturb the peace process. Nor, for that matter, would our friends across the water. It would take something monumental for them to be prepared to risk this. I'm sure you understand.' Bearne felt his phone vibrating in his pocket. 'Ah, excuse me a moment, Sir Duncan,' he said, as he answered it.

Sir Duncan noticed Bearne's face become increasingly grave as he listened to the voice on the other end. He said little in reply, then clicked off the handset.

'Bad news?' enquired Buchanan, as the MI6 chief slowly replaced his phone.

'Your operative in Moscow last year – Brock, wasn't it?'

The herringbone sports jacket of the broad Scotsman seemed to stretch as his body tensed. 'Yes, it was Connor Brock, why?'

Bearne's brown eyes bore into the man across the table. 'Well, apparently he's just assassinated the leader of the opposition in Egypt, Imran Benerzat; who, I might add, was one of our long-term friends.'

Buchanan shot the MI6 director a look of amused cynicism. 'Are you pulling some kind of April Fool's joke, David?'

'I wish I was, Sir Duncan; I wish I was.'

Four-and-a-half hours later in downtown Washington, special assistant to the president Jim Kowalski stared at the cheese bagel which, having been dunked for too long, had dropped into his coffee.

'Just what the hell kind of a circus is your crowd running, Kurt?' he demanded, having just ended his call via a voice-activated phone. Tall, solid and with his head completely shaved of hair, Kowalski, in his early thirties, looked like some blue-suited android with the smooth alloy earpiece and microphone attached permanently to the side of his face. 'You're lucky the earlier reports on Benerzat were in error. He's not dead, but you can bet your money your organization is as good as!'

'When I hear definite news from Van Lederman, who's in Alexandria as we talk, I'll tell you,' answered Williams, relieved that his voice sounded more confident than he felt. 'But my immediate reaction is that Subedei's behind it.'

'Yeah, right, the man planning to fleece the US,' retorted the Washington android, his voice full of sarcasm. 'Some crazy hypothesis which you want me to waltz in and tell the president could threaten his administration.'

The third member sitting in the all-day diner that Kowalski had insisted they had met in because it was convenient to him looked resignedly at the young bureaucrat. As a CIA director, Aaron Hammond had experienced three administrations; each one brought the same type of officious clerk who got their rocks off pushing professionals around. With agendas based on staying in office and rising through the political ranks, they would dangerously wield the pseudo-power they believed their position carried.

Hammond rubbed his temple. He had already known that the reports of any actual assassination were untrue. It always amazed him how the White House's first communication post was either CNN or ambassadorial hearsay, received from foreign-based bureaucratic aspirants also seeking to be noticed. If they were proved misinformed, as they often would argue they maliciously had been, they would turn that to their advantage too, by requesting more budget allocation as their resources were stretched.

'The administration has to be forewarned, but with correct information,' cut in Hammond, sending a definite barb towards the younger man. His pension was already in the bag and he was damned if he was going to pussyfoot around with these guys like he had done twenty years earlier.

'You go along with this hypothetical stuff?' Kowalski said arrogantly. He had not liked Hammond from their first meeting and the director's softly spoken manner and calculating light-blue eyes unnerved him. And he did not like the fact that in the corridors of power the director was spoken of in hushed tones. He found it hard to believe, because to him Hammond looked like a washed-up has-been with his crumpled grey suit and unfashionable tie that no self-respecting Washingtonian in their right mind would be seen dead in.

'Every word of it,' replied Hammond emphatically. 'You see, we too have been investigating Subedei, particularly in connection with a man called Guillermo Nicaros, an oil baron closer to our own backyard in Venezuela.'

'Don't you think that you should have brought that to my attention?' asked Kowalski petulantly.

'Sure, but to do what with? Short of showing your Venezuelan counterpart how clever you are, which I'm sure you wouldn't do, you'd only shove it back on my desk requesting more information, arguing it was too hypothetical.'

Williams bit his lip to prevent a smile as he saw Kowalski redden with annoyance. Inside though his guts were churning, wondering what the hell his crowd had gone and done. Immediately the three had met, he had shared the information he had received via Van Lederman, including that Benerzat was not dead. Kowalski had refused to listen as he had already heard otherwise. Hammond had suggested he make a further confirmatory call.

'Nicaros is a member of the cartel, I take it?' asked Williams, finally sipping from his now-cold coffee that had remained untouched while he had explained the details of the ICE report.

'Yes. Along with another that we know to be a member, Natasha Berentsky. We believe there to be several others but as of yet have no idea as to who they are. Certainly Nicaros and Berentsky are ruthless and between them have a legacy of bribery and corruption, though nothing has been proved. Reading your report certainly puts Subedei in the same bracket, probably more so.'

'Is Nicaros a threat? What's the tie-up?' asked Kowalski.

Hammond said, 'Venezuelan oil, as I am sure you are well aware, is vital to the US. During the country's politically stimulated oil strikes a few years ago, Nicaros began to store oil secretly. Because of the strikes, our own billion-barrel store under the salt lakes was badly depleted and has not yet been restored.' Hammond stared at the special assistant. 'Meaning that if ICE's hypothetical scenario happens, and we lose the Saudi oil – that's twenty-five per cent of our twelve-million-barrel daily requirement – we're hit very hard. And if Nicaros reduces or stops his flow – or even raises the cost per barrel significantly, which is more likely – then a further twenty-five per cent of our oil imports would be affected. And if, at the same time, Berentsky redirects the flow of her vital Kazakhstan and her New Caspian oil to China, then the bottom line is that, with our depleted reserves, we would run out of oil in about ninety days.'

'But the Saudis will just increase their supply,' countered Kowalski, biting into his bagel. 'There's no way that they will not continue to export to us.'

'I seem to remember that there was no way they would ever deal with Russia. Until they signed trade agreements with them last year.'

Kowalski snorted scornfully. 'Yeah, OK. But I can't believe that the Saudis would risk upsetting us. Even if, as your hypothesis suggests, they have no choice – well, what's to stop us simply increasing the supply of our own oil?'

'And attain the elusive goal that five former presidents have pursued, of being self-sufficient overnight, eh?' said Hammond. 'The simple answer is that it's impossible. We consume too damn much!'

Kowalski thought for a minute as he chomped his way through bagel and cheese. 'Run out of oil?' The possibility seemed to occur to him for the first time. He frowned and then said sharply, 'Then the president must be told of this immediately!'

'Bright of you to work that out,' commented Hammond flatly. 'I have a pre-arranged meeting with him this afternoon.'

Kowalski threw down what was left of his sandwich and quickly got up from the booth. 'I'm gonna brief him right away.'

He stalked off without saying goodbye, leaving the check for the other two to settle.

'Nice guy,' said Williams drily.

'I'll make sure the president gets the right picture,' said Hammond. 'We'll liaise with ICE as to our intentions, though apart from the Nicaros tie-up we will probably not want to be seen involving ourselves too much in the Suez or Egypt. We get enough hassle over the two-billion-dollar budget we provide their neighbours every year for defence. The British might take a different view but we're getting too much of a reputation for going to war to protect our oil.'

'Thanks for that, Aaron, but the real threat here, remember, is terrorism not oil, which does concern you. Subedei's aims are tantamount to terrorism at its worst. The economic carnage he could wreak could hit the west harder than ever, with the fall-out being almost impossible to recover from. Whatever he wants he takes, and we don't seem able to do anything against the guy.'

Hammond looked philosophical. 'Perhaps it'll make our

country finally wake up to what's going on in the rest of the world and drive us to become more self-sufficient by reducing our consumption. Though the reality will be we'll just turn to a different energy source, solar or water, something that will keep the environmentalists happy, eh?'

'More likely nuclear energy, I think.'

'Perhaps you're right, Kurt.' Hammond smiled apologetically. 'You know, by the way, that I can't help you out with your operative. Perhaps the correct information will paint a different picture. Though whatever the facts are, he's up to his neck in the proverbial shit, as we all are a bit now.'

Williams shot Hammond a questioning look.

'We've been counting on our friend Benerzat being the future president of Egypt,' added the CIA director, shaking his head as he turned back to his nearly cold coffee.

Hani Pasha returned to the hotel door and knocked, more out of habit than politeness. The 'Do Not Disturb' sign still hung on the door and she could hear the television playing but she knew that the room was unoccupied. It was a ploy many hotel guests used, pretending they were in to prevent their belongings from being stolen.

Reception had informed housekeeping that the missing occupants had only checked in for one night and the rooms were now required for incoming guests. It had been almost the end of Hani's shift and just as she had finished, the head of housekeeping had instructed her to collect the errant guests' belongings and place them in the luggage store. She had cursed her luck that it happened to be on her floor and on her shift. She had wanted to be on her way quickly – her sister was visiting that evening.

She opened the door with her pass key and entered purposefully, eager to get on with the job. If she was quick, she could still be home in time to clean her own small apartment.

Hani breathed a sigh of relief as a brief survey revealed very few items to collect. Deftly, she collected the toiletries and clothes, folding them neatly before placing them in the already half-packed flight bag.

Fifteen minutes later, with the sheets and towels replaced, the room was ready for the next guest. Hani tried the internal door connecting to the adjoining room. It was locked from the other side. Sighing to herself, she returned to the hall, entered the adjoining room and unlocked the connecting door.

She picked up the flight bag; she didn't want to forget it before she started to clean the second room. It caught momentarily on something before coming away from the luggage stand that it was resting on.

Hani Pasha neither saw the nearly invisible piece of cotton nor heard the tiny snap as it broke. A moment later, the unfortunate woman was blown to smithereens as the detonated semtex tore apart the guest rooms of Messrs Brock and Ferguson, reported by management as having left without paying.

Thirty-One

'Welcome,' beamed Ferguson jovially. 'You'll have to excuse the mess, I'm afraid. The maid is unreliable and the neighbours are a bit raucous at times, but the meals are regular and an interesting view of the city can be enjoyed, if you stand on your tiptoes.'

Still wearing his dress shirt and tuxedo trousers, the Irishman, his face covered with four days of red beard, looked like some eccentric cocktail partygoer who had been mugged on his way home. Which was more or less what had happened to him.

'Good of you to invite me,' replied Brock, as he limped into the two-man cell and the door clanged shut behind him. 'Are you sure I'm not putting you out?'

Ferguson let out a loud laugh, surprising the attendant guard, who looked thoroughly puzzled at the inmates' high spirits. 'Chance would be a fine thing!' His voice turned more serious as he saw his friend's face come into the light. 'How are you, Connor?'

After two days in Cairo's prison hospital, followed by two days of intensive interrogation, Brock, his face beaten, cut and bruised, looked exhausted. 'Well, let's put it this way. These cruises down the Nile are not all they're cracked up to be, you know. I certainly don't feel rested. What about yourself?'

'Fine. I've been taking the opportunity to improve my fly-swatting technique. I'm hoping to get into the Olympic team next year.'

'This certainly is a shit hole,' said Brock, as he looked around at the grimy walls of the cell. Two black-stained, infested-looking mattresses lay on the wet floor next to a metal slop bucket. The smell of shit and urine was all-pervasive. A tiny rough hole that served as a window was placed directly below the ceiling, but the ceiling was so low that it was just a few centimetres above Brock's head. Through the hole, Brock could see the smoggy heat haze hovering above the sprawling city roof tops, pierced by minarets and domed mosques.

'What news? Have you learned how Neusheen's father is?' asked Ferguson.

Brock shook his head. 'Every time I ask a question, they whack me. Mind you, each time I answer one, they whack me, so it gets a bit confusing as to what they want. The only thing I know is that they won't listen. As far as they're concerned, I'm an assassin, you're my accomplice and, by the way, who else are we planning on killing?'

'Bit of a leading question, that one.'

'Yes. And as I can't answer it, we might end up looking down the wrong end of a firing squad.'

'Oh. Now, I never like to end a holiday that way. Firing squads are a real downer. The photographs are never much fun to look at afterwards. Tell you what, Connor, let's give that one a miss.' Matt smiled brightly at his friend. 'So, what's the plan, then?'

'Well, no doubt ICE will already be here fighting our corner.' Brock shrugged. 'For the moment, we just wait.'

Thirty minutes later, the door clanged open. Heavy guards came in, hauled the men up and marched them down a corridor to another interview room that Brock had not yet visited. This one contained a weary but relaxed Dr Paul van Lederman and a gaunt Neusheen Benerzat.

Van Lederman took three brisk paces to grasp the shoulders of his investigators. 'Sorry not to have been able to see you earlier. They wouldn't let us know where you had been taken, but the good news is that we will be getting you out.'

'How's your father?' asked Brock immediately, looking at Neusheen's bloodshot eyes.

Neusheen had been shocked at Brock's appearance. His nose looked as if it had been broken; both of his eyes were purple and swollen and his lips were badly split. The whole of his shirt was stained with blood. She threw her arms around him, feeling him wince with pain from what he had already surmised were further fractured ribs since he had left hospital.

'He's alive, feisty as ever, and sends you his best wishes.'

273

'That's one tough politician,' grinned Brock in delight.

'He's certainly a lucky one,' added Neusheen. 'The bullet passed right through his upper chest, deflating a lung and exiting just between the scapula and the backbone, apparently missing his heart by a centimetre. He's comfortable, as they like to say, but he will be out of action for a month; a few weeks if he does what he is told.'

'Well, at least we can't get charged with assassination, only attempted assassination now,' remarked Ferguson. 'Things are looking up: a life sentence in this hell hole, instead of execution.'

'Better than that,' put in Van Lederman. 'Imran is already denying you pulled the trigger, though that is not the reason we can get you out.'

Brock looked at Van Lederman curiously. 'What is then? We can hardly think they're going to allow us bail so that we can leave the country. If Subedei's planned this far, he's not going to make it easy for us.'

'Well, he doesn't have much of a choice at the moment,' said Neusheen, her face brightening. 'The whole event was caught on camera.'

'What?'

'Well, you remember that there were almost as many reporters there as guests, including the top television news teams; all of them invited to record the announcement,' began Neusheen. 'Well, one Cairo Network cameraman, panning the audience to get general reaction shots, was standing just to your side filming our group.'

'They'll never be allowed to show it,' said Brock, surprised at how negative he sounded.

'Our thoughts exactly,' put in Van Lederman. 'But fortunately the programme producer was persuaded to air it an hour ago on the main news before asking the powers-that-be if he could.'

Brock threw his boss a suspicious glance. 'How did you swing that, Paul?'

'More luck than anything,' replied Van Lederman. 'As soon as I saw the airing of the announcement I contacted Cairo Network News asking to buy copies of all of the pre-edited coverage. Nothing unusual in that, of course; it's normal network sharing practice that pays high dividends to TV stations. Their technical department sent the digital package down the line before they were instructed to withhold all unedited copies.

Immediately we saw the shots of you being approached by the security guard, we computer-enhanced it and could see how the real gunman turned and shot Imran and then himself. The weapon could not be made out as it was hidden under his jacket but the moment he passed the gun into your hand was clearly captured. Now we knew it proved your innocence, but we also knew, of course, that such digital evidence would almost certainly receive cries of tampering and be excluded from any trial. So I asked an old friend at Al Jazeera News to call Cairo Network informing them that they were going to air the shots later tonight.

'He must have owed you a big favour?' interrupted Ferguson.

Van Lederman nodded. 'He did, but more to the point I promised him the material if and after he made the call, so that he would be able to air them later tonight. When Cairo's news producer, already dubious about airing such evidence, because of political pressure, learned that it would be seen anyway, he decided to go for broke and put it on the main news under the banner of "Is there a political conspiracy?"'

'We watched the report with Father at the hospital,' put in Neusheen. 'Within five minutes Jumair called the hospital under the pretext of seeing how his political rival was.'

Van Lederman mimicked a quick pompous expression. 'President Jumair was *most* concerned that the announcement *so* valuable to Egypt's future growth would not be diluted by distracting forces intent on bringing the government into disrepute. He immediately informed Imran that the secret service had already studied the tapes, recognized the real assassin as a member of the radical Muslim fringe and had already detained him.'

'This is sounding better,' interrupted Ferguson. 'A life sentence commuted to getting out of this shit hole.'

Van Lederman grinned. 'President Jumair asked Imran if in the interests of quickly diffusing the growing tension incited by the news report, immediately denied by the Muslim Radicals, of course, he would be prepared to join him in an immediate press release to calm concerns about his health and at the same time endorse the announcements that meant so much to Egypt at this time.'

'And father agreed, with several conditions,' added Neusheen, her infectious smile widening. 'Including, of course, that all charges against you two were immediately dropped.'

Ferguson shrugged. 'What riles me is that we didn't even get to eat any of the food from that marvellous buffet; oh, and someone stole my bow tie.'

'I'm afraid that's not all you've lost, gentlemen,' said Van Lederman more seriously a few moments later as the room erupted in tension-relieving laughter. 'Your rooms at the Montazeh Palace were torn apart by an explosion. The maid evidently set off something that was intended for you. She was killed, unfortunately, the only casualty despite the extent of the damage.'

Brock looked monstrous; his cold expression made even more frightening due to the livid bruising. 'When?'

'Three days ago,' answered Van Lederman. 'We only just learned today that it had been you two staying there; the hotel traced you to us through the credit-card imprints you left with reception.'

'Paul, someone knows our movements better than we do! Someone is hacking us. And you'd better make it a priority to find out who it is! But my god, I swear Subedei is going to pay for all these innocent deaths he is leaving in his wake.'

Ayeesha stole a sideways glance at Subedei. Their love-making had been considerably rougher than ever before and it had really hurt her. And for the first time she had not felt in control, which frightened her. Subedei had been like a man possessed; and she had felt used.

Earlier that morning they had watched via satellite the Al Jazeera live report in the Middle East, eight hours behind Beijing time. Placing the blame directly on the Ghulat dar al-harb, the name meaning a fringe group of Muslim extremists committed to waging war against any state or community hostile to Islamic fundamentalism, the broadcast went on to deliver a joint announcement from President Jumair and the opposition leader, Benerzat, before concluding that security forces had detained the Ghulat dar al-harb antagonists who had tried to supplant the news of government initiatives with their own demands.

Subedei had been at first surprised at the news report, then partly confused at Jumair and his rival's joint agreement, but still pleased that his own enemy was incarcerated. Soon after that he had received word from Barracio that Brock and his partner were not the antagonists in question, and moreover had been released from custody. His rage had been furious as he realized that Jumair had succumbed to a knee-jerk reaction to threats of a conspiracy cloud rising over his administration.

'They may have eluded you, My Lord, but they are no match for you,' offered Ayeesha tentatively. 'Everything you have planned is still in place and though they may guess at them they do not know them.'

'Because I do not carelessly share them with *anyone*; no one knows them fully except I; but ICE is an interfering annoyance and the resilient Brock is proving to be more dangerous than I anticipated. As for Jumair, he is a spineless fool!'

'Yet his action has only served to tie him closer to you, My Lord. Now he will have no choice but to accede to your directions.'

Subedei turned to look quizzically at his Egyptian mistress. 'Meaning?'

'His quick denial of any conspiracy has made the Egyptian people, particularly our media, and therefore the world, suspicious. You have only to fabricate a political scandal to create further doubts.' Ayeesha paused for a moment. 'I am speaking in ignorance, My Lord, but perhaps you already have such a tool with the investments you have wisely advised Jumair to involve himself with.'

One of Subedei's rare laughs rose in his throat at the wiliness of the beautiful creature lying next to him, her dark olive and perfectly toned limbs seemingly relaxed, though poised as if ready to pounce like a sleek panther. 'Ayeesha, you are a good student and an adept counsellor; qualities that are matched by your exotic beauty and thoughtful attention.'

Ayeesha almost purred in calculated ecstasy as Subedei gently stroked her breast before pulling her naked body towards his. Back in control, she convinced herself. Good, for the time was fast approaching when she would have to put her own plans into action.

Thirty-Two

The 130,000 deadweight ton vessel the *Riyadh* had been built by Norwegian Shipping for Saudi Oil. With a breadth of forty-two-and-a-half metres and an extreme depth of sixteen metres, she had been specifically designed to pass through the Suez Canal, giving the maximum allowance with her load of one point two million barrels of oil. Only eight years old, the *Riyadh* had been constructed in strict compliance with the Oil Pollution Act of 1990 that was passed as a knee-jerk reaction following the *Exxon Valdez* disaster. The main stipulation of the act pertaining to international shipping was for oil tankers to have double hulls. A double-hulled tanker involves a metre or more space between the outer hull and the inner tanks. The theory was that if the outer hull was penetrated through being grounded, as happened to the *Exxon Valdez*, the inner hull would remain intact.

With a length between her two perpendiculars from bow to stern of 257 metres, the cigar-shaped hull of the Saudi crude-oil shuttle tanker visibly seemed to twist as if flexing her highly toned muscles of iron and steel to wrenching point to compensate against the mountainous rolling green-grey waves of the fathomless ocean that sought to stretch them. The south-westerly wind was moderate increasing to high, whipping the white-crested cliffs of water into an unending stampede that the *Riyadh*'s massive bow unceasingly pushed against.

Standing on the fully-automated bridge, Cadet Youssef Demeri felt a twinge of fear, as he had never seen anything like it before, and stole a glance at the captain. Ake Rejarten, a tall, tanned Dane with greying yellow hair, beard and moustache, who had celebrated both his sixtieth birthday and his tenth anniversary as a captain with Saudi Oil in the last week, had

278

entered the high wide tower a few minutes earlier, following his routine meeting with the chief engineer below. Comfortably dressed, in his habitual ironed white shirt and pressed white trousers, Captain Rejarten noticed the look and grinned, his bright blue eyes twinkling.

'Few imagine that a ship this size will twist like a suspension bridge in a strong wind, but have no concerns, Cadet Demeri. All of our tanks are fully loaded.'

Since this was his first major sea voyage, Demeri appreciated the reassuring comment from the captain. Most of the other twenty-six members of the crew had revelled in the opportunity of scaring him with stories as to why more cadets got lost on tankers than other ships. When he had asked the reason why, they had snorted with delight, telling him it was because the ship was so huge. The captain, on the other hand, never seemed to mind if his questions were naïve. He always took them seriously and explained the answer carefully; unless he asked the same question twice, in which case the laughter left his eyes, and he instantly shot out a stare from under his peaked cap that would wither hardened sailors let alone inexperienced cadets.

'A full load helps, sir?' asked a calmer Demeri, his large, brown eyes looking more attentive than worried, brightening up his pleasant smooth face.

'These beauties were designed for carrying, so, when we are loaded with the correct payload we're actually more stable than when empty. Too much twisting does lead to cracking in a ship's structure. Some much older ships continue shuttling crude despite knowingly having hairline cracks that are continually seeping oil.'

'And that's allowed, sir?'

'No, it is forbidden, but that doesn't stop some outfits doing it. The worst offenders are the freelance carriers. But there is another reason, Demeri, which you must never forget,' added his captain. 'Full tanks are completely safe because there is not enough oxygen to support combustion with oil vapours. But if the tanks are partially full they will contain oxygen, which, if stirred up with building oil vapours, runs the risk of mixing a hazardous ratio that will create an explosive atmosphere.'

The seventeen-year-old Demeri looked doubtfully at the 850 feet of deck that stretched out in front of him concealing over fifty million imperial gallons (227 million litres) of oil. 'You mean the oil could explode? How do you know the tanks are full?'

'Well, first we have an array of electronic equipment here to tell us,' offered Rejarten, turning on his heel and sweeping his outstretched hand around the bridge. 'Secondly it takes several weeks for vapour to accumulate to dangerous amounts; even if that does happen, a spark is still required to ignite it, which is one of the reasons for having a double hull like the *Riyadh*. If her outer hull were to ground and scrape rocks, there would be no chance of sparks igniting the combustible vapour that may exist within the inner hull. Thirdly we have just had our whole structure, tanks and hull overhauled. And fourthly I have made it a habit to check personally all tanks are full before we depart port.'

Demeri was about to ask another question relating to tanks being empty on the return voyage, a thought that suddenly concerned him, when the captain looked at him speculatively. 'Which reminds me, Cadet Demeri, how about servicing your captain with a large cup of strong coffee?'

Captain Rejarten turned to look out at the blackening expanse of water that surrounded the *Riyadh*, making his enormous ship appear insignificant like the evening star that had just become visible between dark, ominous clouds.

It being the first voyage since the refit, he was pleased it had been a relatively smooth one. Following the three-week maintenance check at Port Said, they had sailed down the Suez to Yanbu in the Red Sea, where the oil pipeline flowing from the rich fields across the barren desert of Saudi Arabia terminates. His close-knit crew had benefited from their break and worked through the high-stress situation of loading at a rate of a 100,000 barrels an hour, allowing them a quick turnaround in twelve hours, to pass back through the canal the following morning. From Port Said he had plotted a course west, moving from thirty degrees latitude to thirty-five degrees to skirt the Tunisian headland where the Atlas Mountains jutted out into the Mediterranean, and through the straits of Gibraltar. From there it had been a direct route to the Philadelphian Port of Delaware between Washington and New York.

With the taste of the ocean in his mouth and his lungs

breathing welcome sea air, Captain Rejarten relaxed, a man in his element; a man totally unaware that what he had just explained to the young cadet about the dangers of explosion through combustion, was inexorably building within his own ship; having already reached a point so critical that one spark was all that was required to ignite it.

Seventy-two hours earlier Zarakov had watched the *Riyadh* pass Port Said on her return trip through Suez, her tanks fully loaded *en route* to America. Standing at the far end of the quay that pointed like a giant bent finger into the blue Mediterranean, with his high-powered binoculars raised to his eyes, he could easily see the folds of a Saudi Arabian flag open as they caught in the wind; the two distinct scimitars that crossed over a central palm tree indicating the registered ownership.

'They are ahead of the schedule you originally advised,' Zarakov said in a matter-of-fact way but with enough menace for the man standing with him to feel under blame.

'Only by three hours,' replied the American engineer, choosing acceptance rather than denial as the safest form of action. 'Either their loading or convoy period must have gone better than I anticipated. But we are still within a safe margin. The detonator located between the hulls will deploy itself before they are fully unloaded. There is no way that they could gain another three.'

Zarakov regarded the stocky young American, Joe Hengel, disguising the contempt he felt. Even though Zarakov had been betrayed by Russian comrades, he would never consider acting against Mother Russia. Perhaps this is what his teachers had meant about the dangers of capitalism, where the individual serving himself is viewed as a greater priority than serving his country. He considered the people he had killed during his term with the KGB as a service, in the interests of his country. At least that is what he had been told, and he had believed it. He still did. Perhaps he was becoming too philosophical for his mercenary status; but at least Subedei's operation could only serve Russia. That too he had been told, and that too he believed. Yet he knew it would serve him better.

'Well, in a hundred and twenty hours we will know for sure if they have or not, won't we?'

'You got it, right on the button,' answered Hengel confidently. A former army engineer who had been brought, over eighteen months earlier, to help repair oil wells at Basra in Iraq, he had been accused together with three of his crew of gang-raping local women. Since the problem threatened to escalate already strained tensions with the locals, Hengel and his team were severely punished, being first court-martialled and then placed in a military prison in Kuwait awaiting their trip back to the States. Hengel had escaped, stolen aboard a ship, later jumping it at Port Said, where he had been quickly employed by Subedei Industries.

'I drilled those holes in the hull myself. They're only little but the pressure will force oil out into the empty area between the two hulls. Lots of oxygen there – it will cook up nicely. And after five days, you've got an explosive situation. You gotta trust me on this – I placed the detonator in there myself. I'm one hundred per cent confident that that baby is going to blow right on time.'

'And there is no chance that their instruments will pick up the oil leakage?'

'Nope.' Hengel looked proud of himself. 'I recalibrated the gauges myself. They'll look one hundred per cent full.'

'Very good,' said Zarakov. He turned back to watch the giant tanker heading out to sea. 'This detonating device – is it a timer?'

'Yes and no. It's activated by sensor. Once the combustion level is critical, the sensor will register that, but it won't detonate before a preset time period, so you don't have to worry that it will explode before we can get maximum impact. Once everything is ready, the sensor will send a series of electronic sparks firing outwards until . . .' Hengel grinned. 'Well, until it blows.'

'Very clever,' commented Zarakov. He lowered the binoculars and the *Riyadh* shrunk to the size of a speck on the horizon. 'Now, if you will excuse me . . .'

He walked off along the quay, dialling Beijing on his mobile as he went.

'Lord Subedei, everything is on course as you instructed.'

'Excellent,' replied Subedei. 'Remember that the Americans are to receive your call no more than one hour before detonation.'

'Understood,' answered Zarakov. Subedei terminated the call

without another word, leaving the Russian shaking his head in wonder at the sheer audacity of his employer. Blowing up a fully laden tanker in the Delaware Bay, causing a catastrophic environmental disaster in the rich coastal resort, would outrage the Americans. The loss of one of their proud ships certainly wasn't going to please the Saudis. But the *coup de grace* was strategically brilliant. A nationalist American group would claim responsibility for the act of terrorism – *before* it happened. The damage to the diplomatic relations between the US and Saudi Arabia would be enormous.

Aaron Hammond carried two mobile phones at all times. One was for his colleagues, family and close friends. The other rarely rang but when it did, he held his breath. The number was known to only a handful of people, including the president.

The chief of the CIA's Directorate of Intelligence had just left the office and was halfway through the underground corridor leading to his waiting car when he heard the ring that brought him to an abrupt halt.

He flicked the phone open. 'Hammond.'

'Aaron, it's Moyshe,' said the voice of Hammond's counterpart in Mossad, Israel's secret intelligence service. 'I have bad news. You have a tanker wired for explosion *en route* to your east coast.'

'Details?'

'Not many. Our operative informs us that it is Saudi-registered. The explosion is due at eleven o'clock your time tomorrow morning. The tanker's arrival could be earlier. Credit will be claimed by an American nationalist group.'

'Subedei?'

'According to our operative.'

'Nothing else?'

'Only that it seems unstoppable, I'm afraid, Aaron.'

'Remote control?'

'More chemical reaction, our operative believes.'

'Thanks, Moyshe.'

'Good luck.'

Hammond looked at his watch. There were just fifteen hours to go before the detonation. Briskly, he retraced his steps to his centre of operations.

* * *

Captain Rejarten enjoyed an early breakfast. He had twenty minutes before the pilot came on board to guide him into the giant berth that lay waiting for him, itself dwarfed by the towering containers standing behind it ready to receive his load. The high wind had reduced to moderate but still assisted the *Riyadh* to advance its schedule even more; Rejarten had gained a total of five hours. He decided that while his crew unloaded he would take a short trip to see his American mistress in Delaware City.

It had been seven weeks since their last assignation and he was eager to see her. He was sure Lydia would be too; god, what a whole lot of woman, he thought. Forty-four Lydia he had called her after he had got to know her better two years earlier. She had recently been divorced and they had gone out to celebrate her forty-fourth birthday. She had raucously laughed that her age matched the number of inches her ample chest measured.

The broad smile that his thoughts had woven into place drooped to a serious frown when the pilot informed him that the berth was not ready; he was too early. Three hours later after ensuring the *Riyadh* was securely moored, he oversaw the commencement of the unloading directly to pipe. Calculating that the mostly automated operation would take another eight hours at 120,000 barrels flow rate an hour, Captain Rejarten passed the unloading operation to the command of his first officer. Fifteen minutes later he briskly departed his vessel and walked the 500 metres to the clearing office to collect the waiting taxi he had booked. Just before he closed the door, a noise caused him to look up.

'Now, if I had one of those I could bypass all of the traffic,' quipped the driver.

'Nice idea,' replied Rejarten. The States, he mused, looking up at the approaching helicopter, always so much frantic rushing around. A moment later he was speeding towards the city.

The helicopter carrying special agent Samantha Wellington surprised the remaining crew and dock workers by landing directly on the quay. More fondly than unkindly referred to as Long-Legged Wellington Sam by colleagues behind her back, the lithe, trouser-suited agent leapt from the helicopter and raced toward the moored Saudi-Arabian tanker.

It had taken longer than expected to study the shipping lines. What should have taken Hammond's people no more than an hour had taken ten. The coastal docking ports were numerous and the incoming tankers even more so. After five hours they had been certain that every Saudi ship was accounted for. Hammond's team was also certain that the Saudi tanker arriving at Jackson in Florida was the wired ship. Two local Special Forces teams were despatched immediately to evacuate the ship and tow it out to sea.

There was almost a stunned disbelief at the operations centre when a call passed on from a local radio station claimed advance credit for an explosion about to blow up a Saudi ship at Delaware. Hammond looked at his watch. The time had been ten past ten. There had been no record of a Saudi vessel due into Washington area at all. Clearly the documentation had been electronically altered.

Hammond had sent Sam Wellington to oversee the emergency operation. If anyone could get things done, she could.

On the dockside, Sam worked efficiently. Establishing her authority with her CIA badge, she fired out instructions to the crew and dock workers.

'This tanker has to be disconnected from the berth and oil containers *now*. Understand? We have a serious situation here. Let's go!'

Her team of four agents acted swiftly to ensure that her orders were carried out, while Sam liaised with the Bay Authorities to get the permissions and the vessels she needed. When they understood the grave seriousness of the situation, they came in line instantly. It was a brilliant team effort. Within fifty minutes, all unloading pipes had been disconnected. The huge ship was then released from her mooring lines and four powerful tug boats began pulling the evacuated ship away from port.

'We're underway!' Sam Wellington shouted down the phone to Hammond, the noise of the tanker and its tugs almost drowning her out entirely. 'We're tugging her out to sea.'

'Excellent. How much oil is she carrying?'

'Enough to cause a hell of a problem,' Sam yelled back. 'They'd only been unloading an hour or so when we arrived. Have we done the right thing? Should we have continued unloading?'

'We can't be sure because we don't know what the detonation relies on. The contact said "chemical reaction" but that could mean anything. And there could be a back-up device. Getting her as far out as possible is the only way.'

'OK. I'm going up to accompany her by helicopter. What time is zero hour?'

Hammond paused. 'The event is due at eleven a.m.'

Sam looked at her watch. 'Oh my god,' she breathed. It was twenty to eleven. She looked up at the vast body of the tanker being hauled out of port. 'We'll never make it,' she said. 'We haven't got a chance.'

Running to the helicopter, she tried not to panic. 'Get up in the air,' she panted at the pilot as she climbed in. 'Stay with the tanker but not too close. Be prepared for evasive action.'

They whirred up into the air, and stayed with the giant ship as she moved further away from the port. The minutes seemed to fly by and the ship seemed to move with painful slowness.

'Come on, baby, *move*,' Sam begged. The hands of her watch edged closer to eleven o'clock. She shouted to the pilot, 'Get ready to swing away!'

Ten seconds. There was no way the ship was far enough away for safety. Sam held her breath. Five. She wanted to shut her eyes but didn't dare. Three. Two. One.

Nothing.

Her phone rang. She answered it.

'Sam?' Hammond's voice was brusque.

'It hasn't blown!' she said, hardly able to believe her eyes. The tugs continued to pull the great tanker away. 'It's still in one piece.'

'So it's not on a timer,' said Hammond. 'But that means it could go at any minute.'

'They're taking her to Pond's Point,' said Sam. 'It's a small harbour off the Delaware Channel. We think we can contain any spillage there and minimize environmental damage.'

'In a harbour?'

'It's a former military testing base, enclosed with concrete walls. It's shorter than the tanker but it's our best hope for limiting the damage.'

'How long till you get there?'

'Not much longer now. I'm getting a signal that the tug pilots have sighted it. We just need a bit longer, that's all.'

'Hang in there, Sam. It's gonna be fine.'

Sam switched off her phone and looked down. She could see the enclosed harbour now, further up the channel. It was 400 metres away. They needed only minutes. Surely they were going to make it . . .

'Come on, guys!' she shouted into her headset. 'We're almost there!'

A moment later the port side of the *Riyadh*'s outer hull tore open with a giant explosion, jarring the 200,000-ton weight of combined ship and cargo as if it were a plastic toy. Shrapnel the size of solid oak refectory tables, and just as thick, sliced across the water like spinning stones, slamming into the harbour walls with resounding clangs. A colossal geyser of explosive flame spewed up into the air with the force of volcanic eruption, sending out hot oil, hissing with the sound of a thousand snakes as it rained down on the water. Two of the port side tugs were plastered black as they were helplessly caught in a torrent of crude oil.

The pilot of Sam's helicopter veered to the right, taking them out of range of the explosion, as Sam pressed her face to the window, slamming her fist against her seat. 'No!' she shouted. 'No!'

As she watched, the fearsome flame was blown out as the oxygen mixture that had ignited it burned itself out. The torn ship listed but continued to plough into Ponds Point, the surrounding water thick with oil. One of the tugs, its crew utterly disoriented, was crushed with a sickening crunch; it was too late to extricate itself from between the harbour wall and the oncoming hull.

Around the edges of the Ponds Point harbour stood members of the Delaware Bay Racing Club, which had been allowed to take over the military harbour. They watched in helpless horror as the wounded behemoth, which had attracted their rapt attention, smashed through the fleet as if they were made of matchsticks; demolished the harbour end wall and flattened the brick hut that had served as the club members' room. Finally the pride of Saudi Arabia groaned to a mournful halt in the rear car park where moments earlier had stood a collection of Sport Utility Vehicles with trailers, belonging to the unfortunate members who had run for their lives.

Sam gasped at the devastation below her. The mighty vessel looked like a gigantic beached whale, gushing black blood into the ocean. The faint wail of sirens indicated that the emergency services were on the way.

The ensuing fire that was thought to have been started either by the various oxyacetylene equipment or damaged gas cookers, both of which were being operated at the time, took the combined efforts of four fire stations working fearlessly over eight hours to put out.

The first person to notice Captain Rejarten's return was Cadet Youssef Demeri. Seeing the look of utter confusion and lack of comprehension on his captain's face, Demeri decided it would be a mistake if he was the one to answer the approaching man's questions. With a sigh of relief, he noticed the first officer also running towards Rejarten. Inconspicuously the cadet turned away, deciding that life on board a tanker was not what he wanted after all.

Thirty-Three

The thousand or more bodies slowly and precisely moving their hands and feet back and forth, as if pushing or carrying an invisible heavy weight, looked as if Qin Shi Huang's famous unearthed terracotta army was stretching in preparation for unexpected life. One man, his stooped and wizened frame covered with loose brown trousers and smock, appearing considerably older than his sixty years, blended insignificantly with his host of nameless neighbours; all absorbed in their early morning practice of Tai Chi in the People's Park, before entering the myriad of tiny offices, factories and hotels to continue their other daily routine of work.

The man bent down to pick up his stick and small bag of belongings and began to walk the 800 metres that would take him from the People's Park past the Forbidden City; through a wide underpass, where he would take the time to give a coin to the beggars operating there; then join the disturbed ants' nest of chaotically cycling commuters and drab walkers with their loud colourful chatter, all frantically seeking a way through the busy streets; his destination the warehouse-size offices of the Beijing Museum.

Other than a limp in his right leg, the wiry old man seemed sprightly, though his journey was hampered by having to walk with a stick. Yet he would never allow himself to take the short journey by bus, even when it was raining.

Today was an auspicious occasion for Teacher Tang. The Protectorate of Historical Artefacts, for whom he had so diligently worked as an advisor for five years, was at last being formalized within the Beijing Museum under the new identity of The People's Centre of Cultural Heritage. Tang had been recommended for the new position of Assistant Curator and today would be his first day.

'Assistant Curator Tang,' he murmured to himself as his slightly glistening brown eyes glanced fleetingly at the wide entrance of the Forbidden City; a symbol that seemed to slightly increase the pain in his right leg. 'It has a certain ring to it.'

He liked it – even if his true name was not Tang. He had taken the name from the brand on his arm – Tang 24739 – a constant reminder of the twenty years he had been imprisoned in the Tang Camp, west of Chengdu, in the Sichuan province adjoining Tibet. It was a terrible place, referred to by inmates as the Camp of Lost Souls, a place where the lucky ones died and the survivors simply existed as scavenging animals forced into pointless slave labour. There he had lost his innocence, through brutal treatment by the guards; there he had lost the proper use of his leg, broken in four places from a severe and unprovoked beating; there he had lost even his name: Lu Yen.

He did not know how he came to be at Tang. His interrogators had told him that he had been found wandering the streets of Lhasa in a bewildered state and had been accused of stealing by shopkeepers. He did not remember it. Another inmate told him that Tibetans were giving their own countrymen away to save themselves.

'It will have been your robes, 24739,' whispered the other prisoner. 'Anyone from the monasteries was rounded up. The townspeople were left alone – if they collaborated.'

'I think I was given some food, I could never steal anything from anyone,' Lu Yen had replied.

Number 18129 had not believed him. 'You'd be surprised at what you're capable of when you are starving.'

'Why are you here?'

'No reason,' said 18129. 'I was rounded up and put into a truck when I went to collect the rice for my mother.'

It was twenty-five years since Lu Yen had been one of the few released under Deng Xiaoping's benevolent pardon gesture. None of his friends could leave with him, the last having died two years earlier. Since then, he had become one of what were called the silent numbers. Though only thirty-four when he was released, he had looked much older and was able to find work as a teacher in Chengdu. Eleven years later, he had been sent to Beijing University to represent Sichuan Province under a

Communist Party of China initiative intended to bring closer harmony in education between the provinces.

Through continuous study and research over a further nine years, Lu Yen achieved recognition as the leading authority on dynastic cultural history and, in the Millennium Initiatives, was granted the position of advisor to the Protectorate of Historical Artefacts. It had been the time he had enjoyed most, since it involved research and documentation of many religious scrolls and artefacts taken from his homeland of Tibet.

There had been several occasions when he'd discovered discrepancies in recorded files, mentioning artefacts that were impossible to locate within the PHA vaults. On each occasion he had ignored them, simply moving on to one that did exist. His survival instincts, honed during his long imprisonment, told him that were he to bring the discrepancy to the notice of his superiors he would simply attract first suspicion, then blame, followed by dismissal or even imprisonment.

Lu Yen walked slowly through the wide hall of the PHA. It was adorned with fine artefacts, many similar to the ones he had known in his former days as a novice in the ancient monastery. They always brought back poignant memories of that happy home, but he didn't stop to linger over them. Instead, he made his way to the first floor and entered the director's high-ceilinged office at the exact time that his punctilious super-ior had requested to see him. The room was decorated with framed calligraphy and drawings collected from the late-seventeenth-century Ming dynasty, together with matching furniture comprising four ornate mandarin thrones and a large, intricately carved table, personally chosen by the director to serve as his desk.

'Welcome, Assistant Curator Tang,' boomed Director Guo Jian. 'I see from your face that you are eager to commence your new duties with your famous energy! You must tell me what it is you partake of. I was telling my honourable colleague here that I believe you must live on royal jelly and ginseng!'

Lu Yen bowed politely. 'You are too gracious and too wise. Already you have guessed my secret,' he answered humbly, revealing his few remaining teeth as he grinned.

'I have some exciting news – a first for us at the PHA.' Director Guo Jian peered over his thick round glasses and gave a toothy smile to the person he had seated in the grandest of the mandarin thrones. 'Pardon me, I mean to say the People's Centre of Cultural Heritage. And this is something that requires your unique knowledge, Assistant Curator Tang.'

Lu Yen bowed again. 'You honour me too greatly, Director.'

'Not only I, but our own venerable patron here also,' beamed Guo Jian.

Lu Yen cast a respectful glance at the director's guest, waiting to be introduced. Then, to his astonishment, he felt a sudden stab of anxiety as the black eyes looking back at him seemed to penetrate his own, assessing the very depths of his beating heart.

'Indeed, I have heard much of your ability and knowledge,' said Subedei, without rising. 'This is why I have requested our honourable director to permit me the use of your talents for a short period.'

Noticing the old man's confused expression, the director hurried to explain. 'You are to travel with our honourable patron to Egypt next week with a view to establishing links with your counterpart, Curator Suleiman Attallah of the Supreme Council of Antiquities. More importantly, you are to study a collection of artefacts that venerable Subedei has acquired. He wishes you to advise him as to their nature and use. He is seeking confirmation of his own theories.' The director paused for a moment as he beamed another toothy smile at Subedei. 'And, depending on your services, perhaps our honoured patron may allow an exhibition of his collection at our museum in the near future.'

Subedei nodded benignly, without taking his eyes off Lu Yen.

'Venerable Subedei honours me beyond my ability, I fear,' replied Lu Yen. 'My expertise relates to Asian dynastic heritage, not Egyptian.'

Subedei appeared unconcerned. 'But specifically to foreign religious artefacts imported to China either from Tibet, Mongolia or Persia, if Director Guo Jian informs me correctly.'

'That is indeed correct, kind sir.'

'Then your learned opinion is required,' announced Subedei with finality, as he raised himself from his throne. He delivered a single nod to the newly appointed Assistant Curator Tang in polite acknowledgement and farewell.

*　　*　　*

One hour later Temujin Subedei nodded three times in polite acknowledgement of Xudung Sun, the vice premier of the state council of the Communist Party of China, the sole political party allowed within the People's Republic of China. The third most powerful man in China was seated between the minister for energy, Fu Chen, and the minister for foreign affairs, Zhilun Yang.

The thin lips of Vice Premier Sun drew back into an increasingly broad smile as Subedei delivered the message of friendship sent from President Jumair, and explained how the Saudis and the Stans would shortly be exporting their oil to China.

'Few men of business display their loyalty to the Party as you do, Ambassador Subedei,' he said softly. 'Would you not agree, my respected colleagues?'

The silent nods from the ministers of energy and foreign affairs respectively were all that was expected in agreement.

'Such loyalty will decidedly be rewarded in due course,' added Vice Premier Sun.

Subedei knew that the promise of reward was easily come by. Actual reward was a different matter and was dependent on his making everything come to pass as he had promised. By the same token, the failure of any scheme brought to their attention would be likely to merit severe punishment. Politicians were happy to take the credit for any success, but losing face was unthinkable. Subedei knew that, in the event of failure, he would be held fully responsible. It was why everything he said in this meeting had to be phrased extremely carefully.

'My only reward is to serve the Party that has already been so generous to me,' he said.

Vice Premier Sun liked Subedei. He considered him one of a necessary breed that would bring greatness and power to China. Already things were moving satisfactorily. China was now a preferred destination for foreign investment, ahead of the US and Britain, with an increment of twelve and a half per cent in the last year alone. But foreign investment did not fulfil the increasing demand for energy resources and, if the US was any guide to go by, China would require at least ten million barrels of oil a day to be imported within the next five years, notwithstanding the nuclear programme that was underway. But Sun was also wary of Subedei. He was too ambitious, with Ministers

Yang and Chen already in his pocket. Sun would have to handle him carefully.

'I understand that you have expressed an interest in holding the office of Secretary General of Inner Mongolia,' said Sun lightly.

Subedei was aware of the double edge to the question. 'It is an office that is close to my heart, being Mongolian,' he admitted. 'Since Inner Mongolia wisely came under the protection of the People's Republic, there have been, in my humble opinion, too many unfortunate protests against China. These I would wish to resolve.'

'Some may consider such words a criticism of the handling of Inner Mongolia by the PRC,' commented Vice Premier Sun. 'Though I do not, of course.'

'No such meaning is intended,' said Subedei with a bow. 'Indeed, I would use my office, given the opportunity, as a platform to announce the truth of what great benefits the PRC has brought to her neighbour these past fifty-six years. Such an announcement could not be viewed as a criticism but rather as an honourable defence against misguided world opinion.'

Dangerous and clever, a pure politician, Vice Premier Sun decided. 'Then we must see if such an office can be forthcoming. In the meantime, allow me, on behalf of our president, our vice president and our premier of the state council to wish you continued success in your much-valued entrepreneurial endeavours.'

Thirty-Four

Some 12,000 kilometres to the west of Beijing, deep beneath Washington's domed White House in a richly panelled briefing room, sat a serious-looking Aaron Hammond with presidential assistant Kowalski and ICE director Kurt Williams. Sitting opposite them was President Henry 'Bob' Petersen.

Formerly governor of California, Petersen had a frank enjoyment of the presidential office. There were only two small parts that did not appeal to him. The first was that its seat had to be near Congress, and that meant living on the East instead of the West Coast. And the second was that a mostly Republican Congress dictated budgetary constraints to every policy he stood for as a newly elected Democrat.

Occasionally, like tonight, there was a third niggle. That was when he was forced to abandon something important in his personal life because some crisis demanded his immediate attention. It was all part and parcel of the job, of course, and usually he didn't think twice about it. But tonight was his twenty-sixth wedding anniversary and he hated letting Mattie down. She always claimed not to mind, and it had been her driving force that had brought him this far anyway, all the way from California to the White House. But he still disliked disappointing her, and that was making him cranky.

Petersen scanned the men opposite him with a frown, his voice rough with an edge of strong annoyance. 'I got the Senate, the media and the high voice of indignant Americans screaming at me to break off relations with the Saudis. I got the environmental committee screaming at me to get the Saudi royal family to pay for the damage along the Delaware shore. I got the military screaming at me to place marshals and electronic surveillance equipment on every tanker and cargo vessel – they've even got a new name for them, they're calling them PDCs –

295

Potential Disaster Carriers, or Potential Deployment whatevers. And now you're telling me that not only is the group claiming credit for this terrorist act a bunch of home-grown Americans with some crazy notion about national pride, but that the media has somehow got wind of it and is doing a complete breaking-news report first thing in the morning.'

Petersen paused, and tapped his pen sharply on the table. 'I'm not happy, gentlemen. Not at all. This sure is going to put a different perspective on our commitment to fight terrorism.'

He rested his blue eyes on the chief of the Directorate of Intelligence, a man he both respected and trusted. 'OK, what's the programme, Aaron?'

Hammond's answer was already prepared. He'd rescanned it as he waited patiently for the president to take his annoyance out on them. It went with the territory. He cleared his throat. 'Thank you, Mr President. Three points to start with. First, our view is that the *Riyadh* is not a precursor of a series of terrorist acts to follow. It's a one-off. Second, the group claiming responsibility does not exist. Third, we do know who is behind it.'

'The president's going to need more than just your view,' interrupted Kowalski. 'Where's your proof?'

Petersen turned to his assistant. 'Jim.'

'Yes, Mr President?'

'When I'm here, I can talk for myself. OK?'

Kowalski's bald head quickly nodded in agreement. 'Sorry, Mr President.'

Aaron leaned forward, ignoring the assistant's interruption. 'To fill in the details for you. We know that the sole purpose behind the incident on the *Riyadh* was to cause as much tension as possible between us and Saudi Arabia. The timing could not have been worse for the US because, as you know, Mr President, our relations with them are somewhat strained at the moment.

'Though we do not know fully what he is planning, we do know, thanks to our friends at ICE and in the Israeli Secret Service, both investigating him for different reasons, that the perpetrator behind the *Riyadh* explosion is Temujin Subedei, head of Subedei Industries, and a known associate, possibly within a cartel, of Guillermo Nicaros.'

Petersen nodded. 'The same guy who's been giving us a headache in Venezuela?'

'Yes. According to one of our agents who has been attached to Nicaros for five months now, the two have not actually been seen together, but following information just received we now believe that Subedei arranged the *accidental* hanging of Nicaros's wife.'

The president raised his eyebrows. 'And you say they're associates?'

'Most of the Nicaros's power has come from his wife, whose father was one of Venezuela's original four oil barons. With her death he took control, but he could not take the risk of arranging it himself. When it happened he was as shocked as everyone else because he had no inkling at all of when or how.'

'You say it was an accidental hanging. What in hell's name is that?'

'They were holidaying on a friend's three-mast yacht, a real beauty, apparently, called the *Columbian*. One morning Nicaros's wife was found hanging from the rigging. She had apparently climbed up it to get her cat, which was still up there. Why do we believe that Subedei was behind it? Because the face of one of the other guests, a Russian photographed by our operative, matches a picture sent to us by Mossad, taken by their own undercover operative, standing right next to Subedei.'

'Subedei seems to be a man who specializes in arranging accidents,' said Petersen grimly.

Hammond paused to drink from his glass of water.

'Seems to be his preferred method and we now believe that his intention, as uncovered by ICE, is to somehow "accidentally" blockade the Suez, thus further increasing tension, with a view to diverting the Saudi flow of oil towards China.'

The president leaned back and shoved his hands in his pockets, a worried frown crinkling his brow. 'Y'know, I hear what you're saying but frankly it's hard to credit. Is that really on the cards, Aaron?'

'Yes, Mr President, I'm afraid it is. The Saudi agreement with Russia took us by surprise, and their diplomatic relations with China have been improving for some months now.'

'It just doesn't seem possible that this guy Subedei could manipulate so many people and governments to get the outcome he wants. And correct me if I'm wrong – the Saudis don't get on so well with Iran, so any oil flow will have to be diverted by tanker round India.'

'I know, Mr President. And it's precisely the incredible unlikeliness of it that's allowed him to get this far unchecked. And as for the Saudis using tankers instead of pipelines – you're absolutely right, that would be the obvious conclusion. But we have information that Iran's minister for energy, Mullah Abd al Rahwan, has persuaded his regime to allow Saudi oil to flow through Iran towards Kazakhstan. Their pipes flow direct to China and are operated primarily by Natasha Berentsky, whom we also believe to be a member of Subedei's cartel.'

Hammond gestured to the world map across the wall, and they all turned to study it.

'But any pipe would first have to cross Turkmenistan, wouldn't it?' asked Kowalski.

Kurt Williams pressed the buttons on the computer console in front of him. 'Allow me, Aaron.' He quickly outlined the ICE hypothesis that oil pipelines had already been constructed that were capable of being linked to existing lines, providing the necessary route to Ceyhan on the Turkish coast. 'Since we've drafted this hypothesis, Mr President, we've been able to put flesh on its bones with satellite evidence.'

The president looked confused. He turned back to Hammond. 'If they're already constructed, why didn't we know until now, Aaron?'

'We did. In fact, it was American engineers that helped with the technical specifications. But we can't dictate which country builds what pipe to where.'

Petersen clenched his jaw. 'Maybe not, but I, for one, take a very dim view when they start blowing, blocking or diverting pipes to prevent oil flowing to the States.'

Hammond paused to show that he sympathized with the president's point of view, and then continued. 'Subedei is adept at avoiding any kind of connection with incidents we believe are planned and executed by him. The *Riyadh* is a case in point. The incident has been claimed by a terrorist group – as so many of these disasters are. There's always a convenient faction to act as a scapegoat for Subedei's actions. There's no way that the *Riyadh* can be linked to him. With the media all excited about this so-called – and frankly fictitious – American national-pride group claiming responsibility and the Saudi Kingdom already demanding action, apology and compensation, Subedei has achieved just what he wanted.'

'OK, so another round to Subedei. What are we going to do about it?'

Hammond shifted uncomfortably on his seat. 'I'm coming to that, Mr President. The problem is one of extremely delicate world diplomacy. We cannot be seen to interfere in the domestic policies of other countries, particularly not Arab Muslim ones. We all know what kind of legacy we have from previous administrations. Naturally, this causes immense difficulties in trying to extricate the sharp thorn Subedei has placed in our soft fleshy butt, if you'll pardon me, Mr President.'

'Not helped by the bureaucracy of Congress and carping campaigns against me in the media,' growled Petersen bitterly.

'It's certainly not conducive,' agreed Hammond, casting a look at Williams. 'With our hands tied, we can only provide extremely cautious and covert support for ICE.'

The president looked over at Williams with his trademark charming smile. 'You guys can help us out here?'

'We very much hope so, Mr President. We're working on an idea at the moment. Our friends in Mossad are coming in with us and I believe that makes us much stronger than Subedei can possibly realize.'

Kowalski frowned. 'With all due respect to ICE and our Israeli friends, leaving it to someone else to sort out our problems could be even more dangerous. What if this idea, whatever it is, doesn't work? Who takes the blame?'

The president breathed deeply while rubbing his silver-grey temples with his fingers. 'If we can't stop this guy, then we'll all be in deep, deep trouble. I can kiss goodbye to achieving what I promised during a second term. The fact is, as Aaron quite rightly says, we can't dictate which country builds what pipe to where. There have been an awful lot of people who have wanted to see the US kicked in the butt for a very long time. Well, gentlemen, this time we've been well and truly caught with our trousers down, exposed – and there's little we can do about it.'

Thirty-Five

Ayeesha breathed an inward sigh of relief. At last, she had been taken completely into Subedei's confidence. He had brought her here to his secret quarters concealed within the Alexandrian refinery and told her she was to be present at a most important meeting. At first he had left her in a hidden room, where she could observe his guests from behind a two-way mirror, so that she could study their body language and tell him her observations. Now he was doing her the honour of inviting her to join them all.

She walked out into the magnificent Egyptian throne room where the guests were assembled with their host, her head held high and her shoulders straight.

'Ah,' said Subedei, as she approached. 'Let me introduce you to my associate, Ayeesha Al Fahila. She will be joining us today.'

Each cartel member assessed her, she could see that, although they appeared to accept her warmly. Only Berentsky could not conceal a hostile glare. Lord Somers was clearly dazzled, his attempts at suave politeness coming across as just a little too leering.

'An absolute work of art, another chosen piece you have kept hidden from us,' Somers said, refusing to let go of her hand. 'It is really wonderful to discover that the exquisite voice one has already spoken to emits from such matchless beauty. Not for sale either? Priceless if she was, eh?'

Subedei, somewhat annoyed by the continuing pleasantries or vulgar humour that the Englishman always seemed determined to prolong, ignored the question. He was eager to start. 'Let us begin,' he said smoothly.

They all took their places and waited expectantly.

'My dear colleagues, welcome, and thank you for coming to this meeting, the final one before Operation Genghis Khan commences in forty-eight hours. I take it that all of you have already heard the news concerning the *Riyadh*?'

'An excellent success,' chirped Berentsky sweetly, and she pursed her thin lips into a kiss which she blew at him. 'Such an outrage to learn that Americans, the self-appointed fighters against terrorists, are no better than terrorists themselves,' she added, laughing sarcastically.

Subedei's black eyes gleamed back at her. 'Already Saudi Arabia has announced they are to review their economic relations with the US unless they receive both apology and compensation. The hardliners are even proposing that they send over their own forces to fight terrorism on American soil. Imagine the States swallowing the very same medicine they so righteously dole out to other countries?'

'Yes, but the fact is, I fear that they know who *really* is behind it,' Somers said soberly, attracting everyone's attention.

'Meaning?' enquired Subedei, instantly alert. He would be furious if Somers had been holding anything back.

'Prior to the *Riyadh* incident, I received a report from our own intelligence, hypothesizing a plan by Subedei Industries to control oil in the Middle East. Made light of it, of course, but sent a bit of a shiver up me.'

Subedei's eyes narrowed. 'Did the report mention ICE?'

'ICE put the report together. Actually, there was a request from the ICE chairman, Sir Duncan Buchanan, insisting that we take it seriously and act on it at once. I refused, saying that it was not in the interests of Her Majesty's government to meddle in the commercial matters of foreigners.'

'Hypothesis!' shouted Subedei, scornfully. 'Investigating a large conglomerate like Subedei Industries is hardly unusual, particularly as that is what ICE does, but absolutely nothing can prove their suspicions. And, in seventy-two hours, it will be too late for them to do anything about it.'

'Still, it's a bit close to home,' Somers added.

'Enough, William. The report mentions me. Not you, nor any other members. So let us concentrate on the reason we are here. Now,' he continued, 'this is what we have. On the morning of the fifteenth, the export pipeline that carries crude oil from

Iraq's Kirkuk fields to Turkey's Mediterranean coast will be once again blown up, but this time in four places at main pumping stations. There will be no requirement for any group to claim credit as the guerrilla members of the former Iraq Republican Guard will once more be blamed.

'On the following day, the British-led Caspian Consortium pipeline will be blown up, also in four places, with blame this time being placed on the rebel army of Chechnya, who will claim that this act is intended to draw the west's attention to their oppressed country. It will have the appearance of a copycat attack.

'Natasha, you will immediately call your own network, voicing your outrage over the consortium's loss and proposing that they join with you in choosing to send oil through your own pipes eastward to China, and through our own newly constructed pipe westward to Ceyhan.'

Berentsky's eyes shone brighter than the enormous diamonds set within her earrings. 'They will have no other choice. With the threat of their own pipe being out of service indefinitely, the cost to them in profits will be billions if they do not!'

'Again on the fifteenth, the US cargo ship *Atlantic Valiant*, carrying oil-rig machinery urgently required for Iraq, will be blown up at Al Qantarah on the Suez Canal.' Subedei allowed himself one of his rare smiles. 'Credit for the devastating explosion will be claimed by a group of Saudi fundamentalists in retaliation for the US terrorist act on the *Riyadh*.'

Subedei looked at Mullah Walid Abd al Rahwan. 'My brother, you will immediately contact your Saudi counterpart. Like Natasha, you will voice your outrage and concern and remind him that the services of your new pipeline are immediately available to your Arab neighbour. I will also be contacting him, offering my own pipeline from Suez to Alexandria at a highly discounted price. They will have to agree in any event, because the Sumed pipeline will be required to shut for emergency maintenance repairs if they do not.'

Mullah Rahwan's severe mouth curved into a smile, his lips disappearing within the thick foliage of his beard and moustache. 'My brother, I am confident that my illustrious neighbour will agree that it must clearly be the will of Allah that the enormous black gold reserves of their great country are destined to go east.'

Subedei brought his hands together in a prayerful motion to his chest in acknowledgment of the mullah's statement. 'Finally,' he said, 'the Al Qantarah tunnel, accidentally damaged by the shockwave of the American ship's detonation, will collapse – with a little help from a timed explosive – to be forever flooded by the canal waters.'

Lord Somers looked concerned. 'Forever flooded? I was led to believe that closure of the canal would only be temporary.'

'Forever flooded – for as long as we choose, William. At any time, we will be able to close the hole using our barricade of MM120, which is now firmly in place. When our aims have been achieved and the west has once again become used to living without the benefits of Suez *and* learned to swallow the high price of our oil or do without that also, we will then benevolently repair and reopen the canal. The political gratitude and economic rewards received will be a bonus. And the costs of the entire operation will be reimbursed through insurance policies.'

'Multi-billion-dollar returns for a nominal investment reimbursed by insurance,' said Nicaros, his face triumphant. 'It is a deal like no other in history. Such a shame no one will ever know.'

'The best-laid plans are the best-kept secrets, as they say,' piped up Somers, his eyes bright with greed, any previous reservations forgotten.

'Guillermo,' continued Subedei, turning to Nicaros, 'you will simply have to wait until you receive a call begging for more oil in the short term.'

Nicaros grinned. 'I will be ready and waiting to help the US out in their hour of need, when their oil supply from Saudi dries up. I will offer generous terms for ninety days, to allow them time to renegotiate with the Saudis.'

'Good, and all of us will make sure that the Saudis are fully apprised of what the US is doing,' said Subedei. 'Saudi Arabia will be disinclined to rebuild their severed relations. Nor will they see the need to, while their powerful reserves are being generously siphoned to a more appreciative China. At the end of the ninety days, when it will be too late for them to do anything about it, you will cease your supply.'

303

'And in one fell swoop, the great old US of A will be held to economic ransom by the rest of the world!' finished Nicaros with evident glee. 'Apologies, colleagues, I mean, of course, by us.'

Thirty-Six

Zarakov stared closely at Ayeesha through the two-way mirror. Instructed to observe the cartel from the concealed room once the Egyptian woman had left it, he used his interrogation-honed abilities to note every member's body language, the individual quirks that either proved their avid loyalty and belief in Subedei, or their distrust and concern.

Only the Englishman's mannerisms caused him unease. Zarakov could sense he was weaker than the others, a man whose power rested only on his political position. He would break in a stressful situation, Zarakov was sure of that. Then there was the Iranian mullah; like Somers, he was nothing more than a bureaucrat at the mercy of his regime, and Zarakov's instinct was that he would turn on Subedei in an instant if that was what was required.

Berentsky and Nicaros were two ruthless individuals clearly intoxicated with the idea of more and more power and wealth. They answered to no one but themselves and would probably remain loyal to Subedei, no matter what. They sensed a kindred spirit in him and they would never be able to let go of their yearning for more.

Zarakov frowned as his eyes rested on the slim, elegant form sitting quietly on the edge of the group. The Egyptian woman, Ayeesha, appeared too confident, too much at ease, yet he sensed there was a nervous tension rippling beneath her satin-like toned skin. All of his instincts shouted at him not to trust her, just as they had from the very start. His first impression of her had never changed: she was extremely dangerous.

Then a thought struck him, the kind of insight he had learned to trust over the years, spawned from hard-won experience. It came upon him in a startling flash – but he could hardly believe it when he realized what it was. Before he could consider it further, the meeting ended. The guests rose to their feet, talking quietly, and were led from the room by a servant. As soon as they had gone, Subedei beckoned directly at the polished mirror, indicating Zarakov should join them.

Subedei watched the Russian come into the room. 'All went as smoothly as expected, Rurik. Any comments you need to share with me?'

Zarakov did not have to look to know that the Egyptian woman, who had remained with Subedei, was watching them closely. 'None that relate to Operation Genghis Khan, but I do have one with regard to the Englishman. I sense that sooner or later he will turn his tail, either to save himself from disaster or to gain advantage from it.'

'My own sentiments exactly,' retorted Subedei. 'Arrange an accident for him within ninety days of the start of the operation. By then he will have served his usefulness. Anything else?'

'No, Lord Subedei, nothing of any consequence,' replied Zarakov. It was not the right time to voice his concerns about Ayeesha. Subedei seemed more besotted with this woman than the others. Perhaps that was the secret of her confidence. He would leave it for now.

'Good. Are all of our people ready?'

'I have attended to it myself, Lord Subedei. Each separate group believes they are operating alone. They have all been well paid, though the Chechnyan militia insisted on an extra artillery payment, which I arranged courtesy of the Russian army.'

'Seems reasonable,' laughed Subedei. He seemed to be becoming more alive with every moment, as though he could sense his destiny getting closer. 'Well done!'

The Russian accepted the praise with a modest nod before continuing. 'Our own security will be in force at Al Qantarah and the container of explosives has already been primed on the *Atlantic Valiant*. The container was the first to be loaded, so it will be nigh impossible to gain access to.'

'What about timing? The *Riyadh* did not do the damage intended because of the damn ship running ahead of schedule, which makes it twice that captains doing their own thing have caused us problems; first the dredger and then the *Riyadh*. It cannot be allowed to happen again.'

'Impossible, My Lord. It will be triggered electronically by a short-range receiver as it passes the designated point. Two of our security dressed as local fishermen will activate it, leaving no room for error.'

'And the Al Qantarah underpass?'

'There was a delay in fixing the scaffold, but the explosives will be in place by tomorrow at midnight. Each one has an integrated shock receiver that will be activated from the vibration wave of the massive *Atlantic Valiant* explosion. Only two are required but we have eight to cover all eventualities. However, in the very unlikely event that they do not explode as intended, Qenawi will activate them. He also holds a final back-up receiver for the bomb carried on the *Atlantic Valiant*.'

'And back-up security?'

'There are teams for the *Atlantic Valiant* if required and security to ensure that the underpass explosives experts can do their work undisturbed. Qenawi himself heads up the security team at our Al Qantarah facility, again in the unlikely event that *any* military forces attempt to interfere with the operation. All of our mercenaries have been handpicked from seasoned professionals and are being generously paid. Your own loyal bodyguards will, of course, remain with you here.'

'My dear Rurik, once again you have proved yourself to be my loyal general and friend. You will be pleased to learn that your numbered account has been credited with the amount of fifteen million dollars.'

Zarakov raised an eyebrow in astonishment, then smiled. He had not expected such a generous gesture. It was three times the sum they had agreed. 'Thank you, Lord Subedei.'

'You ought really to thank one of our own thoughtful patrons, Al Kadeh. It was he who was posthumously kind enough to have funds diverted from his personal accounts to yours.' Subedei saw Zarakov stiffen. 'And, of course, in a manner that is entirely untraceable. Now, tell me, is there any news of that idiot Barracio?'

'He is still under instructions to eliminate agents Brock and Ferguson.'

'We'll all be retired by the time the Italian fool achieves it. After Operation Genghis Khan, attend to it yourself. You can instruct Barracio what to do with Somers. Even he should be able to accomplish a simple thing like that.'

Zarakov's eyes narrowed as he thought of his fallen brother Dimitri. Revenge on Connor Brock would be sweet indeed. 'Nothing would give me greater pleasure.'

With his mind centred on receiving fifteen million dollars *and* being offered the head of his personal enemy, Zarakov did not give a further thought to the beautiful Ayeesha as she departed with her Mongolian lover. Ignoring his intuition, which had so often before kept him alive, was an error he would regret.

'How is it you would like *me* to serve you, My Lord?' asked Ayeesha, as the underground shuttle sped swiftly towards Subedei's Nile residence, the Palace of Ammon. 'I need to see Dr Suleiman Attallah in Cairo for some matters, but will change all and everything to suit your convenience.'

Subedei reached out his left hand and squeezed the nearest of Ayeesha's breasts, softly at first, then slowly tightening his grip. He liked it that she did not seem to mind.

'It truly pleases me that you are always accommodating and considerate of me in every way. I would like you to keep your appointment, but I want you to take Assistant Curator Tang along with you. He is to meet with Attallah too. Don't let the two academics get too involved, though. There is much I wish him to confirm for me.'

Ayeesha slowly trailed her fingers around Subedei's neck. 'Leave it to me. I will take care of everything that pleases you.'

The exhilaration of flying through the clouds at supersonic speed, arriving in a culture so utterly different from his own and being fed delicacies he had not known existed, had not fazed Lu Yen at all.

After everything he had seen and endured in his life, he had perfected a form of meditation that inwardly centred him and gave him complete calm. Lu Yen appreciated the special attention everyone seemed to want to give him, though he never asked for anything, merely nodded his thanks politely when receiving something. During the flight, the venerable Subedei had informed him that he would be taken to see some artefacts. All he had to do was come to an opinion as to their authenticity.

Within two hours of the blood-red Concorde taxiing to a halt at Alexandria's airport, Lu Yen had been ferried down the

Nile to an imposing palace. There, a beautiful woman in a cheongsam had carefully blindfolded his face with a silken scarf. It was strange but he had felt no need to question why.

The feel of the woman's hand was cool and delicate on his own as she guided him into what felt like a small room. He jumped a little when he felt the room descend slowly but neither he nor the woman spoke. When the descent stopped, he sensed the door open and he was guided a further distance. The uneven passage beneath his feet pained his leg. The beautiful woman supporting his arm had forgotten to return his stick. Still he said nothing.

Then his guide helped to remove his blindfold, and gestured to him to enter a large well-lit vault. Lu Yen thanked her and she politely bowed her head before closing the door behind him.

It took a few moments for his eyes to get used to the bright-ness as he gazed around him.

Nothing could have prepared him for what he saw.

His inner calm disintegrated as a cry involuntarily escaped from his throat. Instantly, he was transported back to when he was just fourteen years old and the moment his master had shown him the sacred urn in preparation for Monlam, the prayer festival. Lu Yen had been entranced by its intricate design of golden interlocking horns.

The painful memories that he had so deeply repressed over the years flooded into his mind. He shut his eyes tightly but could not stop the shocking images of the past flashing inside his head – the discovery of his master's body; the sight of the holy crypt, ransacked of all of its sacred icons.

Feeling as though he had been transformed back into a fearful apprentice, Lu Yen slowly opened his eyes.

The sacred gold urn was still there, directly in front of him.

He had not imagined it.

Sitting in her office, Ayeesha thought the funny little man had been strangely quiet in the back of the Lexus. During the entire trip to the Cairo offices of the Supreme Council of Antiquities, which had lasted an hour, he had not said a word. She had studied Chinese and, though she could not write it, she had mastered the basics. Enough for an intelligent conversation, at least. It had been important for her to get closer to Subedei.

But each time she had tried to start a conversation with Assistant Curator Tang, she had met with monosyllabic responses.

'I expect you are looking forward to meeting Dr Suleiman Attallah, Mr Tang?'

'Yes.'

'Have you been out of China before?'

'Yes.'

'Do you find the people different in other countries?'

'No.'

She hadn't bothered to continue. This would be an easy job for the translators, there to assist Dr Attallah and Mr Tang. Once they had arrived at the offices and she had introduced the two men, she left as quickly as she was able to, promising to return soon.

Now, in her office, she carefully dialled a number into the telephone. Her call was answered on the first ring by a pleasant voice.

'Celebration Flowers.'

'I would like to order five large bunches.'

'To be delivered or collected?'

'Delivered.'

'Did you say five?'

'Yes. And they must be an assortment.'

'Please hold for just a moment.'

Ayeesha counted the seconds on her watch while the line was being secured, holding her breath.

'What do you have?'

The soft reassuring tones of Moyshe's rich, gravelly voice allowed Ayeesha to start breathing again. Within five minutes she had quickly relayed the details she had learned about Operation Genghis Khan.

'Sorry I can't give you specific locations or times,' she concluded.

'You have done more than we hoped.' The voice paused for a moment. 'You should get out. Do you want us to arrange a pick-up?'

'Not yet.'

'Be careful, my daughter,' came the reply, followed by a click as the call ended.

* * *

She liked the term of endearment the Intelligence chief had used, Hanita Shamesh thought to herself as she checked her reflection in the mirror.

She was not really his daughter, though might just as well have been; certainly she was closer to him than her own father. Moyshe Jamal had trained her to be the best undercover operative in the service. She was prepared to do whatever he told her was necessary, without hesitation.

Over the years, she had learned to perfect the aliases she chose, almost becoming the people she invented. She *was* her character, in every thought and deed, at all times. She enjoyed it, it challenged her. This new one, though, was her masterpiece. Her Egyptian alias, Ayeesha Al Fahila, had exceeded even her own expectations.

Not once had there been so much as a doubtful look from Subedei. She was utterly and completely convincing, and now she had captivated him in every way, just as she had always intended. The seduction had been a little more gruelling than she'd anticipated, but she had managed it. She could cope with it, that was the important thing.

It was only the man Zarakov who she intuitively felt might harbour suspicions about her. She was sure she'd been wise to act as she had, persuading Subedei to treble the sum when he had informed her of the amount intended for Zarakov. It had pleased the Russian, defused something inside him. And she could see that the extra gift of revenging himself upon his brother's killer had bought her some time.

Certainly it had distracted his concentration from her. She'd been sensing his focus on her more and more and Zarakov was no fool. He was dangerous. If he was not taken out during the operation, she would have to eliminate him herself.

As Hanita Shamesh, her real self, the highly trained agent, she recognized the vengeful killer in Zarakov. She wanted him nowhere near her.

The woman gazed seriously at herself in the mirror, considering what she was doing in the name of freedom and security. Then, a moment later, after her reflection had transformed its whole demeanour once more into Ayeesha Al Fahila, and a wide smile formed.

The thought of the million dollars sitting in an account,

arranged by a grateful Subedei in reward for her continual thoughtfulness and devoted service, would bring a smile to any ambitious woman's lips.

Thirty-Seven

The damming report prepared by ICE, picked up by most of the satellite networks, was broadcast shortly after Mossad had wired its sensitive information to Aaron Hammond and David Bearne at their respective intelligence centres.

The CNN North Africa Network was the first to air the exclusive interview simultaneously in Arabic, French and English. The US and Chinese national networks greedily followed suit with the recordings they had been sent.

The spokesman for ICE, Dr Paul van Lederman, stared directly into the camera, the make-up on his face enhancing his light-blue eyes as the camera captured the genuine integrity that flowed from them.

In response to the interviewer's question as to why Subedei Industries was under investigation for fraud, Van Lederman spoke apologetically but with confident gravitas.

'As investigators of corporate espionage it is neither the purpose nor wish of ICE to cast suspicions on companies without firm evidence to back it up. When an organization the size of Subedei Industries is involved we are very conscious of the backlash effect on the thousands of employees and shareholders.

'Our overriding credo is to expose blatant misuse of shareholder funds, government subsidies and licences and wilful political lobbying either through blackmail or financial persuasion.

'No country should be conned by the wilful malpractice and illegal operation of any organization. It grieves us to have discovered that what we considered was a solid organization, run by a generous patron, has to be exposed as being nothing more than a front for organized crime overlorded by a ruthless terrorist.'

The interviewer sitting next to Van Lederman could not

believe his ears. Handled correctly this would confirm his status as a CNN anchorman. 'Strong words Dr van Lederman. What evidence do you have to support your accusations?'

'Sadly I believe we have only uncovered the tip of a very large iceberg. But the two points I intend to disclose today are damming in themselves.'

The interviewer contained his impatience, recognizing that the ICE director was adept in using his own communication skills to add weight to his evidence. He kept quiet, looking expectant.

'First,' continued Van Lederman, 'following an announcement by your own president about the discovery of massive oil reserves that will guarantee a prosperous future for Egypt, we have to disclose that no oil had been found.'

'No oil!' ejaculated the interviewer, who had already invested all of his own personal savings into the offering by Ammon Oil that had been available following the announcement.

'Not a drop of the multi-billion-barrel reserves alluded to.'

The interviewer wanted to demand more but with the producer's voice in his ear telling him he had only ninety seconds remaining of the three-minute slot of prime air time allotted, he moved on.

'And the other point?'

'The second point of evidence relates to Khan Marine and Dredging, another wholly owned subsidiary of Subedei Industries. The company received the multi-million dollar licences and subsidy to ensure safe dredging of the Suez Canal, both licence and subsidy granted coincidentally on the same day as the Chairman and CEO of Subedei Industries, Temujin Subedei, became Patron of Egypt's Supreme Council of Antiquities. To date no dredging has been conducted and in some places we have evidence to prove that the alluvium has risen to dangerous heights, levels that could threaten safe passage through the canal.'

'Are you implying that Subedei Industries intends to close the canal?' asked the interviewer, a clear tinge of incredulity in his voice.

'ICE are not implying anything, we are just informing you of the tangible evidence we have to date.'

'And may I ask how you were able to acquire such evidence?'

'The chairman of Subedei Industries himself extended an invitation to ICE to investigate his company with a view to becoming an associate member; and we obliged. Our representative flew to Beijing and our investigators in Egypt discovered first-hand evidence actually on site. For the sake of clarity, these are not assumptions – they are statements of fact.'

The interviewer could not help his mouth gaping open in astonishment.

Subedei Industries was not informed prior to the airing of the interview, preventing their lawyers from placing an injunction on it. The unforeseen technical 'accident' was later blamed on a virus that had prevented the sensitive information from being received by Subedei Industries prior to the broadcast.

The organizers were prepared to swear under oath that it had most definitely been sent in good time. In accordance with such situations when no response is forthcoming, the interviewer ended his mini-broadcast with the usual prepared announcement.

'Despite CNN's request for a reaction to the allegations against Subedei Industries, the company has declined to comment.'

Over 3,000 kilometres north by north-west, watching the broadcast, Pete Kenachi smiled innocently as he leaned back surrounded by his electronic wizardry. In the same room sat Ferguson and Brock, appearing almost back to normal after the systematic beating reserved for assassins at Cairo prison.

Brock winked at Kenachi. 'These viruses can be extremely damaging, I'm glad you're on our side; as for Paul, short and succinct, his words just as lethal.'

'He certainly looked good,' put in Ferguson. 'I must compliment him on his make-up, took years off him.'

Brock's cell phone playing its familiar anthem halted his reply.

Five minutes later both Brock and Ferguson were speeding towards the airport, where they boarded a waiting private citation jet that flew them south-west to a military base situated eight kilometres from Pafos in Cyprus; 380 kilometres directly north of Port Said.

Without delay the two ICE operatives were transferred to a waiting British marked helicopter that skimmed across the dark swell of the Mediterranean, depositing them thirty-eight minutes later on the broad metal deck of an old but well-maintained Greek cargo ship. No sooner had they lighted from the aircraft than it lifted off, momentarily hovering like some giant insect, before skimming back across the water.

A well-built seaman, dressed in stained jeans and torn jumper, motioned for Brock and Ferguson to follow him down some thickly painted riveted steps to the cargo hold. As they negotiated the high step of the thick metal door at the bottom of the stairwell, it was like arriving at an evening football stadium brightly lit with high spotlights. The difference was there were no spectators sitting on the bulkheads, and where the pitch would be were about three score players, the majority huddled around electronic surveillance and communications computer screens. Within the tired old Greek cargo ship was a state of the art operations centre.

The seasoned SBS – Special Boat Service – leader looked up from his discussion with his three colleagues and watched appraisingly as the two ICE men approached. He noticed that the shorter of the two arrivals was built like a rugby scrum forward with broad shoulders and a thick neck. A mop of red hair and wide-set mouth and jaw that looked as if it would break into a huge grin at the slightest provocation of humour or sign of danger.

His taller partner with the dark collar-length slightly ragged hair framing a weather-tanned face walked with the confidence and presence of a sleek tiger that was casually observing everything within the territory he had suddenly found himself in. The veteran read that the man's medium skeletal structure was covered in supple wiry muscles and carried a constitution that was fit, determined and persistent.

Scanning and appraising the group of people who were watching them approach, Brock's azure eyes picked Beecham and walked straight up to him stretching out his hand.

'You must be Connor Brock,' cut in the other man, getting up from his seat. I'm Colonel James Beecham, representing Her Majesty's Special Forces here.' Beecham turned to his three colleagues, who also raised themselves to their feet. Two were kitted out in black-pocketed fatigues. The third, and somewhat older than his table companions, was in safari shirt and trousers.

'Allow me to introduce Commander John Tilling, my US counterpart; Captain Simon Cousins, John's team leader, and Moyshe Jamal, Director of Special Security for Israeli Intelligence. Moyshe is the reason why we have been brought together now.'

'Good to meet you all,' replied Brock congenially. 'This is Matt Ferguson, my partner in Special Operations for ICE; though you seem to already know that.'

'I had an opportunity to read your file on the way here, my concern being that as civilians your input might be a non-starter, other than strictly in an advisory capacity. But I learned that you were both in Special Forces, and last year you were the duo responsible for getting the PM out of an embarrassing hole with Moscow. So, gentlemen, it's good to have you aboard.'

'I appreciate the confidence, Colonel,' replied Brock evenly. 'I know the reason why we're here, now let's hear the details. Having flown like a bat out of hell for the past three hours, as I am sure we all have, there must be one hell of an urgency.'

Fifteen minutes later, Moyshe Jamal had concluded his detailed briefing outlining the four catastrophic events planned for the next forty-eight hours. The others listened silently, absorbing all the details quickly and precisely. Then Jamal had handed over to Beecham for discussion of the proposed strategy.

'We have the broad outlines for a responsive strategy – that's what we're here for,' said the colonel. 'But the finer details need some work and then we go straight into action.'

'And what's this operation called?' asked Ferguson. 'Can I suggest a name?'

'Go ahead,' said Beecham, puzzled.

Brock slid Matt a warning glance, as if to say that this was not the time for fun and games. Matt ignored him.

'How about Operation Route Canal?' Ferguson grinned. 'About as welcome and as painful.'

Captain Simon Cousins laughed. 'Very good. I second that.'

Beecham looked bemused. 'Very well. Whatever you think. Now.' He turned to the two Americans. 'Can we surmise that the Iraqi pipe presents the least of our problems?'

'Negative,' replied Commander Tilling, a ruddy-faced twenty-nine-year-old man with close-cropped black hair. 'The field commanders know that they are to expect four attempts to disable the pipe. There is already high-level security on the pipeline due to the frequent incursions over the past two years. But the problem is that it's one hell of a long pipe, fifteen hundred kilometres of the mother. Then we have the other pipe to Lebanon to monitor also, another six hundred kilometres.'

'All of it visibly exposed?' asked Brock.

'As good as.'

'Is it not possible for one of your satellites to keep constant surveillance?'

'We have already arranged for two to be centred over it but even that only gives us a window of protection of two hours in every twenty-four.'

'What's the manpower allocation?' asked Beecham, frowning.

'Ideally, it would be three men for every five kilometres, patrolling continuously for the twenty-four-hour period. But the field commander north of Baghdad, the area considered the most vulnerable, can only spare a fraction of the amount required.'

Brock looked at Moyshe Jamal. 'Your operative mentioned that the bombs were to include pumping areas. How many are there?'

'About two hundred, half of which are exposed and vulnerable.'

'Then I'd suggest that's where we concentrate our efforts,' said Brock. 'Holes in the pipes can be replaced without too much difficulty. Disabled pumps are another matter altogether.'

'Good point,' agreed Tilling. 'There is no way we can perimeter the whole pipe. Looking to the most strategic places will give us a fighting chance.'

Captain Cousins pointed at the large map to his side. 'Then it would be a good idea for us to liaise with our Russian colleagues and monitor the pumping stations on the Caspian Consortium pipe too. That could be where the planned Chechnyan strike could happen.'

Tilling nodded in agreement. 'I'm due to receive a call from the CO at his Astrakhan military base on the Caspian. I'll recommend he make contact with his counterparts at the two other Georgian bases.'

Beecham picked up the positive tone. 'If we are successful in preventing all of the planned attempts in Iraq, there is the very slight possibility that the Chechnya nationals won't proceed with their operation. It's unlikely, but it's a ray of hope.'

A look of concern passed over Tilling's face. 'My worry is that the Russians will want to know how we know. And they may ask why they should protect an international pipeline anyway.'

'I'm sure they're going to press for all the information they can get out of us,' replied Moyshe Jamal evenly. 'But in reality, they'll be delighted to foil any kind of Chechnyan operation. And tell them they owe one to Mossad for the advance warning.'

The British colonel nodded in agreement. 'At least the Russians have the luxury of acting within their own country. Even in Iraq, US forces are acting under agreements. Unfortunately, as military personnel, we do not have the same advantage operating in Egypt on the Suez.'

Tilling put up a hand. 'Well, we do, to some extent. Don't forget that the cargo ship *Atlantic Valiant* is US territory. We're covered so long as we stay on board.'

'That's not much use for gaining access to Subedei's Al Qantarah complex,' Brock interjected. 'I'm guessing that's why Matt and I are here.'

Jamal fixed Brock with a matter-of-fact stare. 'From the reports we've received, I understand that you have first-hand experience of the material MM120, know the exact location of it and have already been inside the facility. Who else would be suitable for the mission?'

'We've been there, sure — but that doesn't mean we have an intimate understanding of it,' said Ferguson.

Beecham looked serious. 'It's more than anyone else. You reconnoitred the surrounding area and, according to your service record, you're trained in explosives.'

'True. But more from a setting-up than disposal perspective.'

'What Matt really means is that he prefers blowing up things to switching them off,' explained Brock. 'But he can still do both with his eyes closed.'

Captain Cousins, a man no more than twenty-six, with a resolute firm jaw and broad nose, grinned at Ferguson. 'You are to work with my team in the underpass as guide and advisor.'

'Underpass? You mean under a bloody lot of water,' answered Ferguson. 'That's just great, reminds me of the old days, when I was always volunteering without having to say a word.'

'It'll be a walk in the park for you, Matt. My guys will do all the hard work.'

Ferguson looked at the young captain. Somehow the man reminded him of himself ten years earlier; and somehow he felt that he would be left with plenty to do. 'When do we leave?'

The Mossad chief answered. 'If the information received from our operative is correct, they will be inserting the explosives tonight, under the guise of urgent repairs requiring scaffold. We have already checked the bridge was closed at ten this evening, reopening tomorrow morning.' Moyshe Jamal glanced at his watch. 'It's twelve forty-five local time. We must assume that their work will be proceeding on their schedule.'

'We are to leave at one o'clock with a view to catching them in the act, while all local eyes are sleeping,' added Cousins.

'And do any of your team speak Arabic, in case we're rumbled by passing locals?'

'Two of our team do, and we have three fluent in French.'

Brock had been eyeing the crowd of about thirty tough-looking professionals that had begun to segregate into three teams and recheck their kit again. None of them looked over twenty-five or twenty-six years old. 'How many are in your team?'

'Commander Tilling and Captain Cousins both have a complement of twelve, all hand-picked professionals who have trained together in their respective teams. You and I will run with the British contingent of eight,' replied the colonel. 'A team that operates in unified precision even when blindfolded,' Beecham added with pride.

'And what is it you have conspired for our team to do even before I arrived?' enquired Brock.

'We will fly separately as a back-up to Commander Tilling's team, join him on the *Atlantic Valiant*, locate the bomb and defuse it. From there we progress to Al Qantarah to pick up Captain Cousins and his team and, only if required, secure the complex.'

'This may be a stupid question, but you are not letting the *Atlantic Valiant* through the canal, are you?'

'The captain has already been requested to anchor a short distance from Port Said. What we hope to do is defuse the bomb and allow the *Atlantic Valiant* to continue its course so as not to alarm the facility. We want to try and keep the element of surprise to prevent them setting off any underpass explosives Captain Cousins and his boys may have missed.'

Brock gave Colonel Beecham a quizzical look. 'Requested? I take it the Captain of the *Atlantic Valiant* has no idea that his ship is carrying a cargo of timed explosives?'

'It's a tough call, but we considered it prudent for it to appear as if our request was coming from the Port Authority. I advised them to hold off entering port for just a couple of hours, with the reason that we hadn't received the advanced shipping notice of his arrival.'

'Is the cargo captain going to buy a bar of bureaucratic soap like that after crossing the Atlantic? Somehow I don't think so.'

An expression of annoyance crossed Beecham's face. He was not used to having his decisions questioned. 'Look, Brock, if the crew panics in the knowledge that their ship's involved in a terrorist activity, we run the risk of them dumping their cargo in the sea. God knows what hazard a floating bomb in a sea of a hundred containers will cause.'

Brock had seen the look, recognizing it from his service days. Men like Beecham were trained to follow rules even when their gut, based on years of experience, told them otherwise. It was tough enough having to play god on who died and who lived, a position which did not help when a decision made was later questioned.

'Safer than letting a floating bomb sail direct into a populated port, Colonel. Your prudence is well founded but I respectfully suggest we contact them immediately, if only because we are dealing with an enemy who never plays by the rules.'

Beecham relaxed, momentarily paused and called over his adjutant. 'You're right, Brock,' the colonel admitted. 'These damn commercial sea captains are a law unto themselves.' Quickly he instructed his adjutant to ask communications to make contact with the *Atlantic Valiant* immediately.

Two minutes later the adjutant returned.

Radar confirmed that the ship was indeed heading direct for Port Said, but communication with the *Atlantic Valiant* was not possible. It was ignoring all attempts to contact it.

Thirty-Eight

'Remember, gentlemen, this is a covert operation. Yes, we are doing an important job, but we are not here to be seen. We do not exist. That is the essence of what we do. You are the elite of the elite and I expect everyone to be at the bar this evening. First round's on me. Good luck.'

Colonel James Beecham's final few words of briefing were met with silent nods.

A few minutes later, Teams Blue, Brown and Green, headed by Captain Cousins, Commander Tilling and Colonel Beecham respectively, stood on the deck. Three tilt-wing turbine helicopters emerged on a large platform that rose gracefully from the depths of *Apollo*'s hold, appearing like some three-headed mythological beast guarding the entrance to Hades. The first two teams ran across the deck and boarded their respective machines. As soon as the last man was inside, the two helicopters lifted vertically into the air and disappeared into the black sky.

Brock had kitted up in a black-pocketed jumpsuit. He had chosen a snub-nose Heckler and Koch automatic pistol that fitted comfortably in his hand; he knew it was a highly effective weapon for its light weight. Held with two hands, it could be as accurate as a rifle, though without the distance – but then, sniper shooting wasn't Brock's style. Strapped to his leg was a large Jim-Bowie-style dive knife. Inserted in his ear was a radio transmitter. Each man wore an identical earpiece.

As the eight-man team headed by Beecham prepared to board the last helicopter, Brock turned suddenly to Moyshe Jamal, standing on the deck beside them, watching proceedings.

'Just one question that interests me,' Brock said to the Israeli agent. 'What motive does Mossad have for infiltrating Subedei?'

Jamal stared at him for a moment and then said, 'We suspect him to be the financier behind Hamas. His activities are

322

destroying our peace process. We believe that Subedei considers our painful conflict a useful cause to be kept alive by his petty cash. Unrest in the Middle East is clearly in his interest. But we needed proof before we could block funds.'

'And take him out?'

'That's two questions, Mr Brock,' said the Mossad chief without expression. 'Good luck.'

Radio silence was maintained during the forty-five minute flight. Though the jet turbines of the tilt-wing aircraft were producing a speed of 320 kilometres an hour, their sound was not much more than a whisper. The jet wings that had folded into place for horizontal flight made the machine look like a black sleek cormorant hurled along by a hurricane.

Brock observed two of the younger-looking men checking and rechecking their kit; they were probably new and less experienced, a little unsure of themselves perhaps. The rest of the helicopter occupants sat as calmly as morning commuters on the bus to work, absorbed in their own thoughts.

Mossad had been invaluable in this mission, thought Brock. Their undercover agent had provided all the details of the planned operation. Without that, there would have been no chance. Now they had a good shot at stopping Subedei in his tracks. What kind of person could do that, he wondered. How could someone spend so long undercover in order to get so close to Subedei? He had a theory, based on long experience in the military, that some people were simply addicted to the flow of chemicals that their body supplied them with in stressful situations. Just as sports people loved the charge of endorphins released from the spine when they exercised, or pain and pleasure addicts craved dopamine generated by the brain, so Brock felt that some operatives got hooked on the buzz of fight-or-flight adrenaline that came with danger.

Hell, it was as good a theory as any. It helped explain all this madness.

A reduction in speed told him they were reaching their destination. Beecham's voice suddenly sounded in his earpiece, startling him. The order was radio silence – only something important would make Beecham break it.

'The pilot's seen our target. He says it's on fire.'

* * *

Team Brown led by Commander Tilling encountered fierce resistance within seconds of landing on the container-covered deck of the *Atlantic Valiant*. Before half his men had exited, Tilling heard the high whistle of a hand-launched missile shrieking towards them like a banshee across the 200 metres of the deck. A split second later the short-range shell tore into their aircraft with a direct hit.

Four of Tilling's men never knew what hit them, caught in the full force of the exploding fireball. Two were thrown into the air, spinning like bowled skittles before slamming into the adjoining metal containers. One was killed instantly as his head hit square on, exploding like an over-ripe melon with the force of the trajectory. The other miraculously survived with a broken collar bone, instinctively body-rolling as the blast spat him like corn popping from the heat.

The rest of Team Brown instantly took refuge behind the nearest wall of containers. Standing in what seemed like a metal ditch a metre wide between the container wall and the top of the hull, Tilling momentarily appraised his situation.

'Radio contact is broken with Team Green but at least each of us can communicate,' he rasped to his team, radio silence between them no longer required. 'OK. What we thought was a simple search and disposal is now an all-out defensive attack. First, we must disable the aggressors before our back-up arrives. We don't want them receiving the same welcome as us.'

'Hostages, sir,' said a team member. 'The briefing advised that a crew of twenty-two men are on board.'

'Priority three.' Tilling looked at his men. Two of the three-man team of scanning specialists were missing, the victims of the missile attack. Each had carried a backpack containing state-of-the-art sensory radio wave equipment to locate the explosive device.

He said roughly, 'Priority two is to locate and defuse the bomb. Brown Three and Six, is your equipment operational?'

The remaining members of the scanning team acknowledged his question. 'That's affirmative, sir.'

'Start scanning all the containers this side of the ship.' Tilling looked at the injured man nursing his broken collarbone. 'We will clear a passage forward. Brown Eight, can you function?'

'Every which way, sir.'

'Good, you and Brown Nine, cover Brown Three and Six.'

Including himself, Tilling had an attack force of four. It's small but it'll have to be enough, thought Tilling, knowing that his men were more than equal to the not-so-highly trained mercenaries he suspected had taken control of the ship. 'The rest of Team Brown stay with me. OK, move it.'

Most of the crew of the *Atlantic Valiant*, including the captain, had been asleep when the powerful motor cruiser had come alongside. Only one man expected something of the sort; he was the newest member of the crew, who had joined the ship in Florida to replace a man who had fallen unexpectedly sick. Before he'd boarded, he'd received an interesting request concerning his time on the *Atlantic Valiant*. In return for a little harmless information, he'd be well paid. A minor smuggling operation, the new crewman suspected. He'd heard of this kind of thing in the past. What would it matter if he pocketed a few dollars and turned a blind eye?

The journey had been uneventful up till now. There'd been nothing at all to report to his contact. Then, he'd been in the canteen with his new crewmates having a bit of dinner when he'd heard some of the sailors laughing raucously.

'Say what you want about Captain Grant Lee Carter – and I often do,' declared one, 'he's a born and bred Bostonian with balls. He won't take orders from some goddamn prissy Port Authority!'

'Sooner roast in hell,' added another.

'What's all this?' asked the new crewman, directing the question at one of the men on the next table.

'You don't know our captain yet, do ya?' replied the sailor through a mouthful of meatball. 'He don't like orders, unless they're his own. Apparently the Port Authority don't have their paperwork in order, and we're to wait a while until they do.'

'Damn that for a game of craps!' cried another. 'We wanna be on our way. I don't want to sit round in this hell hole.'

'Stuff like this usually happen?' asked the new crewman idly.

'They don't normally give a shit about paperwork in this part of the world,' said another man. 'The almighty dollar talks louder.'

The crewman turned back to his food, then casually got up and made his way back to the bridge.

'You will maintain a heading to Port,' Carter had commanded before retiring from the bridge a short time later. 'And if any more *requests* come for me, ignore them. I'll be the judge of what's good aboard my ship.'

The new crew member had immediately contacted the number he had been advised to call if any unusual requests were received. He then followed the orders he had received from Zarakov. It had been easy to drop a line to the cruiser that had arrived at midnight, as it had been to block the three access doors to the galley and the sleeping quarters. There were only two remaining crew members to subdue, which the eight heavily armed arrivals from the cruiser had quickly done for him.

The rogue crew member's satisfaction at how easily he had earned his money turned to one of abject horror when he saw what one of the four heavily armed men he had earlier assisted onboard actually did. To blast a helicopter within seconds of its landing into smithereens with a bazooka type projectile he had only ever seen in war films was the last thing he expected to see. Too late he realized he was part of something much more serious than a simple smuggling operation.

'Looks like we're in for a warm reception.' Beecham looked grim as he moved from the front of the aircraft into the back. 'Team Brown's machine is down.'

Brock looked through the observation window. He could see the wrecked remains of the helicopter on the deck of the *Atlantic Valiant* as livid flames licked at its mangled metal structure. He scanned the area surrounding the ship.

'Can you identify the small light lying due west, about two hundred metres?' he asked Beecham, indicating the small beacon. 'Small vessels do not run that close to cargo shipping lines at night.'

Before Beecham could reply, a sea-to-air missile shot out from the cruiser. The pilot responded with lightning reflexes, slamming forward the levers that tilted the machine from horizontal to full vertical. The stomach-churning response was instantaneous as the aircraft jerked into an almost perfect ninety-degree angle. At the same moment the missile flew past, missing its intended target by a metre.

Feeling like he had just descended in a high-speed runaway

lift, Brock crashed to the floor with Beecham. Without discussion, the pilot, as if playing some electronic computer war game, swooped his machine sharply around and within five seconds had locked on to his target. The knuckle of his thumb whitened as he fired one of the two heat-seeking missiles concealed within their reinforced cylinders. A moment later the cruiser erupted in a bolt of flame as the missile struck it amidships.

Brock and Beecham climbed back to their feet, steadying themselves against the hull. As they neared the *Atlantic Valiant*, a voice came through their earpieces. 'Nice shooting. Brown Two here. Welcome to the party.'

'Green Leader receiving, what is your status?' barked Beecham.

'Not good. Unable to confirm ship secure.'

Beecham's jaw tightened. 'Acknowledged, Brown Two. Brown Leader, do you read?'

A burst of static prefaced Brown Two's reply. 'Unable to make contact with Brown Leader.'

'We've got to get behind the bridge,' advised Brock, as he and Beecham viewed the sporadic gun battle that was being enacted below. 'They're in the bridge. If you provide covering fire, two of your men and I could descend on the blind stern side of the bridge.'

Beecham took one look at Brock, momentarily concerned that the civilian was along as an advisor. His knowledge might still be required at Al Qantarah. The penetrating gaze from eyes that glinted like blades in the half light made up his mind. One hurdle at a time, he decided.

The pilot expertly flew his machine directly behind the blind side of the bridge. As he did so he brought to bear his twin rotating machine guns, which instantly began to splatter into the square turret at 1,200 rounds of armour-piercing shells a minute. Under cover of the barrage, Brock, Green Two and Green Five abseiled the short distance from the helicopter to the safety of the rear deck. They were there in less than ten seconds.

Crouching as he ran, Brock headed directly for the metal ladder that led to the wheelhouse roof. At the top, he peered over the side into the wide cabin. The interior looked like a slaughterhouse. The relentless rain of shells had pierced the walls so that it resembled a well-used dartboard. Bodies lay in various grotesque positions, red-stained and puddled with gore.

One appeared to be a crewman dressed in jeans and matching T-shirt. Two were dressed in black fatigues laden with artillery hardware. Two others were unharmed, lying flat to the deck, sheltered by thick metal struts.

Instinctively Brock ducked his head back as one of them spotted him and fired a short automatic burst upwards. Splinters of paint and metal showered Brock. A cacophony of firing erupted in front of the bridge as the remaining terrorists, realizing that they were being attacked from behind, frantically shot their weapons at everything around them.

From his position, Brock counted four as Colonel Beecham's team disembarked from the aircraft hovering over the bow, and ran swiftly and stealthily along a row of containers towards him.

'Green Nine to Green and Brown Teams. Two Blacks inactive, two active in bridge. A further four active directly in your path.'

'Understood, Green Nine. Suggest you avoid crossfire immediately.'

Brock slid down the ladder, joining the two men who had covered him. He mimed instructions to them, then motioned for all three of them to lie down on either side of the bridge, where they were protected by the stairwell bulkheads.

'Green Two, Five and Nine in position,' he whispered.

An immediate launch of stun grenades was swiftly followed by rapid automatic firing. Thirty seconds later, both teams came to a halt and Green Two and Five leapt to their feet and entered the side entrances of the bridge in a pincer movement. In a split second, they located the two active terrorists lying on the floor inside, aimed and fired. Taken completely by surprise, the men slumped on to the deck, a neat, crimson-edged hole in each forehead.

Another silence fell as the gunfire ceased. It was broken by a lone voice.

'Retreat or I will detonate!'

Brock had circled the container that provided cover for the remaining terrorists. He could see that the last four, having somehow survived the earlier onslaught, were huddled together in a tight circle, each covering a different part of the deck with their weapons. 'Retreat or we will all die now!' shouted one again.

'Green Leader, this is Green Nine,' whispered Brock. 'I have them in view. No bluff. One of them is holding what appears to be a radio unit in his hand.'

The mercenary, his ears bleeding from the blast of the stun grenade, knew that they did not have much of a chance. Yet he thought like a professional and not like the suicidal terrorist he pretended to be. Always play for time. While you still lived there was always a chance, no matter how slim. If he was killed so be it. But he and his remaining team still hoped to enjoy a few more years with the money now sitting in their accounts. The stakes in this game of poker were sky-high and involved steel nerves. He called their hand.

'We give you one minute to surrender or we detonate!'

Commander Tilling lay three metres away from the four-point compass of mercenaries. He and his team had been shot down at point-blank range just as they thought they would be the ones doing the overpowering. If he and his three team members had not all taken shots to the head, their body armour may have saved them.

Yet their opponents were as trained and as fit as them and had gained the advantage by a split second. Though Tilling had been concussed by the head shot that coursed his temple, it had been the body shots that had floored him, and the mouth shot through his cheek which had thankfully convinced his killers he was dead due to the copious amount of blood that flowed from his face.

Tilling regained consciousness slowly, pulled back from his concussion by the voices in his earpiece.

I'm not dead, he thought hazily. But he could tell he was badly wounded. There was blood all over his face and his torso was burning with pain. He must have taken a bullet there.

He struggled to get hold of the situation. He could sense his other team members lying close to him. The lack of movement meant that they were probably dead – the chances of more than one of them surviving the attack were slim. He stayed completely still, though he wasn't sure if he would be able to move even if he wanted. Through half-closed lids, he could make out the terrorist holding a detonation device.

Beyond them, Tilling could see Brock edging cautiously round a container, his weapon poised. *Look at me*, he willed. *Look here.*

As if in answer, he saw the Scotsman's penetrating gaze fall on him. Instantly, he opened his eyes as wide as he could and blinked hard. He saw Brock start in astonishment, then acknowledge the blink and curl round back behind the container. A sense of relief flooded him.

From his position, Brock whispered quickly to Beecham.

'Green Leader, this is Green Nine. Brown Leader can receive only. I believe that he is in a position to take out detonator. I will take out active Blacks. Advise immediate acceptance of demand now.'

Beecham knew exactly what was expected. 'Fair shooting, Brown Leader.' A moment later he shouted his answer to the terrorists.

'Terms accepted. Leaving now. Repeat, terms accepted, do not detonate.'

'Good timing,' shouted back the mercenary, not believing the winning hand he had just played. There was no way he would have acceded to such demands, he thought as he relaxed the firm grip on the detonator.

Tilling noticed the all-important grip release; the thumb curling away from the switch it had been touching.

The terrorist standing furthest from Brock's line of vision, next to the mercenary holding the detonator, saw the movement out of the corner of his eye. Though lying stretched prone on the floor, which facilitated his accuracy, Tilling still had to raise his gun barrel to aim.

This time the Brown Leader was a split second faster.

His bullet smashed into the hand holding the receiver, taking the thumb right off; sending it spinning with the receiver from the surprised mercenary's hand. While it was still in the air, a terrorist's bullet drove through the centre of Tilling's exposed head.

Brock sprang from behind the container, his automatic firing directly at the huddled group. He fired below the thickly padded body armour that protected their vital organs. If he did not disable them, they would in turn kill him in an instant. Two instantly screamed in agony as their pelvises were shattered; groins shot away. A third, his back to Brock, was peppered in the buttocks, which sent him howling to the floor. The final mercenary, partially protected by his three colleagues, swirled

330

round to face his attacker in grim acceptance of the death or maiming he knew was an eye blink away.

Brock's weapon jammed.

A fleeting look of shocked surprise appeared on the mercenary's face as he reacted with astonishing speed to pull at the holstered side gun on his fatigues.

Charged full to the brim with adrenaline Brock pulled at his dive knife as he lunged headlong at the killer just a couple of metres away from him. He did not feel either the thump of lead as it tore into his protective vest or the juddering of his blade as it sliced through the unprotected shoulder that had been reactively thrown up in protection.

The mercenary screamed in anger and pain as, having dropped his weapon, he jumped away, his eyes desperately searching for another. In a second he had torn the automatic from one of his whimpering colleagues, shouting a profanity, thinking he had won.

He realized his celebratory war cry was a microsecond premature as the sharpened edge of the Jim Bowie knife thrown by Brock tore out his throat.

Sixty seconds later the Green Team and the remaining members of Brown Team had joined Brock. Colonel Beecham knelt down at the body of Commander Tilling.

'His last shot saved all of our lives; and much more,' said Brock evenly. 'The man died a hero.'

Beecham's voice was granite. 'He always lived as one too, and I swear that he will be bloody well remembered as such, even if we don't exist!'

Thirty-Nine

The tilt-wing helicopter moved smoothly into vertical mode, preparing to land at Al Qantarah. Ferguson directed the pilot first to an open space some 600 metres from the eastern exit of the underpass. There, half of Team Blue disembarked before the helicopter took off again. Three minutes later, it landed again, this time in a derelict yard 400 metres on the western side. The rest of Team Blue, along with Ferguson and Captain Cousins, left the craft swiftly and it rose once again into the air, disappearing into the darkness on its way back to the *Apollo*.

The two groups made their way to their respective exits of the four-lane tunnel, each access one hundred metres from the canal. At one fifty-nine a.m., both groups' team leaders confirmed their status. They were almost exactly on their planned schedule.

Ferguson and Cousins scouted the area round the entrance of the Al Qantarah tunnel. The glow of a red light indicated traffic signals and they approached cautiously. Next to the traffic light was a large sign, illuminated by a floodlight, advising drivers in Arabic, French and English that three of the four lanes were shut for night repairs and to proceed with extreme caution. The access was a steep downward incline, the concrete bank ingrained with grimy black dust. Deep run-off open drains either side were full of filth and litter that had either been thrown or blown there.

'I thought they said the place would be completely closed,' commented Ferguson, as he saw that one of the four lanes was indeed open.

'At least the traffic is non-existent.'

A burst of static in their earpieces silenced them. The group leader of the second team at the other end of the tunnel spoke into their earpieces. 'Blue Two to Blue Leader. Heavy vehicle heading your way.'

Immediately, Cousins, Ferguson and the five Team Blue members dived into the trench at the side of the road to avoid being caught by the approaching headlights.

Despite the filth covering his black tunic, Ferguson grinned. 'You'll find the non-existent traffic is crazy here. They always try and knock you off the road.'

The American looked nonplussed. 'Is that what the British call irony?'

'Now, it's no good asking an Irishman a question like that, is it?'

Conscious that their voices echoed against the tunnel walls, even at the level of a whisper, Cousins ordered the team to keep silence as they entered the tunnel. After two minutes of slow, noiseless pacing in the darkness, they saw the team of fake maintenance workers in a circle of high-powered halogen light. Cousins signalled to the team to halt and press into the shadows of the tunnel wall.

A series of tower scaffolds had been erected within the closed three-lane area, stretching for what Ferguson estimated was sixty metres. In the illumination from the dazzling arc lights, he could make out six towers. The nearest tower had two men working at the top with lance drills over two metres in length. At the base of the first tower stood a group of six men dressed in yellow reflective jackets.

Cousins motioned his team to the ground.

The vibrating sound of thunder warned of the approach of a large truck. From his prone position, Ferguson kept his eye on the group at the base of the tower. They casually turned their backs, their reflective jackets lighting up like beacons as the lorry's headlights momentarily bathed them in their beam. Menacing shadows danced on the concave wall as the lorry passed and Ferguson saw that each man held a lethal automatic weapon.

A warning shout cut through the silence, followed by an ear-shattering ring as one of the top aitch frames of a tower scaffold fell unexpectedly to the ground five metres below. One of the security gang cursed as he ran over to the tower. Ferguson realized that the accident signalled that the operation of inserting explosives in the tunnel wall had been completed; the workers were already dismantling the scaffold.

333

The look between Ferguson and Cousins confirmed that they were thinking the same thing: without the scaffold, it would be impossible to defuse or remove the planted explosives.

'We've got to move fast. But if we use stun grenades, it could activate their shock-responsive charges,' whispered Cousins to Ferguson.

Ferguson shook his head. 'That shouldn't be a problem. With lorries thundering through this tunnel, they would have to be using a receiver that seismically registered specific shockwaves. To do that, they'll have inserted them right through the concrete skin and into earth. Hence the long drills. Nothing will set them off from this side.'

'In that case, the second team should commence attack immediately.' Cousins whispered into his radio, 'Blue Leader to Blue Two. Are you in position?'

'That's affirmative.'

'Blue Leader to Blue Team. Go in twenty.'

Exactly twenty seconds later, six stun grenades were thrown towards the scaffolds. The enclosed area amplified their effectiveness. The tunnel was plunged into darkness as every one of the arc lights shattered.

The four men on the two nearest towers screamed as they held their ears. The heavier of the two on the second tower twirled disoriented in the sudden dark, beginning to topple as he lost his balance. Reactively his colleague grabbed for his outstretched hand as the already unstable scaffold threatened to collapse. Keeping still would have helped but, scrambling to regain his footing, the clumsy man brought about the reverse. Within seconds the half-dismantled aitch frame section of his tower reached its critical balance point and he plummeted to the ground in a tangle of metal.

At the east end of the underpass the security guards, tasked with keeping intruders at bay, were quick to guess the position that they had heard the grenades come from. It has been proven that the deafening disorientation resulting from stun grenades, and blindness resulting from instant light removal will cause a reactive defence by the terrorists it is used against; rarely will it provoke an attack, but these seasoned mercenaries handpicked by Zarakov unexpectedly rushed like an opening six-fingered fist directly towards the six members of the Blue Team; systematically firing their automatic weapons in a sweeping side-to-side motion.

There was no place to go and the Blue Team charged too; their training automatically forcing them to follow suit with their own sweeping automatics. In one of those senseless moments of unrecorded courage, when neither side gives ground nor quarter, twelve professionals cut down their fellow men; six disillusioned individuals fighting for money; six loyal citizens fighting to free a world from terrorism.

At the western end of the tunnel, Captain Cousins had encountered little resistance. In the extra few seconds it had taken for the group of six mercenary terrorists to orientate themselves, the nearest two lay dead and the remainder lay restrained on the ground, their hand and legs quickly bound with nylon locking cord.

Unaware that all of Blue 2 team lay dead, Cousins continued to execute the containment plan they had initiated. Like the rest of the team, Ferguson now switched on his powerful wide beam torch as he ran directly to the nearest tower. Its two occupants were desperately climbing through the frames to gain the ground when the stocky Irishman swung his battering ram of a fist into the nearest.

The man's head snapped back from the blow he had not seen coming, his body falling limply to the ground. The other man, seeing his partner fall, missed his footing and plunged the last two metres, landing on his hands awkwardly; both of his wrist bones cracking with a dry snap like a dead woodland twig.

Ferguson pulled him by the scruff of his neck and threw him to the ground. He could make out from the darting torch lights that the adjoining tower tenants were receiving similar treatment as they each succumbed to the special force team. The priority now was defusing the explosives without delay.

'I would like to know exactly what it is you have primed,' he asked politely. 'If you do not tell me I know a man who is going to kill you.'

The wide-eyed man, in agony from his wrists, looked blank as if he had not heard anything. Ferguson spoke into his radio with the correct call sign he had been given. 'Blue Leader, Blue 7 requires a translator urgently.'

'I read you Blue 7. Arabic or French?'

Ferguson squeezed the man's wrists which released a tirade of profanity.

'Arabic.'

'One minute Blue 7.'

While Ferguson climbed the tower scaffold, literally dragging its former occupant behind him, Commander Cousins tried several times to raise the east side .

'Blue Leader to Blue 2, do you read?'

A burst of static was the response he received.

He tried shouting, knowing his voice would easily carry the fifty or so metres where Blue 2 and his team were moving towards them.

No acknowledgment, only the sound of Arabic expletives punctuated the air.

With a sense of foreboding Cousins began to run, collecting three of his team *en route*.

The driver pressed his accelerator as he guessed the green light was about to change to red. He knew from experience how slowly roadwork lights changed back, particularly with infrequent traffic. He decided it was pointless to waste valuable time bringing his vehicle to a halt and wait a good ten minutes for nothing. The last time they had carried out maintenance, just three weeks ago, he had been stuck in a backlog of traffic for over an hour. Anyway, other than him, who would be crazy enough to be driving around at two in the morning?

The powerful Renault diesel engine instantly responded, effortlessly pulling its forty-ton fully loaded trailer with increasing speed. The driver smiled to himself as he passed the light just as it changed, and his vehicle shot down the incline at fifteen kilometres an hour faster than the fifty permitted. He knew he would have at least three minutes safety margin before the lights on the other side changed to green. He only needed forty seconds. Allah was with him tonight, it had been a good choice.

Dimming his lights as he entered the tunnel he was surprised not to see any of the usual tell-tale lighting and warning signs. 'Typical,' the driver cursed as he switched his lights back to full beam. There was no maintenance work proceeding at all, they had erected signs to inconvenience hard-working gladiators of the road such as him; he who had stupidly promised to deliver his load before dawn.

Something slightly ahead caught in his headlight.

Trying to discern what it could possibly be that seemed to be lying on the enclosed lanes, he focused on it, straining his eyes to see as it quickly approached. My eyes must be deceiving me, he thought. It looks like a pile of bodies lying in the road. The driver's jaw dropped as he continued to gaze, his eyes quickly swivelling to the vehicle's wide side mirror to catch a second look with his rear lights.

In the split-second lack of concentration the Renault truck veered from its restricted lane, narrowly missing a tower scaffold by millimetres. It would prove to be the driver's last piece of luck.

In the moment before the giant truck ploughed into the next tower the driver desperately swung his wheel in a futile attempt to avoid it. In doing so he unwittingly positioned himself directly in the path of the inflexible jutting steel pole of a disconnected safety rail. Like the pointed long pike of a medieval foot soldier, the pole bore right through the toughened windscreen skewering the driver right through his open jaw, killing him instantly.

Cousins and his men dived to safety as the speeding behemoth, free to unleash sheer carnage, crashed through tower after tower; tearing the aitch frames apart in its path like toothpicks. Seeking cover in the service gulley without a microsecond to spare, Cousins caught a fleeting image of the runaway monster as it captured the last tower in the fearsome glare of its headlights.

Ferguson, who had just made it to the top, had nowhere to hide.

The heart-stopping noise of a screeching locomotive, its spinning wheels gnashing against steel rails in the confines of a tunnel, is terrifying. To see such a monster bearing directly at you is enough to make a rational person freeze, like a rabbit trapped in headlights. Ferguson did not act as most men would. If he had, he would have most assuredly already lost his life during previous life-threatening situations he had bizarrely experienced in working with Brock.

By the time the Renault truck had come to a stop, having

tried to circumnavigate the tunnel wall before inexorably falling and sliding on its side, Cousins was already out of his ditch. The Blue Leader raced towards where the tower had been standing. A mangled body lay half in and half out of the shallow service walk that edged the tunnel. Convinced he had lost his Irish explosives expert he rushed over to the body.

'Ah, there you are. Forget the Arabic translator.'

Cousins' neck shot back as he looked directly above him. In the half light he could just make out Ferguson; his arms and legs wrapped around the bracketed metal conduits that enclosed the lighting and communication cables.

'It's a standard plug-in detonator that can be easily removed,' added the Irishman. 'Though you'd better rebuild some scaffolding so that we can do so; and to get me down, of course.'

Cousins breathed an audible sigh of relief. 'You don't hang around, do you?'

'Now would you be giving me an example of American irony?'

Forty

Colonel James Beecham's weary face brightened. Still holding the cell phone from which he had just received an innocuous message about the weather being good, he relayed the information to Brock.

'Good news at last; that was Captain Cousins, they've located all eight of the bombs and safely diffused them. At least the underpass is safe.'

Jammed upside-down in a deep gulley formed by ridged containers where he had been lowered, Brock once more studied the oscillating dial of the delicate scanner he had strapped to his arm so as not to drop it. At last the radio signals, returning after passing through solid objects, produced the perfect match required.

'Well, Colonel, it's in a damn awkward place, but we've found ours too. How's Blue Team? Could they give details?'

'That's excellent, Brock!' Beecham momentarily paused. 'Not able to give too much over a cell call in case of surveillance but he said the sandstorms had been bad this month, which means he encountered strong resistance.'

Brock looked at the luminous dial of his watch. It had already passed five o'clock. Matt and Blue Team would have been at the underpass for three hours by now. He had been so engrossed with helping to search for the bomb, deducing it would have been placed in the very centre of all the containers, that he had lost all sense of time.

'The canal will be opening for the first convoy about now. When Subedei's people do not see the *Atlantic Valiant* pass by, we have to assume that they will resort to a back-up plan to blow this baby.'

Beecham looked at his watch too. They had four hours before the *Atlantic Valiant* would be passing Al Qantarah. 'I'm no explosives expert but do we have a safety range?'

'Afraid not, Colonel; enclosed like this, there will be a GSM receiver similar to a cell phone; they can detonate this anywhere on the planet.' Brock carefully unscrewed the top of the phosphorous marker. 'OK I've marked the spot, pull me up.'

Three minutes later Brock sat on the container with Beecham. 'The only reason that the stooge fishermen that Moyshe's operative learned were to detonate the bomb were needed was so they could gauge the exact spot. Subedei wants the underpass *accident* to appear as a consequence of a Saudi terrorist plot against the US. Remember his plans were thwarted with the *Riyadh* because he did not control the exact moment.'

'The *Atlantic Valiant* would have been passing close to Al Qantarah by eight o'clock. If you're right and they blow it anyway, that does not give us much time to gain access to the container, almost an impossibility in itself; cut into it and then defuse the bomb,' accepted Beecham. 'But we don't have the slightest idea as to what type of a device we're dealing with.'

'But we have its location, which is half the battle.'

'How did you know it would be in the centre on the bottom?'

'More of a shrewd guesstimate based on a little knowledge of explosives, Colonel. We already knew that the detonation of the bomb was to send a shock that would appear to have caused a rift in the underpass. And that the underpass charges were to be set off with shock sensors. By positioning the bomb on the *Atlantic Valiant* where it is, surrounded by densely packed steel containers, the shock blast would be directed downwards, not up; the canal itself absorbing the full force of the vibrating energy which in turn would be amplified by the water mass.'

Beecham set his jaw in frustration. 'I just wish we could have had more time to put together a specific force. Unfortunately under such short notice we were provided with insufficient scanners and cutting equipment; and almost all of that was destroyed along with Brown Team's transport. Still, at least your little knowledge, as you modestly say, has proved invaluable for us, though how invaluable remains to be seen.'

Brock's eyes grinned as he looked up in the sky. 'Colonel, locating it was the medium part; getting it out is the easy part.'

'You have an idea how to get at it?' Beecham raised his eyebrows in cynical astonishment. 'What are you going to do, Brock? Just lift them like plastic Lego bricks?'

'Something exactly along those lines.'

'Assuming you do, I have an awful feeling that I am going to let you down with the hard part, which I assume you mean to be defusing the bloody device.'

Brock looked at Beecham in surprise. 'I appreciate you not needing to know about explosives, you're part of a team. But you're not telling me, Colonel, that on your team there aren't bomb disposal personnel?'

'There *were* three members of our team,' answered Beecham bitterly. 'Two were lost along with their equipment in the Tilt Wing; the third was Commander Tilling.'

Two hours later, the phosphorous-marked container came into view. It had taken every member of the crew working flat out, including Captain Grant Lee Carter, who had finally stopped fuming at being imprisoned on his own ship and then later having the humiliating experience of being released by a British officer. Nineteen containers had been moved to reveal the one with the bomb inside it.

The removal of the containers upset the balance of the *Atlantic Valiant*, even though great care was taken as each one was shifted. The ship listed dangerously on the port side. Immediately the marked container was accessible, the crew began to use their cutting equipment to reopen the door, which had been welded shut. The side door finally clanged aside to reveal an explosive package the size of a small car. Brock stepped calmly into the housing of the onboard loading crane.

'Now the hard part: operation bomb disposal,' said Brock to himself. He settled at the controls, manoeuvred the crane arm into position, deftly raised the opened container up into the air and slowly swung it over the port side. The waters of the Mediterranean now almost level with the listing ship began to seep over its edge. Brock released the safety levers holding the crane's tensile-steel fifty-millimetre cables attached to the weighted unit. Then he released the hydraulic brake, sending the giant container crashing into the water. Sheets of salty water were flung high in the air. With its whole side open to the sea, the container quickly sank.

Captain Grant Lee Carter looked on in horror as he realized

what Brock had put into motion. As the enormous weight submerged, it began to drag at his ship's expensive hauling tackle. The cable, freed from both brake and safety attachments, screeched through the whirring pulleys. Now unstoppable, the thick locking loops caught for a moment in the topmost section of the crane before forcing it to sheer apart as easily as someone ripping a section of aluminium cooking foil. While the Special Forces applauded the unexpected action, Captain Grant Lee Carter stormed over towards Brock, as he slowly extricated himself from the housing of the crane, which was now a forlorn stump of metal.

'Just what the hell-assed game are you playing at, mister? How the blazes do you think we can operate without that?' Do you have any idea as to the cost of your hell-assed plan?'

Brock looked in some bewilderment at the man whose ship they had just saved from being blown to smithereens; as well as him and his crew from a terrorist plot. Brock clenched his jaw, his anger instantly inflamed.

'You have a crew; you have a ship; you have Port Said twenty minutes from here to help you unload. That's one hell of lot more than the nine young Americans who gave their lives to save your ass.'

Brock's hand shot out like a striking cobra to grab Carter's exposed neck; his eyes menacing like icy sapphires. 'Mister, your ass will be joining your precious tackle if it doesn't get the hell out of my sight.'

Zarakov threw the untouched glass of Stolichnaya at the wall in frustration, the leaded crystal exploding into a hundred tiny shards. From his operating base within Subedei's Alexandria refinery, the Russian had been trying without success to raise his men. None of them had reported in as they should have done at four o'clock.

Previously he had always operated at the forefront, but with so much to co-ordinate he had been forced this time to remain behind the scenes. He hated it, the waiting making him feel unusually helpless. Precisely 190 minutes later, almost every one counted by Zarakov, a call finally came through.

'The *Atlantic Valiant* has not been seen at Port Said,' said Qenawi flatly. 'It is not part of the first convoy.'

Zarakov could not believe it. He had received a coded call that his men had taken the ship over and were steaming to port. What could have happened? The mercenaries were the former elite of the Russian military, their leader a man he had cultivated as his protégé for years. And why had his lookout man, the American deserter Hengel, posted on the quay, not reported in? Why had he not received confirmation that the charges at Al Qantarah tunnel had been primed? How was it that Qenawi knew before him?

'How long have you known?'

Qenawi paused, sensing Zarakov was trying to determine the reasons. 'Your man was not on the quay,' he said flatly. 'When I did not receive confirmation from Hengel, as you said I would at five, I immediately dispatched one of my team to Port Said. He confirmed that there was no sign of the American vessel.'

Zarakov inwardly cursed.

Stupid of him to trust the drunk; Hengel would die for failing.

Knowing that Subedei would hold him responsible, he made another instant decision. 'You are to detonate now without delay.'

'Consider it done.' Qenawi said calmly, in the knowledge that he had been ordered by Subedei personally to follow Zarakov's instructions to the letter. 'What about the tunnel? Their shock sensor will no longer operate. Am I to detonate those?'

'For some reason I have not heard from our people there either, but the charges must be in place.'

'My team have informed me that traffic has been backing up throughout the night.'

The information did not unduly surprise Zarakov; they had wanted to close the tunnel at the beginning but to do so would have brought too much suspicion to bear. 'They must have decided to close the tunnel after all. Have you received confirmation from them?'

'Not yet. I have sent one of my team down there but he has not returned yet.'

Zarakov did not like what he heard. What the hell was going on? Why were none of his people coming back to him? Could it be that their plans were known? He made another decision.

'Then we will detonate them too.'

'When exactly, and what about our men there? Perhaps they

have encountered difficulty in setting the charges. They still have thirty minutes before the deadline.'

'Listen carefully, Ibrahim. Something is seriously wrong. We will go straight on to our back-up plan. You are to detonate the underpass at the exact moment you initiate that. I will contact you to confirm these instructions.'

'I will do as you command.'

Zarakov made another decision. 'Ibrahim, if you and your force are attacked. you are to instigate the back-up plan without further instruction. Nothing must stop you, even if you are prevented from coordinating the timing; which will of course mean you actually being there to do it. You do understand what I mean, don't you?'

'I understand what is expected of me.'

Qenawi replaced his receiver. Once again he was back in the Sudan Bush, a guerrilla rebel at the behest of his overlords, loyally following their orders. He looked at the machete that he had earlier strapped to his belt, knowing that he would willingly carry out their will, without question. It was his destiny, as the Mongolian had his.

The Qenawi tribe were warriors. It was rooted deep into his nature and if necessary he would die a warrior, without fear; joining his forefathers in the stars. He sensed his overlord's preferred plan had gone wrong. Let them come, he was ready. He would not fail.

Zarakov heard the phone go down and felt a momentary relief from his gnawing panic. He trusted the Sudanese warrior. He felt instinctively that he would do all that was required of him, even if it meant surrendering his fate in the cause of his master's grand vision.

The tilt-wing helicopter carrying Brock, Colonel Beecham and his team of eight British Special Forces men rose vertically into the air. Just as the pilot converted to horizontal flight, there was a muffled sound like distant thunder. A moment later the *Atlantic Valiant* was rocked to and fro as if a sudden underwater storm had swelled the calm waters of the Mediterranean.

Beecham glanced at his watch, acutely aware that it had been less than ten minutes since Brock had sent the bomb into the depths of the ocean. 'That was little too close for comfort.'

'They've detonated without seeing the ship. I think that we can assume they're mad as hell,' said Brock, observing the badly laden cargo ship roll awkwardly but stay upright. 'And I'd guess that they're going to be expecting us.'

Forty-One

For three weeks Corporal Rawson had been patrolling the same perimeter. Following his quick promotion three months earlier, he had been disappointed that his first command over a team of four had been to stand vigil at a pumping station in the most deserted godforsaken region of Northern Iraq, 180 kilometres from the nearest base. They should have been relieved yesterday but received a radio call that they were to stay on duty for a further forty-eight hours; resources being so stretched.

Then a second intelligence report was received confirming an intent by rebel militia to destroy the pumping station; then yet another message to expect a maintenance unit. The tell-tale dust cloud billowing in the early morning sunrise indicated the approach of a wide Humvee jeep.

'Herve, that'll be the maintenance unit. Check 'em out, then take 'em inside,' ordered Rawson as the Humvee stopped by the enclosed perimeter twelve metres away.

Infantryman R. T. Hervey was only too pleased to have something to do and another soul to talk to. Being on duty since last night had been as tedious as ever; with the corporal it was just plain boring. 'Sir!'

Fifty-nine seconds later R. T. Hervey's body lay motionless in the dust; half his chest blown in by a nine-millimetre hollow-nose shell fired from point-blank range.

Sixty-one seconds after his command, the sharp-pointed shell of a sniper's bullet pierced Rawson's helmet, slicing his brain in two before exiting the back of his head.

Eighty-five seconds after he had given his last order, the remaining two of the corporal's team were dead.

Only 180 seconds after the Humvee had arrived, it departed again.

It was just becoming part of a billowing cloud on the horizon again when the pumping station erupted in a blinding flash of high explosive.

Corporal Rawson's first, last and only command post was utterly destroyed, leaving a swamping lake of crude oil flooding the perimeter: precious black gold, so vital for Iraq's future; so hungrily consumed by a demanding west.

As the pilot nodded that the speck below them was Al Qantarah, Beecham clenched his jaw. He was not comfortable and felt guilty. He had spoken with Captain Cousins. There had been no booby traps, no missed charges exploding, as feared when the *Atlantic Valiant* bomb had been set off. All had been neutralized. But the cost had been sky-high, much more than ever expected, with the loss of fifteen good men.

'Fact is, Brock, our mission is accomplished. Above all we have been instructed not to compromise ourselves by being observed. All we can do is drop down, deposit you, pick up Cousins' team and get out.'

For a moment a tired Brock thought he had misheard; then he realized. He knew the constraints Beecham was under. He had been under the same once. He knew the way the cookie was forced to crumble so often before a mission could be a complete success. He decided to go for the colonel's jugular.

'I'm sure that your fifteen boys will be proud of you following through their actions like that.'

He scored a direct hit.

Beecham's Adam's apple bobbed with emotion and indignant anger, his eyes turned stone-cold.

Brock followed through.

'If you think that Subedei has not got a back-up plan, you're kidding yourself. The order to blow up the *Atlantic Valiant* came through, despite the fact we messed up their well-laid plan. The operative said there was a force at that facility down there. Why?

'I'll tell you why: because I believe they are going to blow up the store of glue cement they have been dumping on the canal bed. When? You can bet your pension it's when the convoy of ships passes over in about twenty-five minutes from now. I have had some experience of that stuff, which is why I was supposedly brought along. And let me tell you, Colonel, when it's released it's going to cause as much damage as any bomb.

'Frankly I don't give a damn about it blocking the bloody canal. But the stuff's lethal, and I do care if it gets into the Red Sea. One sack can sink a ship and there are literally thousands of sacks down there. And there are literally hundreds of resorts in the Red Sea from which thousands of people swim. Think of the lives, many of them children, that will be lost – or does that not bother the conscience of the powers that be because it is not oil related?'

Silence followed Brock's impassioned outburst, the remaining team of Special Forces watching their CO's face expectantly. Brock had already surmised that the Mossad chief had been insinuating that Brock would be expected to do whatever was required, because of his prior knowledge of the facility and MM120. He also remembered what Beecham had said during the briefing – that they would only secure the Al Qantarah facility *if required.*

'Your call, Colonel,' added Brock, breaking the silence. 'Either help us out or drop me down there to join Matt, so that we can finish what you've been ordered not to.'

Beecham looked at each of his men in turn, watching them return his questioning gaze with a nod. A moment later he instructed the pilot to descend, choosing the best cover he could find not too close to the complex. He radioed Cousins and briefed him. Finally he turned to Brock.

'Let's do it,' he said with finality.

'What do they mean by last night's broadcast; there is no oil?' Exclaimed Jumair immediately Subedei had answered his private cell phone, thinking it had to be Zarakov or a member of his cartel.

'Good morning, Mr President. Of course there is oil,' he breathed easily. 'The flow into our refineries at Alexandria begins within seventy-two hours. You are welcome to come and see for yourself.'

Jumair instantly changed tack. 'How dare they try to discredit me – us! These damn media rats!'

'They had to get their story from someone, Mr President. Perhaps it was Benerzat, who is not as supportive of your announcements as you imagine. We have learned that the man's daughter is very close to the ICE investigator who trumped up the false evidence in the report.'

'Then invite them all to the refinery with the media. That way they will be forced to make an apology.'

'Good idea, Mr President, I shall do so right away.'

'Thank you, um, Temujin, my friend. You understand that I never doubted you of course. It's just that I am being hounded by everyone.'

'You did right to share your concerns – your frustrations – with me. That is what friends are for.'

Deciding immediately to take action, Subedei called for two members of his personal guard. The added insurance was important.

After a brief meeting between Colonel Beecham and Captain Cousins, it was agreed that the tilt wing return the whole of Blue Team back to the *Apollo* together with their fallen colleagues.

'Sorry it wasn't the walk in the park I promised, Matt,' said Cousins grimly as he firmly shook Ferguson's hand.

Ferguson saw the controlled emotion in the young captain's eyes: the pain of having lost six of his team and close friends. It would be his job to tell their loved ones. He was a young leader who would never consider delegating the responsibility to another.

'The operation was a success, Simon, purely because of the bravery of your great team.'

'You defused the bombs.'

'I just sat on the park bench and pulled plugs. You made it possible by cleaning the park and by rebuilding smashed benches.'

Fifteen minutes later, Brock and Ferguson, accompanied by Beecham's elite team, were observing the former Al Kadeh facility from the same spot they had eighteen days earlier. The quay had been cleared of the debris caused by the battering dredger. Another smaller dredger was moored up; together with a powerful-looking motor cruiser. In the distance the first of the early morning convoy of giant ships could be seen, sedately but elegantly approaching from the North like a school of trained whales.

Approaching from the south, as yet unseen, was the *Viking Conqueror*, a supertanker weighing over half a million tons; her breadth occupying over two thirds of the Suez Canal.

The wireless transmission navigational network at Port Tawfiq had already informed the receiving stations of the Bitter Lakes, Port Fouad and Port Said, that the state-of-the-art fully laden monster, her belly full to the brim with over 70,000 barrels of oil, almost three million gallons, had started her passage. Each station was to monitor and plan for oncoming traffic to hold in the passing bays as usual.

Al Qantarah was the straightest section of the canal. It had no passing bays. It was the reason Subedei had chosen the fifteenth. The very day the commercial titan, symbol of superior European merchant strength, was to make her bi-monthly pass through the Suez.

The obvious had been overlooked.

'Here come all the ladies carrying their trades to serve the world's consumption demands,' said Ferguson, looking northward unaware that one of the world's biggest ships was five kilometres away behind them.

Brock nodded. 'And very heavy ones by the look of them, which I'll wager Subedei is planning to inconvenience.'

Qenawi watched the approaching convoy from the north through the same high-powered field glasses he had passed to Omar Al Kadeh just three weeks earlier. He had just received the confirmation call from Zarakov telling him to proceed with the back-up plan.

As the *Viking Conqueror* made her pass from the south, he was simultaneously to blow the explosives laid either side of the MM120 mound and alongside the dredger. The charges on the dredger would be enough to cripple the tanker; the MM120 would root her hull in place, blocking the Suez Canal for years.

Qenawi looked at his watch. There were five minutes before the North Convoy would pass him on their way to the passing canal 1,000 metres south of his facility. Ten minutes later the *Viking Conqueror* would pass him by, except she wouldn't be allowed to.

What an honour for him. None of his former rebel overlords would have conceived of doing anything as big. He was pleased there had been no attack force as suspected. He had not been forced to set off the charges early. He would leave in a few minutes to personally set the charge.

*　　*　　*

'The facility appears deserted,' said Brock, tentatively raising his head over the quay.

Beside him crouched Ferguson, frowning. 'It should be teeming with workers by now.'

Brock spoke quietly into his radio. 'Green Nine to Green Leader, we are in position.'

Colonel Beecham had split the majority of his Special Forces unit into two four-man teams. His own was to enter the north perimeter, having already cut through the low-security fence. Green Two's team would converge from the south. The remaining covert operative, Green Three was to provide a diversionary tactic at the front gate, with a Nissan truck they had requisitioned for the purpose. Green Three was to try knocking for attention first. If none was forthcoming he was to smash through the outer gates and keep going through the inner warehouse gates.

'Green Leader to Green Three. Go now.'

'Affirmative.'

Following the commotion at the gate caused by a man in dirty white jeans and shirt, also requisitioned, three thick-set and very fit-looking men walked briskly over to the gates. Openly carrying guns, they each covered the other. If the leader of them seemed surprised at hearing a well-spoken English accent demanding to pick up the materials that had been promised, he did not show it. He simply raised the automatic rifle he held between his arms and replied in broken English for the man to go away immediately or die.

Green Three did not argue but got in his truck and reversed.

As the three security guards swaggered back toward the warehouse they had come from, the Nissan truck slammed through the front mesh gates like a battering ram. The three guards immediately opened fire. At the sound of their colleagues' automatic weapons the majority of Qenawi's twelve-man force appeared from inside the warehouse. Within seconds the driverless truck, a heavy rock laid on its accelerator, began to look like a giant pincushion as nine automatic weapons peppered it with hundreds of furious shells before bringing it to a halt by the closed warehouse doors, which shuddered from the impact.

The experienced ears of Beecham's team seemed to intuitively know when the fast-emptying clips would come to an abrupt stop, requiring replacement. At the exact moment, three groups, including Green Three's single-man unit, converged in a half hemisphere, overpowering the defenders with an awesome combined firepower of 4,800 rounds a minute between them. In a storming twenty seconds it had been their turn to cut down their opponents. A moment later three surviving mercenaries emerged in shock from the warehouse, their hands in the air.

From the rear window of the first-floor office, the devastation was observed. The whites of Qenawi's wide eyes and his white linen suit bore sharp contrast to his ebony black skin as he involuntarily shouted a war cry of rage. Strengthened by a maddening anger he had not felt in twenty years, he snatched at the automatic pistol that lay on his desk and charged down the office stairwell.

As he leapt into the outer hall he pulled out his machete. The lethal fifty-centimetre blade flashed in the daylight, its blade honed scalpel-sharp from years of care. The fearsome-looking weapon had belonged to his rival; the same one who had jealously cut off the arms of the dove-eyed captured girl Qenawi had chosen to take for his wife. Later he had killed his rival with the machete after prising it from the man's severed hand.

When the cacophony of firing had started, Brock and Ferguson had immediately raced towards the offices, Brock having reasoned that any decision-makers or decisive actions would be located or made there. As they reached the door an obese man came running out.

'What the bloody hell's goin' on!' shouted the panic-stricken Maynard. The red-faced man was so desperate to get out he slipped and toppled right into the path of Ferguson, his weight bowling the Irishman over before he pirouetted like an obese ballerina. Ferguson was too winded to notice the engineer's prudent exit with a flurry that defied his bulk.

A moment later Qenawi shot through the door, leaping over the two sprawling bodies and landing like a black panther before racing toward the moored dredger. Brock's and Qenawi's eyes met. In that fleeting moment they both recognized a force that would stop at nothing to do what they had to do. They would kill or be killed.

Brock raced after the machete-wielding madman who was

incongruously dressed in a white designer suit, guessing his intent. Qenawi sliced at the central mooring rope securing the dredger, which immediately began to drift from the quay. A moment later Brock easily jumped the widening gap on to the tarpaulin-covered deck, landing on his feet.

'You're too late!' snarled Qenawi, standing protectively in front of the wheelhouse.

'For what? Breakfast?' shouted back Brock, casting a cautious eye at the approaching convoy of ships that suddenly seemed to be looming towards them. 'Looks like you plan to have us freshly squeezed.'

Qenawi shot the man in front of him a stunned look. How could a man be so casually joking? He then noticed the ships.

'I suppose you don't care about where you stick your chewing gum. What if everyone was to go around doing that?' continued Brock.

Though Qenawi understood English well, he had not the slightest idea what the tall man meant. 'Are you mad?'

'No, but your boss Subedei is if he thinks that gluing up a few ships will bring Europe to its knees.'

'His plan is worthy!' shouted Qenawi. 'Very soon you will see how much!'

Brock saw the slight movement and fired first. The automatic spun from Qenawi's hand as one of Brock's bullets tore into the shoulder it was attached to. His white suit quickly spreading with a red stain, Qenawi lunged, the speed of the man's action taking Brock by surprise.

As Brock stepped sideways, his foot caught on the tarpaulin and he slipped. Crashing down to his knees, he saw the glint of the blade as it quickly rose upward. Brock twisted, his body missing the downward slice of the machete's vicious swipe by millimetres.

Without pause Qenawi continued to raise the machete again and again, each time sweeping its evil blade at Brock's feet and legs as he desperately tried to kick himself away. Clouds of flour-like material began to billow around Qenawi, as his side-to-side slicing action tore deep into the sacks covered by the shredded tarpaulin.

So sharp was the blade that Brock did not even feel the wound that sliced through his trousers into his calf as he once more gained his footing and raced towards the wheelhouse. The moment he reached it he was knocked off his feet again.

Two of the ships in the convoy had managed to avoid the free-floating dredger that had slowly moved into their path. The third, carrying an Italian flag with a cargo of dried foods, had no room to manoeuvre. It hit the dredger broadside.

As Brock once more hit the tarpaulin-covered deck, Qenawi was flung into the water by the collision. In a fury he began to pull himself out, his face turning from rage to confusion as he found it almost impossible. His expression began to turn to horror in the dawning realization of what was happening to him. The MM120 that had covered his suit had metamorphosed into the viscous superglue after its contact with water.

Brock watched as Qenawi, his machete glued to his hand, exerted almost superhuman effort to raise his torso above the water. Underneath the surface, the powder, which had been thickest around his shoes, formed into a moving block of heavy cement.

Unable to hold himself up any more, the recently installed chief executive officer of Al Kadeh Construction sank slowly into the embracing water.

Frantically he fought to extricate himself as he held his breath. In a last futile attempt he slashed at his own legs with his machete. As he sank to the bottom of the canal, Qenawi's mouth reactively opened wide, desperate to release the pressure from his bursting lungs and screaming brain by an intake of air. As water forced its way down his throat and the frantic struggle for life ebbed, his final thought was that he had succeeded.

He had simply died a few minutes earlier than planned.

Forty-Two

Brock heard a shout above the screaming obscenities being hurled at him by irate crew members of the ship that had hit the dredger. Despite their fury, they pushed the dredger back towards the quay. Ferguson was standing there, trying to catch Brock's attention by shouting and waving. Brock turned and caught the rope that Ferguson threw him. He looped it across the onboard stanchions as Ferguson and Beecham hauled him back to shore.

Brock was in the wheelhouse when Ferguson and Beecham joined him on board.

Ferguson saw what Brock was looking at. His eyes narrowed and his tone was grave. 'That is not a sight for sore eyes.'

For Ferguson to sound so uncharacteristically serious, Brock knew that the small device on the wheelhouse floor posed a big problem.

'The timer on the side reads six minutes,' he said evenly.

Colonel Beecham watched as the last two of the remaining convoy of ships passed the dredger. 'The convoy will be long gone by then, which is something.'

Ferguson was already down on his knees studying the device, trying to decipher what triggering mechanism was encased within it.

'This is only a small trigger bomb that will detonate a series of others that are primed and waiting,' he said. 'We can assume that this whole ship and the tonnes of MM120 under the surface will all be activated in a domino effect. Why the hell they want something so big beats me. The MM120 only requires something small to release it.'

'I think I know the reason,' replied Brock, his voice like rough granite.

Beecham followed Brock's gaze. 'Jesus! Look at the size of

355

that! It must be as big as Wembley bloody stadium!'

Even from a distance of 2,000 metres, the *Viking Conqueror* was huge.

Brock's voice was unmistakably tense. 'And due to rendezvous with us in about six minutes. Matt, no pressure, but you better pull your finger out or we're going to have a major disaster on our hands.'

'Another one? I think that's the third today, and it's not even lunchtime yet,' mumbled Ferguson as he finished unscrewing the end of the device. 'Still, the good news is that it is not booby-trapped.'

'How do you know for certain?' asked Beecham.

'Simple. I opened it. Didn't think I had time to waste.'

'What Matt means is that he deduced that there was no necessity for them to set up a booby trap,' explained Brock.

Beecham looked relieved.

'No, what I meant was that I opened it.' There was an increased urgency in Ferguson's voice. 'Connor, while I'm deactivating the trigger, you must find the conduit that leads beneath the surface. There will be a shock receiver attached to it that will set the MM120 off in a prearranged sequence. There should be a switch – push it from auto to off. Do not pull it as it will be weighted and may go off under weakening pressure. A weight at the end of the line will be holding it in place.'

He turned to Beecham. 'Colonel, try and find the main stockpile of explosives, which must be somewhere under this tarpaulin. About a metre away, you'll find the detonator plugs. Pull the ones that lead to the taped charges, not the ones right next to it.' Ferguson glanced at his watch. 'I don't like to hurry you, gentlemen, but you have just over four minutes.'

Brock raced out of the wheelhouse and began searching the edge of the tarpaulin-covered hull. Gently he peeled away the covering, not wanting to tear whatever it was he was supposed to be looking for. After exposing two metres of the hull, he saw it: a thin black cable dangling from the edge like a fishing line. Carefully, he stepped over the edge and lowered himself directly into the water. He pulled in a few deep breaths to take as much oxygen into his lungs as possible, and slowly began to follow the line down beneath the surface.

*   *   *

Beecham and his team worked rapidly but carefully, rolling back the deck tarpaulin to reveal the sacks of MM120. All along the canal side of the dredger were explosive charges, neatly arranged in a long line. At the centre point, surrounded by a dense stockpile of explosives, lay what looked like a black fuse box with a series of thin cables coming out of it like spider legs.

Brock equalized the pressure every two metres down by holding his nose and blowing. Without a mask or light, he could only feel his way and when he reached a depth of eight metres, he began to feel like a dizzy blind man, guided only by the thin line of the cable.

Suddenly, he felt a smooth oval shape, almost like a bar of soap.

Bingo, he thought. Immediately, it slipped from his hand and he blindly felt for the line. With a growing sense of panic, his lungs beginning to demand relief, he swung his arm about him, his fingers flailing in the water.

Something threadlike brushed his face. Quickly he snatched it.

It was the line, but the effects of disorientation had already started to take effect, and he was uncertain which way was up or down.

Blindly, he chose one.

'Everyone, take cover!' shouted Colonel Beecham, as he frantically followed the cables, looking for the detonator plugs. There seemed so many of them spreading outwards in different directions. It didn't help that he hated being around explosives, like some people had a phobia for snakes or spiders.

He heaved off sacks of MM120 and saw a thick bundle of cable entering a series of taped charges. They were about a metre away from the fuse box. They had to be the ones.

Brock knew he could hold his breath for three minutes. As a boy, he had regularly proved it to himself. It was a skill that had come in handy in manhood as well. Forcing himself to count, he tried to concentrate on anything but wanting oxygen.

He released some bubbles of air from his mouth.

His hand slipped around the oval shape once more.

His eyes were tightly shut as he felt for the button Ferguson

357

said would be there. Then it was under his finger. He opened his eyes to see which way to push it but could discern nothing in the murky darkness. His finger felt a double ridge to one side of the sliding switch.

Immediately, he remembered the alarm clock his father had given him when he had joined the services. 'To make sure you don't miss parade,' his father had joked. The central position was off; one way was on; the other auto.

Brock pressed the switch slowly and felt it click into the first ridge.

Feeling blood in his mouth as he bit down on his lip, Beecham deftly pulled out all the plugs that entered the strapped charges, tensing as he did so.

Nothing happened.

He had no idea what was supposed to happen anyway. He opened his eyes.

He was still holding his breath.

Four minutes had passed.

Brock had been submerged for over three minutes.

As he followed the cable up to the surface, he saw flashing lights behind his closed eyes. Slowly he released the last of the stale air he had held in his lungs.

He was desperate to breathe and opened his eyes. There was light, he was certain of it.

A moment later, his head broke the surface.

A mere one hundred metres away ploughed the gigantic bow of the *Viking Conqueror*.

Ferguson made a fervent silent prayer that Brock and Beecham had achieved the impossible. Then he pressed the angled metal edge of his Swiss Army knife against the two opposing circuits.

The timer stopped.

The device was still primed, still unsafe, but the timer had stopped. Nothing could happen.

An instant later, he gained access to the hidden battery and disconnected it. He checked the timer. It had stopped with six seconds to spare. He always said six was his lucky number.

* * *

Neusheen had just left the Cairo hospital where her father had been moved. The news had been good.

'The doctor informs me that you will be out of here in a week,' she had said as soon as she'd entered the room and gone to hug him. She knew he would be in a foul mood at having to spend so many weeks in a hospital bed.

Imran had kissed her hello and squeezed her hand, trying not to look too grumpy. 'I wish it was now. There's so much to do.' He brightened. 'The broadcast last night was dynamite! Did you see it?'

'I missed it, Papa.'

'Then we'll watch it now, I recorded it,' said her father eagerly, and Neusheen had watched fascinated as Dr Paul van Lederman condemned Subedei Industries on worldwide television.

She left an hour later, her thoughts full of the broadcast. Surely Subedei would retaliate against his enemies – but how? What would he unleash on ICE, and on Brock and his colleagues?

She went up to the waiting car that her father insisted that she used, along with his personal driver, Karim. As she approached, she was surprised that Karim did not jump out to open the door for her, as he usually did. He was normally a stickler for these politenesses, even when Neusheen told him it wasn't necessary.

She saw that Karim was too engrossed in reading something to notice her arrival. Bending down, she opened the car door for herself and was suddenly pushed roughly from behind.

She gagged as a thick, unrecognizable odour filled her nostrils. Something was being held against her face. She tried to cry but no sound came.

The taste in her mouth was sharp, clinical.

Then all sense had gone.

PART FOUR

The Circle of
Containment

Forty-Three

Since his meeting with Suleiman Attallah, curator of the Supreme Council of Antiquities, Lu Yen had been struggling to put his mind in some order. He had never known such a ferment inside his head. A torrent of torturing memories and the many questions whirling about made it hard to think. First, there had been the shock of seeing the sacred golden urn, stolen so long ago from his former monastic home. It brought back every terrible moment of the grisly destruction of its patriarch and the holy order. Then, there had been what he had learned from the curator.

Suleiman Attallah had been eager to exchange theories and ideas with his Chinese counterpart. New discoveries were making him fizz with excitement, and he was desperate to share them with someone knowledgeable.

'These finds at Siwa are incredible,' he had explained to Lu Yen. 'We have discovered the Lost Army of Cambyses II. I expect great things from this find. Much light will be shed on our understanding of the ancients and our knowledge of the Egyptian deities. For instance, take the god Ammon. The name Ammon, written in ancient texts as Amen, means hidden god or invisible being, conceived as the breath that animates all living things, a spirit that is present everywhere. And Ammon is much older than people realize. He is considered as an Egyptian form of Zeus, but really he was a primeval deity – he is mentioned in the famous pyramid text from the Old Kingdom of 2686–2181BCE.'

Lu Yen had politely nodded to Attallah after his words had been translated for him. 'What form did the god appear in?' he had asked in return.

'Many manifestations!' Attallah had answered, his enthusiasm growing. 'Usually he is depicted as horned ram, a symbol of fertility. But images of him have been discovered in the form of a goose, the head of a crocodile or frog, even a primeval serpent. In time, Ammon became the one and only supreme deity. All other gods were represented as mere symbols of his power in different manifestations.'

The curator paused to drink the hibiscus tea that had arrived, while his guest listened to the translator.

'Later the god became merged with the visible sun god, Ra, becoming known as the all-seeing Ammon Re; where the *hidden* became *revealed*, representing two opposites of divinity. Depicted with a bright stone in his crown, representing the rays of the sun, the texts confirm that his oracles revealed his secret will with the aid of a mystical seeing stone.'

Lu Yen's ears had caught the last words translated; his interest heightened. 'Where is it possible to see such images?'

The curator had laughed, waving an outstretched arm around. 'Everywhere there are images of Ammon. Over centuries great temples were erected along the Nile dedicated to Ammon, including Luxor Temple and the Great Temple at Karnak. There in the great court is the Avenue of the Sphinxes, each seated sphinx resting its chin on a king, the ram of god Ammon assimilated with the solar symbol of the lion.'

'What of the seeing stone?'

'It is believed that the seeing stone was kept originally by the priests of Thebes, where the god was first deified; then later by the oracle's priest chosen to explain Ammon's secret will. The greatest of Ammon's oracles was located at Siwa Oasis. He is the one that Alexander the Great sought answers from when becoming King of Egypt. Legend says that he was guided by the oracle to go to Persia and retrieve the seeing stone that had been stolen during the sacking of Thebes, of which Ammon was god, by the Assyrians in the twenty-fifth dynasty.'

Attallah paused as he sipped from his tea and smiled. 'Perhaps he retrieved it, perhaps he didn't, though some believe he took it from Cambyses II's father's tomb, Cyrus the Great. But what happened to it or where it is hidden, if it exists; only Ammon knows.'

Lu Yen had asked the curator if he himself actually believed it existed. With an expression of aloof academia, Attallah had said that any opinions he might personally hold would have to be evidence-based. He had gone on to explain how some block statues, popular because their flat sides could be filled with hieroglyphs, did in fact hold evidence of such a stone.

'One such statue records the autobiography of Udjahorresnet, an Egyptian priest. What is interesting is that the engraved statue, which unfortunately is now part of the Vatican Collection in Rome,' Attallah had added with some bitterness, 'tells how the priest introduced Cambyses II to Egyptian religious beliefs.

'And it is of course his Lost Army we have just discovered, which perhaps proves the point that Cambyses II was indeed intending to overthrow the Priests of Ammonium and their oracle. Why? Because prior to this, Ammon had become so powerful that the priests of the deity actually came to rule Egypt during the twenty-first dynasty.

'Cambyses would have considered them as a future threat to his own dynasty. From such evidence, and of course from other somewhat disjointed accounts, usually of a religious basis, we can surmise that such a mystic stone exists or existed.'

Suleiman Attallah had then conspiratorially winked to Lu Yen, as if to admit silently that he believed in its existence but could not possibly divulge the fact to his colleagues by having his view openly recorded by the translator.

Lu Yen was returned to the underground vault, blindfolded as before, to continue the studies ordered by Subedei.

He picked up the urn, handling it with great delicacy. He could hardly believe it was in his hands. It was the very same sacred holy relic that had been kept at his monastery for over seven hundred years. How it had come to be in the monastery in the first place, he had no idea. Perhaps it had been stolen. But he knew without a doubt that the urn had come from some-where else before then. It had never rightfully belonged to the monks. Its ownership disappeared back into the mists of history.

But how had the venerable Subedei come by it? Lu Yen doubted if it had been honestly. His experience in the Protectorate of Historical Artefacts had taught him that history had been plundered and robbed by greedy criminals all too often.

Lu Yen turned his attention to the object that Subedei said had fallen from a concealed chamber in the golden urn. He picked it up and turned it in his hand. It was astonishing that it had never before been discovered by any of the dozens of patriarchs who had guarded the urn over the centuries. But Subedei had shown him how its discovery had accidentally come about. He had ordered Lu Yen to study it, confirm what it was and what powers it might confer on its owner.

The old man had not the faintest idea what he could mean by these 'powers'. But he knew what it was he held in his hand.

Once *hidden*, it had become *visible* again.

Bending down towards the short sword that lay in front of him, Lu Yen slowly reinserted the object into the empty socket that had been expertly fashioned into the hand-worn hilt.

It was a perfect fit.

Once again the sword became as it was when its conquering owner had wielded it. The seeing stone of Ammon glowed as it absorbed the light from the vault and refracted it back towards the opened, smoky white marble sarcophagus of Alexander the Great.

Forty-Four

Subedei paled in disbelief. Ayeesha noticed the whitening of his knuckles at the same time she heard the audible crack of the cell phone's casing. Subedei did not release his grip as he pressed the phone harder against his ear.

She stole a glance at her watch. It was six o'clock. Raising her eyes, she inwardly recoiled at the cold stare that was being levelled at her, but outwardly remained serene, her eyes displaying just the right amount of questioning concern.

'And the news from Iraq?' asked Subedei.

'Only one pump station was destroyed. The three others were forewarned. They were ready and waiting when our teams arrived.' Zarakov sounded dazed. He was still in shock at the almost complete failure of their plans and the loss of his men. His strategy lay in tatters, a sorry joke. 'I have failed, My Lord. Operation Genghis Khan has been utterly thwarted. But I believe that this could not have happened without the intervention of someone else. I believe that there is a traitor.'

Subedei said nothing.

'Forgive me, My Lord Subedei,' said Zarakov, urgency in his voice, 'but we must consider this possibility. The only people who knew the details of this operation were you, myself, and the members of the cartel. And one other. This traitor has to be close to you, *very* close.' He took a deep breath and said, 'I believe it to be your Egyptian woman.'

Subedei listened to his second in command as he continued to stare at Ayeesha. He trusted Zarakov and he was certain that the Russian was right. There was a traitor. It had to be a member of the cartel – the weak Somers had betrayed him. But then, not even the cartel had been given details of the back-up plan. Its utmost secrecy was the key to its success. How then did it fail? How did the *Viking Conqueror* escape destruction?

That was why he could not believe that it was Ayeesha who had betrayed him. She had no knowledge of the back-up plan. And she was still here, where surely a traitor would have fled by now. Only he himself, Zarakov and Qenawi had been in possession of all the plans.

'Have you heard from Qenawi?' he demanded.

'No, he has not been seen. Our security head escaped the onslaught at Al Qantarah. He reported that he last saw Qenawi running towards the quay.'

'And he heard no explosion?'

'None. And the *Viking Conqueror* has passed safely through the canal.'

It was Qenawi, decided Subedei. But then, Qenawi had no idea at all of the Iraq part of the plan – so it could not have been him. Qenawi must have been killed before he could detonate the relay of charges. Subedei had trusted him and he was sure he had not been wrong to do so.

Subedei felt a pain in his chest as the realization dawned on him. For the first time he had allowed a woman to get into his heart and she had immediately repaid him with treachery.

His general was right. It was the Egyptian whore.

But he would not kill her.

'You are right, Rurik,' he said slowly, his eyes still on the woman.

'Thank you, My Lord.'

Subedei felt himself relax. He knew what he would do. Others would pay for their interference before he returned to Beijing. 'I will send the package over to you now. I will dispose of the other one already here when I am safely away.'

'I will not fail you, My Lord. When will you leave?'

'In one hour.'

The powerful Italian Maiora motor cruiser had skirted the Nile Delta for a pounding two-and-a-half hours; five knots over the manufacturer's stated top speed of thirty knots, cutting through the white crested waves like a sharp knife through thick icing.

From the wheel, Brock finally spotted the greater harbour of Alexandria. It was already late afternoon and in thirty more minutes they would arrive at the new port that housed the refineries of South Western Oil and Ammon Oil, both now in

Subedei's control, albeit the former only by licence, ruthlessly acquired.

Earlier in the day Brock had had no idea he would be where he was in the afternoon. He recalled grinning at Colonel Beecham's reaction when he had suggested that there was no need to risk bringing in the tilt wing for a pick-up.

'And just how the hell do you expect us to get back to the *Apollo*, bearing in mind we're not even meant to be here!'

Brock had pointed to the sleek motor boat moored to the quay. 'Including me and Matt, you, Colonel, and your team, there are ten of us in all. That baby cruises comfortably with twelve guests and two crew, so we won't have to crowd each other.'

'You mean to take that?'

'With its three cabins and the excellent provisions which I have no doubt someone has thoughtfully provided, I am going to repay your help by taking you back in comfort! You can be our guests; Matt and I will be your crew. My guess is that's what it was intended for, a quick little escape after blowing up the *Viking Conqueror*.'

They had rendezvoused with the *Apollo* ninety-five minutes later, the team having enjoyed the champagne and caviar that Brock had promised; Colonel Beecham opting for the Jacuzzi tub in the main cabin with a large glass of scotch. Everyone took a turn at the wheel of the powerful water beast that seemed able to fly over the waves with a sophisticated ease.

During the debriefing a communiqué had been received that Neusheen had been abducted, the driver Karim, having been given a message that she had been kidnapped by the fringe group of Muslim extremists, Ghulat dar al-harb.

'Bullshit!' Brock had exclaimed. 'It's Subedei and I bet I can make a calculated guess as to where he's taken her.' Ten minutes later, the twenty-metre Maiora had been fully refuelled.

'Wish I could go with you, Connor,' Colonel Beecham had said sincerely. 'But . . .'

Brock had interrupted him. 'No need to explain, James. I'm just following a hunch, which Matt and I can handle on our own.'

Beecham had watched the cruiser skim quickly away, assisted by its lightened load, before turning to Captain Cousins who had joined him on the deck of the *Apollo*.

'Brock's hunches have saved a hell of a lot of civilian lives today. Let's just hope to God that they don't cost him his own.'

During the trip to Alexandria, Brock had taken the opportunity to correlate all the information he had gathered about Subedei over the past few weeks and put it into some form of order in his mind; the sea air rushing past on the cruiser conducive to his intuitive reasoning.

'So is this the time to ask what's on your mind?' asked Ferguson, now at the wheel, as Subedei's Alexandrian Refinery came into clear view.

'It's simple really. I flew over this complex a few weeks ago with Neusheen. It lies at the head of the same Nile tributary on which Subedei keeps his yacht the *Pharaoh Queen*, and the same tributary that leads directly to where he and the Egyptian president were collected. You remember; the place the sweet marketing girl Fatima referred to as the Temple of Ammon; Subedei's palatial residence he had so generously partly-donated to the president. Well, I believe Subedei follows a pattern of overt secrecy. Whenever he wants to keep something hidden he makes it appear part of something else.'

Ferguson looked confused. 'Simple, you say? It's about as clear as mud to me.'

'The caverns you were kept in at Siwa remained hidden because they were located close to the archaeological dig for the Lost Army. It meant that Subedei could take what he wanted from the Ammon Temple there without being noticed. Or do what he wanted. Remember the large empty urns?'

'Yes, and the dead body.'

'Exactly, what Subedei wanted was in those. I have no idea what, but whatever they contained, he took. Nobody from the Supreme Council of Antiquities has suspected, because they are so engrossed in the nearby dig, courtesy of Subedei. How did he gain the patronage of the SCA? By saying he had discovered oil nearby and would hold off drilling for it so as not to compromise the discovery of the dig.'

'But there is no oil?'

'Never was. But there was an archaeological dig, the details of which I got Pete Kenachi to check after my friend Professor Amuyani told me about a Greek woman who claimed to have

370

discovered the tomb of Alexander around Siwa, as well as remnants of an army. Apparently the Greek government, put pressure on the SCA to not renew her licence, immediately preventing her from continuing her dig. She was not even allowed entry into the country. Now guess which other government has recently received a generous donation as well as Egypt?'

'Greece?'

'Right; and from Subedei Industries. He simply took over the dig and handed it to the budget-tight SCA, saying the whole cost would be covered by his Ammon Oil Company.'

'But why say there's oil when there is not?'

'Because it is the key for winning all the approval he needs to control Egypt. His plan to block the Suez and destroy pipes would cause a real headache for Saudi Arabia. His main intention was to divert the resource to the demanding east, but the Saudi Pipe at Yanbu on the Red Sea could be easily connected to his own pipeline from Suez to Alexandria, for which he was granted a licence because of his oil exploration in Egypt. No doubt he would negotiate a massively discounted price and it would appear that Ammon had discovered oil at Siwa.'

Ferguson looked doubtful. 'But the Saudis might have taken weeks to agree, if at all. Surely he would have been found out?'

'I believe the thought never even entered his head. Everything Subedei owns has been ruthlessly taken from others; built with their sweat and toil first; he has always got away with it, so why should he be concerned about getting found out now? Perhaps he believes he is somehow chosen for a great destiny. However, he is still prudent enough to build in back-up plans to all of his grabbing schemes; like he did with the *Viking Conqueror*, which even the Mossad operative did not know about. So his back-up for oil was to take over John Ridge's South Western Oil refinery. In that way he could provide oil that was really coming from existing reserves further north. He would simply increase the flow via the extra piping he had already constructed.'

'But he still ran the risk of being found out,' Ferguson persisted.

'By then it would have been too late. I believe his intention was to use Egypt as a base to control a Europe that, following the success of Operation Genghis Khan, would be dependent on him and his cartel. Like his ancestor Temujin, the real Genghis Khan, he would rule over Europe, the Middle East and who knows?

371

Perhaps even China as the Emperor of Mongolia. The man is insane enough to think so and has already proven that he will stop at nothing to fulfil what he no doubt believes to be his destiny.'

'With his Alexandria refinery the control centre?'

'Yes. Following the same plan that has worked for him so well at Siwa. Conceal it within an oil refinery, itself a front as the Ammon Oil wells are at Siwa, and link it directly to his Temple of Ammon palace, probably by a pipeline, again in the same way. Hence my expression, overt secrecy.'

'But why Alexandria?'

'That involves his obsession with Alexander the Great and a legend that gave Alexander conquering power. And right now I intend to take us right down the Nile to his Ammon Temple.'

'What's the plan? Are we to just waltz right in?'

Brock shrugged. 'Yes, why not? I'm betting that with his policy of overt secrecy, the part he occupies is a front for something else; why else give almost all of what he had built to the president as a country residence. My guess is that, like Siwa, it is just an entrance to something else; perhaps leading to the original Ottoman palace that was built somewhere around here.'

'Have I missed something?' Ferguson looked puzzled.

'Professor Amuyani also told me about how the first Arab ruler of Egypt, called Amr for short, built a palace on the banks of the Nile outside Alexandria. Perhaps Subedei building his own residence here has something to do with that.'

'And you're thinking that this will be where he is holding Neusheen?'

'I don't know, but I'm damn certain it's where Subedei is. And if we find him, we stand a chance of finding Neusheen.'

'He might be expecting us again, you know. You said he seemed to be prepared for us on the *Pharaoh Queen*. It could be a set-up Connor.'

'It's a risk we have to take. We'll just have to knock on the door and find out. As they say, we'll cross that bridge when we come to it.'

'Fine with me, but just one more question.'

'Fire away.'

Ferguson pointed at the rapidly approaching barrier that blocked their path. 'How do we get past that?'

* * *

372

The high-powered security cameras connected all around Subedei's Alexandrian Refinery automatically recorded the Maiora motor cruiser as it passed by on its way to the temple palace. Only recognizable craft were allowed to enter the private tributary. A craft could only be considered recognizable if it carried an encrypted reference code, similar to a European toll-road barrier.

The security camera read the code and passed it on to the computer, which sought its databank for recognition. In the blink of an eye the information required was retrieved. The Maiora cruiser was currently operated by Ibrahim Qenawi, CEO of Subedei Industries (Egypt).

The computer dutifully raised the barrier.

Brock grinned at the Irishman's mystified look. 'Piece of cake.'

The computer logged the time. 18:01

Forty-Five

She should have been more prepared, but she had not anticipated the sudden backhand blow. It had caught her full in
the face, breaking her nose and splitting her lip. Before she had
time to recover, strong arms forced her to the floor.

Subedei stood over Ayeesha, his eyes full of hate.

She realized at once that she should have got out earlier. Now
it was too late.

Subedei's eyes glittered like black coal. 'I wish I had more
time to deal with you personally, but I'm sure that you'll understand that, due to your treachery, I have to make a somewhat
earlier than anticipated departure.'

As she tried to form a reply, Subedei kicked her viciously in
the mouth, breaking one of her teeth. Turning on his heel
towards his desk, he addressed the Mongolian brute who was
restraining Ayeesha as easily as he would a baby.

'Zarakov is expecting her.' He pressed a concealed button on
his desk and a third of the wall slid away, revealing an open
elevator. 'Take the ugly whore to him!'

Five minutes later, after destroying the hard disc of his
computer, he called for the remaining two of his personal bodyguard.

'I want to leave for the airport in thirty minutes. Get the girl
ready. She will be travelling with us.'

Subedei entered the elevator, which had silently returned. His
private cell phone rang. It would not be Zarakov; it would be
a cartel member or Jumair – no one else had the number.
Subedei dropped the phone and crushed it under his foot. The
incessant ringing stopped.

Mi Ling met Subedei as the elevator door opened and followed
him silently as he walked through the narrow marble passage
toward the vault.

374

'Mi Ling,' he snapped, 'we are to return to Beijing immediately. Make the arrangements.'

'Yes, My Lord. Am I to return to guide Assistant Curator Tang?'

'No, I will bring him myself.'

Mi Ling recognized the cold, cruel look in Subedei's eyes. She had seen it often enough. She swung open the vault door. 'Yes, My Lord.'

'Bit quieter than the last time we were here,' commented Ferguson as he moored up the cruiser.

Brock had studied the building as they had approached. The palace not only looked empty, it did not even look habitable yet. Only the farthest wing did not have its windows heavily boarded with shutters; the same wing that he had observed Subedei and the Egyptian president exit with his entourage.

'It looks like classic Subedei. The main section of the palace apparently donated to the government is not even finished. Like so many of his generous gestures it is empty; which is no doubt an ideal façade for Subedei, being left alone in a government-designated building.'

'Not entirely empty.' Ferguson nodded at the silver Lexus that was pulling up at the far wing. The thickset driver got out of the car and was about to walk towards the ornate door he had parked close to, when he noticed Brock and Ferguson casually walking towards the palace wing. Built like a federation wrestler, his neck was so thick that his hairless head appeared to come directly from his chest. The black trousers and shirt were tightly stretched, revealing muscled arms almost as wide as the huge legs that caused the brute to swagger like a goose as he walked menacingly towards what he considered uninvited guests.

Brock gave his most disarming smile. 'Do you know if there is a fuel station around here?'

One arm pointed firmly back to the quay as if directing a bad dog to get out.

'Perhaps he doesn't know?' offered Ferguson

Brock was about to say something when a cry of indignant rage drew the attention of all three to the opening door. Brock recognized the yelling before he actually saw that it was Neusheen being roughly held around the waist. The huge arm holding the

375

struggling woman in a horizontal position was attached to the twin of the brute facing Brock and Ferguson.

Neusheen's captor, seeing Brock and Ferguson, retreated, slamming the door shut behind him. The two ICE investigators were close enough for the both of them to rush bodily at the monster in front of them with their combined weight. It had the same effect as running into a solid concrete wall.

'That puts a new slant on being built like a brick shit house!' shouted Ferguson. 'Your man here's tougher than a battering ram!'

Brock didn't reply; just lay stunned where he fell. The bodyguard, seeing he had floored one of the intruders, turned quickly to finish off the other, his arms wrapping around Ferguson in an unbreakable bear hug. The pressure on Ferguson's chest was intense. He couldn't move and was certain he heard one of his ribs snap as the man fell on top of him with his full bodyweight.

The automatic tucked in the back of his belt literally came apart in his hand as Brock pistol-whipped the bodyguard's head. Quickly he dragged Ferguson out from underneath the inert human boulder.

'Check the car for another weapon, Matt,' he shouted, running for the door. A moment later, bellowing like a bull, the other bodyguard re-exited the front door and charged at Brock, bowling him clean off his feet. Dazed, Brock felt himself being lifted into the air as the grimacing oriental threw him up behind his neck. The grimace turned to a knowing smile as the brute positioned his victim so as to break his back in two. Helplessly Brock struggled, unable to move as he felt his spine beginning to bend the wrong way.

Brock heard the sickening crunch. Realizing his back must have broken he was surprised to feel himself flying through the air. Was this how a destroyed nervous system momentarily felt?

As he hit the ground the sensation of pain tore through his entire body. His hands, knees, elbows and shoulders were in agony. If he could feel such pain maybe his back was not broken. Slowly Brock raised his head to see if he could move his neck. He could. He opened his eyes.

Directly in front of him was the head of the man who had pinioned him, his face squashed into the ground by the heavy front wheel of the Lexus jammed on top of it.

'You're not going to find what we're looking for down there on your hands and knees, you know,' quipped a relieved-looking Ferguson. 'Get yourself up and let's be finding that young lady.'

'It took Amr Ibn-el-Aas seven years to build his palace. Most of it is long gone now, except for these underground cellars. They are a series of impermeable vaults, constructed to store the works of art he had removed from Alexandria. This is just one of dozens, you know, each one with a combination of weighted locks that took weeks to open. This one is by far the most interesting.'

Lu Yen watched Subedei in silence as the Mongolian walked around the oblong-shaped room filled with priceless artefacts dating from a variety of Egyptian dynasties.

'When the Roman viceroy, Patriarch Cyrus, formally surrendered Alexandria to Amr on 8 November 641BCE, the newly appointed ruler of Egypt insisted on commandeering all of the patriarch's valuable collection of historical items, many of which were believed to have been lost in the great library fire two hundred and fifty years earlier. They'd been secreted away. I know I would have done the same. To experience the sanctity of such things on your own is beyond measure.'

Subedei stopped at the sarcophagus sitting on the pedestal in the centre of the room, its huge lid held open by a secured pulley. 'And to be in the vicinity of Alexander is to feel close to the same power he enjoyed, even if all that my forefathers left of him were his ashes.'

Lu Yen looked at the blackened marble tomb in surprise. 'Your forefathers burned his body, venerable Subedei? Why?'

'I can only guess at the reason. But I believe that they knew more than we do now about the legend that the great empire-builder was buried with the stone that gave him his power. Who would have thought of looking inside the body?'

'This discovery is most wonderful,' Lu Yen said humbly. 'When do you plan to show it? Curator Attallah never made any mention of it. Has he inspected it yet?'

Subedei's demeanour instantly changed. To hear these words, after the failure of his plans, infuriated him. 'Show it! Inspect it! You fool, I have searched for years, spending millions to find

377

it. Do you think I am about to share it now? I will not allow anyone to take this from me.'

Lu Yen bowed, sensing the menacing atmosphere grow in the enclosed room. 'Forgive me. I have blundered.'

Subedei tore open his shirt, revealing his tattoo, his anger increasing. 'Do you see this? I have carried this for most of my life. All chosen members of the Borjigin tribe are tattooed with this sign. See how the stone and the sword hilt match those before you now! The stone is the seeing stone of Ammon. The sword is Alexander's, the son of Ammon. It is destiny that has guided me to bring them together. This is the very God Sword that Alexander built his empire with! You are here because I was misguidedly led to believe that you were an expert on such things.'

Lu Yen bowed nervously. 'Respected sir, I cannot know what you mean.'

Subedei's eyes were blazing as he picked up the sword by the blade, bringing the hilt to his face, his voice resonating within the chamber. 'I took this sword from the Temple of Ammon, where it had been sealed in an urn for eternity by Alexander's general, Ptolemy. There it lay, revered for centuries by priests as a religious artefact, until I was led to it and claimed it. But long before that, over forty years ago, in the same way that the faithful warriors of General Subedei were led by destiny to find the stone of Ammon, I too was led to find it exactly seven hundred years later, again sealed in a golden urn revered by priests who were ignorant of its true purpose. That one there!'

Subedei's voice rose to a shout, spittle flying from his mouth, as he pointed at the urn so familiar to Lu Yen. 'No one but I knows the truth. No other person would understand. But you are supposedly an authority on such things. You must know that what I say is true! And you can surely see with your own eyes that I am chosen for a special destiny! Yet why do you not confirm what you see before you? Alexander sought and received confirmation of his destiny. I want to hear confirmation from you of *my* destiny! Confirmation that fate has guided my hand to this God Sword and will now guide me to greatness.'

Lu Yen was in shock as the words formed on his lips. 'You found the golden urn yourself?'

'Exactly!' laughed Subedei. He seemed to be consumed with

378

madness, losing the control he had always preserved so carefully. 'Just as destiny intended me to. And like my forefathers, who discovered the seeing stone by burning Alexander, I discovered it again by burning the patriarch who was concealing it from me!'

Distracted by the vault door swinging open, Subedei did not see the old man lunge forward. Forty years of pent-up grief, pain and suffering were released in a moment of wild frenzy as Lu Yen clawed at the murderer of his former beloved master, his Patriarch Ti Rinpoche.

Astonished, Subedei flailed back at the old man, easily deflecting the weak arms attacking him, but as he did so he lost his balance and fell back into the open sarcophagus, the God Sword gripped firmly in his hand.

Stunned for a moment at finding himself suddenly lying on his back, Subedei shook his head to clear it. Then he hauled himself up, raising himself on his elbow. He found himself looking directly up into the azure eyes of Connor Brock.

The agent stood looming over the open tomb, his dive knife gripped firmly in his hand. His expression was icily cold as he said, 'Temujin Subedei.'

'You!'

'You remember me. Very gratifying. You know so many important people. Sorry I'm late. Cleaning up Operation Genghis Khan took longer than I had anticipated.'

Subedei's eyes filled with the light of pure evil as he realized that Brock was behind the destruction of his schemes. A strange smile twisted his mouth. 'You cannot defeat me,' he mocked. 'I am too powerful! You will not contain me for long. You cannot change my destiny!'

In one swift movement, Brock sliced through the rope pulley and the heavy sarcophagus lid crashed back on to its massive base.

'Containment seems like a good idea!'

Forty-Six

'It's been too long,' said Neusheen anxiously. She gestured with the gun she had trained on the Chinese woman. 'I say we go down.'

Ferguson frowned and pursed his lips. 'Maybe you're right, Neusheen. Hey, you!'

Mi Ling looked up. She had been kneeling obediently on the floor, staring at the marble tiles. She had done everything that these foreigners had requested, from the moment she had exited the lift to see the tall man flooring the bodyguard, grabbing his weapon and setting free the girl prisoner. The girl had been spitting with rage and, as soon as she was released, she had run at the tall man, hitting out at him and screaming with fury. But an instant later, her face had dissolved into smiles and she had flung herself against him, hugging him tightly to her and kissing him strongly on the mouth. The tall man had winced for a moment at the woman's grip and then had relaxed himself and returned her kiss for just an instant longer than he perhaps needed to.

This red-haired man had grabbed Mi Ling and held the gun to her head, although she had no intention of struggling. The tall man had come over to her and demanded to know where Subedei was. It had been the work of a moment to direct him to the vaults. The girl and the red-haired man had stayed here, making sure that Mi Ling did not escape, though where she could possibly go she had no idea.

Now, as the man shouted at her, she looked up timidly.

'Where did you send our friend?' he demanded.

She bowed her head meekly. 'To the vaults below, where my master keeps his treasure.'

'Take us there now.'

Mi Ling got smoothly to her feet, led them into the elevator and down to the corridor leading to the vaults. They could hear a muffled shouting and knocking and they hurried towards the sound. As they ran into the vault, Mi Ling saw Lu Yen sobbing on the floor, clutching his golden urn, and she rushed over to comfort him in Chinese, as the other two made sure their friend was all right.

They were looking at the closed sarcophagus, which echoed with thumps and shouts from within, when Mi Ling interrupted them in her quiet voice. 'Honourable sir, I believe there is another of your friends in danger. I saw her taken, her face all bloodied. She needs help.'

Brock looked at her suspiciously. 'What are you telling us?'

'Lady Ayeesha. I heard Lord Subedei call her traitor. Then he hit her. He sent her to the Russian by cart track.'

'Ayeesha?' shouted Ferguson. 'Finally had to swallow some of her own medicine at last, eh?'

Brock's face lit up. 'Wait a second, Matt. She must be Mossad's undercover agent! It had to be someone really close to him.' Brock grabbed Mi Ling by the arm. 'Show me where this track is. Neusheen, you get back to the surface. Take this old gentleman with you and wait for us there.'

Within a minute, Mi Ling had led them to the track and Brock and Ferguson were in a cart.

'Please go now, honourable sir.' Mi Ling bowed. 'And I will go too now, please!'

Brock looked at the frightened girl, another of Subedei's innocent pawns. 'OK. You've done a good job. Thank you. Now get the hell out of here.'

A moment later, the cart sped along the track to Subedei's control centre at Alexandria.

Immediately, Mi Ling returned to the vault. She entered tentatively, listening to Subedei's muffled shouts.

Even though the sarcophagus was tightly shut, Mi Ling switched off the lights and turned off the air filters. She then closed the vault door behind her, listening to the weight-activated locks she had earlier emptied as they filled with sand. They took much longer to fill than on the other occasions when she had opened and locked the vault.

This time she had removed the plugs, allowing the sand to fill up the void inside the stone door, making reopening impossible.

Only weeks of careful excavation, or explosives, would open it now. She could not see the Egyptian Supreme Council of Antiquities allowing explosives to be used on such an important discovery: the long lost tomb of Alexander the Great.

Mi Ling knew her husband would be waiting at the Concorde. She had already contacted him to prepare the plane, as instructed by Subedei, but now only she would be arriving, after she had removed some vital documents from the office upstairs. She did not have access to all of Subedei's accounts but she knew enough to ensure that she and her husband could live in luxury, and begin to repair the terrible damage that had been inflicted on them.

The turntable and platform were empty. Brock, followed by Ferguson, headed down a short passage until they reached an elevator with an adjacent stairwell. The stairs circled upwards towards a wide hall, and downwards out of sight.

Brock looked around cautiously. 'These may well join up since they look like part of the giant refinery silo we saw from the outside, but we'll separate anyway. You take the higher one, Matt, I'll take the lower one.'

'An' I'll be in Scotland afore ye,' whispered back Ferguson.

'No doubt. Watch yourself.'

Brock headed downwards as quietly as he could, staying alert. Halfway around the silo, Brock's stairway began to rise again. Then it turned in on itself, opening into an inner hall which led to a series of rooms. One of the doors was slightly ajar.

Brock went forward, pushed the door fully open and entered. It was a small room, with a semi-circle of chairs placed in front of a large viewing screen which seemed to show a much more lavish room. Then he realized that there was movement: it must be a window looking directly into a room beyond this small one. He swerved to the side at once, so that he could not be seen.

Cautiously, he looked around the edge of the window and realized that he was looking into some kind of throne room, crammed with statues and works of art. In the centre was a large table surrounded by chairs and the door opposite was open. Leaning behind the door was a great brute of a man who, though staring directly at Brock, did not seem to show any sign of acknowledgement. Brock moved tentatively back and understood why. This window was a two-way mirror. He could not be seen.

Now confident, he approached the mirror and stared through at the room beyond. In it, Brock counted three people: the brute who was a clone of the two he had already encountered, and a man and woman, both of whom he recognized.

Zarakov, he thought. I wondered when I'd come across him again. And Ayeesha. By god, she's in a bad way. I bet that Russian is practised in some pretty nasty techniques.

Ayeesha was half naked and tied across a chair that had been dragged away from a large boardroom table. Her face was battered and bleeding, with a stream of red coming from her mouth, and she looked exhausted. Zarakov half sat on the table near her, a syringe in his hand.

'As you see, it works admirably without pain, *my dear*. It's just that I had an impulse to have a go anyway. How are you feeling? Now, just a couple more questions and you'll be able to have a nice, long rest. But first things first – why is Mossad so interested in Subedei?'

Ayeesha tried to raise her head to look her interrogator straight in the eye. Before she was able to say anything, a fourth person entered the room. It was Matt. Brock tried to shout a warning as a look of surprise appeared on Zarakov's face, but it was obvious that he couldn't be heard.

The Russian got to his feet and said with a smile, 'Ah. My old friend. I remember you. The man after my own heart. How good of you to drop by.'

Ferguson had levelled his gun at Zarakov but he hadn't noticed the heavy standing directly behind the door. Brock watched impotently as the bodyguard moved quickly, crashing his great fist down on Ferguson's arm, sending the gun spinning from his hand.

Brock had no idea how he would get into the throne room. He couldn't see where the other entrance was from his position. As the brute began to pound Ferguson in the stomach, Brock spotted a microphone at the side of the mirror. Darting forward, he flicked the switch.

'The place is surrounded, Zarakov,' Brock said, trying to sound calm. 'Call off your clown. Drop your weapons immediately.'

The Russian looked about for the source of the voice and

then realized what he was hearing. He turned to stare towards the two-way mirror. 'Now, if my friend here has dropped by, that means Mr Brock cannot be far away. In fact, I recognize your voice! Just the person I was hoping to meet again.'

Brock said with an edge of menace, 'Give it up, Zarakov. Your boss Subedei has already been taken, along with the other pretty boys of his bodyguard.'

Zarakov appeared nonplussed. 'Well, then he is more of a fool than I thought. Why should I care? He has been more than generous to me and my only goal in life now is to kill you.'

'Why bother with me?' asked Brock. 'If Subedei has been his usual generous self I'm sure there are many other goals that you could achieve.'

Zarakov's eyes narrowed as his fingers curled around the automatic pistol tucked in the back of his belt. 'But none of them would give me the same satisfaction as to kill the man who killed my brother!'

Brock noticed the movement. He had already seen the gun while Zarakov had been leaning against the table. 'I didn't kill your brother.'

Zarakov knew exactly where the microphone was. He knew the armour-piercing shells of his Glock would cut through the thick mirror like a red-hot poker in snow. 'Dimitri's body was found at the bottom of the well. Every bone in it had been broken, yet he still lived for an hour; in pain. I intend to break every bone in your body.'

'I would have tried to save him from falling actually, but I was too busy avoiding the bullets he . . .'

With blurring speed, Zarakov brought round his automatic, firing directly at the mirror at the rate of three bullets a second. For ten seconds he fired; every second taking a pace closer to his target.

Brock had pushed himself tight against the far wall, while still holding the microphone. In doing so, he unwittingly discovered the counterbalanced door that Subedei had used to swing unnoticed into the small passage leading to the boardroom entrance.

'Looking for me?' goaded Brock, crouching down on the floor as Zarakov peered through the smashed mirror.

Brock's bullet caught Zarakov right on the chin, shattering

384

his jaw. Two seconds later, Brock had dashed through the passage. In the time it had taken to get round to the entrance, the oriental bodyguard had waddled halfway across the room toward Zarakov.

Spun round by the force of Brock's wounding bullet, Zarakov glimpsed Brock as he entered. He fired immediately; the heavy machine pistol shuddering in his unsteady hand as he fired. Six bullets caught the approaching bodyguard, who seeing what was about to happen, jumped the wrong way, right into them. The pistol clicked. Empty.

Ferguson dragged his battered body over to Ayeesha, who stared into the green eyes that were looking up at her from the floor. He noticed the flicker of recognition in her eyes. 'Is it always this dangerous going on a date with you?'

The woman's swollen lips broke apart into a loose smile.

Forty-Seven

Aaron Hammond leaned back into the wing-backed calf-hide chair; his fingers tapping softly on the smooth leather arm. 'The fact is we cannot do anything about Nicaros, other than to arrange an accident, which we, contrary to popular belief, do not do.'

The president looked at his chief of intelligence, wondering why the man's suits were always so crumpled. Their weekly meeting in the oval room was coming to a close; the last item on the agenda was oil. 'Do we know for certain he was involved?'

'Oh, for sure. We followed him to Alexandria, where, though we didn't see them together, Nicaros was seen entering and leaving Subedei's refinery. Forty hours later, operation Genghis Khan was underway.'

Hammond did not add that his operative had managed to implant the tiniest transmitter in Nicaros's stomach. Having been caught looking stupid with the *Riyadh*, he had decided to increase the surveillance. Their operative, who posed as Nicaros's personal chef, had simply inserted the transmitter into the oysters his patron adored. Swallowed in one gulp, each one lasted twenty-four hours. They had learned first of Subedei's plan; Mossad had confirmed it. There is no way, in his position, he would have authorized the covert assault otherwise, without such first-hand evidence. Certainly, his counterpart David Bearne would not have either. Hearing the evidence against their own minister had prompted swift action from the British.

Petersen set his mouth. 'So, I read in your report, Aaron, fifteen of our young boys lost their lives; that's one hell of a price to pay. Good thing the media hasn't got hold of this.'

'They received a statement after the relatives had been informed,' offered Hammond. 'The helicopter they were all travelling in while on manoeuvres crashed, regrettably there were no survivors.'

'One hell of a reason to take out that Venezuelan son of a bitch.'

Hammond rested his light-blue eyes on the president. 'Bob, I know it sticks in the gullet, but the other fact is that Nicaros is more useful to us alive.'

'I fail to see why.'

'Stability.'

'Based on the devil you know, I suppose?'

'Something along those lines, Mr President.'

Hammond met Jim Kowalski in one of the White House corridors of power. The special assistant nodded acknowledgment as he passed by; the well-cut dark blue suit that matched the president's was in sharp contrast to the grey, unfashionable CIA director's. 'Good result, eh, Aaron?'

Hammond smiled. 'Your oil's safe, until the next time.'

Continuing his purposeful walk to the Oval Room, Kowalski did not hear.

The CIA director allowed himself another smile. He had no doubt in his mind that the British would deal with their treacherous minister in their own inimitable way; but the information he now had on Nicaros and Berentsky would prove very useful, very useful indeed. Somehow, he thought to himself, even Mullah Abd al Rahwan will prove to be extremely valuable in our relationship-building with Iran.

'But it's St George's day on Saturday and we're all planning on going to the races; you know we always do, it's a family tradition. Can't you cancel whatever it is?'

David Bearne was still at his office, expecting a call. His private line had rung exactly at the moment when it should have. But it was his elderly mother.

'It's also William Shakespeare's birthday; perhaps we could see one of his plays in the evening.'

'Now there's no need to be sarcastic, David. If you can't, you can't. We'll just have to plan something else. We hardly see you these days, you know!'

The MI6 director felt the guilt, wishing he could use it as expertly on his own team as his mother did on him and his sister. 'I have to go, Mother; I promise I'll visit soon. Oh, and Mother, please don't use this line, unless it's an emergency.'

Realizing he had just done it back to her, he grinned inwardly. Immediately he replaced the receiver, it rang again; this time with the individual tone he was expecting.

'Yes, Prime Minister.'

'David, I wanted to thank you personally for your, and your team's, excellent work last Friday.'

'Thank you, sir. Credit must also go to ICE for first bringing it to our attention.'

'Sir Duncan Buchanan's outfit?'

'Yes sir, in particular one of their investigators whom you may recall, Connor Brock?'

The Prime Minister paused. 'Yes, the Moscow fiasco. I remember. We must thank him in some way.'

'Yes sir.'

'All safe and secure; no backlash possible?'

Bearne knew there could only be one response, even on a safe phone. 'Yes, Prime Minister.'

'Good. Any plans for the weekend?' Changing the subject entirely before the call ended. 'It's St George's Day, you know.'

'I'm afraid I have to attend a funeral, the minister's.'

'Of course, Lord Somers, so sudden, a good man too. Hunting accident, wasn't it?'

'Yes, Prime Minister, I'm afraid it was.'

'An ironic endorsement for why my government would like to ban it; shouldn't have been doing it in the first place. Hardly sets a good example when one of my own ministers abuses his position, does it?'

'No, it does not, sir.'

'You must let me have your recommendation for his replacement. I've purposely left it until after the funeral, wouldn't be fitting otherwise.'

'Agreed, sir.'

'Right. Well, we can discuss that next week at our usual meeting. Bye, David, and, um, thanks again'

'Good bye sir.'

*   *   *

Energy Minister Fu Chen and Foreign Affairs Minister Zhilun Yang felt the cold stare of the Vice Premier Xudung Sun as it bore into the tops of their heads while they continued to look at the floor in obeisance.

'Where is Ambassador Subedei now? He has still not come to explain that broadcast as I commanded him! Our president is furious at the embarrassment!'

'The man has vanished, respected Vice Premier,' offered Chen.

'You told me his Concorde jet returned from Egypt four days ago! He must be somewhere!'

'Customs have now confirmed that only his personal assistants returned, lord,' answered Yang.

'And where do they say he is?'

Yang wished he had not offered the information, 'They too have disappeared without trace, lord.'

Vice Premier Sun's cold look slowly began to gleam. 'So it seems that he does not wish to appear before me. Do you both agree?'

'We agree with you, respected Vice Premier.'

'Then we must assume that his failure to appear must be taken as indication of the broadcast's truth and of his own guilt. Anyway, it is now of no consequence. On behalf of our president, and the Party, I have decided that Subedei Industries is forthwith to be operated by the People's Republic of China.'

Both ministers paled further; no longer would they receive their generous handouts. Now they would both have to find alternatives to finance the lifestyle they had become accustomed to.

'You are wise indeed, respected Vice Premier,' Minister Chen offered, accompanied by a nod of agreement from Yang.

'Foreign Affairs Minister Yang, I will require you to review all interests relating to Subedei Industries outside China. Any forthcoming lawsuits that challenge ownership, or licence, you are to settle quickly. I will not allow any liable actions that we have no power over to shadow our Party, or China.'

'I will begin right away, lord.'

'Energy Minister Fu Chen, I will require you to continue the negotiations started by Subedei Industries with Russia and Saudi Arabia. Until we increase our nuclear energy alternatives, China needs increasing amounts of oil. We three have been given the rewarding task of serving her demands. I do not expect either of you to fail me. Is that understood?'

The ministers both smiled inwardly. The opportunity for the continuance of their lifestyle had presented itself. It would also bring them closer to the Vice Premier.

'We understand, lord,' they replied in unison, raising their eyes to meet Xudung Sun's smiling ones.

The storm of uncontrollable rage that had possessed Subedei eventually began to wane. In its place came fear.

For what seemed like hours, he had shouted for attention. Shortly after that infernal Brock had entombed him, he was certain he had heard something. He had strained his ears, fearing that the sound was the closing of the vault door. He had shouted his voice hoarse in the belief that it was Mi Ling returning with his faithful bodyguards. Nothing. Not a sound. In fact, it seemed quieter and blacker than ever.

A thought struck him. Yes! He had his phone. Desperately, he twisted within the confines of the stuffy sarcophagus to search each of his pockets. It wasn't there. He remembered. He had destroyed it! How stupid!

Another thought. Zarakov. Of course! His trusted general would already be on his way to release him. He would have killed that interfering Brock. There was not long to wait now.

He checked his watch. Broken. It must have been when he fell. Why did that stupid little man attack him like that? He had shown him things that no other had seen. No one! Yet, on learning of his destiny, his greatness, the man had attacked him. What possible provocation could he have given him?

He had no idea how long he had been there. Every minute seemed to pass like an eternity. The stone felt cold. His fingers scraped the bottom, his fingernails filling with the remaining ashes of Alexander. He turned round and tried to force himself up on his hands and knees, pushing his back against the lid with all his strength. No movement.

Another idea. The sword! He began to use it to scrape around the lid edge where it met the base. Perhaps he could prise open the lid. A few splintering shards of marble motivated him and he went harder at it, the sweat pouring off him. Then – disaster. The sword, weakened by twenty-three centuries of ageing, shattered.

Exhausted and beyond hope of setting himself free, Subedei waited to be released. He knew it would happen eventually. Whether it was Zarakov or Brock, he did not care. He just wanted to get out. He would give anything right now to get out. But no one came.

After two days, Subedei began to hallucinate. His bodily demands for water and food were unbearable. A faint thought came to him. He had remembered what his great uncle, who had survived days without water in the Gobi desert, had told him as a child. Sucking on a stone keeps the saliva flowing. He had a stone. How stupid of him. Of course.

He blindly felt for the sword, breathing a sigh of relief when he found the broken hilt. He felt for the stone. Gone! It must have fallen out. Frantically, he scrabbled for it but it was nowhere to be found. Then, trying to keep calm, he began a systematic search, walking his fingertips methodically around the bottom of the sarcophagus. His fingers touched it and relief flooded him. Gratefully, he placed it in his mouth and began to suck on it.

It started to work. His great uncle had been right. A moisture seemed to fill his mouth. Slowly he felt the fear within him dissipate. His mind seemed to set itself free, unhooking itself from his control and taking him away on a strange flight. He went back through his life, reliving his actions, seeing the faces of the people he had killed or ordered dead. He was pulled right back through his boyhood to his earliest memories, and then back even further. He seemed to be flying over history, watching as it unfolded backwards until he saw Alexander in battle, as clearly as if he was standing next to him. All around lay the dead. He was able to look directly into Alexander's eyes. But . . . what a surprise . . . there was no triumph, no recognition of his extraordinary triumphs, no look of divinity in his eyes. Instead there was torment and guilt. Then Alexander was dying in agony, asking for his sword. Alone, Alexander placed a stone inside his mouth. He looked directly into Subedei's eyes as he swallowed it. Then he spoke.

Subedei knew he was near death, but he was no longer afraid. His death was deserved, he realized that. For those who live by the sword die by it. He had sought to build an empire with ruthless cruelty, destroying the lives of countless people to do so.

He had been wrong and he knew it as he swallowed the stone.

In his last breath he repeated the words he had heard from Alexander: 'The secret to worthy empire-building lies within man's warm heart; let the stone ones remain hidden.'

Epilogue

The face of the new president elect beamed across the world as live television coverage witnessed him and the equally beaming director of the Supreme Council of Antiquities warmly shaking hands.

The formal announcement of the discovery of the tomb of Alexander the Great, together with a great treasure of priceless artefacts, papyrus scrolls and books originally thought lost in the fire of Alexandria, was watched by over a billion people.

Asked what his first reaction was when actually opening the great sarcophagus, Suleiman Attallah answered simply that he had been lost for words.

It was no more than the truth. Raising the sarcophagus and seeing the face of the council's former patron had almost given him a seizure. He had been so startled and flummoxed by it that he'd decided the best course was to say nothing at all.

When asked how long it would be before the public would be able to see the tomb and the body that lay inside, Attallah preferred not to give a date. He explained that the careful exploration of this incredible find would take many months, perhaps longer.

When the president elect was asked how he felt about having his new country residence so close to the lost Tomb of Alexander, he answered that he was, as of today, giving the residence to the Supreme Council of Antiquities to be used as a museum that would eventually house the treasures.

One American reporter took the opportunity to ask a question not related to the immediate purpose of the interview. 'Why do you think President Jumair resigned so suddenly, sir?'

'Quite simply, to be able to spend more time with his family and on other personal interests, after serving his country so well,' replied Benerzat with a smile.

'Isn't it because his oil-for-prosperity promises were meaningless?' persisted the reporter.

'Let me answer you by saying our prosperity is assured,' came back the politician's answer. 'The discovery we announce today is oil in itself to lubricate our most valuable industry, tourism.'

Watching the announcement, Brock laughed as he placed his hands behind his head and relaxed back into the Jacuzzi. 'You certainly have your father's smile, and guile!'

'Well, it's lucky for you I don't get everything from him,' replied Neusheen huskily; pressing her naked breasts against Brock. He put a hand on her smooth back and ran it down over the satiny skin.

He dropped a kiss on her soft, full lips. As he pulled away, she pouted in mock annoyance.

'Champagne first,' he said, reaching for the bottle in the ice bucket at the side of the pool.

'I like this holiday home,' said Neusheen, splashing the water with her hands. 'Do they send you here often?'

'Only when I've been very, very good. They save the Gulf of Aquba for special occasions.'

'Then I'm privileged that you asked me to join you.'

Brock topped up the champagne as a late news report caught his attention.

'Simone Al Kadeh, daughter of Omar Al Kadeh, returned home yesterday after backpacking in Australia for four weeks, with no prior knowledge that all the members of her family have disappeared,' the announcement said. 'Lawyers handling her estate, under information provided by the Zurich based investigation company ICE, have already agreed with the Chinese lawyers now acting for Subedei Industries (Egypt) to make null-and-void the recent acquisition of Al Kadeh Construction; one of our country's leading companies, founded by her father, Omar Al Kadeh; and Ms Al Kadeh has vowed to continue to run the company.'

'Now, where did we get to?' purred Neusheen, switching off the TV screen and putting down her glass, before nuzzling once more into the man next to her.

Brock pulled her even closer. 'You know, I've never made love to a president's daughter before. Is there a certain protocol?'

A slim hand submerged. 'That all depends on you.'
'Well, perhaps some form of security pass?'
'You seem to have one already.'
Brock tried to look innocent.